A SIXTH SENSE

A Sixth Sense

A priestly murder unleashes a lifelong
odyssey of pursuit, hiding, and escape . . .

Alastair Davie

To order additional copies of this book, contact:
Xlibris LLC
1-888-795-4274
www.Xlibris.com
Orders@Xlibris.com
542088

ORIGINAL SIN

From the devil they came and to the devil they will return.
                              —St. Bernard of Clairvaux, 1091-1153

CHAPTER 1

Dublin, Ireland, July 1936

Life's choices are often influenced by a parent's tainted life. The influence of their inherited seed often entraps their children despite efforts to break free from its malevolent clutches. Francis Reagan was about to be entangled in his father's legacy, which would dog him for the rest of his life, despite his best efforts to avoid it.

Sixteen-year-old Francis Reagan was heading home at seven thirty in the evening after work and had turned into Chancery Lane on his way to the tenement where he lived with his mother. He was pleased with himself. He had a plan to lift himself out of the grinding poverty of the Dublin tenements that had bred so much disease and despair among its residents for well over a century. He felt satisfied with the progress he had made so far. His job was the first rung on the ladder to success.

Francis made a living as a delivery boy for a butcher on nearby Camden Street. His burning ambition didn't stop there. He had plans to eventually own his own business. At the moment, he didn't know what type of business this would be, but he was going to do it come hell or high water. Really, he wanted to be a lawyer or doctor, but he knew this was out of the question because he didn't have the education. Still, his ambition was deeply ingrained in his soul.

He delivered meat all over Dublin, and this had opened his eyes to the bigger and richer world outside the constricting tenement life in the Liberties section of the city. He had a vehement desire to take his mother out of their one-room hovel in the vermin-infested tenement where they lived and give her a life free from the fear of daily survival.

In the 1930s, the Dublin tenements were considered the worst slums in Europe, trapping more than twenty-six thousand families in some five thousand dilapidated buildings that were once rich, Georgian houses for the Anglo-Irish gentry in fashionable squares and streets. The movement of these wealthy citizens out of the city after the Act of Union in 1801, which dissolved the Irish Parliament and transferred responsibility for ruling the country to London, was economically disastrous for Dublin. The once-fine houses were sold for a pittance to profiteering landlords who were determined to make money from the wretchedness of others. As a result, these homes, which had housed one family and its servants, had between ten and twenty family members in each room.

By 1936, many of these buildings were so dilapidated that some had collapsed with tragic consequences for the residents. The vast majority that lived in single rooms did everything there, from cooking, sleeping, and bathing. The lavatory was usually an outside privy in the back of the building to be shared by everyone. It is little wonder that an air of sickness and death permeated these buildings. And it was in this environment that Francis was raised.

He was the result of the rape of his mother, Maureen, in 1920. That year saw the last macabre chapter of Britain's cruel rule in Ireland, which was being fought in the streets of towns and cities, such as Dublin. In its attempt to stifle the Irish revolt, the British had introduced curfews and paramilitary units, such as the dreaded Black and Tans, who wreaked havoc among the population with burnings, beatings, and random killings in 1920 and 1921. Officially, the Black and Tans were a special police unit formed to root out members of the Irish Republican Army and suppress the independence movement. In fact, they were nothing but thugs of the worst kind who showed no mercy. The group was made up of out-of-work former soldiers and criminals from cities such as Glasgow and London. This short reign of terror was etched forever into the souls of the Irish people.

One October evening in 1920, Maureen was finishing up a ledger at her father's accounting business. He had already gone home, and she was supposed to leave soon after. But she found a mistake and was so absorbed in correcting it that she didn't realize it had become dark outside. Although it was a few minutes past curfew, she thought it safe to walk the short distance home. About halfway there, a vehicle turned the corner, and in the back of it were six uniformed Black and Tans. The man in charge questioned her, wanting to know where she was going. When she explained, he said he didn't believe her. He accused her of being a runner for the IRA and that they had a way of dealing with people like her. She was dragged screaming into a nearby alley and gang-raped. When they had finished, one of the men took out his revolver and shot her.

The next morning, she was found miraculously alive. Because of the dark, the man had misjudged his aim, and the shot had just glanced off her face, but she was still critically ill from her ordeal. After several weeks in the hospital, she began to recover, but the scars were far deeper than those that could be seen. She had a wound on her face that would be there for the rest of life. Two months later, she found out that she was pregnant.

Maureen was angry and resentful of the world as a result of her brutal attack. Outwardly, she seemed calm and in control, but there was a simmering anger below the surface. This boiled over when her parents tried to convince her to have an abortion, which was illegal at that time in Catholic Ireland. Her body had been violated, and it was not going to be violated again. She had a stubborn nature and would not give into any entreaties from her family or friends. The arguments that ensued in the following weeks turned into angry vitriol, and she spent most of her time by herself in her room. Her friends deserted her, and she took up drinking. The pressure built inside her with such intensity that after a particularly nasty argument with her parents, she left home, never to return. She rented a room using money from her small savings and planned to start her new life.

Her family never reported her rape to the police for fear of reprisals. However, word got out through a police informer that she had survived and that there was a real possibility she might recognize her assailants. One night, her family home was firebombed, and her entire family—her mother, father, and three siblings—were killed. Those who rushed out of the house were shot, picked off by snipers lying in wait. People in the neighbourhood were told that the family was an IRA cell, but they knew better. They were just too frightened to protest or say anything, fearing for their own lives.

Maureen was devastated when she heard the news. Her instinct was to go to the authorities, but she knew that would seal her fate. She just stayed out of sight in her small room and grieved for her family at a distance. She told herself that she had brought this terrible disaster upon them. It was all her fault. How could she ever make amends to them? It was too late. She would have to live with the consequences for the rest of her miserable life. It was then that she started to drink heavily.

Maureen had her baby at Coombe Woman's Lying-In Hospital, and because her money was running out, she took an attic room in a tenement on Chancery Lane. A cousin, with whom she was still in contact, found her a domestic job; and the women of the tenement were very supportive and willingly looked after the baby when she worked.

That was sixteen years ago, and Francis had grown into a large boy who looked much older than he was and was very mature for his age. Outwardly, he was very friendly and helpful to the people who lived in his street.

However, there was a darker side to his personality. The good and caring side could easily turn evil when he was cornered or challenged. The malignant side of his nature had been inherited from his Black and Tan father, who had been a vicious killer and, some years after his mother's rape, had been executed in London for murder. Also contributing to his malicious side was the verbal and physical abuse suffered at the hands of his mother. When he was ten years old, he savagely beat another boy much larger than himself who was teasing and bullying him. It took two men to separate the boys. The other lad had a broken jaw and lacerations all over his face.

Francis had two close friends from the street, Eugene Raines and John Reilly, with whom he played soccer and handball, as well as taking part in pranks on people. Although they were both a year older than Francis, the three of them were inseparable and were just as determined as he to get out of the tenements.

A year earlier, to Francis's great disappointment, the boys had moved away and had joined the far-right Blueshirt movement. This was a fascist party started by Eoin O'Duffy, a former Dublin police commissioner, and had the unofficial blessing of the Roman Catholic Church. The party was organised along the same lines as Mussolini's Blackshirts and Hitler's Brownshirts but never had the same backing and influence. The purpose of the group was to stop communists and socialists from gaining power in Ireland. This was a common fear in many European countries at the time, following the successful communist takeover of Russia starting in 1917.

Francis heard from one of the boys' sisters that they were part of Eoin O'Duffy's personal bodyguard and had taken part in many fights at meetings held by the Irish communist party and the Irish Republican Army known as the IRA. But other than that, he had lost touch with them.

Francis had resisted joining what was called colloquially as an animal gang—a street gang that controlled a neighbourhood. These gangs were a form of protection and helped many residents fight off eviction and hunger. He was not unfriendly; rather, he was focused on his own future, and he hadn't the time or inclination to join a gang. There had been some scuffles with gang members, which he usually won. So eventually, they left him alone.

Francis went to school at St. Brigid's on The Coombe where he learned to read and write. This was a tough time for him as the teachers didn't spare the strap, whether it was for a wrong answer or talking in class, but he learned. He left school on his fifteenth birthday and knew that if he was going to improve his lot in life, he would have to educate himself. As a result, he spent most of his spare time at the local library on nearby Kevin Street. At first, the librarians would not let him in, but when he persisted and gave them a note from one of his former teachers, they realized that he was serious about studying and left him alone. He devoured books on all subjects and was curious about the wider world he had never known.

Living in a tenement was taking its toll on his mother. She often came home from work late, drunk and very belligerent. He always kept a low profile when this happened, often coming home even later to avoid a confrontation. Many times he had felt the lash of her belt. The memory of her family often threw her into fits of depression, especially on the anniversary of their deaths. In her remorse, she spent the afternoon and evening in the pub, drinking away her weekly earnings.

On one occasion, she was so drunk she could hardly walk and had been helped up to her room by neighbours. At the sight of her son, she took her grief out on him. When her rage subsided, he was heavily bruised on his face and had cracked ribs and a broken arm. The next morning his mother, who couldn't remember anything about the night before, was very solicitous and eventually took him to hospital where they set his arm. But he remembered the incident, and it caused him to be even more withdrawn.

For her part, Maureen knew deep down that he was not to blame for her predicament, but she resented him anyway. She worked hard to bring him up as decently as possible, but it was a desperate task raising a child on your own in these conditions. She marveled at the good nature and humour of the men and women around her, some with eight or ten children. She wondered how they did it. But even with poverty, there was a clear sense of community in the tenements, with people helping each other out.

When she first moved into Chancery Lane, there were a number of male suitors, but she wasn't at all interested in men anymore, and after a while, they stopped coming around. Over the years, she began to cling to religion as her solace and had become a regular supplicant at the local Roman Catholic Church, St. Clements. Father Tremain, one of the young assistant priests who heard her confessions, visited her often, sensing her need to open up. With his encouragement, Francis became an altar boy at Sunday services at his church. He liked Father Tremain a lot. He had helped his mother a great deal with his pastoral visits, and he had found Francis his job. She was always in a good mood when he left. For this, he was grateful.

As Francis crossed the street, he waved to the people he knew. He saw a group of men on a corner, busily gambling away at what was known as a toss school. He wondered who was winning today. He climbed the steps leading to the tenement where he lived and was greeted by Mrs. Murphy, a large friendly soul who was sitting on the steps. She was very motherly and always took an interest in what he was doing.

"Hello, Francis, how was work today?"

"It was fine, Mrs. Murphy. They gave me a new route that is little further south than before with more deliveries. I have to pedal hard, though, to make my rounds on time," he said.

"That's good news. It shows they like you by giving you more responsibility. You work hard compared to those laggards over there," she replied, indicating with a toss of her head the group of men on the corner, which included her husband.

"Your mum has a special visitor, Father O'Brien from St. Clements."

"Thanks for the warning, Mrs. Murphy," he said, entering the building. There was no front door, and the stairs he took had no banisters and were missing some of the wooden steps. They had gone for firewood long ago to warm the unheated rooms.

I wonder what Father O'Brien wants, thought Francis. He did not really like this parish priest. He didn't know why, it was just a strange feeling he had. He felt very comfortable when Father Tremain was officiating at services but always felt hairs go up on the back of his neck when Father O'Brien was around. However, like every good Catholic, he had been brought up to revere the authority of priests who supposedly represented God on earth. They were to be obeyed at all times, and their flock was never to question their orders. Blind fealty was what was expected. So Francis kept these thoughts and feelings to himself.

Father O'Brien was in his mid-fifties and heavyset, and his rumpled clothes always looked like he had slept in them. He had a loud booming voice that startled parishioners at services when he first came to head up the parish some eighteen months before. He was a friendly, jovial man who had made many friends and was a complete opposite of his elderly predecessor who had retired. He came from a parish in County Wexford.

Nobody knew why he had been moved because he was only in his previous parish some two years, and it was unusual for a diocese not to promote one of its own priests. Of course, the rumour mill had worked hard to discover the cause with no success. Some said it was his drinking. Others thought that he had embezzled money or gambled, and still others said he probably was involved with a parishioner. Whatever it was, Father O'Brien never let on, so the rumours just continued to fly around.

Michael O'Brien was the seventh son of a farmer in County Wicklow and, as such, was bullied and tormented by his elder siblings. Compounding that, he was physically not up to the hard life on a farm. He preferred his books and was at the top of his class at the local school. His parents were exasperated with him because he was not pulling his weight on the farm, and they didn't think he would amount to much. They talked about their problem son with the local priest who suggested that the young Michael become a priest. So at the age of seventeen, he entered a seminary, never to visit or see his family again.

He thrived at his studies, although he was not a brilliant student. He was ranked in the middle of his class at the seminary and was eventually ordained some five years later. He was appointed as an assistant priest to a parish in Cork and eventually became a parish priest in that diocese. As the years passed, he began to become frustrated with his lack of advancement in the church hierarchy, especially when he saw several of his friends from the seminary get senior appointments. He began to resent their success and wondered what was wrong with him. He began to drink heavily and, in his more morose bouts, doubted his calling and started to think about his latent sexuality.

Father O'Brien became a troubled man. He liked young boys. This sexual drive had come on him some twenty or so years earlier. At first, it was just an attraction to them. He spent time at church-run camps and fishing trips. On one occasion, a particular boy, who was older than the others, joined the group on a camping trip. He volunteered to help the priest find firewood. When they were in the woods, they sat down and talked. It was then that Father O'Brien began to fondle the boy who responded. One thing led to another, and before he knew it, he had sodomised the youth. Panic set in, and he became very aggressive. He warned the boy not to breathe a word of what had happened because it was his right as a priest to do exactly what he wanted and that the wrath of God would come down on the boy if he said anything.

As the years passed, he became bolder and had a number of liaisons with boys, particularly male prostitutes in the seedier parts of Cork. Finally, his activities came to the notice of church authorities in the diocese because a number of prominent parishioners reported rumours to the bishop. After an investigation, he was sent away to a retreat for troubled priests, and after some counselling, he was assigned to a series of parishes. Each time, after two or three years at a parish, he continued to offend and was moved on. Finally, the church moved him into a parish in the tenements in Dublin where they thought he would be less conspicuous and the parishioners were less likely to complain.

As Francis slowly climbed the stairs, avoiding people asleep on the landing, he used the time to prepare himself to face Father O'Brien. This visit certainly was a first. What's he up to? As he approached the room, he heard muffled voices and a giggle from his mother.

When he entered, his mother greeted him, "Hello, Francis. We have a special visitor. Father O'Brien has just been telling me of some of the funny things he's seen since coming here. He has come with some news and has waited for you to come home so he could tell us both together."

"Good evening, Father," Francis said politely, although suspiciously.

"Bless you, my son," said Father O'Brien as he blessed Francis. He and his mother crossed themselves.

"My first bit of news is about Father Tremain. Unfortunately, he has left us. He is replacing a priest in another parish who died suddenly," he continued. "Until I can appoint a new assistant, I'm afraid no one will be able to visit you here. Of course, this doesn't mean you can't take confession at the church, but the pastoral visits are out for now."

"We are very sorry to hear about Father Tremain. He will be a great loss to the parish," said Francis's mother.

"But I have some good news as well. I have been watching Francis very closely at the services that I have conducted, and I think he is line for a promotion. I would like to make him my one of my thurifers. What do you say, Francis?"

Francis was shell-shocked. This was the last thing he wanted to do, but his Catholic upbringing got the better of his natural caution and common sense. "Well, er, I would . . . All right," he stammered.

"Good!" said Father O'Brien. "That's settled then. Brian Gatfield's family has decided to move back to Cork where his father has been offered a job. Maureen, your son will be a fine replacement. Now he has to come to the rectory for some training. How about tomorrow at this time?"

"He'll be there," said Francis's mother without hesitation.

"My other news is really for you, Maureen. I am looking for a housekeeper at the rectory, and I thought you might be interested. It'll mean more pay and will not be too arduous. What do you say?"

She put her hand up to her mouth in shock. "Oh, Father, how wonderful of you! I would be only too happy to take you up on your offer. When would you like me to start?"

"Wonderful, Maureen! How about Monday week? It'll give you time to give proper notice to Mrs. Beal."

After Father O'Brien left, Maureen turned to her son. "What's the problem?"

"Problem, what problem?"

"You know what I mean. You were very hesitant about agreeing to accept Father's proposal. Now I know you, Francis, something was going through your mind. I hope you're not thinking about quitting the church."

"No, it's not that. I was just wondering why Father Tremain left without saying goodbye," he lied. There was no point trying to tell her about his misgivings. She just wouldn't understand.

"It sounds as though he hadn't time to say his goodbyes," she said with a weary sigh.

"I'm so pleased to be working for Father. It's nearby, and maybe we could save enough to get out of this place. I've always dreamed of getting a small flat somewhere."

Francis lay in bed that night wondering what he was going to do. He couldn't sleep, although he heard his mother snoring across the other side of the room. When they went to bed, they put up a curtain between the two sleeping areas to give each some privacy. As the noises in the rest of the building settled down, he was still awake, going through in his mind what he was going to say to his mother.

The next morning, he was up early. He went downstairs with their slop bucket from their room and emptied it into the sewer drain at the back of the building. When he got back, his mother was up and getting ready to go to work.

"Mum, I've been thinking. I don't really want to be a thurifer for Father O'Brien because—"

Before he could go any further, his mother slapped him in the face.

"You will go to the church tonight, mister, no arguing! I don't want to hear any more about it. I have enough problems, and one of them is not going to be you!"

Chapter 2

Francis approached the rectory the next evening with an empty feeling in the pit of his stomach. He waited in the shadows of the church, trying to muster some sort of courage. After a while, he took a deep breath and reached for the large ornate knocker on the door of the rectory. The sound of his knock seemed to reverberate around the inside of the building, and it made passers-by in the street look up. Did they look forlornly at him with pity in their eyes?

He didn't have long to wait. He heard footsteps come down the hall. The door swung open, and the priest beckoned him in.

"Hello, Francis. Come in, come in, boy!" he boomed. "Let's go into the church sacristy, and I can show you first how the thurible works." And with that, he set off down the passageway that led to the church.

This was the first time Francis had been inside the church when there wasn't a service. The emptiness was formidable, and the silence was unnerving to a young man who had grown up in a tenement with noise all around, even at the dead of night. All he could hear was the priest's footsteps echoing in the nave as they walked to the sacristy, which was at the back of the church.

"Come on, Francis, don't dawdle, I have other people to see tonight after we start your training."

When they reached the sacristy, Father O'Brien went to a cupboard and pulled out the thurible. It was a silver boat, which contained incense, and a spoon.

"Now, first, I want you here at least thirty minutes before each service," he said matter-of-factly. "You have to light the charcoal in the bottom of the thurible and make sure it glows. You will have to blow on it to get it red hot so that when I put the incense in, it will burn and make smoke. The key is keeping the charcoal glowing, and I will show you how this is done."

With that, the priest lit the charcoal in the thurible and closed its lid. He showed Francis how to carry it and how to swing it to make sure the charcoal stayed alight during the service. After a few practice turns, Francis grew more confident that he could handle the role of thurifer.

"Let's continue your training on Friday. Brian Garfield will be at Sunday's mass, but I want you to do the theorizer's job. He'll be there to help you. After that, you are on your own. Now here's a little booklet which has a chapter on the role of the thurifer. Read it and we will go over it on Friday. See you at the same time then." And with that, he turned on his heels and marched back down the nave and out of the church.

Francis was left alone in the dark cavernous church, except for the light cast by the votive candles in front of a statue of Mary Magdalene and the sanctuary light. He was puzzled. This was not what he expected. What did he expect? He didn't know. Father O'Brien had been very matter-of-fact and somewhat more friendly than you would think from his gruff exterior. Perhaps he was wrong in suspecting the father's motives, but he was haunted by the troubled pale face of the present thurifer, Brian Gatfield. Since Francis had been an acolyte, Brian's personality had changed quite remarkably from the happy-go-lucky soccer-loving boy to a withdrawn quick-tempered young man. Francis decided he was going to talk to him on Sunday.

Friday evening came, and Father O'Brien greeted him with a broad smile. They sat down in the large rectory kitchen where the priest thought he would be more comfortable. They went through the booklet together with Father O'Brien sitting next to him. He had drink on his breath and a strange odour about him. Francis didn't know what it was that made him so nervous around the priest. Seemingly, the priest was focused on instructing the boy, but his leg was leaning against Francis's leg. Towards the end of the session, he began to rub it up and down. Francis moved away.

Nothing was said, and the priest offered to make him some cocoa. Francis accepted more out of fear of the consequences of disobeying a priest. He was puzzled about what happened. Having no father or father figure with whom to discuss this with, he was left on his own to work this out for himself. In his case, maturity came often with experience. As it was, warning bells didn't sound about the danger he was in and save him from what would be drastic consequences.

Father O'Brien was at the stove, bringing the milk to a boil for the cocoa, when he asked, "How's your mother? It must have been quite a shock when I told her about Father Tremain."

"Yes, it was, Father."

"She has worked very hard to bring you up, so I hope you won't let her down. She needs your help. Don't disappoint her. I am very pleased to see her at church because she needs the comfort this brings."

"Yes, Father."

"Here's your cocoa. I look forward to her coming to work here. I think she'll enjoy it."

While Francis finished his cocoa, he talked about his job and what he wanted to do in his life. Finally, he finished his drink, and the priest let him out of the front door.

On the following Sunday, he took part in the mass celebrated by Father O'Brien. He only had to be prompted once by Brian Gatfield. He saw his mother in the congregation beaming with pride as he performed his duties as thurifer. The mass lasted about an hour, and he was relieved when it was all over. In the sacristy after the service, the priest complimented him on a job well done.

As he left St. Clements Church, he saw Brian Gatfield waiting for him by the street door. "I just want to wish you good luck and warn you to be very careful around Father O'Brien." Francis was about to speak when other members of the congregation came out of the church. Brian signaled him to keep quiet and to follow him.

They walked along York Street in silence to St. Stephen's Green and sat down on the grass in the warm August sun.

"What did you mean when you told me to be careful of Father O'Brien?"

"Well, I'll tell you in strictest confidence. Please don't tell anyone what I'm going to tell you. People won't believe you because they think a priest can do no wrong."

"I promise," Francis replied.

"I was attacked by him one day in his study. He got me to do bad things to him, and he pulled down my trousers and did bad things to me." Brian then began to cry, remembering the details of this first assault.

Through his tears, he continued to tell his gruesome story of sexual abuse. At first, Francis was in total disbelief as he listened. He had only seen fights in the street, often between drunks, not this kind of attack.

"Things got so bad that it was happening to me every time I saw him. I felt sick and didn't want to go to church anymore. My parents forced me though."

He explained how he was paralyzed and numb with fear of what was going to happen to him after each service. He said the abuse was like living in one big nightmare that went on and on. In the end, Father O'Brien insisted that Brian visit him at the rectory, and he would summon him when he wanted. Brian obediently did as he was told.

"Didn't you tell anyone what was going on?" Francis asked.

"I tried to. Father Tremain walked into the study one day, and Father O'Brien left the room fast. I know that Father Tremain had words with him, and maybe that's why he left. I finally told my father. At first, he was mad with me, calling me a liar and a troublemaker. I know he asked around. A few days later, he calmly asked me to tell him again what had happened. After our talk, Father O'Brien suddenly stopped cornering me. Then dad was offered a job in County Wexford, and now we are going to move there.

"I'm telling you all this because we have been friends, and I don't want to see this happen to anyone else. Now I've got to go. Oh, one other thing, beware of the fishing club."

"What do you mean?"

"Father O'Brien belongs to a fishing club, and he took me to it one weekend. In the beginning, it was fun. But the other members of this club were just like him. They also brought along boys, and we were shared out among them. So please be very careful!" With that, Brian jumped up and started to walk. Soon, he was lost in the crowd of couples and families walking around the gardens, enjoying the warm day.

It was some time before Francis realized that he was gone. He was deep in thought, trying to formulate some plan to cope with this crisis. He had to go along with his new role at the church for his mother's sake. She saw her new position as a ticket to a better life. He couldn't disappoint her, but he couldn't end up like Brian. Was Brian really telling the truth, or was he just imagining what had happened to him? Perhaps it was living in such poverty that finally caused him to flip out. A lot of people Francis knew had become very depressed, and some even killed themselves. Whatever the truth, he had to be careful and try not to be alone with the priest.

The next morning, he reported for work as usual, and the butcher assigned him to yet another new route. This time, he was to deliver meat in Ranelagh, which was a small town south of Dublin city limits. This was a plum assignment because the bicycle ride got him out of the depressing city and into the suburban villages and towns where the wealthier professional families lived. It was a pleasant ride in the sun, and it lifted his spirits as he headed down Lower Leeson Street to Ranelagh Road.

After a while, he saw the signs that told him he was approaching Ranelagh. He was awed by the beauty of the Victorian houses he saw as he pedalled his way to make his delivery. The neat gardens and large trees were a wonder to him. This was a beautiful new world, the polar opposite to the filthy tenement and street where he lived. He vowed to himself that he would be part of this one day. The butcher had told him to watch out for Northbrook Road, which was a turn off Ranelagh Road. There it was.

Without any hint of danger, he rounded the corner and made his way to the address he had been given. As he rode down the street, he saw two large men pushing and shoving a well-dressed woman. Both men had filthy ill-fitting clothes and dirty well-worn boots. They reminded Francis of some of the men he had seen at the docks and tenements in Dublin.

Without any hesitation, Francis jumped off his bike and ran over to the men who were trying to wrestle a handbag from the woman. She was screaming at them and fighting back.

"Oi! What's going on?"

One of the men turned and snarled, "Mind your own business or you'll feel the back of my hand. Now piss off!"

Francis got angry at this and pulled himself up to his full height. He knew he had to do something. "I'm not going anywhere until you leave her alone."

"Right, you asked for it."

The man walked over and took a swing at Francis who ducked from the haymaker and punched the man in the abdomen. With a grunt and a yelp, the man fell to the pavement winded.

His partner then let the woman go and came after Francis, swearing and threatening all kinds of punishment for his insolence. The woman ran into a house, which was across the other side of the road. The two men pounded Francis, who fell to the ground with a searing pain in his face. He knew what was coming next and got into a foetal position with his hands over his head. They had started to kick him mercilessly and pummel him. This went on for what seemed to him like a long time.

Suddenly, a voice roared, "That's enough, you two. Be off with you now or you'll feel the end of my shillelagh on your skulls."

With that, Francis's punishment stopped, and the two men ran off. He eventually looked up into the face of a very large man who was smiling at him.

"Me mistress said you were having some trouble and needed help," he said with a grin. "Now let's have a look at you. You've got a real shiner there, and I'll bet you will be sore where they were kicking you. Let's get you up, and Mrs. Haggerty can clean that cut on your face in the kitchen."

He picked Francis up with ease and helped him stand. Francis felt very woozy, so the man put one arm over his shoulder and helped him walk across the road to a large house. "By the way, I'm Joseph Riordan, and I am the butler to Mrs. Ritchie. It was her being attacked in the street by those hooligans."

"Thank you, sir, for your help. My name is Francis Reagan. I hope Mrs. Ritchie is all right."

"Oh, she's fine. When we get you patched up, she wants to thank you. The meat you were delivering was for us."

They went through the servants' entrance and entered a big kitchen. There was a large table in the middle of the room and an equally large stove at one end. At the sink was a maid cleaning pots and pans, and a boy was cleaning shoes.

"Mrs. Haggerty, our hero has arrived!"

Mrs. Haggerty bustled in and tut-tutted at the sight of Francis's face. "Come on, young man, sit down at the table, and we'll get you cleaned up. Ellen, get some hot water and some clean cloths," she said to the maid.

"Bill, go outside and take this lad's bike to the back and bring in our meat," the butler instructed the young boy cleaning shoes.

Mrs. Haggerty finished cleaning the wound on his face and put a bandage over it.

"Now would you like a nice cup of tea?" she asked him.

"Oh yes, please."

They all sat at the kitchen table while Ellen poured the tea. Mrs. Haggerty went to the larder and brought in a fruit cake. As she sliced it, Francis's eyes were bulging at the sight of the first cake he'd ever seen. Mrs. Haggerty smiled and handed him a slice.

Francis took a bite and wondered at the sweetness he felt in his mouth. The cake was so fresh it melted like butter. He had never tasted anything quite like this. He once ate some fresh bread, but this was ambrosial to his taste buds. This was unexplored territory.

"Would you like another slice, Francis?"

"Yes, please."

"Now don't eat it so fast. It's very rich, and you will upset your stomach," she warned.

"Is this your first time in a big house like this?" asked Mr. Riordan.

"Yes, it is. They must be very rich to live in this house. I read a bit about the history of Dublin in the library where it talks about these grand houses. I have been delivering to some fine houses in the city, but I've never been inside."

"It is very grand, isn't it? This house belonged to Mrs. Ritchie's family. Her father was an owner of a linen factory, and he made his fortune supplying the British government in the First World War. When he died about ten years ago, Mrs. Ritchie inherited and then sold the business to an American company. Her mother died when she was four, and she had no brothers or sisters. She was married to a solicitor, but he was killed in the Great War. That, in a nutshell, is the history of this house. Now let me take you to see Mrs. Ritchie. When she speaks to you, don't be afraid to talk. As long as you are respectful, she will listen to you. Follow me."

Mr. Riordan led the way as they left the kitchen and walked through a maze of corridors finally reaching the drawing room. This was a large room with expensive and ornate furniture and a piano at one end. A large bay window looked out on to the back garden, which at this time of year was alive with colour from the flowering plants. This, to Francis, was the epitome of wealth. It was a dream come true.

"Hello, Francis," a gentle voice came from behind him. "Do you like my garden? It's really pretty at this time of year."

He closed his gawking mouth and turned to see an attractive woman standing behind him having just come into the room. Anne Ritchie was in her midforties and tall, particularly in the high heels she was wearing. She wore a tight-fitting dress that amply showed off her figure.

"It's beautiful. I have never seen anything like it," he said with true sincerity.

"Please sit down and let's talk."

She walked over to some chairs and a coffee table and indicated for him to sit down. Francis nervously obeyed.

"First of all, I want to thank you so much for my well-timed rescue. I am very grateful to you."

"Thank you, ma'am. I couldn't stand by and let them hurt and rob you. It's not right!"

"You were very brave, and I appreciate very much what you did for me. Now tell me about yourself, where you live and what you are doing as a delivery boy."

Francis told her about his life and that he lived with his mother in a tenement. He described how they made ends meet to survive the conditions they lived in. Mrs. Ritchie listened intently, and she was amazed at the story she heard unfold. She knew there was a great deal of poverty in Dublin, but this was the first time she had heard it directly from someone who lived it.

She asked him what he wanted to do with his life. He said he wanted to become a solicitor or an accountant, but that was an impossible dream. He'd settle for owning his own business.

"Why is it impossible for you to be what you want to be?" she asked.

"I haven't got an education, really. I left school when I was fifteen, and I haven't passed any exams to get me into university. Anyway, I can't afford it, even if I passed the exams," he responded despondently.

"A good education is the foundation of life, but it can be wasted. I've seen so many well-educated people not using their God-given talents properly. I'll tell you what, let me think about your situation and see whether I can be of any help."

They talked on about other things. Francis told her about his new job at the church and that his mother was going to start work that next week as housekeeper for the priest.

After more than an hour, Mrs. Ritchie finally said it was time they took Francis back. "I'll ask Mr. Riordan to take you back in the car. They must be wondering where you are. He'll explain what happened to you so you won't be in any trouble. Now will you promise to come and see me next Sunday? We can talk some more."

"Yes, ma'am."

With that, she pulled a bell cord, and after a few minutes, Mr. Riordan appeared. "Joseph, would you please drive Francis back to his butcher shop. Francis, I look forward to seeing you on Sunday. Once again, thank you."

This was turning out to be a day of firsts for Francis as he sat in the Mrs. Ritchie's big Austin car. His bike was tied in the boot, and they were driving at least thirty miles per hour. What a treat!

"Mrs. Ritchie seemed very pleased with her talk with you. How did you find her?" Mr. Riordan asked.

"I think she is one the kindest people I have ever met. She was interested in what I had to say."

"That's her, all right. And she is really genuine. There's no nonsense about her at all."

They pulled up in front of the butcher's shop just as Mr. Flynn was putting meat away in his storage locker. He came out of his shop to see them.

"Francis, where have you been? I was just closing up. What has happened to your face, boy? Mr. Riordan, what are you doing here? What has he done?"

"Now, now, Mr. Flynn, your delivery boy here has been quite a hero." Then Mr. Riordan explained what had happened.

After Mr. Riordan left, Mr. Flynn turned to Francis. "It seems you made quite an impression on Mrs. Ritchie. She is a very good customer of mine. Now just be careful in the future. Make sure you are polite to the lady and show her respect at all times. Now be off home with you and well done!"

Francis decided to go to the library on his way home so that he could read the newspapers and look up information on the Ritchie family. He knew his mother would not be home for a while, and he did not enjoy being there by himself.

As he walked up Camden Row, he saw two men coming towards him on the same side of the street. He didn't take much notice of them and wrote them off as a couple of nobs. He was deep in thought as they approached when one of them said, "You've got a real shiner there. Have you been fighting again?"

He looked up straight into the eyes of his old neighbourhood friends, Eugene Raines and John Reilly. "Oh my god, it is you! I must be dreaming! Look at you dressed in posh clothes!"

"How have you been, Francis? We've missed seeing you. What happened to your face?" asked John Reilly, his blue piercing eyes studying Francis.

Francis then told them about how he got the black eye and was surprised at the serious look that came on their faces.

"Mrs. Ritchie is a troublemaker. She belongs to a left-wing socialist group that has caused a number of strikes and disrupted the lives of many peace-loving Christian Irishmen. You can't trust her. You'd be best to stay away from her," Eugene Raines warned.

"Anyway, let's not ruin a perfectly fine reunion, shall we? Come on, Francis, let's go to the nearest pub and catch up with what's been happening to us all," Reilly suggested.

"But I'm not old enough," said Francis.

"Ah, never mind that! You look the part," said Reilly with a smirk.

They went to the first pub they saw, and Eugene Raines bought the first round of beer. Then they told Francis of their adventures and how they lived now that they had broken away from tenement life. They spoke in almost reverent terms about Eoin O'Duffy, who they referred to as the general. They explained that he was the only true Irish leader and would someday lead the nation based on Christian principles against the red menace. They told him that the founders of communism were Jews, and they controlled the banks and commerce. As a result, Irishmen were being ground down into poverty. They had to be stopped.

The beer seemed to loosen their tongues, and they admitted that the Blueshirts had been merged into the Fine Gael party, with O'Duffy as its leader, and were now known as the League of Youth. They told him about how they tried to set fire to the house of a socialist politician and had killed another. However, O'Duffy had been thrown out of the new party because he advocated invading Northern Ireland. He now planned to take a contingent of about seven hundred and fifty former Blueshirts to fight on the side of Franco in the Spanish Civil War, which had begun that year.

To Francis, their views were extreme and didn't make sense. He knew many good storeowners who were Jews, and they were wonderful people who would do anything to help you. Sure there were those that cheated people, but so did other non-Jews. He just kept his mouth shut and let them talk. How had his friends become so radical in their views? Perhaps it was their determination to relieve themselves of their tenement life at any cost that they would turn to anything to achieve that. Did they really believe what they were saying or just mouthing the propaganda that they had been infected with?

"So what are you two doing here in the old neighbourhood?" he asked, changing the subject.

"We wanted to say goodbye to our families. We ship out to Spain tomorrow," Reilly announced. "Then the real adventure will begin. Finally, we will be doing something useful and meaningful."

Francis was feeling a bit woozy. He never had beer before, and he felt it was time to go home.

"I've got a great idea, Francis, why don't you join us? It would be great to have you along," Eugene suggested as they walked along the street from the pub.

"I'll have to think about that. I am concerned about my mother," he replied, not certain he was making any sense.

"If you decide to, we'll see you at noon tomorrow on the O'Connell Street Bridge."

With that, they turned and walked on towards the city centre.

CHAPTER 3

Francis never went to meet his friends that Sunday. He had a raging headache from the drink, and it was all he could do to get through the church service. He had vomited intermittently during the night and had woken up that morning feeling wrung out and wretched. The one piece of good news was that Father O'Brien had been sent on a six-month sabbatical in County Wexford, and there was a temporary priest taking his place. Nobody knew why. It didn't matter why to Francis; at least, Father O'Brien wouldn't be around for him to worry about.

As soon as he could, he left the church and walked over to Iveagh Gardens where he often liked to walk and think. That morning, his thoughts were about his friends. They just saw war as a big adventure, and their reason for joining up was they wanted to get out of Dublin and Ireland. He wasn't sure that they knew what they were doing by going to fight in Spain. It seemed to him their reasoning for taking such a drastic step was not very well thought out.

The stories in the newspapers that he had read at the library about the start of the civil war were pro-Franco, the right-wing leader of the revolt against a democratically elected government. The leadership of the Roman Catholic Church in Ireland had certainly promoted the war at rallies for the Spanish general, calling it a war in support of the Christian religion and against communism. But there had been some muted voices of dissent from Irish labour, socialists, and republican organisations, such as the IRA.

Francis heard a clock from a nearby church strike one o'clock, which disturbed his thoughts. He was planning to visit Anne Ritchie at two o'clock. He was going to be late. He ran towards Camden Street and the butcher's shop. Mr. Flynn had said he could borrow his delivery bicycle so long as he brought it back. He found it in the shed at the back of the shop. He jumped on it and pedaled as hard as he could toward Ranleigh.

He rode up to the house on Northbrook Road and took his bicycle to the side of the house and knocked on the servants' entrance door. It was opened by Ellen, the maid, who gave him a warm smile. "Nice to see you again," she said pertly. "Mr. Riordan is in the kitchen."

Francis found the butler sitting at the kitchen table, reading a newspaper, and drinking a cup of tea. "Come in, Francis. Would you like some tea?"

"Yes, thank you."

Ellen brought over another cup and poured him some tea from a large enamel teapot she had taken off the stove where it had been warming. He added some milk and sugar.

"Now let's have a look at your ugly mug and see how it's healing," Riordan said with a smile.

"Not bad. You will be your same ugly self again soon," he said with a laugh. "What's been happening to you this last week? Been getting into to any more fights?"

"Some friends of mine have joined up to fight for Franco in the Spanish Civil War at the urging of their Blueshirt leader. They wanted me to join them, but I am not interested. I don't know why they chose to do this," Francis admitted.

"I think you made the right decision, Francis. It seems that they are heading for trouble," said Mr. Riordan.

A bell rang, and Ellen went scurrying off.

When she had gone, Mr. Riordan's mood changed, and he said bitterly, "I want to tell you something now that the girl has gone upstairs. I've just been reading in the newspapers how some young Irishmen are going off to fight in this war in Spain for General Franco. You'd think that our politicians would have learned their lesson from the Great War. They called it the war to end all wars then, and now look what's happening. Mrs. Ritchie's husband was killed in the last year of that war. I was his platoon sergeant and by his side when he got it. I know that war is not glorious and rots the brains of soldiers on both sides. They are led to the slaughter because some general has decided one last push and they would have the enemy on the run. Millions of men died needlessly."

"I didn't know you were in the war, Mr. Riordan," Francis said.

"Yes, I joined the Royal Irish Rifles and was posted to France after basic training. I was in the trenches for just over two weeks. Before that, I had had a job providing the lines with rations and ammunition in the regiment's supply company. When they were running out of men, we got sent there. We didn't know what we were in for. In fact, often, we would gain a hundred yards or so, losing a lot of men, and Gerry would take it back the next day.

It was a stalemate, except for the killing of men on both sides for no gain. It was awful.

"I suppose what I remember most wasn't just the mud, the bad food, and the lack of sanitation, but the rats and the flies. After Mr. Ritchie was killed, I was badly wounded in the leg when I was on a reconnaissance patrol. They just left me there with the flies. God, those flies! I managed to put a tourniquet on the leg. I lay there during the hot day, pretending to be dead, so that snipers would not pick me off. When night came, I painfully crawled back to our lines. They took my leg off and that, fortunately, was the end of my war.

"I don't like to talk about it, and you will never hear me mention it again, but I don't want you to get caught up in the false euphoria that is going on at the moment and enlist. Think very carefully about it before you sign up. Don't waste your life. That's all I'm going to say."

Just then, Ellen came back, as if on cue. "Mrs. Ritchie will see Francis in the study now," she announced.

When Francis entered the study, Anne Ritchie was sitting in front of a large oak desk that looked out on to the garden. The study was a large room with shelves of books that went up to the ceiling and filled three sides, except the side with the door from which he had entered, and a stone fireplace. In the middle of the room was a big table with discarded newspapers and magazines. At one end of it, and near the desk, were two comfortable chairs.

"Come in, Francis. Please take a seat. I won't be a moment," said Anne Ritchie, finishing up some papers on her desk.

Francis took a seat and watched her as she finalised and assembled some documents she had been working on. When she had finished, she put them to one side and put a paperweight on them.

She walked over to the other chair, sat down, and turned to face him. "I suppose you are a little curious to know why I wanted to see you. I realise today is your day off and you might want to do other things rather than talk to me."

Francis began to protest, but she raised her hand to silence him.

"After our talk the other day, I asked around about you, and my inquiries confirmed my feelings. You are honest and hardworking, as well as brave. I am most grateful to you for protecting me from those men last week. You are just the sort of person I would like to help me with one of my projects. You talked about bettering yourself, and I would like to see you achieve this. What do you think of that?" she asked.

"I'm all for that, ma'am. I don't want to be a delivery boy all my life," he commented.

"Let me explain then what I have in mind, and you can tell me what you think. I am on the board of Kiernan House on the outskirts of Dublin. This is an orphanage where, apart from giving them a home, we educate the youngsters, and when they get older, we train them for different kinds of trades. Unlike most of the church-run orphanages, we take in boys and girls. It is important for their social growth that they meet and understand the opposite sex as early as possible. A lot of people see this as too radical, but so far, we have had no problems. At the moment, we have about sixty children, but we plan to expand the number. The demand is so great it's outstripping the places we have available.

"We have an administrator, Mrs. Hennessey, who tries to cope with the mounting paperwork. She needs someone who she can train as an office clerk and eventually take some of the burden off her. I know you can read, write, and do your sums because I have made some inquiries about you with your former teachers. This would be an opportunity for you to grow, and in the evenings, you could study. Also, your pay would be double of what you are getting now. Does that sound interesting to you?"

"I don't know what to say, ma'am, but thank you for thinking of me," he responded unenthusiastically.

She was surprised and puzzled by his response. "But what?" she asked.

"Oh, it's nothing, ma'am."

"Come on, Francis, something is bothering you. I thought we were friends. Tell me what it is. You know, I believe in straight talk and discussing what bothers me. I'd like you to feel the same way."

"You've been so kind to me I don't want to hurt your feelings," he responded.

"Do you trust me? Are you suspicious of my motives? Come on, Francis, please tell me. I promise you my feelings will not be hurt," she begged.

Francis swallowed hard and took a deep breath. "It's not me, ma'am, I've heard people say bad things about you. I am very confused about what to think." Then he told her about his friends volunteering for Franco in Spain and what they had said about her.

When he had finished, there was a long pause before Anne Ritchie said anything.

"It must be confusing for young people of your age to understand what is going on in this world of ours. The fact that you didn't join your friends tells me that you are a thinker and you make up your own mind about things. Francis, remember that there are always other beliefs or philosophies on any side of an issue. Look at every side of an argument and always decide for yourself based on your own common sense. Don't believe everything I or anybody else says. Check it out and then make up your own mind.

"As far as this wretched civil war is concerned, I think a lot of young people are getting sucked into supporting the fascist cause. Here in Ireland, many people are following the Catholic Church's lead and believe they are on another crusade. Yes, I am against the coup attempt by some army officers in Spain because they are trying to impose their will on a democratically elected government. I have always believed in democracy, despite its faults.

"Also, not all priests believe in General Franco's cause. Fr. Michael O'Flanagan is one of those who support the elected government in Spain. In fact, he'll be speaking at Engineers' Hall in early December if you want to go along and listen to him.

"I believe that everyone should have the opportunity to better their lives, no matter where they come from. They should not have their lives dictated to by someone else, be it in Ireland's case, the British, or some other privileged minority. They have the right, within a democracy, to express their views peacefully and without prejudice and to persuade others of their point of view."

"Well, I don't know much about this, ma'am. I mean I haven't been educated properly. But I do know that there are a lot of things in this city that aren't right. Take where I live—the building's roof is leaking, there are too many people living in it, there are rats as big as dogs, and the O'Malley kids in the basement live in the dark because their parents can't afford the rent to live upstairs. We pay rent to some man who always has some toughs with him. Fall behind and you're out. I've seen many families put out on the street because they can't pay or borrow what's owed. There are too many men without regular work, and when they get a job, they spend their wages on drink. They don't have a trade. Now I know that's not right," he said with conviction.

"That's exactly my point. Our work at this orphanage is a start. It will give these kids a chance in life."

"What about the kids that have mothers and fathers? Who is going to help them?"

"Unfortunately, there's not much help. You have to pay a fee to go to a training school, and many poor families just can't afford it. I hope the government will do something to help soon."

There was another long silence while Francis absorbed what he had been told and made his decision. "I would be willing to look at the possibility of working at the orphanage."

"That's wonderful! You will have to see Mrs. Hennessey, and she will tell you all about the job, as she will be your boss. I was hoping you'd say yes, so I arranged for you to see her at 2:00 p.m. tomorrow, if that's all right. I've already cleared this with Mr. Flynn, and he was very supportive of you improving yourself, although he'll miss you. You see, Francis, there are a lot of people who believe in you."

Francis was stunned by this and couldn't believe his luck. Maybe his mother and he could find that small flat they'd always wanted after all.

"There's one other thing," Mrs. Ritchie continued. "And that's your education. If you agree, I will arrange for a tutor to meet you at the orphanage so you can study. I would like to see you go to university when you pass their entrance exams."

"I think that would be wonderful, but I can't afford a tutor, let alone go to university," he said.

"Don't worry, I'll take care of the expense. You just have to study. I have a tutor in mind, a Mrs. Couch. I'll let you know when you and she can get together. Now tomorrow morning, I want you to meet me at Brown Thomas on Grafton Street at nine, and we'll buy some clothes for you that befit your new position."

She got up from her seat and went to a bookshelf and looked for a book. Finding it, she returned to her seat. "I am serious about you understanding both sides of an argument before making a decision. Here are two pamphlets giving arguments for and against the war in Spain. I think it will give you some good information. Also, this book talks about the history of democracy. I think it will interest you. If you have any questions, I'll be here to answer them for you. In the meantime, I'll see you tomorrow morning."

She got up and pulled the bell cord.

When he got home that evening, he told his mother his good news about a possible new job. This was the first time he'd seen her smile since Father Tremain left.

"That is wonderful news, Francis. We both have new jobs that pay more! Let's go and celebrate, shall we?"

Reluctantly, he followed to the nearest pub. This time, he limited himself to one drink. His mother was in deep conversation with a group of women, so after an hour, he slipped away home to bed.

The following morning, he was at the store before nine when Mrs. Ritchie arrived in her car driven by Mr. Riordan. As he opened the door for her, he winked at Francis. They went straight to the men's department, and a snooty sales clerk helped them choose a suit, other clothes, and shoes. He then went straight home to change for his meeting with Mrs. Hennessey. Mr. Flynn let him borrow his delivery bicycle again which he rode to the town of Terenure, which was just south of the city limits.

The orphanage was a very large Victorian building on Prescott Street. It had four stories and wings on either side of the centre section. He could see children's swings, a large slide, and a roundabout. He was struck by how neat and tidy everything seemed.

"What do you want?" said someone as he passed through the gate.

He turned to see a small boy in a rumpled suit sitting behind the low wall that surrounded the front garden.

"Who's asking?" Francis responded with a smile.

"Me."

"Who's me then?"

"My name is Charlie Simon, and we don't like strangers 'round here."

"Well, Charlie, I've come to see Mrs. Hennessy. Can you show me the way?"

"I suppose so," he said reluctantly and ambled off towards the house with his hands in his pockets.

Charlie led Francis up the path to the front door, which he pushed open, revealing an enormous wood-paneled hall with a regal staircase looping upwards. The floor was made up of different coloured stones woven into an intricate pattern. The ceiling was a classic hunt scene with the mythological characters in plaster relief that stood out from the light blue ceiling. It was clearly a house once occupied by some rich Dublin family. But unlike the city houses that had become tenements for the poor, it had been preserved and put to good use by its caring owners. The hall had a strong aroma of polish and disinfectant.

There was a great deal of noise from the children playing in the hall and, it seemed, in all rooms leading off it. There was a Ping-Pong table surrounded by a cheering crowd of children egging on two players. In the middle of the front hall was a door with a wooden sign that read "Staff Room." Charlie knocked on the door, and a voice said, "Come!"

Charlie opened the door and announced, "Someone to see Mrs. Hennessey."

Just then, a bell rang, and the noise grew louder as the children filed into their classrooms. Adults, presumably teachers, came pouring out of the staff room. Charlie had disappeared, and Francis was left standing there by himself.

Then Mrs. Hennessey appeared at the door. She was a corpulent lady in her fifties and had a winning smile and a jolly face.

"You must be Francis. I've heard so much about you from Mrs. Ritchie. Let's go to the office and talk."

They went down a corridor that led to one of the wings of the house and entered a large room. This was the general office, which had three desks, typewriters, and filing cabinets. Sitting on one desk was a telephone. This was the first time Francis had actually seen one, although he had read about them in a science book at the library. When it rang, he nearly jumped out of his skin. Mrs. Hennessy was laughing as she picked up the receiver and sat down at her desk. Soon, she was deep in conversation with the person at the other end.

Francis took in the scene of chaos. Mrs. Hennessey's desk was covered in mounds of papers, some more than two feet high. There were similar mounds on the other desks and on the floor in the same state of confusion.

"Well, Francis, this place needs someone to tidy it up and keep it that way," she said when she finished her telephone call. "Do you think you can handle it?"

"I think so, ma'am. I will give it my best effort."

"Good lad. What I need is someone who can file and keep this office organised. A lot of paperwork comes through here all the time, so it will keep you pretty busy."

They talked for another thirty minutes, and then Mrs. Hennessy gave him a tour of the orphanage. It was quite remarkable. On the first two floors were classrooms and workshops, and on the third floor were the dormitories, the boys in the left wing and girls in the right wing. The fourth floor was the preserve of the resident staff. On the ground floor to the right were a library, a billiards room, and an auditorium, which had been the ballroom in Victorian times. To the left of the main hall were the dining rooms and a huge kitchen. Mrs. Hennessey introduced him to the cook and her assistants. Francis was amazed at the cleanliness of the kitchens and the friendly people who had started to prepare the evening meal, although it was only three fifteen.

Seeing his surprise, Mrs. Hennessey said, "We are very lucky in that we have a very rich benefactor in Raymond O'Donovan who lives in America now. He was brought up in an orphanage in Dublin and went to America when he was seventeen. He made his way up the business ladder and became a rich banker. He never forgot his roots and set up this orphanage about five years ago. He was determined that the children here would not suffer the same indignities that he did and that they would be properly trained to take their place in society. The rest was up to them."

"Does he come here often?" Francis asked.

"About every two years. He made sure he had people like Mrs. Ritchie on the board who have a great concern about the welfare of children. What do you think of this orphanage and its facilities?"

"I would never, in my wildest dreams, have thought that a place like this existed. It's wonderful! I will certainly do my best. I won't let you down, Mrs. Hennessy," said Francis excitedly.

"I certainly hope not. Now can you start on Monday?"

"I'll be here."

He left the orphanage in high spirits, thanking God for providing him with this opportunity. As he walked down the path towards the gate, he saw Charlie waiting for him.

"Get the job then?"

"Yes. What's that you're holding?"

"Ain't you ever seen a football before?"

"Yes, but not such a nice one. Bet you can't play!"

"Of course, I can."

"Let's see what you're made of then."

They went to the back of the house where there was a playing field with goal posts. Francis played goalie, and Charlie practiced shooting the ball at him. Within ten minutes, they were joined by another four boys and were all having the time of their lives. Finally, a bell rang, and they all raced towards the building.

"Hey, where are you all going?" cried Francis.

"To supper!" shouted Charlie.

Suddenly, they were gone. Francis picked up his coat and cap and let himself out of the front gate.

As he put his bicycle back in the shed behind the butcher's shop, Mr. Flynn came out and greeted him. "Hello, Francis. How did it go?"

"They have offered me a job and want me to start Monday. I am sorry to hand in my notice to you. You've always been very good to me."

"Don't be. The past two years have been good to both of us. I've had a good, reliable worker. I knew you would eventually find something better. So how are you going to get to your new job every day?"

"I hadn't thought about that," said Francis with a look of concern on his face.

Mr. Flynn laughed. "Look, lad, I'll give you that bicycle. It's about time I got a new one anyway. And you can store it here. Otherwise, it'll get stolen if you take it home."

"Oh thanks, Mr. Flynn. That's very generous of you."

Francis walked home that evening full of himself and on cloud nine.

Chapter 4

The next few months went by in a whirl of activity. Francis enjoyed his work at the orphanage, and Mrs. Hennessy turned out to be a good teacher. Between them, they had organised the administrative office, so it ran very efficiently. He got over his initial fear of the telephone and had become quite proficient in answering it. Mrs. Hennessy had given him responsibility for ordering stationery and other supplies they needed. After a rocky start, he got the hang of it, and his confidence grew.

Also, Mrs. Ritchie was as good as her word. He met Mrs. Couch, his tutor, twice a week and was enjoying the intellectual stimulation that these sessions brought.

As if his plate wasn't full already, he had become a mentor to Charlie and his friend, Bernard. He helped them with their homework and played football with them after he had finished for the day. It was strange playing with a real football and not one made of rags like he and his friends played with at home. There were other boys from the orphanage who wanted to play, and soon, there were enough for two sides. He chose captains for the day, and they selected their own players.

At home, life became more pleasant. He and his mother had moved into a small flat within walking distance of the church where she worked as a housekeeper for the priests who lived there. They could now afford to have a better home because their combined income enabled them to move up from the awful tenement conditions. With a small loan from Anne Ritchie, they had bought some secondhand furniture to furnish the flat. It was small, but they had their own bedrooms. There was a small kitchen, dining room, and front room combined. But what was so wonderful was the small bathroom down the hall, which they shared with other residents. For the first time, they were able to luxuriate in a bath.

However, their landlady, Mrs. Rogers, was stickler for her rules and had given Francis's mother a dressing down when she came in drunk late one night. This wigging seemed to have had a salutary effect on her because she stopped going out on her binges and stopped drinking cold turkey.

Francis was a frequent visitor to the Ritchie household. In fact, he went with Mrs. Ritchie and Mr. Riordan in December that year to listen to Father O'Flanagan who spoke to supporters of the Republican cause in Spain. He likened the attempted coup d'état by the right-wing Spanish generals to the British use of the Black and Tans in Ireland to quell the will of the people. He was a very forceful speaker, and a lot of what he said made a great deal of sense to Francis.

Mrs. Ritchie had joined the Women's Spanish Aid Committee, which was formed by some leading Irish women to support the Republican government in Spain. Francis had attended some of their public meetings. At one of these, which was held at the Gaiety Theatre in Dublin, a Spanish priest talked about the deception that been played on the Irish people when they were led to believe that the fascist leaders were fighting a war to defend Christianity.

One Sunday some months later, Francis's euphoria for his new life suddenly came to a crashing end with the news that Father O'Brien was coming back to St. Clements the following week. His old inexplicable dread came back. He would have to be on his best behaviour in order not to ruin the gains his mother and he had made. His melancholy was noticed by people at work and his friends in the Ritchie household. He would not tell anybody what was bothering him and retreated into his shell.

Then it happened one day when he was walking home. A voice boomed, "Francis, how are you, my boy?" He turned to see Father O'Brien walking toward him with suitcase. "I've just got off the train. How have you and your mother been?"

Francis offered to carry his suitcase, and as they walked up the street to the rectory, he filled in the priest on what had happened since he'd been away.

"This sounds very exciting for you both. You must work hard to be a success and make us all proud of you. Don't let us down now. Why don't you come and see me some time and we can talk longer about your career?"

"Yes, Father," he said without enthusiasm. They came to the front door of the rectory, and the priest took his case and went inside without another word.

Two days later, his mother came in from work with some news. "Father O'Brien told me today that he is planning to hold confirmation lessons for older parishioners who have not been confirmed yet by the bishop. He said he knew you hadn't been, and I said that you would be willing to join the group," she told an appalled Francis.

"But I'm not interested in this, Mum. Why did you volunteer me?" he asked.

"It's your duty, as a good Catholic, to be confirmed. I didn't do it when you were thirteen because we couldn't afford any new clothes that would be suitable for you to appear in before the bishop. Father O'Brien said that the bishop would be here in two months, and he has to prepare people to be confirmed. Classes start tomorrow evening. Francis, please do this for me. I've got to keep my job, and he would see your refusal as a slight. I've got to be careful. Please!" she begged.

Francis knew she was right, and he reluctantly agreed. What had made her so worried? He had never seen her so nervous before, and there was relief on her face, as if a great load had been lifted from her shoulders, when he said he would do it.

The next evening, he dutifully arrived at the rectory. His mother showed him into the library where four other people were sitting in chairs set up facing a comfortable upholstered chair by the fire. There were three women and a man. The women seemed to know each other, and it turned out that they were shop girls from a big clothing store on Grafton Street. They were talking among themselves when Francis came in, and they stopped to look him over. They continued their conversion having decided, as if in unison, that he was not worth bothering about. However, one of the women glanced surreptitiously at Francis and turned away when he looked up.

Francis sat down next to the man who was in a chair some feet from the women. The man was in his early twenties and appeared very surly. Francis tried to make conversation with him, but it was like drawing blood from a stone. However, he did find out that he was a clerk at the Guinness factory and his name was Tom Murphy.

Just then, Father O'Brien made his entrance with a flourish and a booming "Good evening, everyone." He sat down in his chair and surveyed them.

"Now this will be a very concentrated course because I have been away. What would normally take at least three months to prepare you must be squeezed into two months in order to be ready for the bishop's visit. So we have to meet at least twice a week if we are going to get through all of the required material," he intoned.

Then he began by asking each of them to tell the others about themselves. Two of the women seemed to have no trouble talking about themselves. Francis thought they seemed very arrogant. The woman who had taken a second look at Francis was named Rachel Pearce. She was tall and skinny but full-bosomed. What attracted him to her was her pretty face and smile. She was not as self-confident as the others and quieter.

When the priest asked Tom to speak, he was very reticent and had to be prodded to offer up information. It was obvious he was very embarrassed. Francis, on the other hand, had no trouble telling the others about himself and what he did. Then the priest talked for about an hour and a half and answered their questions. He then invited them to the kitchen for cocoa. When they had finished, the priest saw them out of the front door.

Francis wished the women good night and waved to them as they went giggling down the street. As they reached the corner, Rachel looked back momentarily and smiled before they disappeared around the corner out of sight.

He found himself thinking about Rachel as he walked home. She was attractive and articulate. She seemed interested in him. He decided to get to know her better, but he had to admit to himself that women like that were not interested in the likes of him because they considered themselves as a class above his status. He knew this was defeatist thinking. Why wouldn't she be interested in him? He was fairly good-looking, interested in learning more about politics and society, determined to improve his lot in life, and had a fine job. No, he had nothing to be ashamed of at all. But what if he was wrong about her interest in him? He would be acutely embarrassed, especially in front of her friends. He would have to take this situation slowly, not appear to be too interested until he had a real sense of how she felt.

These long and boring confirmation sessions would turn out to be fun after all when he could sit there and fantasise about Rachel. What surprised him the most was his sudden and strong interest in the opposite sex. It had come on him like a fever with no warning and had made him unexpectedly light-headed. He hadn't really thought about girls before, and none had shown any real interest in him until now. He had seen his mother naked once, accidently, when she took a bath, so he knew what they looked like. He had heard some of the dirty jokes the older boys in the tenement told. He had laughed knowingly but hadn't really understood what they were talking about. He and his friends had whistled at young couples as they walked down the street hand in hand, but he didn't know why.

No one had taught him about sex and how to handle his feelings. His mother never bothered, and he couldn't ask Father O'Brien. What did a priest know about women? How could he advise him if he never experienced what it was like to be attracted to someone of the opposite sex? All a priest knew about sex was what he had been taught when he was studying in the seminary. No, he needed to talk to a man of the world. He decided to talk to Mr. Riordan the next time he went out to Ranleigh.

The two days before the next class session dragged by slowly. At work, Mrs. Hennessey sensed something and quite innocently said, "Francis, you seem in a daydream, lad. What's wrong? Are you in love?" and she laughed at her own joke. Francis went red in the face and apologised. He said nothing was troubling him. And from then on, he focused on what he was doing.

He was the first to arrive at the next class and sat in a seat that would put him next to the group of women. The three women arrived, talking among themselves as usual, and took little notice of him. Tom followed them in. Rachel sat next to Francis and gave him a smile, which made him go red in the face. The other women giggled, and Francis, dying of embarrassment, hung his head in shame. Just then, Father O'Brien came in, and the session started.

Afterward, when they went to the kitchen, Francis hung back from the group and busied himself helping make the cocoa. When this was done, he handed everyone a steaming mug. When he came to Rachel, she thanked him and whispered, "Please don't be embarrassed. There's no need to be." And with that, she joined the other women.

Tom came over to him. "She's taken a real shine to you. You'd better watch out, or she'll get you in her clutches," he commented and walked away, laughing. This took Francis by surprise. It was quite out of character for Tom to say anything, let alone crack a joke. Did he have a point?

He arrived at Mrs. Ritchie's house that Sunday and had tea with Mr. Riordan. They always talked about many things—the political turmoil in Ireland, the war in Spain. When they had exhausted these subjects, Francis asked Mr. Riordan if they could talk about a personal matter that was bothering him.

"I met this girl, you see, and I don't know quite what to do," he pleaded.

Mr. Riordan smiled. "Let's take a walk and talk about it."

As they walked up the road, Francis explained what was bothering him, and it became quite evident to Mr. Riordan that nobody had told him about the wonders of sex and the love of a woman.

"Your feelings are quite normal for a young man. I know I was confused at your age. No one told me a thing about women or sex. I had to learn as I went along. But I learned that your feelings are natural and nothing to be ashamed about.

"When I left the army, I met a woman, fell in love with her, and married her," he told Francis. "She was a wonderful person, and we were great friends as well as lovers. Unfortunately, she died in childbirth, and the baby was stillborn. I was left alone with my memories. Loving a woman is not all about sex and having children, despite what the Catholic Church teaches. It's about compatibility, respect for each other, and building a future together. Sex is part of this equation, but it's not the be-all and end-all of a relationship. My advice to you is if you are really interested in this woman, take it slowly and develop a meaningful relationship with her first. If it's just sex you want, you can go to Whitefriar Street to one of those bad houses and get that."

They walked on in silence into a nearby park and sat down on a bench. "What do you know about having sex with a woman?" Mr. Riordan asked bluntly.

"Er, not much really," said a red-faced Francis.

They talked for another half an hour and then walked back to the house.

As he cycled back home that evening, his brain was feverishly sorting through his conversation with Mr. Riordan. The more he thought about it, the more questions he had. He would have to save them up until next Sunday when he again visited Ranleigh. One thing was quite clear, he was going to heed Mr. Riordan's advice and take this relationship slowly if it was going to go anywhere.

Class resumed the next evening and followed the usual pattern. When they were leaving the rectory, Rachel hung back from the other women and said to Francis, "Will you walk me home, Francis?"

Francis was flummoxed, and it was all he could do to stutter, "I would like that very much." And they set off down the street.

When they were by themselves, Rachel said to him kindly, "You haven't had much experience talking to girls, have you?"

"No, not really. I don't know what to say to them. It's not like talking to my friends. This the first time I have talked to someone like you," he said after some hesitation and suddenly realising his mistake.

"Should I take offense at what you're saying? Who is someone like me?" she teased.

"No, I don't mean that. The only other women I talk to about things are my mother and Mrs. Ritchie." Now he thought he was making a fool of himself.

They turned into Grafton Street, and Rachel said, "I tell you what, let's go to Bewleys and get some coffee. What do you say?"

They got their coffees and sat down at a table. "Now tell me all about Mrs. Ritchie," she said.

They spent the next hour in deep conversation, and Francis found himself relaxing in her company. She was so easy to talk to, and it turned out that she was interested in the same things he was. He told her all about his life and how his grandparents were killed by the British, forcing his mother into tenement living. He told her about his friends in Ranleigh. He found out that she was an only child and that her family owned a small woman's clothing shop in Henry Street. She was learning the business at the large store on Grafton Street so she could take over the family business.

Eventually, they left the café after getting unsubtle hints from the staff that it was time for them to leave so they could close up. They turned on to Henry Street and walked towards her home, which was above the shop. When he saw her to her door, she turned to him and said, "I have really enjoyed our talk. Can we do it again?"

"I would like that. Let's do this after each class. It would be fun."

"Yes, let's."

With that, she disappeared behind her door. Francis felt on top of the world and headed home. Tonight had been a revelation to him. He didn't know girls were so interesting.

They followed this routine after each class in the subsequent weeks. After a while, they had held hands as they walked up the street. Francis's first clumsy attempt at this was seen by the other two women and had caused them to titter. Embarrassed, he immediately dropped her hand. Rachel didn't care. She grabbed his hand firmly as they walked along.

One Sunday, they visited the Municipal Gallery of Modern Art and spent the afternoon viewing the works of both Irish and British modernists. It was after this visit that Rachel kissed him on the cheek as he saw her to her door. Before he could respond, she was gone.

Their assignations didn't go unnoticed. Unbeknownst to either of them, someone from the rectory's second floor window was angrily watching as they left after class.

One evening, as they approached her home, Rachel grabbed Francis and pulled him into the darkness of an alley next to the shop. She slowly began to kiss him on his mouth, and he responded until their tongues almost tangled up as they wanted each other so much. Then as they kissed, she rubbed her hand against his hardened groin, and he stroked her full breasts. Suddenly, a light went on in an upstairs room, illuminating them and destroying the moment. They stopped, wondering what to do next.

"That's my parents. I'd better go in," she said with a sigh and disengaged herself from his arms.

"Do you have to go?"

"I'm afraid so. They will come looking for me if I don't. It's late, and they're probably worried where I am. Look, I've really enjoyed this evening. You are the most interesting man I have ever met. I hope we can be close friends because we have so much in common."

"I hope so too. It has been a wonderful evening for me. Thank you."

"Let's do this again, shall we?"

"Yes, please."

She turned, unlocked the door, and went into the shop. Francis let a yell of delight and went skipping down the street with nary a care in the world.

The wait was killing him as he dashed to the rectory two days later for another class. When he entered the library, he was puzzled not to see Rachel in her usual place. The other women and Tom were there. Perhaps she was late or maybe sick. Before he could ask the others where she was, Father O'Brien came in and sat down in his chair.

"Before we start, I have a small announcement to make. You will have noticed that Miss Pearce isn't with us tonight. Her parents have sent her to stay with an aunt in Dun Laoghaire. Her aunt is in poor health and needs day and night care. I'm sure she will be missed by all of you. Now let's begin," he said matter-of-factly.

This news hit Francis like sledgehammer. He was thunderstruck. It was all he could do to concentrate on the class. When it was over and they were in the kitchen, Father O'Brien asked him to stay behind.

When the others were gone, the priest turned to Francis. "I saw that you were really affected by my news about Rachel. Was she a particular friend of yours?"

"I met her here, and we had some good times. When will she come back?"

"I don't know. Her father indicated that it would be some time. So I don't know. It seems a shame that your friendship with her has been interrupted in this way. Anyway, you have other friends," he said putting an arm around him.

Francis began to cry and then moan. "What am I going to do? I miss her so much already," he sobbed.

Father O'Brien went over to a cabinet and poured himself a large whiskey and brought a clean glass over to the kitchen table. He poured a large glass for Francis and said, "Here drink this, and we'll talk about it." He took a sip, and his mouth was on fire. He took some more, and it felt better. The priest went on talking about relationships and how it must be God's will that Rachel went away. Francis began to protest, but the drink was having its effect. He felt a little light-headed and very woozy.

The priest went on talking about the parish and its needs for a priest of the people such as him. Then he turned to Francis and confided in him, "We priests are a rum lot. We have taken a vow of celibacy, but in fact, we are human beings, just like everyone else. At least some of us are. I suppose we have an aura of authority about us because of the religious rituals and mythology we have weaved over the centuries.

"People hold us in some sort of awe or superiority because we have seemingly removed any sexual feelings from our lives. In my experience, that is not so. Many of us have wants and desires, but we can't express ourselves. We are locked into a surreal world where everyone regards us as eunuchs. No one knows how lonely our lives really are and how isolated we feel. Take this large house, for example, with just one occupant. Although sometimes there's an assistant priest staying here, I'm usually by myself. I'm busy all the time, going here, there, and everywhere. I have no time for myself," he slurred.

"But you have your parishioners and your work for them, Father," said Francis through a haze of alcohol. He was now feeling woozier from the whiskey.

"But I have no real friends. No one I can talk to. No one I can confide in. I'm all alone really, and no one really cares! That's the heartbreak," he responded. "Will you be my friend, Francis?"

This took Francis completely by surprise, despite feeling the effects of the whiskey. Here was a priest, who was supposed to represent God on earth, asking him to be his friend. Reverence for priestly authority is deeply ingrained into a Catholic's soul from early on in life. He had been taught to fear and respect priests who are regarded as father figures by their parishioners. Father O'Brien's revelations were something he didn't know how to handle.

"I suppose we can be friends, if you would like that," Francis slurred out, not realizing what he said and the consequences.

"Good lad. You see, what I really like is a little massage." And with that, he grabbed one of Francis's hands and rubbed against his crotch.

"Why don't we go into my study where I have a fire going and we can get more comfortable?"

He led a stunned and now completely drunk Francis from the kitchen across the hall to the study. When he closed the door and Francis could see the priest's erection, he felt powerless to stop what came next in front of the fire. A fear and loathing closed in on him like darkness as the priest went to work on him. The pain was overpowering, and he cried out. This seemed to excite the priest who pushed even harder.

When he had finished, he got up and pulled his trousers back on and said to the hurt and humiliated boy, "You don't need a girl to have fun, do you? What has just happened is between the two of us. If you breathe a word to anyone, I'll make sure that you and your mother never walk the streets of Dublin again. Do you understand me? In any case, no one will believe you. Now go home."

Francis just nodded. The pain was subsiding, but when he got up, he had difficulty walking.

"I'll see you on Sunday. Don't be late," said the priest as he left the room.

Francis staggered to the study door. He must find his way home. When he let himself out of the rectory, he collapsed on the pavement, crying. Fear and loathing engulfed him. He found his way home, somehow, and made it to his room. He got into bed, curled up in a foetal position, and just sobbed.

CHAPTER 5

Dawn eventually came up over the horizon the next morning, revealing a shattered human being lying on his bed. Francis had not moved all night and had just lain there, eyes wide open. He was paralyzed and numb with shame and disgust. He had been awake all night, trying to fathom what had happened to him, and he was feeling very sick. One moment, he had been on top of the world, and the next, he was in the depths of despair. It was something he didn't understand. What he did not know then was that this emotional roller-coaster ride would set in motion a chain of events that would turn him into a hunted animal.

Francis had grown up in the church as a Catholic believer, where priests were regarded like little tin gods by their parishioners. They could do no wrong. After all, weren't they supposed to be God's representative here on earth, or so the Catholic faithful were taught? They were your soul's gateway to heaven. Why would Father O'Brien harm him in such a degrading way? Maybe he'd said something to the priest to encourage him. Maybe he was at fault. If the priest was God's representative, maybe he was sent to punish him, but why? What had he done to deserve this? But he had been taught that God was a merciful God, so why this punishment? It didn't make sense.

He remembered his conversation with Brian Gatfield who warned him to be careful of Father O'Brien. The same thing had happened to him. No, this can't be right. He knew good priests like Father Tremain and Father O'Flanagan who would never do this. If you can't trust a priest, who can you trust?

Francis grew angry. Some inner strength, which he could not explain, rose up inside him. Why should anybody do this to him, even if he was a priest? He had no right to treat him like that. He vowed to himself that this would never happen again, whatever the circumstances. He won't be tricked again into submitting.

He heard his mother stirring in the other room. He knew there was no way he could tell her what had happened since she wouldn't believe him. Apart from that, she was desperate to keep her job and the pay so that they wouldn't have to live in a hovel again. He knew that she would hang on to her new life at all costs, even if she knew the priest was abusing her son. What an indictment, but he knew in his heart that would be the case. He couldn't trust his own mother.

He heard his mother in the kitchen making some tea. "You'll be late for work if you don't hurry!" she shouted.

He appeared at his bedroom door. "Mum, I feel too sick to go to work."

"Now look at you. You look as though you haven't slept all night! Go back to bed, and I'll bring you a cup of tea."

A few minutes later, she came in with the tea. "Look, I'll call Mrs. Hennessy on the rectory phone when I get to work. I must rush or I'll be late." With that, she left him lying there in his misery.

His mind was in a whirl. He had to think about what to do. He had to tell someone. Who could he confide in? Not Mr. Riordan, he would be too embarrassed to tell him. He knew that he couldn't tell anyone because no one would believe him.

He wished Rachel was there; she'd understand because she knew the priest and his demeanour. But would she? The more he thought about it, the more he realised he couldn't tell her because that was something you don't tell a girl in whom you are interested. It would make him sound like damaged goods. But he needed her company badly, if only to talk about other things and find out the real reason she left so quickly. He had to find her somehow. He wouldn't tell everything that happened, but he would talk about his fears. Father O'Brien said she had moved to Dun Laoghaire. He didn't know where that was. How could he find out? The library, of course.

He got out of bed very stiffly and walked slowly to the library on Kevin Street. By the time he got there, his body was beginning to loosen, and he was finding it a little easier to walk. When he walked in, he was greeted by Susan Gilks, one of the librarians. "Hello, Francis, what can we do for you today?"

"Mrs. Gilks, I need to get to Dun Laoghaire."

"That town is on the sea, very close by to Dublin. Come over here, and I'll show you the map."

He followed her over to reference department, and she got out a large atlas. She found Ireland and showed him where Dun Laoghaire was.

"The best way to get there is by train from the Amiens Street station here in Dublin. I've made the trip there before, and it only takes about an hour. I don't know what the schedule is. You'll have to check at the station.

You have to go across the River Liffey at O'Connell Street." She showed him the route on a street map.

"Thanks for your help, Mrs. Gilks," he said as he left.

He decided to go to Dun Laoghaire that Saturday. He asked one of the other thurifers to stand in for him at the Sunday mass. He had some money, which he had saved up, and he got it from his room where he had hidden it. That Saturday was going to be another first for him. He had never travelled on a train before and had never even seen one.

When he got to the Amiens Street station that Saturday, he stood there in amazement at the hustle and bustle of this train terminal. He had never seen so much commotion. There were family groups, young people, and the elderly all planning to go somewhere and looking for the right platform or coming off platforms and being greeted by friends or other family members. And the cacophony of noise was deafening from the sound of steam coming from engines, whistles announcing train departures, to a voice over the loudspeaker broadcasting the imminent departures of trains from certain platforms.

When he had got over the shock of seeing this sea of humanity, he looked around for where he should go and saw a large sign that said "Tickets.'" When he got to the office, there were three windows with clerks selling tickets. Signs above them said "First Class," "Second Class," and "Third Class." Judging by the dress and demeanour of people in each queue, he decided that third class would be the cheapest.

Eventually, he reached the window, and the clerk looked him up and down. "Where do you want to go, lad?"

"Dun Laoghaire, please, sir."

"Are you coming back?"

"Oh yes, as soon as I can."

"You'll need a return ticket then, and it will cost you five shillings."

Francis handed over the money, and the clerk told him the train would be on platform two and was leaving in fifteen minutes. He thanked the man and went off to look for the platform. He found it and showed the ticket collector his ticket. He walked up the platform to the engine and took a good look at it.

After a few minutes, he went back to the third-class section, climbed into a carriage, and found a seat by a window. There was already a family in the carriage—a jovial man who was the father, his rotund but happy wife, and a boy and a girl, who must have been about nine or ten. They were deep in conversation about the trivia of family life, such as school and visiting relatives. They observed Francis when he got in, ignored his presence, and carried on with their conversation.

Francis's fascination with the station and the train had temporarily taken his mind off his troubles. As he sat down and waited, they soon returned. Sitting there, he quietly cried as the memory of the rape by the priest flooded back into his mind.

As the time for departure neared, other people climbed in, and before long, all the seats were taken. The train jolted as it started up, which woke Francis from his daydream. He looked mindlessly out of the window as the train ran over viaducts and across the Liffey river. He was seeing Dublin from a different perspective. He was able to look down on the buildings, both grand and small, whereas he was used to seeing them from the street. It was beginning to drizzle with rain, and the city was enveloped in a dreary mist, which matched his mood. The train then came to a grinding halt at Tara Street station.

There was a lot of door slamming, and then a whistle was blown, and the train was off again, gathering speed. It wound its way through the small towns that made up suburban Dublin. The train stopped at another three stations. After the train pulled out of Sydney Parade station, it wended its way east, eventually revealing the countryside and the beautiful panorama that is Dublin Bay. Then it turned south and ran parallel with the sea. This was the first time Francis had seen the sea, and his mouth opened in surprise at the sight. He had seen the large ships that unloaded their cargo at the docks in Dublin, but he had never seen from where they had come.

The train reached Dun Laoghaire, and Francis stepped out and showed his ticket to the ticket collector at the gate. The bracing sea air took his breath away. He breathed in deeply to take advantage of the fresh clean air, which felt totally different from the smoky rancid air of the city.

With all the excitement of the journey, he never gave a thought to how he was going to find Rachel. Now he had a problem. He walked along Harbour Road to take a look at the ships coming in. When he reached the harbour, he sat down on a bench and started to think about how he was going to find her. He could walk through the shopping area of the town in the hope of spotting her. This seemed a waste of time because the chances of running into her were very slim. Then it came to him that she was Catholic, so she would probably go to church the next day, which was Sunday. The question was which church?

He saw some men and a woman mending their fishing nets and approached them.

"Excuse me, could you tell me where is the nearest church?" he asked politely.

One of the men looked up from what he was doing. "Now why would you want to know that?" the man said suspiciously.

"Well, I'm visiting from Dublin, and I want to go to church tomorrow."

"Why should I tell you? We don't like strangers 'round here asking questions, especially them from the city."

"Come on, Cyrus, stop pulling the lad's leg," said the woman.

Cyrus smiled a toothless grin. "That would be Father Randolph's church. It's called St. Michael's, and it's up on Marine Road. You go past the station towards the Royal Marine Hotel, and it's up there on your left. How long are you here for, boy?"

"Just for the weekend. It's the first time I've ever seen the sea. I've never ever seen anything quite so beautiful."

"Ah, but it can be a cruel master to us fishermen. I lost my father and brother out there in a big storm once. It's dangerous because of the currents at low tide at the entrance of the River Liffey. See all these ships in the harbour? They're waiting to go upriver to unload their cargoes in Dublin. They can only do this when the tide is right."

Francis thanked the fishermen and walked back along the harbour wall towards the railway station. He wanted to see St. Michael's before it got dark. He followed the directions he had been given and soon found the church, which was on the corner of Marine Road and Upper George's Street. Now he had to find a place where he could sleep that night.

He decided to walk around the town and get something to eat. He walked down Upper George's Street and saw a grocery store. He bought a loaf of bread and some cooked sausage and then crossed the street to a park, which had benches and a bandstand. He sat down and started to eat. He didn't realise how hungry he was. He decided to keep some of the food for breakfast in the morning.

It was now dark and about eight o'clock by a clock he heard chiming in the distance. He walked to Lower George's Street and saw a pub on one of the side streets. As he approached, he could hear that the evening was in full swing. When he entered, he saw a small group playing a banjo, penny whistle, and spoons. A woman singer was singing popular songs, and the people in the bar were joining in with the choruses.

Francis went up to the bar, ordered a beer, and took it to a quiet corner table. He enjoyed seeing the happy faces and drank in the warmth of their good cheer. After a few minutes, he was singing along with everyone else. During one of the breaks in the singing, a young couple came up to his table.

"Do you mind if we join you?" said the man with a friendly smile.

"Of course not," Francis replied.

"Thanks. My name is Dermot Williams, and this is my wife, Margery."

"I'm Francis Reagan."

They sat down with their drinks.

"We live just around the corner, and we come here every Saturday night. It's always such fun. Do you live close by?" asked Margery.

"No. I live in Dublin, and I'm down here just for the weekend."

"I've been to Dublin a lot," said Dermot. "I follow the league champions Shamrock Rovers soccer team."

"Ah, you haven't seen real football until you've been to Dalymont Park and watched the Bohemians play. They are in a class of their own," Francis replied.

Then they spent the next thirty minutes in friendly banter about their teams and other soccer topics.

Dermot bought a round of drinks. When he was at the bar, Margery asked, "So what brings you to Dun Laoghaire?"

Francis then explained that he was looking for Rachel Pearce who used to live in Dublin. "We were very close, and she left all of a sudden without saying goodbye. I just want to find out why. Her family said she had come here to help out her aunt. I thought I'd wait at St. Michael's in hope of spotting her."

"This is a small town, and apart from the holidaymakers, we pretty much know one another. I can't say I've come across her though," she said sympathetically. She sensed his hurt and wanted to suggest something that might help. Then Dermot returned with their drinks.

"Dermot, Francis was telling me that he was looking for friend of his called Rachel Pearce. She came here to help an aunt. Ring any bells?"

"Fraid not."

Francis changed the subject and asked Dermot about his career. It turned out that he was an accountant at a firm in the town. His new friends were very interested in hearing about Francis's work at the orphanage.

They talked and joked until closing time. They got up together and walked out of the pub. Francis thanked them both for a great evening and was about to leave when Margery asked him where he was staying.

"Nowhere. I'll probably sleep on one of the benches in that park across from here."

"No, you will not. Apart from the police patrols, you are not dressed properly to sleep outside. You can sleep on our sofa in our front room. No argument." she said emphatically.

He hesitated and then said, "Thank you. I would like that. You're so kind."

They went up the hill and turned into another street, which was lined with terraced houses. Dermot got out his keys and opened up the front door of number sixteen and ushered Francis in. The inside of the house was warm and welcoming, and it reflected the personality of its owners.

"Francis, would you like some cocoa?" Margery called from the kitchen.
"Yes, please."

Dermot came into the front room with a pillow and blanket in his arms.
"This should keep you warm," he said.

Margery came in with the cocoa, and they sat down to drink it.

It was after midnight before Francis settled down to sleep on the sofa. He felt very comfortable with his newfound friends. He drifted off to sleep easily that night.

The next morning, he was up early because he wanted to be at St. Michael's for the first service at eight thirty, just in case she went at that time. He was surprised to see Margery and Dermot in kitchen. They greeted him warmly.

"How was your night?" asked Dermot.

"It was very comfortable. I slept like a baby."

"Well, come and sit down and have a cup of tea. Breakfast will be ready in a jiffy," said Margery.

Francis sat down, and Margery served him with a plate of fried eggs, bacon, and fried bread. He began to eat.

"So what's your plan for the day?" Dermot asked.

"Well, I was going to the church, waiting to see whether Rachel comes to one of its three services. If she does, I will be able to talk to her. If not, I will go back to Dublin. I have to work tomorrow, so it's now or never."

"Look, please come back to tea before you go, say three o'clock. We want to hear whether you met up with her or not. Then you can go back. If you haven't seen her, we can ask around and send you news if we locate her. Here, write down your address on this piece of paper," said Margery.

When he had written down his address, Francis walked to the front door and wished his newfound friends goodbye. He headed down the hill on Patrick Street towards the church and reached it at about eight fifteen. He walked into the courtyard of the church and positioned himself in a quiet corner facing the main door. Parishioners for the first mass started to arrive. They were mostly elderly people, and he didn't see Rachel. It was a long wait until the next service at ten. Now there were families arriving, and many more young people. Still, there was no sign of Rachel. Then there she was, running towards the door, late.

Francis called out her name, and she turned and gave him a broad smile. He offered her his arm, and they walked into the church together. They sat down in a pew at the back of the church and looked at each other longingly.

When the service was finished, they walked out together, not saying a word. When they got clear of the other people coming out of the church,

Rachel turned to him. "What a surprise to see you. How did you know where I was?"

"Father O'Brien told everyone you had come here. I wanted to see you to find out why you left so suddenly. I wanted to know what I did wrong."

"You did absolutely nothing wrong. It was very strange. It all happened so quickly. Look, I've got to get my aunt's lunch at twelve. Can we meet, say at one thirty, down at the harbour? I'll tell you all about it then. If I don't go home now, my aunt will worry where I am, and that would mean trouble."

"That would be great. I'll see you then," he replied.

She walked off towards the town centre. He looked after her. She was a very pretty curvaceous woman and confident in herself. She was not like her friends in Dublin who were full of themselves and thought they were God's gift to men. He liked her for that.

The next hour and a half passed excruciatingly slowly. He walked down to the quay where the ferries arrived from Holyhead, which is on Anglesey, an island off the Welsh coast. He watched as they crept in and docked with a gush of water that put the ferry in reverse just before it hit the dock, bringing it alongside perfectly. Once docked, large gangways were attached to the ferry, and passengers and cars were unloaded. Having watched the ferry start its return journey, Francis walked along Harbour Road and on to the east pier to one of the two lights that guarded the entrance to the harbour. By the time he walked back, it was almost one by the town hall clock.

Francis was getting anxious because Rachel was nowhere in sight. It was now twenty minutes to two. Perhaps she's had second thoughts, or maybe her aunt kept her back. And then a voice behind him gently called his name. He turned, and there she was.

"Sorry, I'm late. My aunt asked me to do some things for her," she said.

"I thought you might have had second thoughts about meeting me."

"Not at all, Francis. You shouldn't put yourself down so. Let's walk up to where the yachts are, and we can talk."

They walked arm in arm towards the yacht basin without saying anything and sat down on a bench.

"I want you to understand that I had nothing to do with my moving here. It was my father's idea, or should I say order, really. He was visited by Father O'Brien one evening. I was dismissed from the room, but I managed to listen to most of their conversation through a crack in the door. The crux of it was that I had made bad friends, and he particularly named you. Then he said that you were a product of the tenements and were looking to ingratiate yourself above your station. He said that you were a thief and womaniser not to be trusted, especially around pretty girls. He seemed to have it in for you.

"When Father O'Brien left, I had a terrible row with my father and mother who said that they would make arrangements for me to leave Dublin. They believed that, at nineteen, I should be married, and they would look for a suitable husband for me. They said that there were too many negative influences in the city that would turn a girl's head. So they contacted my aunt, and here I am, very sad and lonely. It's like being sent to a nunnery. I can't contact any friends and especially you. I'm glad you found me," she said with a smile.

At first, Francis went cold, and then a white hot anger grew inside him.

"But you know none of this is true, and so does Father O'Brien," he said hotly. "I'll have to go and have it out with him!"

"I wouldn't do that, Francis, if I were you. Think of the consequences. You facing him down will alert him to the fact that you've talked to me. I don't want to disappear again because I want to go on seeing you. I would just let it be. What I don't understand, though, is why he did this?"

"I don't understand it either," Francis lied because he knew why. "He's always been good to me and my mother. Well, what should we do now?"

He was very angry, but this wasn't the time to decide what he must do. He was with the girl he loved, and he was going to enjoy the short time they had together. He'll deal with the priest later.

"We should arrange to see each other as often as possible, though it is going to be very difficult to communicate without causing suspicion."

"Can you get to a telephone?" he asked.

"Yes. There's one at my aunt's—no, that won't do because she sees the calls on her monthly bill. I could always go to the post office and call."

"Great! Have you got a piece of paper and a pencil?"

She rummaged around in her handbag and found what she was looking for. He wrote down the orphanage's telephone number.

"You can call me on this number anytime during the day. Now you said you don't have any friends here. Well, I'm going to introduce you to two people who I think you will like. They put me up last night, and we had a wonderful evening together. They've asked me to tea at three. What do you say?"

"I would enjoy meeting your friends," she replied.

They talked on for another half hour and then made their way to the centre of town and to Margery and Dermot's house. They were welcomed with open arms and ushered in to the lounge where Francis had spent the previous night. The talk was warm, and everybody enjoyed one another's company. Time flew by, and at four thirty, Rachel said she had to go because she was due back at her aunt's house at five and wanted to see Francis off at the station.

Margery made arrangements to meet Rachel later in the week. Then she and Francis said their goodbyes and set off for the station. They reached it and, in a quiet corner out of anyone's sight, kissed and promised they would get together soon. Eventually, Rachel said she had to go and left his arms. She said a sad goodbye, smiled, turned, and walked towards town. He watched her longingly as she turned the corner.

Francis had to wait an hour for the train, and he sat deep in thought in the waiting room. What was he going to do about Father O'Brien? Rachel was right—he couldn't confront him, but he had to escape his abusive clutches. The more he thought about it, the more he knew that he didn't owe anyone anything, not even his mother. She had been very abusive to him, forcing him into situations that only had her interests at heart. He was determined to be true to himself and not be a slave to the conventional wisdom of the society in which he lived. Mrs. Ritchie had taught him that. He'd have to tell the priest he was not going to allow him to do things to him ever again. Physically, he was big enough, but he wondered if he had the courage to face his aggressor.

He eventually arrived in Dublin about seven. He reached home and climbed the stairs to the flat he shared with his mother. When he let himself in, she was waiting for him. She was very drunk.

"Where the hell have you been?" she demanded.

"Thinking."

"Thinking!" she screamed. "An idiot like you doesn't think. I'm going to take my belt to you right now," she said getting up.

Francis got angry and pushed her back down hard into her seat. He snatched the belt from her hand and threw it across the room. He felt himself go cold with rage.

"No, you won't do anything of the kind. Time has come for you to stop treating me like a child. We afford this place only because we both work. If I could do it, I would find my own place. We are stuck with each other until I work out where I am going to live."

"You can't do this to me, you ungrateful little bastard. You're just like your Black and Tan father, cruel and vicious. You've got his genes all right," she slurred. "I'm not going back to live in that tenement, do you hear me?"

She started to sob and then looked up at him. "You're going to pay for this, you mark my words," she said with a venomous tone to her voice.

He looked at her, and his eyes narrowed. "No, I'm not. I am not, at all, like you. You're a drunk who makes pathetic excuses for your sad life instead of picking yourself up and going back to being the accountant you once were. What happened to you was terrible, but you can't live forever feeling sorry for yourself."

"It's all your fault. If I hadn't had you, I would be living in a house with a loving husband, far from this dump and the people in it," she wailed.

"Don't blame me for your problems. They are partly of your own making. I'm going places, and I'm not going to let you and our circumstances get in my way. The sooner you understand that, the better. I am not sticking around to see you wallow in your own self-pity. I've places to go."

"Oh, aren't you the Mr. Big Shot? Is that what Mrs. Ritchie has taught you?"

"She has taught me that there's more to the world than this."

His mother grabbed for the whiskey bottle, but Francis snatched it from her. He poured what remained of it down the sink. His mother began to cry.

"Why don't you go to bed and sleep off the whiskey! You've got work in the morning."

"Don't you tell me what to do!"

Francis went in to his room and got ready for bed. When he looked out of his room, his mother was fast asleep in her chair with her head on the table. He picked her up and put her to bed. He took the precaution of putting a chair under the knob of his door and went to bed.

The next morning, he left early for work, before his mother was up. He had started catching up with the work he'd missed on Saturday when Mrs. Hennessy came in.

"Good morning, Francis. How are you feeling?"

"Much better, Mrs. Hennessey. I don't know what I caught."

"There's been quite a bit of flu going around this autumn. I need to talk to you about your work here," she said.

Alarm bells went off in Francis's head. What had he done?

"The board have asked me whether you'd be willing to take the boys for sports in the evening. We've seen how you've played soccer with them and would like you to do this officially so we can have our own team to play other kids. You'd still work in the office during the day. It would mean more money, which I'm sure you could find some use for," she said, smiling.

"That would be wonderful, Mrs. Hennessey. Yes, I would love to do it. When do I start?"

"We've got to work out the details yet but probably next week."

For the rest of the day, Francis was elated, yet he was anxious about seeing Father O'Brien again that evening for one of his confirmation classes. After lessons, he played soccer with the kids as usual but decided not to go home before going to the church so he would not have to face his mother. He couldn't face her right now when he had to focus on how he was going to deal with the priest.

He arrived for class on time and took his seat next to Tom Murphy. "Where have you been? Father was mad as hell when you missed the eleven-o-clock service on Sunday," he said.

"I was sick. Probably it was the flu. My mum told him though."

"You'd better watch out, he was as mad as hell."

Just then, Father O'Brien came in and saw Francis. "So the prodigal has returned."

"I was sick, Father."

"So I believe. Stay after class, and we will talk."

After the others had gone, Father O'Brien turned to him and gently admonished him. This took Francis by surprise.

"I've got a treat for you this weekend," the priest began. "I belong to a fishing club, and we have planned a trip to the Camcor River for trout fishing. I want you to come."

Francis was stunned. Now he will have to deal with this priest earlier than he had expected. Remembering what Brian Gatfield had said, he was angry at the thought of going away with him and being used as a sex toy by him and his sick friends. Again, he felt a cold, calculating rage rising in him.

"I won't be going on any weekends with you. You are a sick man who is a loathsome evil person who shouldn't be a priest," he said very calmly. He was just about to hit out when the priest grabbed his testicles through his trousers.

"Listen, you little prick, you will be there or else. Do you understand?" He squeezed and twisted his testicles, producing a pain so excruciating that Francis almost passed out, but instead, he vomited over the priest. He let go immediately, and Francis lay on the floor, writhing in agony. The priest swore and kicked him.

"I don't want to see you ever again! There will be repercussions, mark my words!" he shouted at the top of his voice as he left the room.

When the pain subsided a little, Francis picked himself up and made it to the front door. He vomited again when he was outside. He felt a little better now, and he began to think about how he would handle his predicament. He couldn't go home to face his mother. He couldn't handle her right now, and anyway, he couldn't tell her what happened. He went into a local pub, bought himself a beer, and sat down to contemplate his future. When news got out about what had occurred, or Father O'Brien's version of it, he couldn't go home. His mother wouldn't want him around.

He went home eventually when he knew his mother wouldn't be there. He went to his room and went to bed. He heard his mother come in about midnight. She didn't bother to see if he was in.

The next morning, he left early again and was at his desk by seven thirty. Mrs. Hennessy and he were very busy all day because there was going to be the monthly board meeting the next day. They had to prepare the financial statements and other material that was needed. He finished putting everything in the conference room when Mrs. Hennessy told him to go home.

It was about seven by the time he turned on to his street. He had decided that he would tell his mother he was going to find his own flat. That should give her plenty of warning so she could find something else. He entered their flat and saw a half-empty whiskey bottle and a note. He picked it up and read it. It was from his mother who, in her drunken state, said she had been sacked by Father O'Brien and was not going to live in a tenement again. She called Francis a callous son who cared for nobody but himself, and she didn't want to see him again.

Francis wondered where she was and decided that she was lying down on her bed. He opened the door and stood aghast at what he saw. There, dangling from a beam on the end of a rope, was a grotesque rag doll that had been his mother. Her eyes were wide open and bulging. It was as if she was saying "See what you have done to me." Spittle in the form of foam was coming from her mouth. He ran.

CHAPTER 6

Francis went racing down the stairs and ran into Mrs. Rogers. "Francis, don't run on the stairs. You'll cause an accident," she scolded.

"What's wrong, lad?" she asked, seeing his grey pallor and distress.

"It's me mum! She's killed herself!"

"Oh, God in heaven. Wait here."

She ran upstairs to their flat and was soon back, looking shaken. She took charge at once. "Francis, run and find a garda. There's probably one on Mount Street. Go, lad!"

He woke up from his stupor and ran to find a police officer.

The garda followed him back home and went up to the flat. Mrs. Rogers and Francis were left sitting on the stoop outside, not saying anything. The officer soon came out and told them not to touch anything and to let no one into the building. He rushed off towards the nearest garda station to report what he had found.

About half an hour later, a garda wagon turned up followed by an unmarked car. A dishevelled-looking man got out of the car. He looked as though he hadn't slept for several nights, and his clothes bore witness to that fact.

"I'm Detective Sergeant McFadden. Now who found the body?" he demanded.

"I did, sir. It's me mother," Francis responded.

"I see. Your name?"

"I'm Francis Reagan, and this is our landlady, Mrs. Rogers."

"Did either of you touch anything?" he asked tersely.

"Only the note she left. It's on the kitchen table."

"All right. Wait here, and I'll take a look."

After a while, he was back. "According to her note, she seemed to be angry with you and a Father O'Brien," he said to Francis.

"Yes, she was angry with me because I had had a big row with Father O'Brien, our parish priest. He must have taken his anger out on her by sacking her. She was his housekeeper."

"What was that argument about?"

Francis hesitated and then told him a half-truth. "He had told lies about me to the parents of a girl I was seeing. They made her leave town."

Sergeant McFadden looked directly at Francis. "Is this all you rowed about?"

"Yes, sir," responded Francis, going red in the face.

"Where were you this afternoon?"

"I was at the Kiernan House Orphanage. I work in the office there. I left work at about six."

"All right, lad. We'll have to determine at what time she died and then check your story out with your employer. It's just routine and has to be done. Also, I'll talk to Father O'Brien. Ma'am, did you hear or see anything?" he said, turning to Mrs. Rogers.

"I heard her come in about two this afternoon. I remember thinking how early it was, and then I went on with my housework, not giving it another thought. I didn't hear anything after that."

"That's very helpful because it gives us a timeframe. Having examined her and seen her note, I don't believe there was any foul play."

"What'll happen to her?" Francis asked between sobs.

"We'll take her away to the city mortuary on Store Street, and she'll be examined by the doctors there so that a death certificate can be issued. Then it's up to the coroner who will hold a short court session, probably next week, and officially announce her cause of death. He'll then release her body to you, and you can make arrangements to bury her," he said gently.

Just then, two men came out of the building. Between them was a stretcher with Maureen Reagan's body on it, covered in a blanket. Seeing this, Francis broke again into tears. He then realised how alone in the world he was now.

"What am I going to do?"

"Have you got friends you can stay with tonight? You can't stay in the flat until we've finished our investigation," the sergeant said.

"No," sobbed Francis.

"I'll take care of him tonight," said Mrs. Rogers. "We'll have to talk tomorrow about what's to happen."

Francis settled down to sleep early that night. He was exhausted and mentally drained. He fell asleep quickly, but it wasn't deep and restful. That night saw the start of his nightmares. They were repeated night after night for the next ten nights and would recur every so often for years to come.

The nightmares were always the same. He dreamed that he was in this dark prison cell which was illuminated by a single light bulb. In the corner, sitting in the shadows on chairs, were two prison guards. On the table in front of him were two documents, his mother's suicide note and a warrant for his execution. He didn't know what crime he had committed, and the two guards would not talk. They just stared at him.

There were two doors to his cell, one to the outside world and the second to the scaffold. Suddenly, the door to the outside swung open, and Father O'Brien marched in. He was there to give Francis his last rites, but he couldn't contain himself. He laughed out loud between prayers. He leered at Francis and told him that should he have been a good boy, then all this wouldn't have happened.

All this time, a red mist came seeping gradually through the open door that the priest had come through. The mist enveloped everything.

Then the door to the scaffold opened, and the guards manhandled Francis towards the noose. Just then, his mother appeared and put the rope around his neck, smiling at him all the time. She walked over to the lever that activated the trap door and yanked it. As Francis fell and before the rope tightened, he became suspended in the air. Then he saw a strange creature which was part man, part goat with cloven feet. It had fire in its eyes, and there was the red mist coming from its enlarged nostrils.

The creature was about seven feet tall, and it beckoned him to follow. It said in a menacingly, gravelly voice, *"You belong to me now, Francis, just like your father."* The creature took the noose off Francis, and he followed it through the red mist. *"Let me introduce you to your father. He's an accomplished disciple of mine, and he will follow you from now on."*

Out of the mist came a figure dressed in leather and wearing a black beret.

"Hello, Francis. I see your bitch of a mother has finally met her end. I should have made sure of her in 1920, but we were too busy looking for IRA killers. I am glad she had you though. You can follow in my footsteps and carry on the good work I started. First, you have to deal with that miserable priest. He was the one who drove your mother to kill herself. Now I will visit you from time to time."

With that, he turned back into the mist and disappeared.

Francis screamed after him, "No, no, no. I won't!" It was then that he woke up. His bed was rumpled from his thrashing around and was damp with sweat. He found himself in Mrs. Rogers's spare room and was unable to sleep anymore. He lay awake, shivering.

The next morning, a wrought Francis was treated to a large breakfast. Mrs. Rogers had been very kind to him and had fed him well, although he didn't feel like eating. She persisted saying he had to keep his strength up so that he could make some important decisions for his future. Then she raised a subject she been dreading bringing up.

"Francis, I have a problem. I depend on the income I get from the rent of the flat that you and your mother were in. Now I don't expect you can afford the rent on your own. You will have to find something smaller."

"Oh, how long have I got?"

"You need to be out at the end of the week," she said quietly.

"That doesn't give me much time."

"I know, but I can't afford to have less money coming in."

He didn't argue or plead with her; he just didn't have the energy. He decided that the best thing was to go to work. There was nothing he could do at that moment.

When he got to the orphanage, he found Mrs. Hennessey in the office as usual.

"Good morning, Francis," she said gaily when he walked in. She then saw his downcast demeanour and realised something was awfully wrong.

"What's the matter?"

He then poured his heart out to her. She was aghast at what he told her.

"You leave it to me, Francis. I'll see what I can do."

She made him a cup of tea and then went scurrying off out of the office.

He busied himself with some routine chores, and when she got back about an hour later, she told him that Mrs. Ritchie would like to see him in the boardroom.

He knocked on the door, and he heard a voice saying "Come in." When he entered, Mrs. Ritchie was sitting at the end of the long board table.

"Hello, Francis. Please sit down. I can't tell you how sorry I am to hear about your mother. It must have been quite a shock for you to discover her like that."

"Yes, ma'am. I still can't believe it. I blame myself because I had a bad row with her the day before. I don't know what I'm going to do. I have to bury her, and I don't know where to start. I can't go to Father O'Brien, our parish priest, because he was the one who sacked her. I would feel really uncomfortable talking to him. So I don't know where to begin. Also, I've been given notice by our landlady, so I will have to start looking for somewhere to live too."

"Francis, first things first. We are very happy with your work here, especially what you have done with our kids. We don't want you to leave us. So we would be very happy for you to stay in one of our staff rooms at the top off the building. You can eat with the kids. You will always have a roof over you so long as you are with us.

"Now your other problem is trickier. I will help you arrange to bury your mother. I will contact an undertaker and make arrangements. The unfortunate thing is that she committed suicide. The Roman Catholic Church has some archaic notion that people who commit suicide should not be buried in consecrated ground and have a priest say mass. She will have to be buried at the one of the plots for suicides, and I can arrange for a priest to bury her. Did the police say when you could have the body?"

"They told me the coroner would rule on her death sometime next week."

"Fine, leave the arrangements to me. Now what you need to do is to pack up your things and move in here."

"Thank you, Mrs. Ritchie. I just can't thank you enough."

"Just don't let me down."

Mrs. Ritchie was as good as her word. They buried Maureen Reagan ten days later at the Ballyborough Suicide plot. Francis moved into the staff accommodations at the orphanage and began to settle into his new life.

Weeks later, a tall elderly stranger arrived at the orphanage, asking for Francis. Mrs. Hennessey found him playing soccer with the kids.

"There's a gentleman looking for you. He looks very serious. Be careful what you tell him," she advised.

Francis went inside to the front hall and walked up to the man who was sitting in one of the stuffed chairs.

"Are you Francis Reagan?" he asked kindly.

"Yes, sir."

"What was your mother's Christian name?" he asked.

"Maureen, sir."

"Well, Francis come and sit down. I have some good news for you."

Francis sat opposite him.

"My name is Robert O'Leary. I was your grandfather's solicitor. He had written a will, leaving his estate to his wife and then to his children. After he, his wife, and three sons were murdered by the British, your mother inherited his estate. However, she ran away before we could talk to her, fearing for you and herself. So we were never able to find her. I saw the short piece in *The Irish Times*, reporting on the coroner's court finding of suicide. After a few more questions of the garda, I was able to trace you."

Francis opened his mouth in surprise.

"I don't know what to say. I am shocked. How much would I inherit?"

"Enough to give you an income of about two thousand and five hundred pounds a year. There will be taxes to pay on the principal, of course, and it will take about six months to go through probate."

"It's a pity my mother isn't alive to enjoy this news. She always wanted to get out of living from mouth to mouth. After all she went through, she could have lived a different life. If only she knew."

"You will have to decide what you are going to do now. You have enough to live comfortably."

"I hear what you are saying, but I can't desert my friends and the people who believed and trusted in me. I will certainly move out of the staff quarters here at the orphanage and find myself a flat somewhere. I don't think I will make any other changes."

"I admire your loyalty. Your grandfather was like that too. There's no rush to do anything right away. Just give it some thought. Here's my card. I'll be in touch with you when I have more news."

Francis met with Mr. O'Leary several times after that to discuss the will and its ramifications. Some six months later, the will had cleared the probate court, and the principal amount was made available to Francis. Mr. O'Leary helped him set up some investments and a bank account. This, of course, was new to Francis, but his good sense and intelligent questions helped him start to understand the complexities of his new life. Also, with the help of Mr. Riordan, he found a suitable flat.

He spent many weekends visiting Rachel and the Williams's in Dun Laoghaire. They were very happy for him when he told them of his good fortune. When they all went out together and spent money on food or drinks, Francis, for the first time, was more comfortable with himself and now felt he wasn't a cadger of their generosity.

As the weeks went by, Francis noticed that Rachel wasn't herself. Usually, she was very bubbly and gregarious, but now she was deep in her own thoughts and seemed distracted. This mood had been coming on slowly, and Francis wondered what was troubling her.

One Sunday, they were walking as usual along the harbour wall when she sat down on a bench and turned to him. He could see tears welling up in her eyes.

"My parents want me to get married to this man I hardly know. Oh, he's very kind and considerate, but I'm not in love with him. They have been putting pressure on me for some weeks now."

"You should have told me."

"I couldn't. I suppose I was hoping that I could put them off indefinitely. Then I told them about your good fortune and how you had come into a bit of money. I thought this would change their minds about you. It was the wrong thing to tell them. They were mad at me for defying them and being in contact with you. That hastened their decision. I have to marry this man next month, otherwise I will be cut off from my family."

She started to cry, and Francis put his arm around her for comfort.

"Then we'll have to elope!" he said.

"We can't do that. I love my family. I have this terrible choice to make. If I choose you, there would be no reconciliation with them—ever. I can't do that. It would hurt them irretrievably. I love my parents, and they mean the world to me, but so do you."

She took a deep breath, dried her eyes, composed herself, and continued, "I have decided that I must obey them, and I'm afraid, Francis, this means we have to part as friends and lovers. Please don't think badly of me for this decision. It is probably the hardest one I will ever make."

Francis didn't know what to say. He was speechless. Here was the girl he thought the world of saying she didn't want to see him again. He felt hurt, angry, and sorry for Rachel all at the same time. It was that damned priest's fault.

"I must go. My aunt is taking me back to Dublin today. I am so sorry, Francis. I would give anything to change the situation." And with that, she kissed him on the cheek and walked away. He watched her go, knowing that this was probably the last time he would ever see her.

Going home that night, Francis was in a deep depression. So the priest had finally won. He had lost his mother and his girl, let alone being raped by the man. He resented Father O'Brien with an ice-cold detachment that frightened him. Part of him wanted to take revenge; the other urged him to let it go. There was nothing he could do without getting into trouble. He had to look out for himself now and concentrate on his own future.

The following week was the most difficult for Francis because of his conflicting emotions. To overcome these, he managed to absorb himself in his work, but it was difficult to forget the past. His nightmares had returned, and they left him psychologically devastated. He had nobody to talk to now about his feelings and what had happened to him. He felt totally alone in the world.

That Sunday, he was due to visit the Ritchie household, particularly the staff who had been so kind to him. He was looking forward to it, and his spirits were uplifted at the thought of the insightful conversations he usually had with Mr. Riordan and the wonderful tea prepared by Mrs. Haggerty. So it was with a sad feeling that he set off for Ranelagh. He arrived at exactly three o'clock and knocked on the door. Ellen, the maid, let him in.

Mr. Riordan was in his usual chair, reading the newspaper.

"Hello, Francis. How's the world treating you?" he asked cheerfully.

"Oh, all right, I suppose," he replied sullenly.

Sensing something was wrong, Mr. Riordan suggested they go for their usual walk to the park. On the way there, they talked in generalities about politics and the Spanish Civil War. When they reached a bench near the duck pond, they sat down, and Mr. Riordan turned to Francis.

"What is bothering you? Are you thinking about your mother?"

"No, not really."

"Then what is it?"

"I don't want to talk about it."

"Please yourself. I thought it might help if you talked about it. Something else has happened to you, hasn't it?"

"Don't you understand, I don't want to talk about it! Just leave me alone!"

"Fine, Francis, but I'm always willing to listen. If you don't want to tell a friend what's bothering you, I'm not going to ask again." And with that, Mr. Riordan got up and started to walk on the path which went around the pond.

Francis began to sob. "All right then, I'll tell you!" he shouted after Mr. Riordan who came back, sat down, and didn't say anything.

"First, you must promise not to speak to anyone about what I am going tell you. Promise!"

"I promise, Francis. This will be between you and me."

"Rachel's parents are forcing her to marry someone else, and she told me last week she can't see me anymore."

Then the whole story came gushing out about Father O'Brien's assault, his interference with Francis's relationship with Rachel, his attempt to get him to go to his fishing club, and his attack when Francis said no, resulting in his vomiting over the priest and to his mother's firing. The sad tale came out between sobs, and when he had finished, he told Mr. Riordan of his rage about what the priest had done to him.

"You don't believe me, do you?" accused Francis.

"Yes, I do, absolutely."

Mr. Riordan then sat there in silence for what seemed a long time, contemplating what he was going to say. "What I am going to tell you must likewise go no further than the two of us. Nobody knows this. I was sexually abused and beaten by some Catholic brothers when I was very young. This continued on and off for years. My mother had put me in an orphanage when I was eight, which was run by a Catholic religious order. She was a single mother, and the local parish priest wanted her to do this to remove the stigma of having an illegitimate child so that she could marry. Although she married later, I never saw her again, and she certainly didn't want to know me. I left the orphanage when I was sixteen and worked as an under-gardener for a rich family in Rathfamham. As soon as I was old enough, I joined the army."

"How do you deal with the shame you have suffered?"

"At first, I was angry with everyone around me. I was frightened, had panic attacks, nightmares, and sudden fits of uncontrollable anger. You name it, I had it. I didn't trust anyone because it seemed to me that I had no control over my body and what these perverts did to me. I developed a defensive wall to shut everything out.

"I told you before that I was once married. She was a kind, caring person, and I was lucky someone like that took an interest in me. My problem was that I couldn't talk about my feelings, and I couldn't have a close relationship with anyone. I couldn't trust anyone, you see. Janet was patient and slowly brought me around from the depths of despair that had been festering in me for many years. But with her death, my dreams of a stable home life were shattered once again."

"My story is nothing compared with yours," Francis said after some reflection. "How do you cope with it?"

"Slowly. I had to realise that what had happened to me was not my fault. You have to develop the determination not to let it affect your life. This is easier said than done, but gradually, you make it happen. Having someone to love me and care about me helped a lot. I sometimes get flashbacks, but on the whole, it's now a distant memory."

"What do you suggest I do?"

"First, understand that it happened to you only once and that you will never get into a situation where it will occur again. What happened with Rachel was unfortunate, but you will get over it and meet someone else. I am sure you don't think this right now, but believe me, that will happen. Time is a great healer. You are doing a wonderful job at the orphanage. Focus on that."

As they walked back to the house, Francis felt that a great weight had been lifted off his shoulders. Someone now understands what he had been going through. This was someone he could confide in.

Monday morning came, and he went to work in high spirits. At the weekly staff meeting, Mrs. Ritchie announced that the board had decided to appoint a chaplain for the orphanage and had asked the archbishop of Dublin to nominate a priest to take this part-time position. She said he was coming to see her that afternoon and asked all members of the staff to welcome him with open arms. Francis didn't think anything of this and went about his daily responsibilities with a happy and positive attitude.

Lunch time was the usual raucous occasion in the large dining hall. The kids were abuzz with the coming soccer match against St. Ignatius School the next day, and they kept pressing Francis for his opinion on how the game would go. He always enjoyed this banter with the kids and had hardly touched his meal when the bell went for the first period of the afternoon.

As he walked back to the general office, he saw Mrs. Ritchie ushering a man in black into her office. He couldn't see his face because his back was towards him. He didn't think anything of it as he began his work. Sometime later, Mrs. Ritchie came in to the office followed by Father O'Brien.

"I would like you to meet Father O'Brien who has been appointed as our chaplain by the archbishop," she said. "I'm just showing him around the orphanage to meet people before he starts here next week. Father, this is Mrs. Hennessey, our office manager, and this is Francis Reagan, her assistant."

Francis's jaw dropped, and he managed to politely say, "Father O'Brien and I are well acquainted."

Father O'Brien flushed a little, gave a wintery smile, and mumbled a general "hello" to them. Then he and Mrs. Ritchie were off.

Francis just stood there not believing what he had just seen. Father O'Brien would be here among these impressionable kids, and they would be a source for his perverted pleasures. He would be like a predator licking his lips as he circles his prey, deciding which one would fulfill his insatiable appetite.

"Francis, you look as though you have seen a ghost. Aren't you going to sit down, or are you going to stand there all afternoon?"

Francis woke up from his trance. "Sorry, Mrs. Hennessey."

He sat down, and for the rest of the afternoon, his mind was not on his work, and Mrs. Hennessey had chided him several times.

Francis made up his mind that he would have to confront the priest. He knew that Father O'Brien took confessions on Wednesday evenings between six and eight o'clock. He realised that this would be his best chance to get him on his own so they could talk.

On that Wednesday evening at seven thirty, Francis watched from the street as people were coming and going from the church. When he saw the last person go in and then come out, he realised that the session was winding down, and it was time to move. He crossed the street, quietly entered the church, and sat in a back pew in the shadows. The priest came out of the confessional and started to switch off the lights and tidy up the pews where people had been waiting.

"Good evening, Father!" said Francis from the shadows.

The startled priest dropped the books he was carrying. "Who's there?" he demanded.

"It's Francis Reagan."

"Ah, Francis, this is a surprise to see you. What are doing here?" he said nervously.

"I have come to listen to your confession and give you absolution for your sins!"

The priest laughed nervously. "Always the joker, aren't you, Francis? They always said you were."

"I have come to talk to you, man to man, about what you did to me and demand that you relinquish your role at the Kiernan House Orphanage."

The priest laughed out loud. "You've got to be joking. We'll let bygone be bygones, won't we? Now let me be clear, if I get a whiff of a problem from you, I will make your life impossible. Do you understand me?" he threatened.

"Yes. But I will not let you harm those children. I'll be watching! I know you well enough. You're a pervert and should be locked away," he said coldly as his rage grew.

"You cheeky bastard! I can make more trouble for you than you can ever make for me. See this collar? People wouldn't believe you. They'll believe me, though, because I'm a priest. By the time I've finished spreading word around, they'll think you want to keep the orphans for yourself. Now be a good boy and don't rock the boat or else. Now get out of my church before I call the garda!" he screamed.

Suddenly, the red mist began to fill the church as Francis now seethed with anger. He became so angry that he felt himself go cold and that strange feeling came over him again. Something had to be done to stop this priest. He mustn't be allowed to molest one more child.

A voice in his head said, *"Are you going to let him get away with that? I know your father wouldn't. Don't let him insult you. Didn't he really murder your mother? What about poor Rachel, eh? Think of the children at the orphanage. Who will stop him if you don't? Perhaps you don't care. Why not just walk away? No one would blame you."*

He turned on his heels and marched towards the exit. He slammed the door but didn't go out. He crept around the inside perimeter of the church and entered the vestry. He grabbed the thurible around the chain and waited behind the door.

After a while, Father O'Brien came in. Too late, he felt the cold chain go around his neck. It tightened as he began to cry out, wringing the life out of him. He put his hands up in an effort to tear the chain from his throat, but it tightened even more. And then it was oblivion.

CHAPTER 7

Father Ashley was late as usual. He hated early morning services. He thought they were a waste of time. Not many people came at six thirty in the morning, but the church insisted on holding them twice a week. As the junior priest in the parish, he was responsible for officiating at these services.

As he approached the door leading to the church, he got a bunch of keys out of his pocket and started to put one of them in the lock. It was then that he noticed that the door was open. He mumbled to himself about how senile Father O'Brien had become by leaving the church unlocked after he took confessions the night before. And look, he even left the lights on. He'll have to have a word with him. He walked down the aisle and found the front entrance door open as well.

He turned and walked back up the aisle. It was then that he saw something lying on the altar. When he reached the sanctuary, he recognized the naked body of Father O'Brien. He was lying face down with the chain of the thurifer around his neck and a crucifix stuck between his buttocks. His eyes were bulging, his hands were gripping the chain, and saliva had dripped from his open mouth on to the altar.

A piece of paper lay on his torso. When the priest got close enough, he read, "Know me, for I have sinned against my God and his people." The paper had been torn from a prayer book, and the message was written in pencil, using just capital letters.

With a scream, Father Ashley ran out of the church, stopping only to vomit in a corner as he went. In the rectory study, he made a telephone call to the garda. He knew it was too early to call the diocesan office since they wouldn't be there until eight o'clock. What should he do now? He turned deathly grey, thinking about what he had seen, and fell to his knees, praying for the soul of Father O'Brien.

About ten minutes later, two uniformed garda officers arrived. The senior officer introduced himself to Father Ashley who showed him where the body was. The other officer stood guard at the front entrance to the church to prevent anybody from coming in. The senior officer asked Father Ashley whether he'd touched anything.

"No. I was so disgusted at what I saw from a distance I didn't go any closer. The lights were blazing, and both doors were open. That's all I know," he responded.

"Do you know the person on the altar?" the sergeant asked.

"That's Father O'Brien who is the parish priest here."

"Thank you, Father. Would you please remain in the rectory? The investigative team will want to talk to you further."

"I'll be in the study, working," he said as he walked away.

Det. Sgt. Bill Maloney arrived shortly afterward. He was just leaving the police station after pulling an all-nighter when he got the call about the murder. The elder uniformed officer briefed him on what he had found. The sergeant took a quick look at the body and went into the rectory to talk to Father Ashley. He knew it was important to interview the first person on the scene of a crime as soon as possible. First impressions and thoughts were essential to any investigation.

Father Ashley was seated at the large mahogany desk, working on some papers when Detective Sergeant Maloney came in. The policeman settled in a chair and took out his notebook.

"Father, I understand you found the body?" he said.

"That's right. I've already told the other officer this."

"Please go through the details again in case you have forgotten something. It's very important that we get all the details."

"Well, if I must," said the priest with an irritated sigh. Then he reiterated his story about finding the body.

"When did you last see him?" asked Maloney when the priest had finished.

"At supper in the rectory at about seven last night. He left at about seven thirty to take confessions."

"Weren't you concerned about his whereabouts later last night?"

"Not really. After supper, I went to my room to work on a sermon for Sunday. I went to bed early because I was taking the early morning service."

"Thanks, Father. That will be all for now."

Det. Insp. Brian O'Hanlon arrived at the church about half an hour later. Although he was up and dressed, he didn't have time for breakfast that morning when the station contacted him, which made him grumpier than usual. He was a big man, standing at about six feet three inches and had a well-trimmed beard, which was going grey. He had been in the Irish police force or garda for fifteen years and had seen just about every crime imaginable.

He greeted Detective Sergeant Maloney, who met him at the front entrance to the church. "Hello, Bill, what have you got to delight me first thing in the morning?"

"A dead priest. Wait until you see this one. I thought I'd seen everything. It's so macabre," he responded.

When they got to the altar, O'Hanlon let out a low whistle. He examined the body closely from many angles and read the note several times. He then turned to the sergeant.

"Someone doesn't like priests, or maybe this priest in particular. He was undressed, carefully laid out, and the crucifix stuck up his backside. I'll bet my pension that his crime has sexual connotations. The message on the paper indicates some sort of retribution. What do we know about this priest?"

"Not much. Father Ashley, who found the body, could fill you in on his background."

"Fine, I'll go and talk to him. Bill, in the meantime, organise a search of the church for any evidence and inform the coroner's office."

"Right, sir."

The inspector entered the study and found Father Ashley on the telephone. He finished his conversation quickly and put down the receiver.

"I'm Inspector O'Hanlon. I'm in charge of the investigation into the murder of Father O'Brien," he told the startled priest.

"I was just on the telephone to diocesan office to tell them what had happened. I am sure the bishop will want to know immediately."

"I would like to ask you a few questions. What can you tell me about Father O'Brien?" the inspector asked.

"I didn't know him that well. I've only been here three months. Father O'Brien and I had a friendly but strained relationship."

"What do you mean?"

"He had been running this parish for several years by himself. I used to work in the diocesan office, and the bishop appointed me to be his deputy. I think Father O'Brien saw me as a spy for the bishop."

"What makes you think that?"

"Oh, I don't know. It was just a feeling I got. He always seemed cautious around me."

"Do you know of anyone who had a grudge against him?"

"No, no one I can think of—wait a minute, there was the housekeeper he fired because he said she had been stealing. She killed herself though. That's all I can think about. He wasn't back here that long. He'd been on sabbatical for six months and had returned about the same time I came to the parish."

"Sabbatical? Where did he go, and what did he do?"

"I believe he went to some religious order in County Wicklow, but I don't know what his assignment was."

"Thank you, Father. You've been very helpful. Now I'd like to see his room," O'Hanlon said, terminating the interview.

The priest hesitated. "I will have to get permission from the bishop for you to see his private room."

"Look, Father, this is a murder inquiry, not an afternoon tea party! If you don't show me, I'll find it for myself!" he barked.

"All right, but I do so under protest. My superiors will hear about this," he said snootily.

"Fine."

They climbed the very ornate oak staircase to the second floor and walked to the front of the rectory to a room that overlooked the street below.

"Thank you, Father, that will be all," he said, dismissing the priest and closing the door before he could say anything.

The room was large but austerely furnished. There was a single four-posted bed on one wall, a small desk with papers scattered on it, a large crucifix on another wall, and a chest of drawers. Inspector O'Hanlon started with the chest. There was nothing unusual there but a few clothes. He sat at the desk and went through the papers. There was nothing there too. What struck the policeman was how impersonal this room was. There were no photographs or pictures. There just was nothing to tell you about the occupant. There must be something.

He took the drawers out of the desk and looked behind them. There was nothing. Then he did the same to the chest of draws. And then bingo—he found two envelopes behind one drawer. He opened the first which was full of bank statements, and the other had photographs of naked boys in various poses. "Well, well, what have we here? The secret life of Father O'Brien," he said to himself.

He pocketed the envelopes in his raincoat and went downstairs to the entrance hall of the rectory where he was met by Father Ashley. "Did you find anything?" the priest asked.

"Nah," was his response, and he walked back into the church to find Detective Sergeant Maloney.

"How's it going, Bill?"

"There's not much here. We found this cap at the back of the church. It's one worn by hundreds of workers in this city. No knowing who it belongs to. We found the priest's clothes in the vestry. Judging by the mess in there, that was where he was killed. Our victim put up a tremendous fight for his life. His body was probably undressed there and then taken to the altar. The crucifix had been torn from the front of the pulpit."

"When the police surgeon arrives, ask him to look under the priest's fingernails for any skin. Our murderer might have been scratched in the fight. I doubt it though because he was probably attacked from behind and was fighting for his life by clutching at the chain and trying to tear it away from his neck."

The inspector took the two envelopes from his raincoat pocket. "I found these in his room. One has bank statements, which we can go over at the station. The other envelope was more interesting. It contains some pornographic pictures of boys. We must keep this to ourselves for the moment, but it would be interesting to find out if any of these lads are in this parish. We can start with the current altar boys and other boys that help with services.

"It would help if the police photographer could blow up just their faces so we could show the head shots around," he said.

"I can't believe a priest would be guilty of such a crime. The church wouldn't allow it," Sergeant Maloney said incredulously.

"I suppose it happens in the best of circles. Get these pictures down to the photographer and see what he can do with them. Make sure he doesn't breathe a word of it to anyone, and don't tell him where you got them. We might have come across a paedophile ring, and it might be related to this murder.

"Bill, I'll organise a door-to-door canvas to see if anybody saw anything last night. I don't hold out much hope though. People around here don't trust the garda, so it will be like squeezing blood out of a stone," said Inspector O'Hanlon, and with that, he left for the garda station.

Inspector O'Hanlon set in motion the door-to-door canvas of the neighbourhood. He briefed three constables on what to ask and arranged to meet with them at the garda station in three hours to evaluate what they had found out.

Then he began to sift through some of the material he had found in the priest's room. There were at least five years' worth of bank statements, and after about an hour of carefully checking these, a pattern began to emerge. He soon came to the conclusion that Father O'Brien had been siphoning off money, probably from the church collection. Each week, there had been small cash deposits made at a Limerick bank's Dublin branch. These amounts were five to ten pounds and, when added up, came to a sizeable amount. "So, Father, you were an embezzler too?" O'Hanlon said to himself.

He wondered to himself whether anyone else knew about the priest's scheme and was blackmailing him. He was now getting a clearer picture of him. One question he had was why Father O'Brien had had a six-month sabbatical. He would have to ask the diocese this when he met with them. However, he was not naïve enough to think he would get a straight answer. The church regarded itself as an authority unto itself and not answerable to anyone outside its precincts. Knowing the church as he did, they would be covering up any wrongdoing by one of theirs and presenting a picture of a fatherly parish priest. He knew, in dealing with the church, his inquiries would probably be futile. He would have to be very subtle and careful in questioning them.

His experiences with the church had been mostly positive at the parish level, but he had come across some priests who were arrogant, socially inept, secretive, or thoroughly dishonest. He wondered why these people ever entered the priesthood. Were they running away from something and finding sanctuary from the world within its walls? Were they succumbing to family pressure that said one of the sons has to become a priest, however much they didn't want to commit to a lifetime of poverty and celibacy? Was it to hide an inadequacy, which would be revealed if they weren't cloistered in this artificial life? Or were they hiding from a deeper anxiety than any of these? It just didn't make sense to him. He knew that some priests had a genuine calling, but so many men? It was hard to believe.

He was woken from his musings by Sergeant Maloney who had debriefed the three constables. "As you thought, sir, our canvas brought up nothing, except some people who were applauding his death. They said it was God's punishment for breaking his law. But they had nothing specific to say about the crime or suspects."

"I think I'll pay a visit to a local watering hole around closing time. There should be looser tongues then. What's the nearest pub to the church?" O'Hanlon asked.

"There's a poor excuse for a pub called The Rising. It is in Claremont Alley, which is across from the church. You can't miss it. It's a real dive of a place where the locals from the tenements go to get drunk."

"Thanks, Bill. Now let me tell you what I have found out about our victim." He then proceeded to show the surprised sergeant the bank statements he had been studying.

At about ten thirty that evening, Inspector O'Hanlon approached The Rising. He could hear the loud chatter of the people inside. Suddenly, the front door swung open, and a large man threw a much smaller one down the steps that led to the front door of the pub.

"Now don't come back unless you have the money to pay for your drinks!"

With that, he slammed the door. O'Hanlon, watching from the shadows, saw the scruffy man pick himself shut up, swear, and go staggering on his way. The inspector then went into the pub.

Sergeant Maloney had been right about the place. There were benches around a large room and a counter at one end, which served as the bar. The pub had previously been a shop, and it was quite obvious that the place had not been cleaned for a long time. About fifteen customers, mainly men, were either sitting or standing in groups, busily talking. They were dressed in ill-fitting clothes of the poor, with the dirt of their labours on their faces and hands. Three women sat on one of the benches and eyed O'Hanlon suspiciously as he walked to the bar.

Sensing his presence, a hush fell over the pub. O'Hanlon walked up to the bar and, in a loud voice, ordered a beer. He then said, "I'm Inspector O'Hanlon of the garda. I'll stand a beer for anyone who can give me information about Father O'Brien. Now I'll know when you're lying, so don't try it on."

"What do you want to know?" asked the landlord.

"Anything about him that could help catch his killer."

"Why should we care about him? He was a nasty piece work," one of the women responded.

"What do you mean?" the inspector asked.

"He would give us a hard time about drinking and not going to mass. He would stop you in the street and give you hell. While he was doing that, his breath smelt of drink. Talk about a hypocrite!" she said angrily. "We have enough problems just living. We didn't need his holier-than-thou attitude. I think he enjoyed bullying people."

"Too right. He refused to let me sister's kids be confirmed because she didn't go to church," said another of the women. "Then there was Maureen Reagan who was his cleaning lady. He suddenly sacked her. He said she had been stealing, but nobody believed that. She was so upset that she killed herself, poor lass! She was one of us, trying to make a living."

"What about her family? How did they take this tragedy?" O'Hanlon asked.

"She only had a son, and he moved away when he came into some money. He works at an orphanage in the office there."

"There's one other thing," the third woman said. "It seems that Father O'Brien liked boys. It's pure gossip, mind, but I know at least two families who have moved away after their sons had become altar boys. Word had it that he was sent away by the bishop to some order in County Wicklow for six months."

"Could you give me the names of the families?"

"One was the Stevens, who went to a place on Mount Street near Merrion Square, and the Gatfields, who now live in a town in County Wexford."

"Thank you, ladies, you have been very helpful," O'Hanlon said. "Here's a few shillings for your cooperation."

He turned and walked out of the pub and took a deep breath of the night air.

*   *   *

Francis had woken up that morning with a piercing headache. Had he been drinking or involved in an accident? How did he get home? He could not remember anything from the time he left work the day before to when he woke that morning. He tried to reconstruct his movements, but it wasn't coming to him. It was a complete mystery why he had no recollection of anything that had happened the previous evening. It was blocked completely from his memory.

What was strange was that Francis felt very stiff in his arms and shoulders. Both of his hands had burn marks. He stared down at them for a long time. He could make out an outline of a small chain on each hand. How did I get these? He shook his head and started to get ready for work.

His route to work took him past St. Clements Church. As he turned the corner on his bicycle to ride by the church, he saw a garda officer standing outside the main entrance, talking to two people who wanted to go in. He wondered what was going on. He was tempted to stop to find out, but he was late already and had to pedal hard to be on time.

It wasn't until late that afternoon that he knew what had happened. Mrs. Ritchie called the staff together and announced that Father O'Brien had been found dead that morning. She said the bishop had called to give her the news and said he would appoint someone else as chaplain. She did not go into the cause of death or give any more details because that was all she had been told.

Francis didn't know how to feel. Part of him was sorry that the priest had died, but on the other hand, part of him was glad his nemesis was no longer there to taunt him. For the sake of the boys at the orphanage, he was relieved that one predator was no longer there. He was curious about how he had died, and he was interested in finding out what happened.

On his way home, he got off his bike at the church and joined a group of some twenty people gathered at the steps leading to the front entrance. A garda officer was still stationed at the door. Francis recognised his former landlady Mrs. Rogers and went over to her.

"Mrs. Rogers, what's going on?" he asked.

"It seems that Father O'Brien was murdered last night in the church when he was taking confessions. They took his body away late this morning. That young arrogant priest, Father Ashley, announced a few minutes ago that when the police have finished here, the church will be closed because it has to be reconsecrated by the bishop. He didn't know when that would be," she said.

"How did he die?"

"They won't say, but I heard from someone whose son is in the garda that he was strangled. It seems they are talking to all the altar boys, acolytes, and anyone else who worked with him."

"I wonder why them."

"It seems that they think he had a problem with one of them. Anyway, we now have to go to St. Athanasius for services until they reopen the church."

"Thank you, Mrs. Rogers," Francis said as he walked back to his bicycle.

Francis mused that it wouldn't be long before they talked to him, and what could he tell them? If he said he was angry with Father O'Brien because of what he had done to him and his mother, they would immediately suspect him of the killing. If he said nothing, they would hear things from such people as Mrs. Rogers, and his goose would be cooked. He decided that the best course of action was to be honest and not to lie but not volunteer information. He'd have to have an alibi for last night. The trouble was he couldn't remember where he was. He'd have to think of something.

Francis didn't sleep again that night. He did nothing but toss and turn. He kept on going through in his mind his story and all the possible questions the police could ask him. By five in the morning, he gave up trying to sleep and made himself a cup of tea and some breakfast. He left home at six and picked up a copy of the *Irish Times* so he could see what the newspapers were saying about the crime.

Arriving at work at six thirty, he spread the newspaper over his desk and started to thumb through its pages. The local news was on page four, and when he turned to that page, the headline of the main story blared at him, POPULAR PRIEST MURDERED IN CHURCH. When he read the article, he couldn't believe the fiction he was reading. There wasn't much information about the crime itself, but it said the police were exploring several avenues, including talking to everyone who had been on his staff.

What he couldn't believe was the sickening statement from the bishop, lionising Father O'Brien as a true parish priest who had always put his parishioners and their concerns first. He said that he would be a considerable loss to his community and greatly missed by those that knew him. According to the bishop, he was a shining example of what a parish priest should be—unselfish, giving of himself, kind, and understanding.

When Francis read this, he grew very angry. Why are they hiding his true character? Why do they hide all the lies? This was an evil man who deserved what he got. They don't care about what had happened to him and to countless other boys during this man's reign of terror. Francis thought back to his conversations with Mr. Riordan. Maybe the Workers' Party was right when it accused society of being made up of elites, such as the church, who didn't care about ordinary poor people so long as they remained in control. From that moment on, Francis was determined that he would do something to mend the hate he felt and correct the imbalance of power that was rife, as he saw it, in society.

About half an hour later, staff members at the orphanage began arriving for work. Francis put the paper away and focused on his work for the rest of the day.

CHAPTER 8

It wasn't until the following Monday that Francis was interviewed by the police. He was beginning to think that they had forgotten about him, and as a result, he was feeling more relaxed.

Mrs. Hennessey answered the telephone when it rang. "Right away, ma'am."

"That was Mrs. Ritchie. She wants to see you now, and she has some visitors with her," she told him.

He stiffened at the news, and his positive demeanour was instantly washed away. He hesitated.

"Go on, lad, she's waiting for you!"

With this, he left his desk and began to walk towards the main staircase which took him down to Mrs. Ritchie's office. He walked slowly, as if he was heading to his execution. He wanted to gather his thoughts before he faced the police.

His hesitant knock on the office door was answered right away with a "Come in."

Mrs. Ritchie was sitting behind her desk, and opposite her were the two policemen, one a tall man and the other a heavy-set one. They both turned as he came in.

"Come in, Francis," said Mrs. Ritchie. "I want to introduce you to Inspector O'Hanlon and Sergeant Maloney. They are looking into the death of poor Father O'Brien. I'll leave you to it, gentlemen." With that, she got up and left.

Inspector O'Hanlon turned to Francis and began gently. "We are talking to everyone who has come in contact with Father O'Brien recently."

"Yes, sir. How did he die?"

"He was strangled with chain on the thurible. I understand your mother worked for him. How did that come about?"

"She went to his church, and he took her confession weekly. I suppose he knew her background and how she had fallen on hard times," said Francis.

"Tell me about it."

Francis then explained what had happened to her, how she came to have him, and the fact that they had to live in a tenement.

"I suppose he wanted to help her, so he offered her a job as his housekeeper. The money helped us move out of the tenement and into better lodgings. I know Mum was really grateful to him for his help. It was then that I became his thurifer."

"Why did he sack her?"

"That's a mystery," Francis lied. "He accused her of stealing, which wasn't true. She would never steal. I don't know what the real reason was."

There was a long silence. Then Sergeant Maloney asked aggressively, "Why did you stop being the thurifer for Father O'Brien after such a short time?"

"Er . . . I don't know," Francis replied with obvious surprise at the question and the sergeant's menacing tone.

"Come on, lad, you can do better than that! You had an argument with Father O'Brien. Isn't that the truth?"

"No! No! That's not true!"

"Then why did you leave?"

By now, Francis was getting very flustered at the aggressive questioning and blurted out, "I didn't like the way he treated us. He was not very nice and made doing the thurifer job very difficult. He was always finding fault with everything I did. I just got fed up with the constant criticism."

"Now we are getting somewhere," said the sergeant. "Where were you Wednesday evening?"

"I went to the Bohemian football game at Dalymount Park. They were playing Sligo Rovers."

"They don't have night games!"

"Yes, they do. This time of year, with the light evenings, they kick off at five," lied Francis, surprised at his own inventiveness.

"What was the score?"

"The Bohemians won two to one. Marshall scored the winning goal just before the final whistle," he replied with satisfaction. He remembered reading a report on the game the following morning in the newspaper.

"Where did you go after the game?"

"I stopped by a pub near the ground. I had a couple of beers and went home."

"What was the pub's name?"

"I have no idea. I can take you there if you wish."

"You said that you didn't like the way Father O'Brien treated you. What do you mean by that?" O'Hanlon asked kindly.

"As I told you, he was very critical of me. I probably asked for it."

"Is that all he did? Was there something more personal? Did he touch you somewhere where he shouldn't?"

"No! Absolutely not!" an angry Francis replied, turning a deep crimson.

"Come on, we are all men of the world. He's dead, so he cannot hurt you anymore."

"Nothing happened! Why can't you leave me alone?"

"I believe that Father O'Brien was instrumental in separating you from your girlfriend Rachel Pearce," O'Hanlon said, suddenly changing the subject.

"It wasn't him. It was her parents," Francis responded, knowing the real truth.

"So it seems that you were really angry with Father O'Brien," continued O'Hanlon, ignoring his response. "Your mother killed herself because of him, you lost your girlfriend because of him, and he did unspeakable things to you. These would have been enough to send anyone off the deep end and kill him!"

"No, that's not true," said Francis between sobs. "All you are saying are lies. I want to go now."

"We haven't finished yet."

Francis's sobs turned to a white anger, and some inner strength enabled him to face down the two policemen. He looked them straight in the eye and said coldly, "Well, I have. If you aren't going to charge me, I'm leaving."

This transformation in his demeanour surprised the policemen, and they knew they weren't going to get anything more out of him. O'Hanlon just said, "That will do for now. We haven't finished. Don't leave town."

With that, the officers left, and Francis sat shaking in his chair.

After a few minutes, Mrs. Ritchie came back into her office. She took one look at him and realised that the interview hadn't gone well. "Would you like to tell me what happened?" she asked softly.

"I think they thought I had killed Father O'Brien, or at least their line of questioning seemed to indicate that." He then told her all that had happened.

"The trouble is I don't remember where I was last Wednesday. I told them I'd been at the soccer game just to answer their questions. If I told them the truth, they wouldn't have believed me anyway."

"That's a problem, Francis, because if they were ever to find out that you lied, they would have a good reason to arrest you. It seems to me that you are damned if you do and damned if you don't. The problem is that we don't know how much they really have on you. Leave it with me, I'll try and find out, and I'll let you know."

"I don't want to cause you any trouble, ma'am," he said.

"It is no trouble. Ever since I've known you, Francis, I have admired your resilience to what life had thrown your way and your hard work at the orphanage, let alone what you did to help me. I'd hate to see your talents go to waste. It seems that the police have a lot of circumstantial evidence but no proof. I suggest you keep a low profile and not give them any cause to suspect you further," she instructed him.

On his way home that night on his bike, Francis went through the interview in his mind, trying to work out some sort of strategy to get the police off his back. He couldn't just let things take their course. He had to pre-empt them somehow.

As he rounded the corner on to the street where his flat was, he saw a figure of a man in an alleyway who dissolved into the shadows when he approached. *So they are watching me, hmm*, he thought to himself. *I best do as Mrs. Ritchie said and act as normal as possible.*

He climbed off his bike and walked it through the alleyway that led to the back of the building in which he lived. He put his bike in the shed and walked back to the front door. He went up to his flat but did not turn on the light. He walked over to the window that looked down to the street below. Yes, there was someone there all right. He could make out a tall figure in a raincoat with his collar turned up against the autumn wind and wearing a trilby hat.

He turned on the light and started to make his supper. As he was eating it, there was a knock at his door. When he cautiously opened it, there was Mrs. Docherty, his landlady.

"Hello, Francis. I thought you might want to know that the garda were here today asking questions about you. You've always been a good tenant, never any trouble. I told them that. I hope you are not in any trouble."

"No, Mrs. Docherty. I knew Father O'Brien who was murdered last Wednesday. They are talking to everyone to try and work out who killed him."

"Good. Well, they searched your room anyway," she added casually.

"I see. Did they take anything away with them," he asked as calmly as he could.

"Not that I saw."

"Thanks, Mrs. Docherty."

After she left, he ran to his bedroom where there was a table with papers stacked on it. Yes, someone had looked over his papers. He checked everything, and after a while, he concluded there was nothing missing. It seemed to Francis that the police were very suspicious of him, and he would have to be extra vigilant.

When he got into bed that night, he began to go over in his mind his interview with the police. They seem to suspect him because he had a motive to kill the priest. Then he remembered the burn marks on his hands and his stiffness and the police telling him that Father O'Brien had been strangled with thurible chain. Then it came to him—he was the murderer.

I couldn't have done this! I might have hated him, but I wouldn't kill him. Killing a priest is a terrible sin. My god, it was me! What am I going to do? I need to run. But where?

*   *   *

Detective Inspector O'Hanlon had his feet up on his desk and his hands behind his head and was sucking on his pipe. "All right, Bill, what have we got?" he asked Sergeant Maloney who sat opposite with a notebook open.

"We know Father O'Brien liked young boys. We haven't been able to establish yet who he abused. We talked to altar boys and others that served with him at services as well as their parents. Everyone we talked to clammed up when we started to talk about the priest, and one of the constables said he had seen fear in some parents' eyes. I think that someone has put the fear of God into them. We were able to establish that the good father had been pastor in at least three other parishes and had been moved mysteriously before his term was up.

"Most people we talked to hadn't a good thing to say about him. In fact, many seemed to hate him but not enough to kill.

"The other thing we've established is that the priest had been squirreling away small amounts of church funds over many years. As a result, he had a tidy sum in his bank account," Maloney concluded.

"Our only suspect seems to be Francis Reagan, but we have absolutely no proof he was at the crime scene or that he had been abused by the priest," said O'Hanlon. "He probably had motive with the sacking of his mother, her suicide because of it, as well the abuse he suffered. Also, he was angry because of the break up with his girlfriend, which was engineered by the priest. Did you find anything when you searched his room?"

"No. However, he has private income from his deceased grandfather. It's not much, but it helps pay the rent for the flat he lives in," Mahoney responded.

"Somehow, we have to get a confession out of him," O'Hanlon continued puffing out a large cloud of smoke. "My instinct tells me he's our murderer. He certainly has the motive and probably the opportunity. Before we drag him in here and try, we need to get more information about his mother and her relationship with Father O'Brien. Maybe she found out about his secret bank account. After all, she was his housekeeper and, I am sure, cleaned his room.

"Also, I want to find out more about this priest's predilection for young boys, who took those photographs, and whether there are other like-minded acquaintances of his. Pedophiles, often, are in contact with one another. Maybe we have found a group of these sick people. This case is high profile because it involves a priest, so we have to ensure we have our facts straight before we make a move."

Just then, the telephone rang on his desk. "Yes." O'Hanlon listened carefully and then said, "Right away, sir."

"That was Commissioner Davis. He and I have been summoned to a meeting at St. Mary's Pro-Cathedral with none other than one of the vicar generals, Auxiliary Bishop Taylor. Now this should be interesting!" he said to Maloney as he gathered his notebooks and put on his coat.

Comm. George Davis was about fifty and was a short wiry man with a military mustache. He was not a policeman but a magistrate who ran the city's police department. He had been a prominent solicitor in the city and his was a political appointment by the lord mayor of Dublin.

As they were driven to the meeting, Commissioner Davis turned to O'Hanlon. "I don't suppose you have ever dealt with the church before. You will have to be careful what you tell the bishop. Just give him the facts and don't give any opinion. The church is very concerned and sensitive when one of their own has been killed, and it is very likely that we will be told to tread very carefully."

The car turned on to Marlborough Street and pulled up at the cathedral's main entrance. They went inside the basilica-styled building and were met by a young priest who obviously had been waiting for them. He led them to the back of the cathedral to the parish house and let them into the library.

"Please take a seat, gentlemen, I will tell his grace you are here." With that he disappeared back through door.

Commissioner Davis and Detective Inspector O'Hanlon sat down at the conference table and waited. Half an hour had passed slowly when the door swung open and two priests came in.

"Thank you for coming to see me, gentlemen," said the taller of the two and who was obviously the bishop. Both men rose from their chairs and ceremonially kissed the ring on his outstretched hand.

He waved them to their seats and introduced the other priest. "This is Monsignor Thomas who is on my staff and is helping me develop a report for the archbishop about the tragic demise of Father O'Brien. Inspector, tell me what you have found out so far in your investigation."

Detective Inspector O'Hanlon spent the next fifteen minutes going over the facts of the case from the discovery of the body, the pictures, the bank statements, and the interviews he had conducted so far. The faces of both priests turned ashen as he proceeded with his presentation. When he had finished, there was a long silence before the bishop spoke.

"Obviously, the church is very concerned about these findings. Have you any suspects?"

"Just one at the moment, your grace. As yet, we can't prove his guilt. It's just our suspicion, but we are working on it. We are trying to piece together the father's movements in the last year. I understand he was on sabbatical for six months. Can you tell me what he was doing?"

"That is church business. It won't help you in your investigation," he said pertly.

"It would help if we knew, your grace, because it might help us solve the case," he prodded.

"I'll judge what is relevant for the church to reveal!" he said in a raised voice, turning bright red.

"Now I want to make our position clear, we don't want anything revealed to the public about Father O'Brien's problems. It would be unsavoury for the church to be cast in negative light by the salacious evidence of this type."

"If we arrest anyone for this crime, their defence lawyers would reveal his abuse of children as a mitigating evidence for their client," O'Hanlon persisted.

"If you can't make a case without this coming to light, then the archbishop has instructed me to tell you to drop it. Do you understand, Inspector and Commissioner?"

I understand that the church wants us to pervert the course of justice, thought O'Hanlon.

"I think what the Inspector means is that we want to make sure there are no embarrassing surprises if we should make an arrest. You have my assurance that we'll make every effort to make a case without revealing any sexual abuse connotations," Commissioner Davis soothingly replied.

"So long as we understand each other in this matter, I think we can proceed. I rely on your discretion. I want you to update Monsignor Thomas on the case weekly so we can monitor your progress. Thank you for your time, gentlemen." And with that, he got up and left the room, with Monsignor Thomas following in his wake.

"Well, if that doesn't take the cake! The arrogance of it!" exclaimed an exasperated O'Hanlon when they got back in the car. "We might as well turn the whole case over to an ecclesiastical court for investigation just as they did in the Middle Ages," he fumed.

"As frustrating as it is, there's nothing we can do about it. The church is too powerful to fight. They have the ear of the Taoiseach (prime minister) and the president who will just shut down our investigation. We'll have to achieve a conviction without any mention of Father O'Brien's perversions. Do you think you can squeeze a confession out of the boy you suspect?" the commissioner asked.

"I can try, sir. He has quite a strong alibi, which will be difficult to break. We'll need to do some more digging."

*   *   *

Mrs. Ritchie called Francis into her office at the orphanage the next morning.

"We have been able, through some contacts, to find out something about the investigation into the murder of Father O'Brien. The garda have been very busy interviewing just about anyone who had any dealings with him. They have been met with a wall of silence, and I imagine that the church ensured that this would happen. The truth is that you are their prime suspect. It seems they plan to interrogate you soon and try to get some sort of confession."

Francis was thunderstruck by this news. "But I told them I wasn't anywhere near the church that night," he said.

"Nevertheless, they believe your motive was revenge for your mother's death and Father O'Brien's interference with your relationship with Rachel. It doesn't matter what we think. The fact is that you are very likely going to be charged with this crime. Neither Mr. Riordan nor I believe you did this, but we have to take action to get you out of the country and away from Ireland."

"But I've never been outside of the country. I'd rather stay and protest my innocence," he pleaded.

"And be hanged? Because that will happen if you are found guilty. They need to solve this case as soon as possible so that the crimes of this priest can be forgotten quickly. You're the scapegoat they are looking for. Don't be fooled into believing that you can beat this charge. You've got your whole life ahead of you. Don't throw it away," she urged him.

This was the first time he had realised that he could be hanged for something he didn't do, or did he? He wished, more than ever, that he could remember what had happened that night, but he was pretty sure that he had killed the priest. He trusted Mrs. Ritchie, and when she said he had to go away, she said it was for his own good.

"If you put it like that, ma'am, I suppose I should leave as soon as possible. But where should I go? I don't know anyone outside of Dublin," he said reluctantly.

"That's where I can help you, Francis. One of the organisations I do voluntary work for is the All-Ireland Spanish Aid Committee. We raise funds for the republican government of Spain. One of our current projects is supplying the Spanish Republican Army with ambulances and drivers. The drivers we recruit wear Red Cross armbands and do not take part in the fighting but are responsible for transporting the wounded to aid stations. You would be joining other lads in providing a valuable service to a very just cause," she said.

"I've made arrangements for you to stay in London with an old friend of mine, and she will arrange for you to go to Spain. After work today, go home as normal, and then when all is quiet, come to my house in Ranleigh with just a few belongings. I've arranged for you and Mr. Riordan to catch a mail boat from Dun Laoghaire to Holyhead in Wales and then a train to London," she said.

When Francis turned on to his street, he saw the same figure in the gangway opposite the building where he lived. He continued with his routine of taking his bicycle around the back of the building, but instead of putting it in the shed, he hid it in some bushes off one of the side streets.

He walked to the front of his building, making sure the garda officer saw him, and went inside and up to his flat at the top of the building. Now he had to plan his escape. The buildings in the street were all attached with a low roof at the back. The roof was easily accessible from a window in the upstairs hall. He tried the window, which was stiff at first, but it eventually loosened up. It would be easy to go from roof to roof and drop down into an alley that led to the street on which he had hidden the bike.

He started packing a small bag and took out the money from a hidden crevice on the wall under his bed. Now he had to wait. Dusk was falling, and lights were going on in the houses around. Before he switched on his light, he took a look out of the window. All was quiet. Then suddenly, a car turned into the street and came to a screeching halt in front of his building. Two men climbed out and looked up at his window. The larger man signalled to the officer who had been watching to go around the back.

It was time to move and to move fast. Francis grabbed his bag and ran down the stairs to the next floor and slid open the window that led to the roof. He closed the window behind him and started climbing along the slate roofs. It was slow going because the slate was slippery from the rain. One time, he lost his balance completely and was only able to save himself by grabbing at a down spout.

Finally, he made it to the last house. He looked both ways up the alley, and seeing no one, he dropped to the ground some eight feet below. His landing was rough. An excruciating pain shot up one of his legs, and he lay on the ground doubled up in agony. Then he heard footsteps coming along the alley. He forced himself to get up and began to hobble in the opposite direction. The footsteps came closer, and it was then that he lost all consciousness.

Francis was shaken awake by a violent rolling motion. When he opened his eyes, it was pitch black, and it seemed to him that he was in some sort of metal coffin. His leg still hurt like hell, and when he tried to move it, he blacked out again. He was going in and out of consciousness and felt very nauseous. Between the bouts of throbbing pain, he began to take in his environment. As his eyes got used to the dark, he realised that he was in the boot of a car. He could make out the spare wheel and some tools. Next to him was his bag that he had dropped after his heavy fall.

About an hour later, the car stopped, and he heard someone get out and come around to the boot. As it was opened, he could see the stars blinking back at him.

"All right, lad, I think the coast is clear, and you can sit up front with me," said a beaming Mr. Riordan.

"What happened?"

"Quite a bit. But first, I want to take a look at your leg. Fortunately, we have a first-aid kit in the car so we can try and wrap it."

He helped Francis get out of the boot and supported him as he guided him to the front seat. Francis sat sideways in the seat, with his feet dangling out of the open door. They were in a country lane. It was very dark, and the only light came from the torch that Mr. Riordan was using.

"I'll strap your leg up as best I can. When we get to London, we'll have a doctor look at it," he told Francis. He whistled quietly to himself. "You've a real corker there. I wouldn't be surprised if it's broken."

"Where are we?" Francis asked.

"We are just outside Dun Laoghaire. It's about eight o'clock, and the mail boat leaves at just after nine, so we have little time to spare."

"How did you find me?"

"Well, we got a tip that police were going to arrest you, so we knew we had to take some action. I thought you might go out of the back once they came knocking, so I hid in some bushes. I saw you come out across the roofs, so I knew what direction you heading."

"What happened to the garda that came around the back?"

"I took care of him when I saw you. He'll have a sore head and a bruised ego, but that's all. He didn't see me because I hit him from behind. Then I carried you to the car, put you in the boot, and drove off. I thought we were caught at one stage when I came to a junction and a police car pulled up next to me. They only saw an older man by himself and not a young man. After that, I took a very circuitous route to make sure I wasn't being followed and then drove down here."

"I don't know how to thank you."

"Don't. We have to go now."

As they descended into sleepy Dun Laoghaire, they could see the harbour lights gleaming. When they reached the harbour, Mr. Riordan parked the car, and they made their way to the quay, bought two tickets, and sat down in the stern cabin of the ship.

Right on time, he heard a roar as the engines began to turn the propellers. As the ship pulled away, Francis went out on the deck and watched the harbour lights disappear. He could see in the distance the lights of the city he had left behind. Little did he know that he would not see Dublin again for some years.

TAINTED CHOICES

A tragic situation exists precisely when virtue does not triumph, but when it is still felt, that man is nobler than the forces which destroy him.
—George Orwell, 1903-1950

CHAPTER 9

Irish Sea, May 20, 1938

When the lights of Dun Laoghaire finally faded away, Francis turned and entered the main passenger cabin and sat down next to Mr. Riordan with a sigh of resignation. They were the only passengers and had the cabin to themselves. Conflicting thoughts were tumbling through Francis's mind. He wasn't certain that he was doing the right thing. However, he thought about the options he was faced with; he came to the same conclusion that he must leave Ireland or face the hangman's noose.

But was he doing the right thing by going to Spain? Once the garda had realized he had disappeared, and because this case was so high profile, they would probably contact the British police who then would be on the lookout for him. He had no alternative. He would have to disappear for a while and take up a new identity. Spain offered a good opportunity to lie low, and then he could return at least to Britain, find work, and start anew. Little did he know that the garda and the Roman Catholic hierarchy in Dublin were relieved that he had gone because there would be no public trial, and there was no risk of Father O'Brien's past being revealed.

"Penny for your thoughts, Francis," said Mr. Riordan.

"Oh, I was wondering if I was doing the right thing by running away. I've caused you and Mrs. Ritchie so much trouble. I hope you won't have a problem with the garda when you return to Dublin."

"Don't worry yourself about that. I go to London every three months or so. Mrs. Ritchie has some property there, and I meet with the property management company to inspect the buildings to assess whether repairs have been done as instructed. Also, I get a chance to see me sister in Hammersmith. This is one of those trips, except I am going to drop you off at Lady Alvin's house in Hampstead. So don't be concerned with us. We'll be fine. What's really worrying you?"

"I am nervous about going to Spain and to a war. I know I won't be fighting, but I don't know what to expect. I understand that sometimes we have to stick up for what's right. But I don't know how I can help, or how any of us can for that matter," he said thoughtfully.

"I know I warned you off going to Spain to fight with your friends because of the carnage I saw in France in the Great War. And I saw the Blueshirts for what they were, another fascist movement that would lead Ireland down the wrong path. What we are asking you to do is different, and the situation has become urgent. The Spanish government needs as many volunteers as possible to help them. Some of these volunteers are coming from as far away as America, Australia, and Canada.

"Mrs. Ritchie, through her contacts in the All-Ireland Spanish Aid Committee, saw a desperate need for medical services, and this fits in with her pacifist beliefs. A lot of people fighting for the elected government are dying because there are very few medics. I saw the value of these men when I was on the front in France. As a medic, you will be able to help the men who are fighting Franco and not get involved in the killing.

"This is an opportunity for you to escape from your problems at home. There will be danger, yes, but it will be something you'll never forget as long as you live, and you will be a part of something bigger than yourself," he said emphatically.

"I suggest you get your head down and sleep. It's nearly nine thirty, and this trip to Britain will take just over three hours, that is if the weather cooperates. Oh, by the way, the lavatory is over there," he said, pointing to a door in the corner. "I'm going to try and get some sleep myself."

And with that, he lay down on one of the bench seats and closed his eyes. Francis did the same, wondering why Mr. Riordan had felt it was important to point out where the lavatory was. He closed his eyes and finally drifted off to sleep.

He was rudely awakened about an hour later when he fell on to the floor. When he opened his eyes, the cabin was swimming around him. He closed them tight to shut out the sight, and then his head started to pound. He felt nauseated and ran staggering towards the lavatory where he unloaded the contents of his stomach. Although his stomach was empty by now, he gagged and retched for at least another ten minutes. He lay on the floor still feeling very nauseated and too weak to move because of all the retching. He felt exhausted and fell into a fitful sleep. But the rough cold steel floor was very uncomfortable, and he could not sleep. He decided to move back to the cabin, but he couldn't stand, so he had to crawl.

As he crawled back in to the cabin, Mr. Riordan let out a big laugh. "Francis, you have turned green! You were a long time in there. I was beginning to think you had died. Welcome to the Irish Sea, one of the most unruly on this planet. We must have hit some bad weather, which is not unusual. I suggest you go out on deck, it will make it easier to cope with gyrations of the ship, and you will feel less sick. But be sure to hang on to the railings, we don't want to lose you overboard."

Without a word, Francis went outside hanging on to the ship's derricks, eventually reaching the railing. He breathed in the salt air and began to feel a little better. He took stock of his whereabouts. It seemed as though the ship was the only one in the huge vastness of the ocean. It was raining, so there was hardly any visibility. The lights of the ship moved from side to side and up and down with the thrashing of the waves. He watched them, hypnotised by their movement, and then felt sick again. He switched his gaze to the horizon, which helped him counteract his nausea.

"*You did very well disposing of that worrisome priest,*" said a voice behind him. He swung around, and there was his father surrounded by a red mist. "*I particularly like the way you laid him out on the altar. That was a nice touch.*"

"I had nothing to do with that," protested Francis.

"*Yes, you did. I was there and watched you. The Irish police believe you did it, and that's why you are on the run. No matter, I just wanted to say I'll be watching you, and beware of anyone who offers to rescue you from hell. Spain is really a cauldron of blood, and you will cut your teeth there on the way to being a man.*"

"I don't want your help and advice because I'm not like you anyway!" screamed Francis.

"*We'll see!*" he said and disappeared into the mist.

"How are you doing, Francis? You look as though you have seen a ghost. I thought you were talking to someone," said Mr. Riordan as he approached from the cabin.

"I'm fine, Mr. Riordan, really. There was no one here," Francis said.

As time passed, the swell began to slow as they stood there looking over the railing, and after a while, it had stopped. There was an eerie calm over the sea, and the mist had turned into a heavy fog. The ship slowed down and was creeping along. Suddenly, they were startled by a loud blast from the ship's horn. This was answered by a fog horn in the distance.

"We must be approaching Holyhead harbour," said Mr. Riordan. "In this fog, they are using horns to find their approach so they can avoid rocks and other vessels."

After a time, Francis could see the navigation lights from a lighthouse and then gradually the outline of the breakwater, which led into the harbour. Some fifteen minutes later, the ship had manoeuvred itself towards the dockside. The fog was still strong, but he could just make out the lights of the buildings. Dockers could be seen catching the ropes that had been thrown down to them. Others were manhandling a gangplank which they attached to the ship. Next to the dock was a platform where a train was waiting.

"Time to go," said Mr. Riordan. "If anyone stops us, you're my son, and your name is Peter. Sometimes there is a plain-clothes policeman who checks on travellers from Ireland, but this early in the morning, there might be no one here. Let me do the talking."

Francis nodded in agreement, and they picked up their bags and walked down the gangplank. When they reached the dockside, they crossed over to a small railway buffet, selling tea and cakes.

"The train leaves in about an hour, so we have plenty of time. Let's get something to eat before we board," said Mr. Riordan.

"I don't feel like anything right now. I still feel a little woozy," Francis replied.

"Try to get something inside you. We have a long night ahead."

Reluctantly, Francis had a cup of tea and a piece of cake. The tea was sweet, and he began to feel better.

As they sat and ate, a very dishevelled-looking man came into the buffet. He walked up to them and demanded to know where they were going.

"Who wants to know?" said Mr. Riordan.

"I'm Sergeant Hoskin from Holyhead CID," he replied with a heavy Welsh accent as he flipped out his warrant card. He was about fifty, a bachelor, and had a chip on his shoulder. He was an angry man because he had been passed over for promotion several times. He was known for his quick temper and harsh treatment of prisoners. He had a number of run-ins with his superiors who had assigned him to the graveyard shift at the docks. He hated it, but he needed the job. He was looking forward to retirement and a pension in a few years.

After examining the warrant card, Mr. Riordan said, "Me son and me are headed to London on business for our employer Mrs. Anne Ritchie. She owns property in London, so we are visiting it and reporting back to her on repairs she has been asked to do by her tenants. This will be the lad's first time visiting London."

"Where are you going to stay?"

"With me sister in Hammersmith."

"All right, but stay out of trouble. You Paddies are always troublemakers. You've been warned." With that, he turned and walked away.

"Aren't you going to say something?" an incredulous Francis asked.

"There's no point. You learn to keep your mouth shut and your eye on the prize, which is getting you to London. If I had said something, we would have been taken down to the police station. Once he started rummaging around, he might have discovered that you're wanted by the Irish police. If he didn't bother to check with Dublin, the least he would have done would have been to put us on the next ship back to Dun Laoghaire, and then we'd be in a fine pickle.

"Finish your tea and we'll go and find seats on the train."

They crossed the station concourse to platform one where the train was waiting. They climbed into a third-class compartment, placed their bags on the rack above their seats, and waited for it to depart. There were two other people in the carriage, and they were already sleeping. In the meantime, men were seen finishing loading mail and other crates into special freight carriages that were attached to the rear of the train. After some fifteen minutes, the train was ready to depart, a whistle was blown by the guard, and they were off.

As the train climbed above Holyhead, Francis could see the lights of the town, despite the fog and rain. Once clear of the town, there was nothing to look at, so it was easy to fall into a much-needed sleep as the rhythm of the wheels on the track had a soothing effect. When they reached Chester some hour and a half later, he awoke as the train came to a screeching halt and shouting porters loaded and unloaded. Then they were off again, and he slept through the stop at Crewe. He woke again when they reached Birmingham because of the slamming of doors, as a lot more people got on, and their carriage was almost full. The last stop was Rugby, and there was standing room only as the train pulled into Euston station in London just after seven in the morning.

Francis and Mr. Riordan walked to the main station concourse to the Euston underground station's Northern Line. Francis's ankle was hurting, and it was hard keeping up with Mr. Riordan. Despite the pain, his eyes were as big as saucers at this first sight of London. He always thought Dublin was a big city, but London was much busier, and he was struck by the number of people, even at that time in the morning, as they bustled away to their destinations.

"You haven't seen anything yet. They have trains that go underground," said a bemused Mr. Riordan. "Now keep close to me. There will be a big crowd using the train."

They bought their tickets and went down some stairs to a lift that took them down and deposited them at an entrance to two platforms. Mr. Riordan checked the sign and found Hampstead. They walked on to the platform and waited for a train. Suddenly, there was a roar, and a Northern Line train appeared out of the tunnel.

"This is for us! In case we get separated, get off at Hampstead. It's five stops from here!" shouted Mr. Riordan. People began to surge on to the train, and it was with difficulty that Francis kept Mr. Riordan in sight.

They got off at Hampstead and took another lift up to the street level. Mr. Riordan pulled out a map and studied it for a few moments. "All right, Francis, follow me."

They left the station and crossed over to Holly Hill Road. As they climbed up the road, Francis saw the fine houses which reminded him of Mrs. Ritchie's street in Ranelagh. His ankle was really hurting now. At one of the houses, they stopped.

"This is it," said Mr. Riordan, and they went up an alley to a side door. Mr. Riordan knocked. After a while, the door was answered by a tall elderly and smartly dressed man with a military bearing.

"Yes?"

"My name is Joseph Riordan. I am butler to Mrs. Anne Ritchie of Dublin. She arranged with Lady Alvin for me to bring this young man to her. His name is Francis Reagan. We just arrived in London early this morning from Ireland."

"Come on in. I'm Charles Thomas and the butler to Lord and Lady Alvin. The family are away at present, but they should be back tomorrow. We've been expecting you," he said with a welcoming grin. "Have you had breakfast yet? We were just having ours. Would you care to join us?"

"That's very kind of you. We'd like that."

They entered a large kitchen. Around the table were six people, and Mr. Thomas introduced them. At one end, Francis saw a pretty girl whose eyes were looking down at the table when she was introduced. She looked up at him and smiled. Her name was Nancy Neal.

Francis was very hungry and wolfed down the bacon, eggs, and toast Mrs. Ratcliff, the cook, had prepared. "My, you'll eat us out of house and home, young Francis," she said, smiling.

"It's delicious!" he replied.

When he had finished, Mr. Thomas instructed a footman named Barry to show Francis where his room was in the servants' quarters at the top of the house.

When they had gone, Mr. Thomas turned to Mr. Riordan. "Now tell me all about Francis. Maybe you would like to join me in a pipe in my office."

"Certainly, Mr. Thomas."

They got up from the table and went into a small office off the kitchen.

Meanwhile, Francis followed Barry as they climbed up the back stairs to the servants' quarters. Finally, they reached the top, and Barry opened the door to a room.

Barry Trevelyan was a young man of twenty-two, taller than Francis by an inch, and heavyset. He hated his life in the Alvin family home where he thought he could do better than being just a footman. He was determined that service, which had killed his father, was not for him. He was destined for greater opportunities. He had come to the Alvin household after he had been given a second chance. He was caught shoplifting in Selfridges some two years previously.

Barry's father had been butler to the Alvin family for more than twenty years when he had died suddenly of a heart attack. With his father gone, Barry had run wild with a group of boys in Chatham where he lived with his mother. She could not cope with his anger and devilry, and in desperation, she had written to Lady Alvin about her son, asking for help. Lady Alvin agreed to vouch for the boy and took him into her household after extracting a promise from him never to steal again. He resented Lady Alvin's offer, but he was faced with certain prison instead of probation if he did not agree.

Barry knew Mr. Thomas disliked him, and he had been passed over for the under-butler position by that upstart Nigel Winslow. Now he had to put up with this Irishman who seemed to get favourable treatment from everyone. He'll have to be put in his place.

"You're in here with me. Now I want to make it quite clear, you're here because I was forced to have you in my room. I don't want any mess. You Irish have a reputation for being pigs, drunks, and living in squalor. Well, you're not bringing your dirty habits here. Is that understood?" he said very angrily.

Francis was taken aback by this sudden onslaught, and it was all he could do to mumble back a yes.

Barry picked him up by his lapels and shook him. "I'm glad we understand each other," he said with a smirk.

Inside, Francis fumed, but he remembered what Mr. Riordan had said about keeping calm, despite the insults. He eventually found his voice. "I know where I stand, although I don't understand what I have done to upset you. I'm only going to be here for a short while, so I'll make sure our paths cross as little as possible."

"That's great with me. One other thing, keep your eyes and paws off Nancy, or you'll have me to answer to. She's spoken for," he threatened. He left the room slamming the door as he went. *Now that's why he is being so aggressive*, thought Francis.

Leaving his bag on his bed, Francis went back down to the kitchen. Mr. Riordan and Mr. Thomas could be seen talking, so Francis went up to Mrs. Ratcliff and asked her whether there was anything he could do.

"Bless my soul, Francis, thank you for asking. There's a bowl of potatoes in the sink over there that need peeling for our dinner tonight."

About ten minutes later, Mr. Riordan and Mr. Thomas came back into the kitchen.

"It's time I left. Mrs. Ratcliff, thank you for the marvelous breakfast," said Mr. Riordan.

"It was my pleasure, Mr. Riordan," she replied, blushing.

"Francis, walk me to the street so I can say goodbye."

When they closed the door and began walking down the path to the street, Mr. Riordan began to speak. "I've told Mr. Thomas most things about you, except, of course, your problems with the police. I told him you had volunteered to go to Spain because of what you had read in the newspapers. He's a very interesting man. He was in the Great War, and we had a long talk about our experiences, which only a fellow soldier would understand.

"Francis, it's time to say goodbye. Remember, be true to yourself, keep an eye on where you want to go, and don't act impetuously. There will be many temptations out there, so I believe in the old saying "When in doubt, don't." When a little voice in your head tells you something smells fishy, it probably is. Now don't forget us in Ranelagh. Write to us from time to time and let us know how you're getting on wherever you are."

Tears filled Francis's eyes as he took Mr. Riordan's hand to shake it.

"I will never be able to thank you or Mrs. Ritchie for what you have done for me—never. You have been a father to me, and I could always come to you for advice. I'll miss that. I will let you all know from time to time how I'm doing, and maybe I'll see you all again one day."

He watched Mr. Riordan walking down the street until he was out of sight. He turned and walked leadenly back into the house.

He busied himself helping Mrs. Ratcliff until dinner. They all sat around the kitchen table and ate in silence. Mr. Thomas then began to tell them of the threats from Hitler he had read about in the paper that day and how his followers had been harassing and arresting Jews.

"Serves them bloody well right, if you ask me," volunteered Barry from the far end of the table. "They're nothing but bloodsuckers. Mosley is right what he says about them."

"Mr. Mosley is just a right-wing agitator who it would be best to ignore. He and his Blackshirts have no place in our society. He just breeds hatred and not peaceful coexistence. What Hitler is doing to the Jews is just plain wrong and evil. These fascists influence the worst elements of society, like the ignorant, those that feel unfulfilled, or are disaffected. The sooner we wake up and realise this about them, the better it would be for everyone. Now that he has annexed Austria, who will be next?" asked an angry Mr. Thomas.

There was a silence around the table at this outburst.

"We live in very perilous times. What do think, Francis?" asked a calmed-down Mr. Thomas.

"I think you are correct, Mr. Thomas. We have the Blueshirt movement in Ireland. They are bullies and do what bullies do. They beat up anyone who disagrees with them. Fortunately, very few people take any notice of them. Is the same thing happening here?"

"Yes. We get the occasional street fights, but after the Cable Street demonstration in the East End, their influence is beginning to wane," Mr. Thomas said.

"From what I can read in the newspapers, the biggest threat is coming from Hitler and Mussolini. They seem to be spreading their right-wing beliefs and have taken over other countries," Francis responded.

"It would be great to see them marching here in London. They would rid us of all the riffraff communist troublemakers and the unions that are pulling this country down," declared Barry as he volleyed the criticism at the other end of the table.

"So how would you deal with the people who have no money or jobs?" Francis asked.

"I would do what Hitler does, round them up and put them in camps so that their illness would not infect the rest of the country. They're wasters, and we should have no time for them. Rule by dictatorship is the way to go," he responded.

"I've seen first-hand how neglect can destroy people and their dreams," said Francis with feeling. "It reduces them to nothing short of animals, doing anything to survive the next day. They live in squalor because nobody in the government recognises their God-given potential and tries to harness this for the betterment of the country."

"It sounds to me that you are a dirty communist," sneered Barry.

"No. I'm just someone who grew up in the Dublin tenements and a lucky break enabled me to escape from that terrible place. Tell me, would you say that Stalin is a dictator?" Francis asked.

"I don't know anything about him, except that he's a communist," Barry admitted after a pause.

"Well, he is another kind of dictator. Hitler and Mussolini are right-wing fascists, but Stalin is a communist. However, they are all dictators trying to put their extreme stamp on their countries and eventually the rest of the world."

Sensing the discussion temperature was getting too hot, Mrs. Ratcliff asked, "Pudding anyone?"

"That would be a good idea, Mrs. Ratcliff," jumped in Mr. Thomas, sensing he should calm everyone down.

"You have both voiced interesting ideas, which are worth thinking about," said Mr. Thomas. "Now it's time to review more mundane things such as our tasks for tomorrow."

After a fifteen-minute briefing on what was to happen on the following day, Mr. Thomas turned to Francis and said that Lady Alvin wanted him to help Alfred, the gardener, with clean up in the garden.

Once the meeting finished, they settled down to their evening chores. When these were completed, they were free to do whatever they liked. Barry disappeared down to the local pub, Nancy and the other maids went to their rooms to do some laundry, and Mr. Thomas and Mrs. Ratcliff sat around the kitchen fire, reading books. Francis joined them and began reading Mr. Thomas's *Times* newspaper. He was fascinated by the stories and articles in it and was so absorbed that he didn't hear Mrs. Ratcliff ask him an hour later whether he would like some cocoa. A hand on his shoulder woke him from his preoccupation.

"Francis, would you like some cocoa?" Mrs. Ratcliff asked again.

"I'm sorry, yes, please."

By this time, Nancy had joined them and was sipping her cocoa. She was about eighteen with a trim figure, which was very evident even in her maid's uniform. Her cheeks had a rosy hue as was befitting her country background. She had grown up on Lord Alvin's Norfolk estate, which was near Chedgrave, some ten miles from Norwich.

Nancy's father was the gamekeeper on the estate. Nancy had worked as a maid at the big house, and Lady Alvin was very taken with her. She was not shy, had a ready smile and an inquiring mind. She didn't talk for the sake of talking but rather voiced her opinion only when asked, even among the servants. Those opinions were always sound and pragmatic. Her sense of humour leaned toward observances of absurdities she witnessed in life.

"What is Dublin like, Francis?" she asked.

"Oh, it's a very impoverished city, not like London. It has a lot of tenements with many really poor people. There isn't much work, although the docks employ people as well as the Guinness factory. Despite being poor, many of the people there would give you the shirt off their backs. Mind you, they would go around half naked if they did because that's the only shirt they have."

Nancy laughed at his joke. They talked for a while until Mr. Thomas suggested bed. Francis was tired, having slept little the night before, and was quite happy to climb the stairs to his room. He got undressed and got into bed. He thought how interesting Nancy was, and he looked forward to talking with her again.

He began to settle down with the book Mrs. Couch, his tutor, had given him—*Hard Times* by Charles Dickens. He had read the first few chapters and was surprised how closely it resembled life in the tenements. He was also amused by how Dickens's character names bore a close relationship to their activities, like Mr. Gradgrind and Mr. Bounderby.

After a while, he put the book down and began to drift off to sleep when, suddenly, the door flew open and standing before him was Barry. He started to scream obscenities at Francis and was obviously very drunk. He grabbed the sleepy Francis by his collar and dragged him out of bed and started to pummel him in the ribs.

"So you think you'll make a fool of me in front of the others," he began to mumble. "Well, I'll show you, you Irish pig!"

Francis, now fully aware of what was going on, kneed him with force in his groin. With a shriek of pain, Barry let go and grabbed himself. Before he could recover, Francis punched him hard in his stomach, which made him collapse on to the floor, groaning. He then started to stomp on Barry as he lay there.

"You made a fool of yourself and have nobody else to blame. I promise you one thing, though, if you give me any more trouble, I'll put you in hospital for a long time! Do you understand me?"

Between breaths, Barry pleaded for him to stop and finally agreed not to interfere with him again. Francis stopped stomping and let him get up. Barry staggered to his bed and collapsed on to it.

As Francis lay there, he wondered why this man had been so aggressive towards him from the outset. He obviously had a chip on his shoulder about something, and Francis thought that he had better watch out, as he would likely try to take revenge. Only when he heard the snoring from the other bed did he then allow himself to drift off to sleep.

He woke early the next morning, and Barry was still asleep. Washed, shaved, and dressed, he went down the stairs to the kitchen. Mrs. Ratcliff was busying herself with breakfast and set Francis to work, getting coal from the outhouse to stoke up the stove. When he came back in with the coal, Mr. Thomas had arrived and was reading his newspaper.

There was a knock at the door, and a strong wiry man came into the kitchen. He was of an indiscernible age. He was dressed in corduroy trousers and jacket and a shirt with no collar. His hair was unkempt and looked as though it hadn't seen a comb in some time. He was holding an old woolen cap that had a cut in the back of it where someone had obviously expanded the size of the band so it would fit his head. When he smiled, he showed a row of decaying yellow teeth and gaps where others had been. His hands were large and gnarled with calluses across his palms.

"Alfred, have you taken your boots off before coming into my kitchen?" said Mrs. Ratcliff.

"Yes, ma'am, I left my boots outside the back door," he responded in a thick Norfolk accent.

"Then sit down and help yourself to some tea. Breakfast will soon be ready."

"Francis, I'd like you to meet Alfred Sharpe. Alfred, Lady Alvin wants him to help you in the garden for a week before he goes abroad," said Mr. Thomas.

Francis put out his hand to shake hands, but Alfred didn't respond. He looked Francis up and down and then at Mr. Thomas.

"Don't need no help."

"Yes, you do. I'm sure you can find something for Francis to do. How about trimming the bushes that Lady Alvin wanted you to take care of sometime ago and general spring cleanup? Spring is usually a very busy time for you. I am sure you need some help getting the garden ready."

"That's true enough, but he'll have to be willing to work hard. I won't have slackers and people that can't pull their weight."

"Thank you, Mr. Sharpe," said Francis. "I will do my best to help you."

"Francis, I have some gardening clothes for you to wear. I put them in your room, so after breakfast, you can go up and change into them. Tomorrow morning, first thing, I've arranged for you to see Dr. Ambrose about your ankle," said Mr. Thomas.

The next morning, Dr. Ambrose examined Francis's leg and declared it was badly sprained. He wrapped the ankle in a heavy bandage which helped Francis walk without pain.

Francis and Alfred became firm friends as the days passed. Both were wary at first, but then their friendship grew. As far as Alfred was concerned, he was impressed by the volume of work Francis was able to achieve each day. Francis found Alfred a great teacher and a veritable encyclopaedia of gardening. Also, he discovered that Alfred had a witty and wicked sense of humour, which came out when they saw various people visiting or passing by the house. At the end of the first day, Francis had trimmed the bushes in the front of the house and had dug two of the beds. From a distance, he had seen Lady Alvin and her entourage arrive. He returned that evening to the kitchen tired and ready for dinner.

When he entered the kitchen, everyone seemed in a whirl of activity. Mrs. Ratcliff was putting a joint of lamb on a platter, and Nancy immediately carried it out of the kitchen and up to the dining room where Lady Alvin and her son, Phillip, were dinning early before going to the opera. When everything had been delivered and served in the dining room, Mr. Thomas, Nancy, and Nigel Winslow came back down to the kitchen.

"Francis," said Mr. Thomas, "Lady Alvin would like to see you after her dinner and before she goes out to the opera. Go wash and change your clothes. Your dinner will be ready when you come down."

When he went to his room, he noticed that Barry's bed had been stripped and his belongings gone. Puzzled, he washed, changed, and returned to the kitchen. Everyone had gathered, and as soon as he arrived, they all sat down in their places.

Mr. Thomas cleared his throat and made an announcement.

"I am sure some of you are wondering where Barry is. The truth is we just don't know. He left late this morning in a foul mood and just told me he was leaving. He wouldn't say where he was going and said he wasn't coming back. Then he walked out. He looked very much the worse for wear and was clutching his sides in pain as we spoke briefly. Perhaps he had too much to drink at the pub and got into a fight. I know he had some personal problems, and he had been talking about joining the army with some friends. Likely, he has gone down to the Pirbright army recruitment centre. We shall be looking for a replacement for him, so if anyone knows a good candidate please let me know. Now let's say grace."

They ate their dinner in silence. Their sombre mood was broken with the sharp ring of a bell.

"That's Lady Alvin in the drawing room. Nancy, take up the coffee and Francis and I will follow you," instructed Mr. Thomas.

Francis followed Mr. Thomas and Nancy as they entered the main part of the house. When they reached the door to the drawing room, Mr. Thomas told Francis to wait. He opened the door for Nancy, and they both went in. A little while later, he opened the door and beckoned Francis in.

Francis entered and wondered at the richness of the room and the furniture. It was far grander than Mrs. Ritchie's drawing room. It was designed in the art deco style of the 1930s, and the furniture was highly polished with satinwood and lacquered wood pieces. He had never seen furniture like this before. At the focal point in the room was a fireplace in the same style as the furniture. Next to the fire were two chairs, one occupied by a very thin lady dressed in a white gown, which was V-shaped, showing her fulsome figure. Lady Alvin's hair was blond and short. From her ears dangled two large diamond earrings. She was smoking a cigarette from a long holder and casually flicked the ash into an ash tray on a table beside her. She looked up at him as he entered the room.

"So this is the famous Francis Reagan who Anne Ritchie wrote to me about," she greeted him with a warm smile. "Come over here and sit in that chair so we can talk. Thank you, Mr. Thomas, I'll ring when we've finished," she said, dismissing the butler and Nancy.

When they had gone, she looked at Francis. "I have known Anne Ritchie for many years. We were, in fact, at school together. She sent me a long letter about you. She told me about the good work you have done at the orphanage as well as problems you face in Dublin and how you can't go back there. She highly recommends you to help out on our medical mission to Spain. It's not a picnic over there by any means or pretty, but with the danger comes the satisfaction of helping people who will depend on you to save their lives. The government of Spain's forces are on their heels at the moment, taking many casualties, but we hope that their luck will turn around. Do you still want to go there?"

"Yes, ma'am. Mrs. Ritchie has told me about the reason people from many countries want to support the legitimate government there. I am willing to help out the best I can," Francis replied.

"Good. Now here's the plan. We will arrange transport next week for you to go down to the home of Mrs. Charles Gordon in Elmsted in Kent. She has a training school of sorts there, where she trains ambulance drivers in basic first aid and how to deal with wounded soldiers so they can be taken back to aid stations and seen by doctors. She will arrange for you to go to Spain once your training is finished. It's a short course because of the dire need for medics."

She stood up and pushed a button at the side of the fireplace. "Meanwhile, I hear you are helping Alfred in the garden. He is good but slow. Your help will speed up the tidying up that has to be done after the winter so that he can plant."

Mr. Thomas came in, and the interview was over. They went back to the kitchen and returned to their nightly chores.

As the days went by, Francis's life had become a routine, and he longed to get started for Spain. The one highlight of his day was the time he spent talking to Nancy, whether it was over meals or at cocoa time each evening. One day, Alfred joked about how she always looked and smiled at Francis when she brought their tea to the garden shed each morning. "She's got the hots for you, mate," he guffawed. Francis turned red, and Alfred, again, burst out laughing. Francis wondered about their relationship and whether it was obvious to other people. He was certainly attracted to her and she to him. They hadn't even kissed, but that didn't mean anything.

The evening before he was to leave for Kent, the staff threw a party for him in the servants' quarters. Even Alfred came. They had a marvellous meal and a never-ending bottle of wine. Nancy was very quiet, although she was drinking wine. At the end of the evening, when the others had gone to bed, Mr. Thomas and Francis sat by the fire, drinking brandy.

"Francis, we have all enjoyed having you here, however brief it was. You are going into danger, so watch yourself always. If you come back to London, there's always an opening here for you," he said.

Finally, Francis climbed the stairs to his room. He realised that he hadn't spoken to Nancy all evening. He'll have to find time in the morning. He climbed into bed and fell asleep. About an hour later, he felt someone getting into bed with him, and when he opened his eyes, he saw it was Nancy. As she settled in beside him under the covers, he realised she was naked.

"I want to give you a special farewell gift of my own," she whispered.

"I don't think we should be doing this. What happens if you get pregnant?" asked Francis.

"Let me worry about that. Let's just enjoy ourselves while we can."

When Francis woke up the next morning, Nancy had gone, and all he had left was the fond memory of the previous night. He remembered that she was a good teacher and was patient with his inexperience.

He went down to the kitchen where Mrs. Ratcliff was preparing breakfast.

"The van taking you to Kent will be here soon. You'd better get a good breakfast inside of you," she said.

About half an hour later, there was a knock at the door, and a middle-aged man came in. "I'm Rodney Callaghan, and I've come to pick up Francis Reagan," he announced.

"Come in and sit yourself down and have a cup of tea," said Mrs. Ratcliff.

"Don't mind if I do," Mr. Callaghan replied.

"Francis, go get your things, it'll be time for you to go when Mr. Callaghan has finished his tea."

When he came down again, Mr. Thomas, Alfred, Nancy, and Mrs. Ratcliff were waiting for him. Nancy was smiling, and her cheeks were all aglow.

"We got together and got you a small going-away present to use on your travels," said Mr. Thomas handing him a package. Francis opened up the package, and inside was a large leather wallet with "FR" inscribed on it.

"It's something to keep your worldly goods in," said Mr. Thomas. "Keep it by you at all times and remember us."

He said goodbye to his friends and walked down the garden path for the last time, following Mr. Callaghan.

CHAPTER 10

Elmsted, Kent

They drove in silence along the A5 into Central London. They reached Parliament Square and crossed over the River Thames at Westminster Bridge. Francis was deep in thought when they had left Hampstead but was now riveted by the sights and grandeur he saw before him.

Sensing his change in mood, Mr. Callaghan pointed out some of the buildings as they passed them. The scene changed when they crossed the Thames into Southwark. The housing looked poorer, and the people on the street were not as well dressed as those on the north side of the river. They turned on to the A2 Dover road, and some hours later, they passed Bexley and Rochester.

As they drove along, Mr. Callaghan told Francis that he was an ambulance instructor and that he would be joining a class of four people who were to become ambulance drivers in Spain. Mr. Callaghan had been a medic in the Great War and had joined the London County Council's Ambulance Service after he was demobbed. He had been asked to help with training recruits for Spain by Mrs. Gordon who had been a nursing sister in the casualty department at St. Thomas's Hospital in London where she had met him. She had married Charles Gordon, a leading heart surgeon, five years previously and had become involved in the work of the Spanish Medical Aid Committee. She was given the task of training ambulance drivers for the front.

After Mr. Callaghan drove through Chatham, Francis began to see the picturesque Kent countryside. At Canterbury, they took a secondary road, south to Elmsted, and arrived there at about three o'clock. Just south of the village, they turned into a driveway that had a large iron gate at the entrance. The whole property was surrounded by a high wall and guarded by a gatehouse. As they approached, a man came out of the gatehouse and swung the iron gate open for them to pass. The driveway had woods on either side, and when they turned a sharp corner, Francis saw a large Victorian house. To the left of the house were stables, but instead of horses, there were two ambulances parked in the yard. They drove up to the stables, and Francis got out.

There were three other men playing soccer against a wall. They stopped when they saw him. Francis walked over to the group, and Mr. Callaghan introduced him.

"Gentlemen, let me introduce you to Francis Reagan. Francis, this is Doug White, James Cameron, and Tom Harrison. I have the unfortunate task of trying to instil in all your heads something about first aid and showing you how to drive an ambulance. We've only got two weeks to do this in, so the course will be very intensive starting tomorrow morning at eight sharp. After dinner, I suggest you get your heads down, and I'll see you lot in the morning."

When he had gone, James Cameron came over to Francis. "Let me show you around our digs," he said with a thick Scottish accent. "By the way, everybody calls me Jimmy."

They walked into the stables, and in each stall, there were two beds. "You're in here with me," said Jimmy. "Put your bag on the bed and I'll show the rest of the set up."

They went into a large room which was where feed for the horses and tack had been kept. Now there was a long table and a blackboard at one end. "This is a combined dining room and lecture hall. Actually, everything is very comfortable. The only negative is that we have to go over to the house to wash and shave. We all came here last night. Doug and Tom are from London, and I'm from Sterling in Scotland. And where do you hail from?"

"Dublin, Ireland."

"Well, welcome. I think you'll find it comfortable here, certainly better than what we'll face in Spain, from what I hear. Do you play soccer?"

"You bet I do."

"Let's go and show those two Sassenachs how the game is played!"

They played soccer for about an hour, and they began to build a fierce but friendly rivalry. When a bell rang for dinner, they all went to the house to wash up for the meal. They continued the friendly joshing as they took turns at a sink. After dinner, they gathered around the dinner table and played cards. Francis had never played poker before, and Jimmy taught him. They weren't playing for any high stakes, so it was more fun. The London men were good at the game and easily got the better of Jimmy and Francis. They all turned in by nine o'clock.

The next two weeks passed quickly. Mr. Callaghan was a strict teacher and expected nothing less than the full attention of his students. "Someone's life might depend on you one day, God help them, and you have to be prepared," he often told them. On the first day, he gave them each a first-aid manual, which he insisted they carry on them at all times. "You will find it a good source of information and a reminder of what I am going to teach you," he declared.

The course was mixture of classroom lecture and practical experience all crammed into an intense two-week period. They learned how to deal with such things as blood loss, open wounds, shock, partial amputations, chest wounds, head and spinal injuries, and how to administer morphine and chloroform.

Each afternoon at four o'clock, they had driving lessons on the two ambulances. None of them had ever driven before, and they had difficulty using the clutch and long gear stick. Francis found, after many tries and stalls, he was beginning to get the hang of driving and had become very proficient when the two weeks came to an end.

The day before the course ended, Mr. Callaghan said that Mrs. Gordon would like to see them. They all went over to the house and were shown into Mrs. Gordon's study where there were chairs set out for them in a circle. They sat down and talked in hushed whispers. Finally, a door opened, and they all stood up.

"Please be seated, gentlemen. I am sorry to take you away from your bumps and bruises, but I want to brief you on your travel plans to Spain."

Mrs. Gordon was in her late thirties; she was small, plump, and had an infectious laugh. Francis instantly liked her. She sat down on one of the chairs.

"Mr. Callaghan tells me that you have done well and are now ready to go to Spain. How we get you there is complicated, but let me explain. You will be taken down to the ferry at Dover. Because the British authorities are trying to discourage men from going to Spain, you will have to travel in pairs. Any bigger numbers would attract their attention. You will each receive weekend return tickets to Calais because this is the only way you can travel to France without a passport. Once there, you will catch a train to Paris where you will be met by a volunteer for the International Brigade carrying a copy of the *Financial Times*. You'll easily see your contact because of the pink colour of the newspaper. The French are more sympathetic to our cause, but don't flout your beliefs. Otherwise, they will arrest you and return you to Britain. In other words, keep a low profile at all times.

"We will give you fifty pounds each. This is not to be squandered on liquor or a good time but must be spent on train tickets and any other emergencies. Once you have spent this money, you're on your own, and we cannot help you. You will each receive a uniform, Red-Cross armbands, and a satchel with basic medical supplies in it. Please don't wear these until you are in Spain, or the police will pick you up. Are there any questions?" she concluded.

Jimmy put his hand up. "We don't speak the language. How do we get tickets to Paris and then to Spain, ma'am?"

"The only hurdle you have is getting a train to Paris. We will give you each a typed card in French so you can hand this to the clerk at the ticket office in Calais. Our contacts in Paris will make sure you are on the right train to Spain," she responded.

"If there aren't other questions, I want to wish you the very best of luck in your endeavours. Get plenty of rest because you will be extremely busy where you are going," she said, getting up and leaving the room.

When they returned to the stables, sitting on the table in the dining room was a small keg of beer and several glasses. Mr. Callaghan came in and made an announcement.

"The beer is compliments of Mrs. Gordon. We thought we'd have a little goodbye party. Some of the volunteers you nearly maimed for life will be here also. Now Jimmy and Francis will be the first to go tomorrow morning and then Doug and Tom the next day. You will catch a ferry that leaves at eight-thirty in the morning. The trip takes about two hours, and be warned, it is usually a rough crossing at this time of year. From Paris, you will all be traveling to Barcelona, and then it will be up to the International Brigade there to assign you to medical teams at the front.

"I just want to say it was a pleasure helping you lads learn something about ambulance work, but your real learning will only happen with experience at the front. Remember, your job is to save the life of each soldier you help. Now let's enjoy ourselves," he said.

The next morning, Jimmy and Francis left early with Mr. Callaghan who drove them to Dover. He parked the van, and they walked up to buy tickets from a kiosk at the entrance to the ferry port. Then they walked along the pier to the packet steamer, which was to take them to France.

"I'll leave you here, boys. Good luck, and God bless," said Mr. Callaghan. He turned and walked away.

Francis and Jimmy showed their tickets to a collector who waved them on. In front of them and by the gangway that led to the ship, was a customs officer who inspected their tickets.

"Why are you going to France?" he asked in a bored voice.

"We thought we'd see the lights of Paris for the weekend," replied Jimmy with a twinkle in his eye.

"All right, lads. Just be careful," the customs man replied.

Francis and Jimmy walked up the gangway to the ship and settled in the passenger cabin. The ship began to move about half an hour later, and remembering his experience on the overnight ferry from Dun Laoghaire, Francis told Jimmy that he was going out on deck.

"I'll stay right here, nice and cosy," he replied.

As soon as the ship left the shelter of the harbour, it began to toss up and down as it met the notorious winter storms in the English Channel. Francis was prepared for this and just held on to the ship's rail. About two hours later, the ship docked at Calais, and Francis returned to the cabin to look for Jimmy. He found him groaning as he lay across two of the seats.

"Come on, Jimmy, let's get on to dry land," he said kindly to his friend. He pulled him up and helped him onto the ship's deck where they joined the other passengers disembarking.

They found the train station just outside the harbour and handed the clerk one of the cards they had been given with some money. They walked towards the platforms, and Francis said to a ticket collector, "We want to go to Paris."

The man looked at them, frowned, and pointed to a train. "Ici, monsieur."

They thanked him and, when he had punched their tickets, climbed on board the waiting train. Some five hours later, they arrived at Gare du Nord in Paris. As he got out of the carriage, Francis was overwhelmed by the majestic beauty of the station. It was far larger than the terminuses in London and Dublin and on a much grander scale.

"Come on, Francis, stop gawking," Jimmy urged. "You'll catch a fly with your mouth wide open like that. We have to look for our contact."

As they went through the barrier, they started to look at the people waiting but couldn't see anyone with the right newspaper.

"We'll just have to stand here like real charlies until someone comes," Jimmy said resignedly.

As the crowd dispersed, they noticed an old man dressed in weathered raincoat and wearing a classic French beret. He was sitting at a table at a concourse café and was sipping a glass of wine while he read the *Financial Times*.

"Excuse me, sir, are you expecting to meet two people?" asked Francis.

"Yes, lad. Name of Francis and Jimmy," said the man in a thick Yorkshire accent. "Is that you?"

"That's us," said Jimmy.

"I'm Alec Hardy. I'm one of the members of the British Communist Party's membership committee and on loan to the International Brigade here. Why don't you boys sit down here while I finish my wine?"

They chatted away for another ten minutes. It turned out that Alec had been a miner in one of the Yorkshire pits and was injured in a freak accident. He was a shop steward for his pit and, because he could not work anymore, was offered an organising position with the National Union of Miners in the Yorkshire region. He was a committed communist, believing that Britain should be run by the party, along the same lines as Lenin had done in Russia. He felt encouraged by the communist government in France and hoped it would lead to others seeing the light. He railed about the nationalists in Spain fighting against the socialist government there. To him, the civil war was an opportunity to add another country to the list of those that are run by a communist government. Francis and Jimmy listened to him but didn't say anything.

Finally, they got up and followed Alec out of mainline station to the Paris Métro station, Barbès-Rochechouart. They took line two to Pigalle and changed to line twelve which went north to Lamarck Caulaincourt in the Montmartre district. They walked to an address on the Rue Lamarck, which was a union hall run by the French Communist Party. In the hall, there were a number of camp beds and about fifteen men milling about.

"Dinner's in about an hour. Choose a bed and make yourselves comfortable, boys," Alec said and left.

"I hope they are not all like him," Jimmy whispered to Francis as they sat on two available beds. "I'm not sure about the politics of the war, but I am someone who believes in justice and that the likes of Hitler and Mussolini need to be stopped from trying to take over a legitimate elected government. That's why I'm here to help."

"Me too," said Francis. "Back in Dublin, I listened to the speeches of Father O'Flanagan, who criticised the church's support for the nationalists, as well as one by a Spanish priest who couldn't understand why the Irish people had been so deceived by the propaganda from the right. Both men had convinced me that something had to be done. So when I got the opportunity to go to Spain, I took it. But this communism thing sounds like another type of dictatorship where people haven't got a chance to have their say."

"You're right. I think we have to avoid any conversations that are political. We just have to do our job and keep out of any arguments," Jimmy said.

As they were sitting on their beds talking, a tall skinny man walked up to them. He was in his thirties and was wearing a dirty suit, which was several sizes too small, and a cap with a red star on it.

"So you're the two new recruits that Alec brought in today," he said in broken English. "I'm Alexi Radanovich. I represent the International

Comintern. We are glad you have come to help us with our glorious revolution in Spain."

"Mr. Radanovich, we are here as ambulance drivers for the government forces," Francis replied.

"Good. Our valiant soldiers need medical care so they can get back to the fight."

"Will you be joining us to fight at the front?" Jimmy asked.

Mr. Radanovich turned red and replied, "I am too busy here helping organise recruits and supplies. Someone has to do that, you know."

"I was just curious. With the older men here, it would free you up to join the fight. I hear they need every able-bodied man they can get."

A look of embarrassment came over Mr. Radanovich's face, and he blustered, "Must get on now, so much to do." And he beat a hasty retreat.

Both boys laughed. "I don't think he will be back," said Francis.

Dinner was announced. Francis and Jimmy lined up with the others and helped themselves to a stew and bread. They sat down at a table and poured themselves some wine that was provided from two large pitchers. Three other men were at their table, and they introduced themselves.

The leader of the group, Raymond Folds, smiled at the arrivals. "I see you've already encountered Red Alexi. I don't know what you said to him, but he hurried away very quickly.

"We've been here for a couple of days. All three of us are trade unionists from Leeds, and we are very easy-going socialists. You will find some fanatical communists in the International Brigade, like Alexi, though. You have to ignore or put up with them because most of the volunteers are communists and that's just a fact of life. Us, we're simply antifascist. Our leaders back in Leeds reckoned that the fascists had to be stopped otherwise they would come knocking on our door soon. They asked for volunteers, and here we are," said Raymond.

"It sounds as though we have a lot in common because we feel the same way," said Francis. "Jimmy here was a messenger in the City of London, and I was an office clerk at an orphanage in Dublin."

"We will be shipping out to Spain tomorrow afternoon. We'll have to go by sea because the French have again closed the crossings that go across the Pyrénées. We're going to a place called Pujalt, near Barcelona, for training. I would imagine you'll be joining us," said Raymond.

They talked for some time and then played cards for the rest of the evening.

The next day found them still waiting. They killed the time by playing cards. Alec came up to Francis and Jimmy and told them they would be met in Barcelona by someone from the British medical unit. At about four o'clock, a lorry pulled up, and they all got into the back. They drove through the centre of Paris, across the Seine, and to Gare d'Austerlitz. They got out of the lorry and were taken into the station to a train which was departing for Perpignan.

As the train pulled out, they began to settle in for what they were told was an overnight journey to Southern France. Hours dragged by as they went through Limoges, Toulouse, and as the dawn was coming up, the train pulled in to Perpignan. After that, it was several local stops to Banyuls-sur-Mer, a local fishing town. Their guide, who met them at the station, took them to a house in the town. He explained that because of the daylight bombing in Barcelona and the naval blockade of the city, they will have to travel clandestinely by night. In the meantime, everyone was to get some rest and not leave the house.

The time passed slowly, and Francis was able to get some sleep. At five o'clock, the guide was back and took them in pairs down to the harbour. They all embarked on a small fishing boat and were ushered below deck. The captain of the boat came down to see them and spoke to them in French. This was translated into English by the guide.

"We will be pulling out of here shortly, and everyone is to stay below deck until it is dark and we are out at sea. The journey will take some hours as we have to hug the coast in order to avoid the Italian navy. There will be no lights on the ship, and those that smoke mustn't do so unless it is below decks. We should get to Barcelona just before dawn," he told them and then went up on deck.

A few minutes later, the engines started. Some two hours passed, and Francis and Jimmy changed into their uniforms and went on deck. They could see the high rugged coastline and the lights of towns and villages on shore. An hour later, there were no lights, just the black cliffs. The guide explained that they had now crossed into Spanish territorial waters and that there was a blackout because of the air raids and bombardment from the Italian navy. Also, he told them to disembark quickly when they reached the harbour because the captain wanted to get under way well before dawn.

Several hours later, they pulled in to Barcelona's harbour. It was still dark. The sight and smell that greeted them was unimaginable.

CHAPTER 11

Barcelona, Spain, June 18, 1938

As soon the boat docked, they got off quickly and followed the guide up the stone steps to the quay. Before they reached the top of the steps, the fishing boat had already cleared the dock and was heading out to sea.

At the top of the steps, they couldn't believe the utter devastation that was in front of them. There were fires from the mangled remains of buildings. A once proud avenue was crumbled to the ground, leaving girders carelessly pointing upward and at grotesque angles. Incredibly, there were some buildings that seemed untouched, as if a mighty giant had decided to just randomly wreck what was before him. In the dark, Francis could make out shadows climbing out of the pile of bricks, carrying with them what was left of their belongings.

An odious stench wafted its way towards them, and it was a smell never to be forgotten. It was the putrid odour of burning and decomposing flesh from the casualties still under the rubble, as well as from horses and mules that lay at the quayside and in the streets, their life's work done. Added to this was the stink of raw sewage from the broken mains and the contents of the burning buildings.

"Welcome to Spain," said a voice behind them. They turned and saw a young man in a crumbled uniform wearing a Red Cross armband. "I'm Vincent Price from the British medical unit here in Barcelona. You're a sight for sore eyes. We need all the help we can get in dealing with the causalities. The Germans and the Italians have been bombing this city since the middle of March, and last night was another raid," he said as he shook their hands. "Soon, there will be nothing left to hit.

"We'll have to walk a bit because I couldn't get the lorry close enough. The streets around here are blocked with collapsed buildings."

Francis and Jimmy said goodbye to their fellow travellers and their guide, who they thanked especially, and followed Vincent along the quay. They turned into a side street, which was narrow and steep. All around them was devastation, and many times they had to climb over rubble.

"It's amazing how people can stand this on a daily basis. How do they cope with the continual bombardment?" Jimmy wondered out loud.

"The people of Barcelona are very resilient, brave, and determined not to give in. Franco is going after this city because it is the capital of the Catalonia region, which heavily supports the rightful government. People live underground in bomb shelters most of the time and only go out to scavenge what scarce provisions there are," Vincent explained.

"It's the children I worry about the most. They don't know what's going on. We've seen many dead kids, and those that we pick up are badly mangled and burned. The latest fascist trick is to drop antipersonnel bombs marked 'chocolatti,' and when the children, who haven't had chocolate for some time, pick these up, they have their faces or hands blown off."

After a thirty-minute scramble up the destroyed streets, they came to a square where the lorry was parked. They climbed in, and Vincent started the engine, and they began to drive a very circuitous route out of the city.

"We are heading to Huete, which is a little village just northeast of Barcelona where we have taken over a small hospital. It's from there we fan out and bring in the most desperately hurt people who need attention from our team of doctors and nurses," Vincent briefed them. "There are five of us ambulance drivers, and we are kept very busy. I hope you can work on four hours or less sleep because that's what we have to do to meet the need for our services."

They finally were able to speed up along a windy road and eventually reached the small hospital in Huete. They went through the front entrance and found themselves in what had been a reception area of the hospital, which was now a ward with patients on makeshift beds. The nurses could be seen bustling between patients.

Vincent led them down a corridor and knocked on a door.

"Come in," said an authoritative female voice. They entered, and sitting behind a desk, smoking, was a middle-aged woman dressed in slacks and short-sleeved shirt.

"Miss Anthony, here are the two new drivers you asked me to pick up."

"Thanks, Vincent," she said, dismissing him.

When he had gone, she smiled. "Welcome, gentlemen, please sit down. London told us you were coming, and we are glad to see you. Let me tell you what we are doing. We have been helping people in Barcelona, of course, but we have also been staffing hospital trains which travel to the front and pick up the wounded. The first task is getting these people to the trains, and this is where you come in. These trains have operating theatres, and emergency surgeries can take place before patients are brought here or to other Barcelona hospitals for further attention or to recuperate."

Pointing to a map of Spain on the wall, she continued, "The front is bounded by the Ebro River where we have set up field hospitals in some of the caves that overlook it. The fascists have been able to push the government troops across the river and have basically cut us off from the main republican territory to our south and west in Valencia, Madrid, and Castilla-La Mancha. To our north, our forces are holding a line that runs north eastwards to the Pyrénées. I'm telling you all this so that you can understand the situation. Although things are quiet on the fronts at the moment, we expect a push from the fascists probably on northern front. So we have to be prepared to help the wounded if this should happen," she said.

"I want you to team up with our more experienced ambulance drivers for a few days so that you can get some experience of the conditions we face here in the city and learn the lay of the land. I want to transfer you both to the front lines as soon as an offensive begins because your skills will be needed there. Francis, I want you to team up with Vincent, whom you met tonight, and Jimmy with Bill Grafton whom you will meet later. Do you have any questions?" she concluded.

"We only brought with us some rudimentary first-aid equipment. Where do we get a supply of equipment and drugs we might need?" Francis asked.

"The ambulances you will drive have equipment but only a limited amount. Frankly, we are so short of medical supplies that we have to ration it, and our staff has to make do with whatever we have. Normally, you might carry a supply of morphine, but only the doctors have it to use as a last resort. I'm afraid you will have to use your own initiative and improvise," she replied.

"When we were in Paris, we met a man who said he was a commissar of the communist party, and he gave us a talk about the fight here being for the good of the proletariat in Spain. We volunteered because we believe in democracy, as simple as it may seem, not because of some ideology. Is it very political here, or was it just him letting off some steam?" Jimmy asked.

"You'll find all sorts here. I myself am a member of the British communist party. There are anarchists, socialists, trade unionists, and "non-political" people like you. We all have our reasons for being here. In this unit, our mission is to look after the sick and wounded, no matter who they are. If I were you, I'd avoid discussing politics with anyone, just focus on your job," she replied.

Sensing they had no more questions, she thanked them for coming and called out to Vincent. He guided them back outside and showed them a dormitory of beds in a barn next to the hospital building.

"So how did you like our Miss Anthony then?"

"She seemed a bit bossy," said Jimmy.

"Yeah, that's the first impression she gives you. In fact, she has a heart of gold. Now drop your things here, and we'll get going."

They walked to a copse of trees where there were two dilapidated lorries with red crosses painted on their sides that were hidden from aerial view. Another ambulance driver was waiting for them, and he introduced himself as Bill Grafton.

Vincent tossed Francis the keys. "You drive. You'll have to get used to these jalopies. They have a mind of their own and must be nursed along," he said with a smile.

Francis started up the lorry. After grinding the gears and trying to manage the fierce clutch, he slowly moved along the track that led to the road.

"We are headed for the outskirts of Barcelona," said Vincent. "Last night, the rebels tried to bomb the munitions factory in the Poblenou area, and in doing so, they have done major damage to some homes that were in their flight path. Although most people probably went to the shelters, there may be a few stragglers that got caught. We've been asked to check for wounded."

It took them a good half hour to reach the site of the bombing. They parked the ambulance, and with the stretcher and first-aid satchels, they made their way slowly through the rubble that lay in the streets. They stopped every few minutes to listen for any sounds of people under the debris and then moved on. After about twenty minutes, they came across a knot of women who were in distress, wailing and beating their chests. When they saw Francis and Vincent, they ran up and started to gesture wildly.

"I don't know what they are saying," said Francis. "But they want us to follow them."

"My Spanish and Catalan are not good, but it seems that someone is trapped under the rubble. Let's go and see," said Vincent.

They followed the women into a small square where some houses had stood and pointed to a particular pile of bricks and wood.

Vincent let out a big "Shhh!" Finally, the women were silent, and they all listened. After a few seconds, they heard a soft "meow."

"It's a bloody cat!" exclaimed Vincent. "What a waste of time!"

They picked up their things and were just beginning to walk off when the younger of the women cried out in Catalan, "My daughter is in there!"

Francis and Vincent stopped. "Do they expect us to dig out their wretched cat?" said Francis.

"No, I don't think that's it. I recognised some of the words. I think she was referring to her daughter. Let's find out."

They took off their jackets and started to peel away the rumble. It was getting hot, as the sun rose, and they began to sweat profusely. Every so often, they would stop, order silence, and then listen. After a while, they could not hear the cat anymore, but they kept going. As they progressed, the women began to help them, and they were able to clear a way through the debris.

Then all of a sudden, they saw a little hand. Now they dug more carefully and were able to see a leg and then the torso of a little girl who was no older than seven. On top of her body was a dead kitten. The girl was unconscious and not responding to them when they raised her hand to feel her pulse. Francis tried to find it, and after a few seconds, he felt a weak rhythm.

"She's alive but only just," he said. "It looks like one of her legs is broken, and I do not like the look of that gnash on her head."

"Let's put a splint on the leg, clean off the wound on her head and bandage it to stop any more infection. And then we can get her to a hospital," Vincent responded, after taking a good look at their patient. "The nearest one to here is Sant Pau."

They worked feverishly for the next fifteen minutes or so, and then their patient was ready to be put on a stretcher.

Vincent stopped and said to Francis, "I'm concerned that she may have damaged her spine, and carrying her on the stretcher might do her more harm. She needs a firm surface for her to lie on, not the sag of our canvas stretcher. Let's find a plank of wood and carry her on that."

Among the rubble, they found what they were looking for and gingerly lifted the girl on to it, keeping her as level as possible. They then tied her down with some rope so she couldn't move, and they were ready to go.

Their way back to the ambulance was tortuously slow as the macabre little procession of the two men carefully carrying the girl followed by the women. When they finally reached the ambulance and had lifted her on board, Vincent signalled to the mother to climb up. The other women tried to follow, but he waved them away. They drove to the hospital, which was one of the biggest in Barcelona, and reached the emergency department. A nurse and a doctor took a look at the patient in the back of the ambulance and then helped carry her into the hospital.

Tired out, Francis and Vincent sat down on the grass outside the hospital and began to eat the bread they had been given for lunch. After a while, the doctor came out, looking for them.

"Maria is in the operating theatre right now," he said in English. "The way you handled her saved her life because one of her vertebrae is fractured. She is a lucky little girl. Her mother tells me she went searching for her cat just before the air raid. Thanks for your care. I must get back. We have many casualties to take care of after last night's raid." And with that, he left.

Francis and Vincent got back into their ambulance and drove to the west of the city where there had also been bombing the previous night. They spent the rest of the day cleaning and dressing the wounds of the people they found in the streets. As dusk began to creep in and there were no more patients who needed their services, they set out for their base. The route back took them down the Ronda de la Universitat, past the headquarters of the Catalonian Communist Party in the Hotel Col n in Placa Catalunya, and then east on Ronda de Sant Pere. There were a number of communist placards on the walls and in the square.

"Wow! Look at all those placards. I wonder what they say," said Francis.

"It's basically a lot of propaganda by the communist party who are now part of the republican government. There's been a lot of infighting going on between the various communist organisations. The radical Trotskyites, who were one of the communist party's political factions, and the anarchists have been purged by the Stalin-leaning Communist Party of Spain. As a result of this civil war between supposed allies, we came across many bodies in the street that have been shot at the height of the purge. Some were brutalised before they were killed. This has been going on since May Day. Many on the losing side have gone to ground or fled the city, but we keep on finding some bodies still," Vincent commented as they drove along.

As they were driving around the large mountains of debris, Vincent suddenly shouted for Francis to stop and back up to an alley. They stopped the ambulance and walked into the alley. Lying there was a man covered in blood. He had obviously taken a beating and bleeding from two gunshot wounds.

"See what I mean? We better check him out," said Vincent.

When they walked up to the man, he started to crawl away from them.

"It's all right, mate, we're medics. Let's take a look at you," said Vincent.

The man let them examine him, but he eyed them warily. He was young, likely around his mid-twenties. He looked slim and very fit, which probably helped him survive.

"We'll have to take you to hospital to get those wounds seen to," said Vincent after a close look at the bleeding holes in his body.

"I can't go to a hospital," he replied in English. "They will kill me. I have to get away from here because they will be looking for me."

"Look, you are in no condition to go anywhere. Perhaps we can take you to the British medical unit we belong to, and they can patch you up. What's your name?"

"Pierre Bouton, and I am French," he replied as he winced in pain. "I belonged to a commune that was set up here in Barcelona. We were attacked by some communist thugs, and most of my friends were killed in the raid. Those of us who were later captured were tortured and our women raped. Their screams will be with me forever. Last night, we were taken out to be shot. I am the only survivor because I played dead when they shot me. Lucky for me, they were in a hurry because an air raid started, and they ran for cover. Such cowards!"

"Look, here's what we'll do. We'll put you in the ambulance and hide you in the back among our stores. We'll put you under a blanket and load up some wood to cover you," said Vincent.

Francis and Vincent carefully lifted him into the ambulance and collected some wood from the bombed buildings. When they had finished hiding their patient, they climbed back into their seats and began to drive along Ronda de Sant Pere and turned left at a junction. As they did so, they ran into a patrol of six men and were ordered to stop. A rough unshaven man stepped forward and demanded to know what they were doing. At first, neither of them could understand what he was saying until another man asked them in English.

"We are from the British medical unit and have been taking a patient who was wounded in the air raid last night to the Sant Pau Hospital. Then we helped others," said Francis.

They were ordered out of the ambulance at gunpoint and told to open up its back doors. Vincent obliged. After a cursory glance inside, the leader wanted to know why they were carrying so much wood.

"We need it for fuel so that we can heat our hospital and sterilise our operating instruments," said Vincent.

This seemed to satisfy them. The man that spoke some English told them they were looking for an anarchist who had escaped the night before and if they see him, they should report it immediately. They assured the men they would do so and drove off.

The drive back to Huete was uneventful, and they arrived there a little after eight o'clock. It had been quite a day for Francis. They carried Pierre into the hospital, and the nurses began to work on his wounds.

"Let's get something to eat," said Vincent, and they joined Jimmy and Bill Grafton in the small dining room. As they ate, they swopped stories of the day's events. Suddenly, there were distant explosions. They rushed outside and looked down at the city from the hilltop, on which the hospital was perched. They saw a ball of fire begin to creep from one side of the city to another as the planes flew across it and dropped their incendiary loads.

"Oh my god, I've never seen anything like this. How can people survive?" said a shocked Francis. He, like everyone else, was stunned by the carnage they saw below them.

"The German and Italian air forces are experimenting with a bomb that sets fire to whatever it hits," observed Susan Anthony behind them. "At first, they used explosives, and they have progressed to this horrible weapon. They have flattened whatever factories there were here, and now they are just going after the people. Thank goodness most people are in air-raid shelters, but God help anyone caught out in the open in that inferno. You'll have your work cut out for you in the morning. It's going to be a busy day!" She turned and walked back into the hospital.

Francis went to see how Pierre was doing and was told that he had been taken into the operating theatre. He decided that it was time for some sleep and went out to the barn. He lay there thinking about the day's events. He couldn't sleep and got up wondering what lay before them in the morning.

"Well, now you see a little of what war is about, sonny!"

Francis turned suddenly to see, standing by the door, the ghost of his father.

"Tonight's bombing was awesome. That will teach those commie bastards to resist. You mark my words, when Franco takes this city, he will grind them into the dust. Right now, he's just playing by giving them a taste of what's to come."

"But there are innocent people out there who just want to get on with their lives—people like that little girl and her mother we helped today!"

"That was a waste of time, wasn't it? You should have let the little brat die! She's no use to anyone. Anyway, she'll die soon in one of these air raids, and your 'good Samaritan' act will have been for nought. I see I have to show the realities of life to convince you."

He disappeared before Francis could respond.

Francis was now teamed up with his friend Jimmy. Their routine for the next week was that they would get up at four o'clock in the morning and arrive in Barcelona by five. They would spend their days giving first aid to the shell-shocked residents. After the raid the previous night, there would be fires still burning everywhere and people trying to fight the blazes with buckets of water drawn from tankers that had been filled up with harbour water. Others were using sewer water. Francis had never seen such teamwork from the lines of weary and destitute people passing buckets from hand to hand. On the streets, they would pass incinerated bodies in agonised poses that bore witness to their last torturous moments on earth.

One day, Francis and Jimmy were busy giving first aid as usual to a number of people. As they were working, a father approached them, and in his arms was an almost naked teenage girl. She was crying out in pain and had what seemed like burn marks down one side of her body. Part of her clothing had burned into her skin, and she was covered in sores that were oozing puss.

The man's eyes were filled with tears, and between sobs, he said in Catalan, "Please help us!"

Francis got the stretcher from the back of the ambulance, and they laid her gently on it.

"We have to carefully put sterile gauze on her to try and prevent any further infection and get her to a hospital. It seems like a lost cause because so much of her body has been burned," said Jimmy.

They worked furiously to cover what they could of her burned skin and then gently laid a blanket over her. She began to shiver and then convulse as if she was having a fit. Her eyes started to roll, and she let out a frightening scream. Suddenly, she raised herself up a little and then fell back dead. Her eyes stared into oblivion.

Francis and Jimmy just stood there looking down at what had been a pretty young woman who had had her whole life ahead of her. Francis was grief-stricken and, although he never knew her, he couldn't believe what he had just witnessed. Tears started to well up in his eyes, and he had difficulty outwardly controlling his feelings. He ran to a corner of a building and was violently sick. He knew he had to become as anesthetised as possible to the slaughter around him, otherwise he could not function at all, but it would be difficult to achieve.

The grief-stricken father broke through their thoughts as he pushed them out of the way and grabbed the girl's body off the stretcher. He carried her away, wailing.

Francis mechanically did his work for the rest of the day, not speaking much to Jimmy. He was in a dreamlike state and couldn't get the girl off his mind. When they pulled into their base that evening, he told Jimmy he was going for a walk and took off down a path to a rock face that overlooked the city. He sat there in the dark for over an hour when Susan Anthony approached and asked whether she could sit down next to him. He nodded, and she sat down.

After a few moments, she started to speak gently.

"Was that the first violent death you've seen?"

"No, not really. I found my mother when she hanged herself."

Taken aback, she replied, "I'm so sorry. How long ago was that?"

"About two years ago. But I've never seen a young person die in such a tormented way before."

"You'll never forget it, nor should you. However, you must try and compartmentalise it. I had to. That's the only way I can do my job. A year ago, my fiancé was brought in from the front badly wounded. The doctors patched him up, but he was mentally depressed. One day he took a revolver and shot himself. I found him, and that scene is etched on my mind. There are many people dying, and what we saw in the Great War is only repeating itself. History has a habit of doing that because we never learn from it."

They sat there in silence for a while. Miss Anthony then said, "Now there's a young man who's asking for you. His name is Pierre, and you brought him in a few nights ago. Why don't you go and cheer him up?"

"Thank you for your advice, Miss Anthony."

Francis found Pierre in bed, propped up some pillows.

"You're looking much better than when we picked you up. You've got some colour in your cheeks," said Francis enthusiastically.

Pierre smiled. "I feel a little better now that they have dug out those two bullets. I wanted to thank you for saving my life. I was really in a desperate position."

"How come your English is so good?"

"I was a student at Cambridge University before this war broke out. I was studying philosophy and would have graduated last summer. My parents live in Paris, so I stayed with them during the holidays. It was on one of those breaks when I decided to come here and help with the revolution. The anarchist movement started in France, and I firmly believed in their cause of creating an equal society. I had heard that they had set up a large commune here in Barcelona and were living their dream. So here I am."

"What happened?"

"The communists began fighting among themselves for control of the city and turned their anger on us. I was lucky to escape when I did because a number of my friends were executed. Six of us got away from the round up and hid in a cellar of a bombed-out building. We decided to wait out the purge to see how things turned out and then either re-emerge or quietly go home. Unfortunately, someone tipped off the commies to where we were, and they rounded us all up. We spent about a week in stinking prison, and then we were taken out to be executed. You know the rest."

"What are you going to do now?"

"Once I am well enough, I will head back over the Pyrénées to France and then to Paris. Frankly, I've had enough of Spain and have become very disillusioned by what's happening here. It will be wonderful to see my girlfriend again. I've missed her so much. After that, I'll see where life takes us. I might go back to Cambridge and finish my degree, who knows? What about you, Francis?"

"I've only just arrived, and there seems a great deal of demand for our services. I'll probably stick it out for a while. I have no home or girl to look forward to seeing, so I'll probably end up back in London, looking for clerical work."

"Well, if you are ever in Paris, you can look me up, and we'll have a fine time on the town," he sighed as he laid his head down and closed his eyes. "I feel very sleepy now, so can we continue talking tomorrow."

"Of course. Get well, Pierre."

He got up and left, not knowing that would be the last time he would see his new friend.

The next morning, they began their routine again. This time, Jimmy drove, and Francis looked for casualties. There had been no air raids the previous night, so there wasn't such demand for their services. By midday, they had very little to do, so they headed back to the hospital. When they arrived, there was the usual chaos. When Miss Anthony saw them, she called them into her office and closed the door.

"I'm glad you're back because we have a serious problem. Some men representing the Communist Party of Spain came here this morning looking for Pierre. Someone must have informed on us. Anyway, they dragged him away. They asked where you and Vincent were too, and I told them you had been assigned to the front.

"We need to get you out of here because whoever told them about Pierre would certainly rat on you. In fact, we have had orders to send all our ambulance drivers to the Ebro front because there is big build up going on, so you will be joined by Bill and Vincent. It sounds like there is going to be a big advance over the river, so your services will be sorely needed. Let me tell you now, what you've seen here in Barcelona was a picnic compared to what you're about to deal with when the offensive gets started.

"Now there is a hospital train, which we run between here and the front, leaving for the Ebro this afternoon. You all need to be on it."

"What will they do to Pierre?" asked a shocked Francis.

"He's probably already dead. The same fate will happen to you if we don't get you out of here."

"But we only helped a wounded man," Francis stammered.

"They're paranoid. They will eliminate anyone who they see as a threat to their hold on power."

"What about you, Miss Anthony? Aren't you in danger too?"

"I will handle them if they come back. I know how to appease them. Besides, they recognise the help we are giving to the cause and probably will not bother us.

"The plan is to base you both at a cave hospital near a small village called La Bisbal de Falset, which is near the front. Vincent and Bill will report to a field hospital near Mora la Nova. You will get a ride on the hospital train as far as La Torre-Pradell station, and from there, an ambulance will take you to the hospital. This station is near the village of La Torres De Fontaubella and is the closest the train can make it to the front. The tunnel there provides it with protection during the day from air raids. The train transports wounded men back to Barcelona or Tarragona for treatment and convalescence. Your job will be to pick up the wounded from the battlefield, take them to the cave hospital, and, when they are ready, transport them to the train.

"Now collect your bags and meet the group of nurses and doctors who are returning to the front after some R & R. They are gathering by the lorries in the copse."

All four of them picked up their things from the barn and joined the group. There was no talking, and it was as if each person was in their own tormented world of introspection. Francis wondered what was going to face them.

CHAPTER 12

They all clambered onto the lorry in silence. The atmosphere was tense as they rode to the train station in the south western part of Barcelona. They boarded the hospital train and settled into the staff quarters, which was the only carriage with seats.

As the train began to pull out of the station, a woman carrying a clipboard came in and began checking off the names of the nurses. Then she turned to the four ambulance drivers.

"You must be the ambulance men who we are taking to the front. I am Amanda Jefferies, the head nurse for this train," she said matter-of-factly. "We plan to get as near as we can to the river Ebro, but that depends on whether there are any air raids going on when we get there. Put your things down, and I'll show you around."

They followed her, and she showed them one of the four operating theatres. "We transport the wounded soldiers whom you will collect from the battlefield," she said with no emotion in her voice. "The most critical patients are either operated on in one of our field hospitals near the front or in one of our operating theatres on this train. We categorise the wounded when they come in as serious, medium, or light. We can't do much to help those soldiers with severe abdominal or head wounds, except give them morphine for their pain. It helps comfort them before they die."

She showed them one of the twelve convalescent carriages. These had three stretcher tiers on each side so that some thirty people could be transported in each carriage.

"Have you any questions?"

"I noticed that the nurses and doctors who came with us hardly spoke and seemed in their own world. Why?" asked Francis.

"They have all been through what we call the valley of death, which are our field hospitals. Most of them were in the chaotic retreat from the Aragon front that ended when the government forces crossed the river Ebro into Catalonia. They have often witnessed excruciating deaths and have been frustrated because they can't do anything to help. It's hard uncompromising work that takes a toll on you physically and plays havoc with your mind. They are exhausted. They work until the last patient is taken care of and then get two or three hours of sleep before the next wave of casualties arrives. And this goes on week after week, day after day.

"Apart from the stressful conditions they have to work under, they also have to cope with an on-going lack of medical supplies. A number of them have had nervous breakdowns and have been sent home. Unfortunately, you will be facing the same stress, so you'd better prepare yourselves for it. At the moment, our soldiers are facing daily artillery barrages from across the river and bombing from the air. The casualties have been lighter recently because the river has kept the fascists' advance at bay. I suggest you get some sleep now because you don't know when you will get any later," she advised.

All four of them settled down to sleep on the stretchers in one of the carriages. Francis could not sleep. In his mind, he was going over and over the atrocities he had already seen, and doubts about his decision to come to Spain began to enter his thoughts. He wondered what future horrors were awaiting him. Eventually, he dozed off and slept fitfully. The train slowly made its way, stopping in tunnels to make sure air raids were not taking place. They reached La Torre-Pradell station at about two in the morning as the train came to a shuddering halt, which woke them with a jolt.

They looked out of the carriage and saw a sea of wounded men on stretchers. As soon as the train pulled up, stretcher bearers started to load the casualties onto the train. The doctors and nurses had suddenly broken free of their lethargy and began to quickly examine the casualties and direct the stretcher bearers where to take their wounded.

"Come on you lot, don't dawdle! We need you to help loading!" shouted Amanda Jeffries. "We have to get the job done before the German or the Italian aircraft take aim at us!"

They jumped down from the train and quickly followed her to a group of patients.

"The men in this group can be loaded into the hospital convalescent carriages. Make sure they are comfortable, with blankets over them, and then come back for others."

They all worked feverishly for about an hour, and after the last casualty was loaded onto the train, they retrieved their belongings and started to look for their ride to the cave hospital. Amanda Jefferies thanked them and wished them luck. Then the train pulled out of the station for its return trip to Barcelona, and they were left in the darkened station.

Francis and Jimmy found a line of parked lorries and asked whether any of them were from La Bisbal de Falset. Finally, a voice in a strong Cockney accent said, "Sure, mate. I'm Tony Sligo from the cave hospital. Sling your stuff in the back and let's get out of here before Gerry finds us."

They shook hands with Vincent and Bill and wished them all the best. Then they joined Tony in the cab of the lorry and pulled away from the station. The lorry had thin light beams for headlights that enabled the driver to follow the side of the road so that there was not too much light to attract the attention of a passing aircraft.

"We've got about thirty miles to go, which normally would take just over an hour. We can't take the fast route along the river because of the bombing. Going across country, the road winds as it climbs uphill, and with these lights, it's really slow-going," Tony announced. "We have to hug the hills and the forests so we don't let the fascist pigs know where we are."

They passed through the small town of Damos. Everything was in darkness. It was an eerie experience as nothing moved, and the only sound was the lorry's engine. Exiting the town, they made very slow progress as the lorry negotiated hairpin bends. Tony was always dropping down a gear as the lorry climbed up the steep road which hugged a mountain. They passed through small villages, which were again in darkness. Finally, they were able to make progress as the road ran flat for some miles. They were high enough now and could see fires in the distance along the river Ebro.

"The poor bastards are getting it tonight. The Ities and Gerries pound our forces from the sky day and night, and this is backed up by the fascist artillery. We pick up many wounded soldiers after one of these raids. Right now, there is a big build-up of our troops, so we expect a major push soon. That means we will be extra busy," Tony said knowingly.

Just then, there began a slow rumble. Tony hurriedly drove the lorry off the road into an olive grove, switched off its lights, and ordered his startled companions to take cover behind some rocks. The noise grew even louder until the ground around them was shaking and some loose rocks began to fall. When they looked up, they could see the outline of about a dozen bombers of the German Condor Legion flying low overhead. Seconds passed as the bombers began to disappear into the night sky, and the shaking stopped.

"That, my friends, are aircraft returning from pummelling our people," said Tony angrily. "If you hear the sound of them approaching, always take cover because you don't know if they will unload any unused bombs or strafe you. They have no regard for our medical unit tents or ambulances that are marked with red crosses. They strafe and bomb these willy-nilly."

Tony drove the lorry back on to the road, and they continued their slow journey. Finally, as the dawn began to come up, they reached the small village of La Bisbal de Falset. It was set on a craggy outcrop of rock and looked down on the road and the valley below it. About a mile on the other side of the village, they turned on to a track that took them towards a sheer rock face, which was the western edge of the Montsant mountain range.

As they got closer to the rocks, they saw the outline of the entrance to a large cave, which nature had chiselled out of the rugged mountainside. There was a large slab of rock that overhung the two-hundred-foot wide entrance to the cave. The sun, as it rose higher in the morning sky, began to throw more light on the cave entrance. Francis could see people inside feverishly working. Below the cave was a large tent that was the dining area for the staff, the administrative offices, and supply storage for the cave hospital. There were other smaller tents dotted around that were sleeping quarters. Also, several lorries were parked under trees as some crude attempt had been made to camouflage them. A small, narrow pathway led up from the valley below to the cave entrance.

"Welcome to our little grotto," said Tony sarcastically. "The locals call this Cova de Santa Llúcia. We have an abundant supply of fresh water from the spring inside the cave. It's an amazing piece of natural rock formation that gives us protection from bombs. There are two levels, so we have room for an operating theatre and for beds. The floors are very uneven, so the beds are set up in disorderly rows. We have electric light run off a generator so the doctors can operate on the badly wounded. It's near the front so we can get casualties here pretty quickly. This is done at night because of the aircraft flying around, looking for targets during the day."

As they were talking, a slow procession of people carrying three stretchers began to make its way down the path from the cave. On each stretcher lay a body of a dead man.

Seeing Francis and Jimmy staring at the sombre spectacle, Tony explained that they were the casualties who had died in the night, and they were being taken by the locals to a mass grave in the cemetery at La Bisbal de Falset.

The next week went by quickly as Francis and Jimmy learned the best routes that gave them good cover from attack and were the fastest to the cave hospital. The work they were doing was very similar to what they had been doing in Barcelona, except the casualties were soldiers. This routine was about to change.

The much anticipated Ebro offensive began on July 25, 1938, and would last until November 16 of that year. It was hailed as the bloodiest and cruellest battle of the Spanish Civil War and the last major conflict. Franco was able to destroy the republican army in the battle, and after it was over, the Spanish government would soon capitulate to the pro-fascist nationalist forces. What started out as a successful surprise attack by the republican army degenerated in the late summer into trench warfare reminiscent of the Great War. The slaughter on both sides was enormous as both armies fought for a few yards of land. Some thirty-six thousand five hundred men died, fifty thousand were wounded, and twenty-four thousand captured.

Francis and Jimmy were thrown into the thick of the initial fighting. The night before the offensive started, they had been assigned to a medical team and were sitting under the cover of some rocks. They were just north of the town of Vinebre, about a mile from the bank of the Ebro river, across from the town of Ascó. The plan was as the troops advanced, groups of doctors and nurses would cross the river and set up medical aid stations in various towns. They would triage as many wounded as possible before ferrying them back across the river and transporting them to the cave hospital or to the hospital train for further treatment.

An hour before midnight, small groups of republican soldiers soundlessly crossed at various points along the Ebro River and, with knives, silenced the nationalist guards on the other side. They then set up guide ropes across the river, which enabled the small boats carrying the main assault divisions to cross to the other side. This was achieved without incident and was a complete surprise to the nationalist army. The surprise was such that, by the end of the first day, the republican front advanced some nine miles from the river. Despite the very rugged terrain, the vanguard had reached the outskirts of Gandesa, one of the major objectives.

Francis and Jimmy were catnapping and were woken by the shuddering sounds of artillery, explosions, and rifle fire as the main assault started. As they watched from the high ground, they saw fires on the other bank of the river and smoke rising from the buildings in Ascó. At dawn, they could see boats full of men still crossing the river and engineers positioning pontoon bridges. Their medical unit was ordered to move out, and as they went down the road to the river, they saw a wooden bridge structure being put in place, ready to span the river so that heavy equipment and supplies could be transported to support the army as it advanced.

They reached the river, and the unit was directed to a pontoon foot bridge which had been set up during the night. The bridge they crossed felt very unstable as it swayed back and forth because of the strong river current, which created eddies as it hit the pontoons. Some of the nurses balked at using the bridges and went over in boats with the medical equipment.

When they had disembarked, Dr. David Roberts, who was in charge of the unit, gathered everyone around him.

"We have to set up a field hospital near Ascó. Once the bridge is completed, Jimmy and Francis can bring their ambulance over. In the meantime, as we set up, they will advance with the troops and bring back any wounded to us here," he said, pointing to a burned-out single-story farmhouse set on the side of a hill overlooking the river and the main Ascó road.

Francis and Jimmy climbed up a path that led to the Ascó road and began to walk with their stretcher towards the town. They soon came upon bodies of nationalist soldiers, some of which had been decapitated. Those with a leg or an arm missing, their uniforms were burned where the impact of the explosion had struck them. Others had been disembowelled when shrapnel had hit them in their abdomens. There were those that looked as though they were alive, save for a small dried blood on their foreheads or on their uniforms. These were bodies with no hope, lying there in the sun being devoured by flies and, at nightfall, by voracious rats or other rodents. War had written the final chapter in these men's lives and taken them away from those who loved them.

Francis and Jimmy surveyed the gruesome scene. They checked those they thought might still be alive but found no one. They continued on their way in silence. They heard a feeble groan, and looking around, they found a badly wounded soldier lying on a pool of his own blood. He was partly hidden from view by a dead colleague draped across him. They lifted the dead body to one side, and Francis put a tourniquet on his leg to stop the bleeding.

The soldier was no more than twenty years old, and his unshaven face was ashen and wracked by fear.

"Please don't kill me!" he begged in Spanish.

"Sorry, mate, we don't understand. We're taking you to hospital," said Jimmy. And with that, they put him on to the stretcher and began their slow journey to the field hospital. Suddenly, there was an explosion and machine-gun fire, which sent them scurrying for cover. The Italian and German air forces were bombing and strafing the pontoons and boats in the river. They were also going after the troops on the river bank. As Jimmy and Francis kept their heads down, shrapnel whizzed above their heads. After ten minutes of this prolonged barrage, there was suddenly silence.

They scrambled from their hiding place and continued on their journey. When they reached the field hospital, there was utter chaos as the medical staff worked on scores of wounded republican soldiers.

"This is no good. We can't walk and pick up one man at a time. It's going to take too long. We need transportation!" exclaimed Francis. "We can't use the bridge until it's finished, and then it will be too late for some of these men. Let's go and see whether we can find an abandoned lorry and use that."

They made their way again up the Ascó road and approached the town, which was set on a hillside overlooking the Ebro River. They were struck by the narrow streets, which seemed to have been cobbled together in a haphazard way. Most of them were blocked off with rubble. There were wrecked vehicles dotting the streets, but none could be used. It started to look as though their mission was a failure. As they were about to turn back, they came across a group of six men who were resting in the cool shadows on one side of the street and were sitting on three ammunition boxes. They all had rifles, wore dirty civilian clothes, and had ammunition belts strapped across their bodies. When they spotted the Red Cross armbands on Francis's and Jimmy's arms, they waved and called out to them.

"We're glad to see you, guys," said a tall wiry man with an American accent. "We're from the Lincoln Brigade, and we have some wounded colleagues up on the Fatarella Road. We've taken the town easily, but a sniper held us up a bit and got two of our guys. We're here to get some ammunition for our brigade. By the way, my name is Michael O'Malley."

"We would love to help you out, but we have no transportation until they finish building the bridge. We're trying to find an abandoned lorry to use as an ambulance. Have you seen any?"

"No, we haven't. Most of the vehicles we've seen are beyond repair," Michael responded.

Then one of the other Americans had an idea. "We passed a garage on the outskirts of town. It was all shuttered up, and the large wooden doors were bolted. The building was lightly damaged, and I'm wondering whether there is something inside. Let's go and take a look."

They climbed up a steep street and were soon on the outskirts of the village. On the side of the road was a building that had once been a commercial garage. There was rubble blocking the two large wooden doors that led to the repair shop.

"Before we waste time clearing away the debris, let's see whether we can get a look inside," said Francis.

He scrambled over the bricks and other debris. There weren't any windows on one side, and he had to climb over some barrels, old cars, and engine parts at the back of the building to get to the other side. There was a small window on the other side of the garage, which was not big enough to climb through. It was so dirty he was unable to see in. Francis broke the glass and peered in. He smiled to himself and gave a thumbs-up sign to the others. When he got back to the group, he told them that he had seen a lorry.

"I hope it still works," he said.

They all took their jackets off and set about clearing the bricks and stones from the front of the garage. This took them a good fifteen minutes. The next task was to open the padlock on the door. Michael picked up a large rock and started to smash it on the padlock. After his sixth or seventh attempt, the lock started to give way, and with a final heave, it dropped off. They all started to pull at the doors, which slowly opened to a reveal a Dodge lorry.

"Well, what have we here?" said Michael. "Wow! Look at this workshop! I have never seen such chaos, and the equipment is so basic. In Brooklyn, where I come from, no mechanic worth his salt would work with these tools and in such a mess."

Inside was a clutter of parts lying carelessly on the floor. The workbenches were covered in dirt and tools. From the ceiling, there hung a chain hoist, which was used for removing engines. Under the lorry was a pit where the mechanic worked on the underside of vehicles. On the back of the lorry were empty casks, which indicated that it was from a local winery.

"Let's see if she works," said Jimmy, and he jumped in the driver's seat. Michael went to the front.

"Let me give it a few turns first, and then you pull out the choke. When the engine catches, push the choke in halfway so you don't flood the engine!" Michael directed.

He slowly started to crank the engine and then signalled for Jimmy to pull out the choke. After a while, the engine began to splutter and then roared into life with a cloud of blue smoke, which made everyone cough. As he pushed in the choke, the engine began to purr.

"Well, I'll be darned!" Michael exclaimed admiringly. "Despite having the most arcane equipment, this mechanic knows how to tune an engine."

Jimmy put the lorry in gear and slowly drove it out of the garage. They loaded the ammunition, everyone jumped in the back, and they all headed to Fatarella.

Although only seven miles away, the journey took them some thirty minutes because it was a very hilly climb, and the road chicaned. They reached the village and located the brigade headquarters. Francis and Jimmy found the two wounded men lying on a counter of the village store. One had been shot in the leg, and it was broken. The other, who had a head wound, was more serious. They changed their bloody bandages, applied splints to the broken leg, and, with the help of Michael and his friends, moved the patients on to the back of the lorry.

They made their way back to the field hospital and helped move their patients to the line of wounded waiting to receive attention. Dr. Roberts came out of the tent, which was the temporary triage centre.

"Ah, Francis and Jimmy, I see you have been successful in finding transportation. Good. They have finished building a wooden bridge across the river, so tonight I want you to take back some of the wounded to the cave hospital. Also, bring back any medical supplies you can lay your hands on and your ambulance."

"Right you are, doctor," replied Jimmy.

When nightfall came, Jimmy and Francis drove their lorry with six wounded soldiers towards the wooden bridge that had been built that afternoon in Ascó. It was a single lane bridge, and soldiers were acting as traffic controllers, letting lorries come across in one direction at a time. When it was their turn, they were told to cross as fast as possible and not to stop for any reason. Jimmy, who was driving, gunned the lorry as they started to cross.

Just as they reached the centre of the bridge, there was a roar of aircraft engines, as two bombers descended on the river, starting a strafing run. As they passed over the bridge, they released two bombs. The boys watched in horror, certain that death was about to descended on them. It seemed that everything was in slow motion, and they were helpless to avoid what was about to happen. They closed their eyes, as if protecting themselves from the impact, and suddenly, a plume of water hit them. The aircraft had missed their target, and the bombs had exploded harmlessly in the river.

Both were shaking uncontrollably with blind fear, and it was only when the lorry behind them started honking that they pulled themselves together enough to quickly exit the bridge.

They did not speak on the drive to La Bisbal de Falset. Each was deep in thought and realised that what they had just survived was probably only the beginning of their nightmare. As they approached the cave hospital, they snapped out of their melancholy just enough to function and began to robotically unload their charges. When they had finished, they sat on the ground near their lorry just staring into space.

As they lay there, another lorry arrived, and the ambulance men unloaded their wounded. Jimmy and Francis didn't even notice them until one of the drivers walked up and greeted them.

"Hello, boys, how's it going?" said their friend Vincent. "Busy night?"

Francis glanced up, and Vincent could see by his sullen look that something was terribly wrong.

"What's wrong?" he pressed.

"We had a near miss on the bridge at Ascó," said Francis eventually, and then he explained what had happened.

"Phew! You were lucky. But you have to keep going somehow. Everyone you see around you is doing just that," he suggested.

"I know. We've seen enough death and destruction in Barcelona and now here. Why we ever decided to come to Spain, I don't know," Francis responded quietly. "You think to yourself, 'There but for the grace of God go I.' We always come to help them after they were wounded. We weren't there before it happened. We didn't know them. For the first time tonight, I saw what these men face every day, and I don't think I can cope with this. I'm scared."

"It's a very realistic fight we all have with ourselves," said Vincent. "I think of it this way, I'm resigned to the fact that I'm going to die, and I might as well make the best out of things before it happens. Call it fatalistic if you like, but it helps you cope. Survival is the name of the game now. This offensive is going to go nowhere. It will take a lot of lives, and you might be one of them. You've got to go forward somehow, otherwise you'll be a liability for the very people you are trying to help and yourself," he said, getting up.

Vincent walked over to the cab of his ambulance and brought over bag. He pulled out a bottle of Spanish brandy.

"Here, take a couple of swigs. I stole it from the table of a fascist colonel in Miravet. Go on, try it!"

Reluctantly, Francis took a gulp and passed the bottle to Jimmy who did likewise. It burned as it went down. They took another gulp and began to feel a little better. The brandy took the edge off as they both became a little light-headed.

"We do have an option though. We could just leave and go back to Paris, I suppose," said Jimmy.

"I wouldn't do that if I was you. I heard that an order was passed on down from General Rojo to shoot anyone who deserts. Even if you reach Barcelona, the Comintern there would hunt you down. No, we've got to make do with what we have and survive," Vincent cautioned.

"So we're trapped!" Francis said angrily. "You mean we can't go back! We have to put up with this whether we like it or not!"

"Unfortunately, that's the rub for all of us," replied Vincent.

"Jesus! I wonder what the good people who encouraged us to come here would say if they saw the true picture," replied a bitter Francis.

Then the hospital administrator, Anne Frobisher, walked up to them.

"The stores for Dr. Robertson are ready to be loaded. Follow me," she ordered.

Jimmy and Francis said goodbye to Vincent and sullenly followed her. They loaded up the supplies and climbed into the cab of the lorry.

"Tell Dr. Robertson to limit his use of morphine because we have a dwindling supply, and we don't know when we will get more," Miss Frobisher said. "The other thing is that you have to go back via Flix and across the steel bridge there. The wooden bridge was bombed earlier tonight and is being repaired."

They drove off in silence and eventually joined the convoy of supply trucks, artillery, and tanks as they lined up to cross the Ebro river. They looked anxiously around, trying to spot any bombers as they got nearer the bridge. They felt a great relief when they reached the other side of the river. Now that the tension had passed, they began to banter as they drove from Flix to Ascó.

They arrived at the field hospital and unloaded the medical supplies. One of the nurses, Penny Armitage, walked up to them as they lay on the grass.

"We need you to take another group of wounded to the cave hospital," she said matter-of-factly.

"Tonight?" questioned Francis.

"Of course. When do you think, next week?" she said sarcastically. She turned on her heels and returned to ward in the tent.

"Bloody bitch! Who does she think she is?" exclaimed Jimmy.

"I agree, but I suppose we have no choice but to take them across. These men need us to help them," Francis said resignedly. They shuffled off to the makeshift ward in the tent to pick up their charges.

They loaded up the wounded men on to stretchers, and those who were walking wounded sat in the back of the lorry with their feet dangling over the tailboard. Just before they were to leave, Dr. Robertson came up to them.

"We have been ordered to move our field hospital to Corbera d'Ebre, which will be nearer the front line," he told them. "The advance by the republican army went faster than anyone thought, and they are in the outskirts of Gandesa. So when you get back, follow the road to Corbera d'Ebre, and we'll see you there."

It took them another three hours to reach the cave hospital and make it back across the river. Dawn was just breaking as they reached the outskirts of Camposines, and they started to pass columns of soldiers on the Corbera road heading to the front. As they reached the outskirts of Corbera, they started to look for the field hospital and eventually found it set up in the village centre in a square in front of the Baroque church of Sant Pere.

Other volunteer ambulance drivers greeted them, and they sat down to a breakfast of tinned sardines left behind in a food store by the retreating fascist army. They were told that there would be a briefing of ambulance staff at nine that morning to give them their assignments. After eating, Francis and Jimmy settled down in the back of their lorry to get some sleep while they could. They were so exhausted that sleep was easy to come by.

At the briefing later that morning, Jimmy and Francis were assigned to cover the battle for Vilalba dels Arcs. The fifteenth International Brigade had met heavy resistance in the town and was taking many casualties. Added to the republican army's problems, General Franco had ordered the lock gates opened on the river Ebro at Tremp and Camasara in the north, which raised the level of the river Ebro, so that the pontoon bridges and other crossings were temporarily closed. As a result, staging areas for casualties were set up near Ascó and Móra d'Ebre.

Jimmy and Francis set off towards Vilalba dels Arcs with Monica Evans, one of the nurses, and three other medics. They planned to set up a dressing station as near as they could to the front line and transport the wounded at night to staging areas along the Ebro river. A mile from the village, they came across the reserve elements of the Abraham Lincoln Brigade who were resting at the side of the road out of the dusty heat in the shade of an olive grove.

Francis looked out for Michael O'Malley and his friends and saw the big American cleaning his rifle. They waved to each other as they passed by, and soon, they came upon the forward elements of the International Brigade. They heard the chatter of machine guns and rifle fire nearby, which fell silent after a while and then started up again with more intensity.

After a brief discussion with an officer, they set up their dressing station about half a mile from the front line, which straddled a four-way crossroad, and was about a mile from the village. They had just unloaded their supplies and set up their aid station when they heard a piercing whistle, as bombs rained down on the nearby republican soldiers. Taking cover behind some rocks, they saw enemy bombers dropping their deadly cargoes and fighters strafing soldiers on the ground. Francis and Jimmy and the other medics grabbed their stretchers and ran towards the soldiers.

The scene was one of utter desolation as wounded men cried out for help—some screaming, others sobbing. The scene was like that of an abattoir. There was blood everywhere, and there was the smell of rotting, burning flesh.

Francis's first patient was a man who had a shrapnel wound to his face, and he bandaged him up. Then they found a soldier with a serious wound to his stomach. He was bleeding to death and holding his intestines in as he lay there staring at his wound. There was nothing they could do for him, and so they moved on to others.

The team worked hard for the rest of the day between the constant air raids, taking the wounded to the dressing station. Soldiers were now removing their dead comrades and placing their bodies on top of each other in gruesome piles of wasted humanity. These would be removed later for burial by the locals when there was lull in the fighting, but in the meantime, the bodies would remain there as an ugly reminder to the living of the futility of war.

But the worst was yet to come.

A respite came in the early evening, and they sat in the olive grove resting and eating bread and the rest of the sardines they had scavenged from the fascist store. As they sat there, soldiers began to move along the road to the front. Francis recognised Michael O'Malley and walked over and greeted him.

There was a decided change in this previously ebullient American. He seemed quiet and withdrawn. When Francis finally got him to speak, Michael told him that they had been ordered forward to prepare for an assault in the morning. He said that there had been strong resistance from the fascists, who were dug in and difficult to extract.

"It's going to be hard to make any headway, but we need to take the village and move on," he said. "Trouble is we are being shot to pieces by the defenders and by the bombs from their aircraft. We are supposed to have an air force. Where the hell is it? Where are the antiaircraft batteries? Where is our artillery to give us cover? God, this is a total shambles!"

"What are they going to do then?" asked Francis.

"They are going try and overwhelm the defenders by sheer numbers of attacking soldiers. That's why we're moving up to the front now. You'll be busy in the morning, you mark my words! I must go now. See you on the other side," he said with forced enthusiasm.

And with that, he joined the others and marched off up the road, turning once to wave. He was soon out of sight in the gathering darkness.

Francis and Jimmy spent a good part of the night ferrying wounded men to the staging areas by the Ebro river. Finally, at four in the morning, they were able to rest and fall into a light sleep. Francis had difficulty sleeping as his thoughts were with Michael. He was haunted by his last words. Michael's personality had changed so much in just a few days, and it seemed that now he had a death wish or didn't really care what happened to him. Francis knew in his heart he would likely not see his friend again.

The assault began just before dawn the next morning as the night time shadows were dissipating. From his vantage point in the top floor of a house, Francis saw that the republican army was beginning to make progress in reaching the village's defenders, but his hopes soon were dashed with the arrival of enemy bombers and fighters. The attack waned, and eventually, troops started to retreat back to their original positions.

Once again, the medics began to help the wounded, and once again, the survivors collected the dead. Francis was in the thick of the action, sorting through the carnage and helping those he could. Then he saw Michael lying on the ground like a limp rag doll. Francis ran over to him.

He was bleeding heavily from a wound in his chest. He was ashen. His breathing was laboured and raspy. Francis could see that there was no hope for his friend. Tears began to well up in his eyes, and he held Michael's hand.

"Well, I guess this is the end of the road," Michael said between his teeth as the pain rose and fell. "We nearly had them. Promise me something, write to my mother in New York and let her know I'm gone. You'll find her address in my pocket."

"Let me put a field bandage on it to stop the bleeding," said Francis.

"Don't waste it on me, Francis!"

Then he began to cough up blood. When this subsided, he lay there wasted. Suddenly, he gripped Francis's hand very tightly, lifted himself up slightly, and, with a sigh, fell back dead.

Francis sat there looking at Michael's body, mesmerised by the deformed corpse that lay before him that was now just a grotesque caricature of the friendly human being he had known.

He took the letter from Michael's uniform pocket and read it. It was from a warm, loving mother who was begging her son to come home to his family. She reminded him of the wonderful holidays they had had and that his job as a store clerk was being held open for him. It told of everyday life of this close-knit family, of the loves and silliness of his three sisters, and of the machinations of the neighbours. Francis longed for a life with a normal family just like this one. Why had Michael given this all up and come here, he didn't understand.

As he sat there fixated on his anguish, a hand gently rested on his shoulder. Francis swung round with anger and hit out at whoever it was.

"Steady on, Francis!" said a surprised Jimmy. "I was only going to suggest we move along before the bombers come back."

"Since when are you giving me orders? Just leave me alone!"

Seeing the wild look in Francis's eyes, Jimmy backed off and walked away. As he left, he shouted over his shoulder, "Fine! When you've calmed down, you'll know where to find me."

Now you know what it's like to lose someone you admire, Francis.

He looked round and saw his father standing there.

"I don't need you! I'm not like you. You're a butcher and a rapist!" Francis shot back.

"Ah, but you are. You'll see. You're on your own. Nobody is going to help you. You'll find out soon enough that you will do anything to survive, even promising allegiance to the devil. And then you will be in the devil's grip, and you will do

anything he tells you. Mark my words! The priest was a good start, but now you have to earn your spurs."

And with that, he disappeared into the red mist and left Francis alone with his thoughts.

Suddenly, there was the all-too-familiar sound of aircraft and bullets starting to fly as the pilots took aim at the stragglers caught in the open. As the fighters began their strafing runs, Francis ran from cover to cover. At one point, he was caught in the open and could only hug the ground. Miraculously, he was not hit, although shells had passed on either side of him.

He made it back to the aid station and went in search of Jimmy. He found him catnapping under a tree. Francis apologised for his anger.

"That's fine, mate. I know you were upset seeing Michael like that," said Jimmy. "How about eating some bread and those bloody awful sardines? We have a long night ahead of us."

They had made two trips after dark to the banks of the Ebro River with the wounded and were finished by about one in the morning. Their third trip promised to be their last that night, and they were looking forward to getting some much-needed sleep when they got back. As usual, the going was slow. On the way back from the last trip, they had just turned left at Camposines and started to follow the road which climbed up the mountainside. They joined the Fatarella to Vilalba road and were passing through the woods, which were on either side, when they saw three soldiers waving them down.

"They're not our lads. Hold tight!" shouted Jimmy, who was driving, as he gunned the lorry past the soldiers. Then there was a volley of rifle shots, and the lorry began to swerve uncontrollably across the road. It ended up in a ditch at the side of the road. Francis was semiconscious with a large graze on his forehead where his head had hit the dashboard. Jimmy was in worst shape. The steering wheel had hit him in the upper part of his rib cage, and he was unconscious.

The soldiers pulled Francis roughly from the cab of the lorry. They tied his hands behind his back and gagged him with a cloth. Another longer rope was attached around his neck.

"This one will do," said the sergeant in charge of the patrol in Spanish.

Sgt. Alberto Farina was about six feet tall and very muscular. He had a scar down one side of his head. He was an angry man and always had a scowl on his face. He had become cruel and uncompromising after the massacre of his brother, who was a priest, and the rape and murder of his sister and other villagers by militia members belonging to the republican government. The crime took place in his home village in Northern Aragon. It was part of a wave of massacres of Roman Catholic priests and those associated with them that were sanctioned by the republican government. He was an olive farmer and had been away from the village selling his crop, so he had avoided the massacre. After the killings, he had joined the nationalist army and had been wounded at the Battle of Jarama.

He leaned into the cab and shot Jimmy through the head with his rifle.

"Now let's go before someone comes to investigate the shooting," he said.

When Francis saw what happened to Jimmy, he flew at the sergeant but was brought to a crashing halt by the rope around his neck. The sergeant hit him hard in the stomach, which took the wind out of him, and he fell to the floor. He was then kicked by him in the face. The soldiers dragged him to his feet and pushed him into the woods, where they joined three other members of the patrol.

His nightmare was just beginning.

Chapter 13

Francis was aching from just about every bone in his body as well as from his heart. Two friends had been killed that day, and he swore to himself that, somehow, he would get his revenge on that sergeant. This may not happen today or even in the coming weeks, but he would seek him out and punish him for Jimmy's death.

The patrol began to move along the tree line, using it for cover as they started to climb upwards and across country away from the road. It was hard going as the ground was very rocky, and the darkness made footing particularly treacherous. Several times, some of them slipped, sending down a cascade of stones. Once, Francis fell and was dragged roughly to his feet by his captors who yanked on the rope around his neck. Sergeant Farina stopped them frequently and listened. When he was satisfied that they had not been discovered, he waved them on.

It seemed to Francis that they were taking a circuitous route because they were not heading straight for Vilalba dels Arcs but going north. After an hour of heading in that direction, they turned east and continued on this course until they were challenged by a sentry. The sergeant gave a password, and they were allowed to proceed. Now they were well and truly behind the nationalists' line.

When they reached the village, it was in darkness, except for some campfires that were being used to cook meals for the soldiers. These were well hidden from view of the republican lines, which were more than a mile away. The patrol stopped, and the sergeant took over, leading Francis along a street, while the others went back to their respective platoons. They came to a very old building, which had bars on the windows, and Francis thought this might have been a police station or a jail at some time. The sergeant opened the door and pushed him inside.

The room he fell into was an outer office lit by an oil lamp with a desk and a chair in front of it. Maps and papers were spread over the desk in a chaotic jumble, and a leftover meal was on a plate which had been pushed to one side. In the corner was an unmade bed.

"Get in there, you commie bastard!" said Sergeant Farina as he kicked Francis into a back room, which was being used for storage.

The sergeant then threw a rope over a beam and attached one end to Francis's hands which were tied behind his back. He put a hood over his head and pulled on the rope so that Francis's toes were just touching the ground. He fastened the other end to one of the bars on the window.

With a laugh, he said, "This will help loosen your tongue!"

The pain was excruciating. His arms felt as though they were coming out of their shoulder sockets. Through his pain, all he could hear were muffled noises and screams. After a while, numbness to the torture started to come over him. It still hurt like hell, but mentally, he was beginning to come to terms with what was happening to him.

"Well, well, well, we seem to have got ourselves into a real mess this time," he heard his father's voice. *"They want to know the layout of that rabble called an army that you belong to. If I was you, I'd give them what they want. Your friends are doomed anyway, so you might as well save your own hide. Watch out for that sergeant though. He's dangerous."*

"Go to hell!" shouted Francis through his pain and the gag in his mouth.

"I'm already there, and I'm waiting for you. Don't disappoint." Then he was gone, leaving Francis to his misery.

He had been in this stressed position for about an hour when he heard the door suddenly swing open. The hood and gag were roughly removed by the sergeant, and the rope to the beam was undone. Francis collapsed on to the floor as his stressed muscles could not hold his weight and he began to whimper. He was pulled to his feet and dragged into the main room and tied to a chair in front of the desk. The pain started to subside a little, and he was getting the feeling back in his arms as blood started to circulate. He sat there frightened and wondering what was going to happen next.

An officer entered the room through the front door, and the sergeant came to attention.

"Now you are going to tell me about where your forces are and their strength," he said in Spanish.

"I don't understand a word you are saying," Francis responded. The sergeant slapped him in the face.

"Now, now, sergeant, he's English and doesn't understand us," said the officer.

The officer turned to Francis and said in good English, "I'm Captain Francisco Estrada. So what's an Englishmen doing here in Spain?"

"I'm here to provide medical care for the wounded. Also, I'm Irish, not English."

"Forgive me. You see, I'm just a Spanish peasant, and I don't understand these things," he said sarcastically. "Which are you, a communist or an anarchist?"

"I'm neither. I came here to help people because I believe in democracy. That's why we take care of your wounded as well as our own. I'm just caught up in this war like so many others with no opportunity to leave. Either you'll shoot me or those communist fanatics will. I'm stuck with no way out."

Captain Estrada sympathised with Francis's situation because he too felt the same about his own position. He was also disillusioned by the war, which had dragged on too long and many of his friends had died. There were fanatics on both sides like Sergeant Farina. The generals didn't care about men like him who were in the front line. Their attitude was to win at all cost, no matter how many men die.

Still, he had a job to do because there was going to be another attack in the morning, and he owed it to his men to be as well prepared as possible. That's why he had sent a patrol out to capture someone from the republican army so that he could get some information. The sudden attack across the Ebro river had caught everybody by surprise, and he needed to find out the strength of the enemy.

Captain Estrada studied Francis, and it was a long time before he said anything.

"What is your name?"

"Francis Reagan."

"Well, Francis, before we let you go, I want to know about the International Brigade we are facing outside this village. How many men are there, and do they have artillery and machine guns?" Francis grew angry. "I won't betray my friends."

"Your friends! You just said you wanted out. Look at them. They are fighting among themselves. They are a complete rabble, and people like you get caught up in this nightmare. Isn't it about time you thought of yourself and your family? The quicker we can end this, the quicker we can all go home."

"I have no family or home to go to."

"You don't understand the seriousness of your situation. I can have you shot right now," he said, ignoring Francis's comment.

Francis was silent and just stared at him with utter hatred in his eyes.

Seeing this, Captain Estrada said, "Perhaps my sergeant can help you remember."

"Soften him up a bit more," he told the sergeant in Spanish. With that, the captain got up and left.

Sergeant Farina started to beat Francis, and he soon lost consciousness. He was woken up when a bucket of water was poured over his head. He was again strung up on the beam and hooded. Hanging there, he drifted in and out of consciousness. He had a dream that he was back at the orphanage and smiled at the remembrance of the happy times he had had.

Finally, fully alert, he began to think about his situation. The captain was right when he questioned whether he had friends. He had no friends, apart from Michael and Jimmy, and they were gone. He knew none of the soldiers who were fighting against the nationalists. If he was going to survive, he had to give the captain the information he needed. He realised that his cooperation would mean the deaths of more men, and he wasn't proud of that, but to him, his survival was more important. They would die anyway, so what's the harm?

Francis was once again placed in the chair opposite the desk, but this time, he was not tied up. Captain Estrada then began to question him.

"I'm sorry we have to go to such lengths to make you cooperate. Are you willing to help me?"

"I suppose so," Francis said morosely. "What's going to happen to me once I give you the information you need?"

"You will be sent to a prisoner-of-war camp. Your war will be over. Now let's start by outlining where their troops are."

Captain Estrada and Francis spent about forty-five minutes going over the layout of the Third Division, and he was asked a lot about the morale of the troops. When they had finished, Captain Estrada took two glasses and a bottle of brandy out of the desk draw. He poured some brandy into each and offered a glass to Francis who took it.

"Thank you for your help, Francis. We won't tell anyone about your cooperation. They might not like that."

Francis finished his brandy, and Captain Estrada turned to Sergeant Farina and said, "Take him and put him with the other prisoners."

"Shall I take care of him permanently?" asked Sergeant Farina.

"No! He has been of help to us," said Captain Estrada firmly.

Reluctantly, Sergeant Farina marched Francis down a narrow street to the outskirts of the village where there was a large barn. This building was guarded by three soldiers. When they saw the sergeant coming with a prisoner, they sprang to attention and started to unlock the barn door. The sergeant pushed Francis through the door, and as a farewell gesture, he hit him with his rifle butt in the middle of his back.

"Good riddance, you commie bastard!" he snarled in Spanish

The barn door slammed shut, and Francis peered into the pitch black. Eventually, his eyes began to get used to the dark, and he could make out about a dozen sets of eyes on him. No one said a word.

"Hello, I'm Francis Reagan. I was with a medical team until I was caught tonight."

"You have to excuse our reluctance to welcome you," said an English voice. "They have been trying to frighten us into giving them information. We expect to face a firing squad in the morning, so we aren't as outgoing as you might expect. I'm Charles Farmer of the British Battalion. They seem to have given you a proper going over. Did you give them any information?"

"No, not that I'm aware of. I was surprised they stopped beating me though," lied Francis.

He found some straw and lay on it, resting his battered body. He soon fell into a troubled sleep.

He woke to the sound of gunfire. The dawn was just piercing through the wooden slats of the barn. He studied his fellow prisoners for the first time. Some were still asleep, and others were stretching themselves. They were unshaven, dirty, and ragged-looking. When he tried to get up and move his muscles, they seemed to be locked together by a large vice and he moaned at the pain.

"Take it slowly, Francis, and your muscles will soon loosen up," said Charles Farmer as he helped him to his feet. "We've been in this barn for three days. We were caught on the first day of the offensive as we advanced through La Fatarella towards this village. Silly, really. We were told to stop and rest so that we could be resupplied, but this was delayed because of the bombing of the bridges. We sat down in a wood, and sometime later, we were surprised by a platoon of nationalists who came out of nowhere. So here we are.

"We're waiting for them to take us out and shoot us. They've been doing this to other prisoners they've caught, even to medics like yourself. It seems they are too busy at the moment defending the village to bother with us," he said as he peered through an opening in the barn door.

Charles and the others in the group discussed where they were from. One man was a coal miner in Wales; another was a blacksmith from Sterling in Scotland. The others were from England—from the Midlands, Yorkshire, and London. Francis was reticent about telling them too much about himself, except that he was born and brought up in Dublin and he described his work in Barcelona.

By nine o'clock, the barn was stiflingly hot as the sun outside blistered the dry mountainous sierra. The barn doors swung open, and two soldiers brought in some cans of sardines, water, and bread. When these had been delivered, they slammed the door shut.

"Bloody sardines again," said the blacksmith. "I suppose it's better than nothing, but we're going to turn into sardines soon. I'm already growing a tail!" Everyone laughed, and they ate their meal in silence.

As they finished eating their meal, there was the sound of a lorry pulling up in front of the barn. The barn doors swung open again, and several soldiers herded them to the back of the lorry, and they were told to get in. When they were inside, two armed guards climbed in with them, and the lorry set off. Soon, they reached Gandesa, and other prisoners were picked up. There were some thirty men now crammed into the back of the lorry. They were all from the International Brigade, mainly English, Irish, and a smattering of sultry Scotsmen. Then the lorry was off again and joined a convoy of others that were heading back to pick up supplies for the front.

The journey was long and boring. They all tried to relax in the heat and the stuffiness of the canvas-draped lorry. Arguments broke out now and then as the restive men tried to keep as cool as possible and took turns to sit on the outside next to the guards to get what fresh air there was. Finally, at four thirty in the afternoon, the lorry drove through the outskirts of Saragossa, and Francis saw another devastated city. This time, the bombing and artillery shelling had been done by the republican government mainly in the previous year and, whilst it was not as bad as the bombing in Barcelona, it had destroyed chunks of the city, particularly the industrial area.

The lorry drew up to some railway sidings in what had been the city's main goods yard. The prisoners were hustled into an old engine shed, and the doors were closed by the guards. As their eyes got used to the darkness, they could make out the railway lines and the pits, where mechanics were able to work on the underside of engines. There were empty work benches and discarded wooden rail ties. There was nowhere to sit, except on the floor, but at least, they were out of the back of the lorry and its stifling heat.

They sat in groups on the floor and started to guess where they were going and what was going to be their fate. Some believed the plan was to execute them, others thought they might be repatriated if they promised not to return to Spain, as others had, and some said they were heading to a prisoner-of-war camp. Francis thought that the speculation was a useless exercise and lay resting on the stone floor.

The door suddenly opened, and another six prisoners were pushed in. Francis's attention was drawn to a man with what looked like a serious wound to his arm. He sat separate from the others, hugging his arm. Francis went over to look at his wound. The man was sweating profusely, and Francis could smell the gangrene that had set in on his arm. When he looked at the black flesh around the wound, it was oozing puss. He realised the man didn't stand a chance of living. His arm should be amputated, but there was no chance of getting any medical help, and even then, there was no guarantee that he would survive.

"I guess I'm done for now," he said to Francis between the waves of pain. His name was Peter, and he was a twenty-five-year-old from Ilkley in Yorkshire. Francis told him that the arm needed to come off if he was going to survive at all, but there was little chance of getting any medical help. "I can't take the pain anymore! I don't want to hang on. I know the pain will get worse. Can you help me on my way?" Francis said he had nothing that he could use but thought to himself he couldn't steal himself to do this. He left Peter lying there delirious and covered him with his overcoat. He was shivering and crying between the bouts of pain. Francis hoped Peter's end would come soon.

In the middle of the night, they were woken by the sound of a steam engine braking and steam being released. The doors of the shed were opened, and the guards started to hustle them towards a freight train that had pulled up near the shed. One of the car doors was open, and they were told to get in and encouraged to move fast with rifle butts. Francis helped Peter climb in. Once all of them were in the freight car, the door was slammed shut and locked. After twenty minutes, the train juddered to a start, and they were off.

Several hours passed as the train made its way slowly, stopping frequently. At these stops, there were loud voices barking orders, and the prisoners who spoke Spanish said that they were loading supplies. With the dawn, Francis was able to peer between the wooden slats of the freight car and saw the mountainous countryside they were passing through. At midday, the train came to a halt at a station, and Francis could see from the signs that they had arrived in a city called Burgos.

The car door was opened, and they were ordered to disembark. Peter handed Francis his greatcoat.

"I won't need this, but you will need it to keep warm," he said.

Francis argued with him, but he wouldn't listen. Francis wondered why he had given him the coat. He hadn't long to find out.

The soldiers lined the prisoners up in pairs, and Francis stood behind Peter. The soldiers handed their charges over to five armed Guardia Nacional Republicana—the federal police. These men were notorious for their brutality, and they just stared at the prisoners for a long time. Then the staff sergeant in charge spoke in English.

"You scum will regret ever being alive, let alone coming to Spain. You communists and anarchists will be put on trial and executed. We have no time for you. You will be shown no mercy, and we will cleanse our country of vermin like you. Now we have a long march ahead of us. What are you smiling at?" he screamed at Peter.

"I was just thinking how stupid you are! You bloody fascist pig!"

The staff sergeant marched up to Peter and, with a primeval roar, hit him in the face with his walking stick. Undeterred, Peter spat in his face. The guardia pulled out his pistol and shot him between the eyes.

"Let that be a lesson to you all. The same will happen to you if you insult the guardia. You two pick up his wretched body and put it in the cart over there."

Francis smiled ruefully to himself. Peter had got his way.

As they set off on their seven-mile march, the prisoners' mood was sombre, and nobody spoke. Most were thinking about what they had just witnessed and were full of fear for what they might face at the end of their journey. The staff sergeant was leading the way on his horse, and the rest of guardia followed in the rear in the cart, which was drawn by an emaciated-looking horse.

They were soon on the outskirts of Burgos and passing through woods on either side of the road and into a small village called Las Rozanoas. The street was deserted, and there was no one to be seen. The heat was beginning to affect them since most of the prisoners had kept their heavy clothes to protect them from the cold nights. The route was undulating, and it took a toll on their stamina. The speed of their march had slowed, and the guardia screamed at them to pick up pace. There was no water, and most were now suffering from blisters on their feet.

They now entered the larger village of Careñajimeno. As they shuffled along, the villagers came out of their houses and stared in silence at the line of unkempt men who passed before them. Then two women broke from the crowd and ran up to them and spat at them. Others in the crowd began throwing stones.

"Communist filth!" they screamed in Spanish.

The guardia did nothing to stop the crowd venting their anger at the prisoners. The area was a nationalist stronghold with many Franco supporters, and the police felt that they were entitled to take their anger out on the enemy. In fact, the guardia just grinned and encouraged the crowd to throw stones. Even when stones hit the men, they did nothing but laugh.

Finally, they were clear of the town, and the road began to flatten out, and there was an open sierra on both sides. They trudged on for another two miles until they came to a turning, which was an earthen road. They followed this road, which wound around, until they were marched through a wooded area, and finally, the road started to drop down. Through the trees on the right side of the road, peering at them was a large brooding castle-like building with a high Romanesque tower that overlooked the countryside.

As they marched on and got closer, the building seemed even more ominous. Some of it was in disrepair, particularly part of the roof and all of the grounds. They had arrived at the nationalist concentration camp at San Pedro Monastery at Cardeña, parts of which were built in the ninth century and added to in the thirteenth and fifteenth. The monastery had been empty and abandoned for more than one hundred years and had been taken over by the nationalists as one of their primary prisoner-of-war camps.

In the courtyard in front of the building was a large statue of Christ, which was incongruous in a place of pain and death such as this. On either side of the front of the building were two towers. Above the main entrance were ornate marble carvings, which were badly in need of restoring.

On their approach, the heavy wooden doors swung open, and they were marched into an inner courtyard. The doors slammed behind them. Francis would not see the outside world again for almost a year.

Chapter 14

San Pedro Monastery de Cardeña, Burgos, August 1938

Francis and the other newly arrived prisoners were marched into the monastery's cloister and then into its quadrangle. There was a sergeant of the Guardia Nacional Republicana at a large desk.

The prisoners took turns in going up to the desk and stating who they were, what country they were from, how old they were, and what division or brigade they had been in before capture. They were each handed an empty sardine can to use as a plate for food. They had to empty their pockets and the contents confiscated. One prisoner objected when a photograph of his family was taken. Two of the guards immediately beat him with their canes.

Francis decided that he would hide the slip of paper with the address of Michael's mother. He folded it and slipped it into one of his shoes. He had an eerie feeling he was being watched closely, not by the guards but by others who were in the darkness of the rooms off the cloister.

When it was his turn, he gave the information to the sergeant who, to his surprise, spoke passable English. He emptied his pockets of coins, a bandage, and a pair of surgical scissors. He pulled his pockets inside out to show that they were empty and was dismissed.

The new prisoners were assigned to the third floor and told that they were not to leave it unless ordered to do so. As they were marched up the stone stairs, Francis saw prisoners everywhere in the monks' cells, in what had been their dormitories, their infirmary, and their refectory. Everywhere he looked, there were wall-to-wall prisoners talking in many languages. In fact, there were some six hundred and fifty International Brigade prisoners in this prison camp. There were few windows, and those he saw had only bars with no protection from the cold sierra winds which blew in during the night. Sanitation was minimal with a small room on each floor to serve as the lavatory and washroom. The smell was putrefying in these rooms.

Once they had been dismissed by the guards, a man came up to him and, in an Irish brogue, asked him whether he liked what he had seen of the San Pedro Grand Hotel.

Francis had to grin. "You seem to have a fine establishment here! My name is Francis Reagan from Dublin."

"Ah! I'm Patrick Tierney from Cork. I've been in here for about six months, although it feels like a lot longer. I was captured during the retreat through Aragon," he said. Francis guessed that Patrick was in his late twenties. He had bright red hair when it was washed and was extremely thin. In fact, his clothes looked at least four sizes too big. He had a ready smile and a friendly demeanour, which warmed people to him immediately.

"How come you ended up here?" Patrick asked.

Francis explained what had happened to him and said he was surprised he hadn't been shot as this was the fate of many of the International Brigade.

"They have been shooting some of our lads, particularly those who were communist leaders or officers, but word has it that Franco ordered a stop to executions of foreigners so he could curry favour and acceptance by other countries," he said. "The Basques and Spanish prisoners, who are kept in a separate part of the prison, are here for re-education, fascist style, and then they are sent to labour battalions. There are some executions of these poor sods when they find a commissar among them. This is a grim reminder of why we all volunteered to be here."

"Things look appalling. How do you cope with the conditions?" Francis asked.

"Well, it's really a mind game. Always do what the guards want, otherwise you are in for a beating, or worst of all, you will be thrown into the black hole, and I can tell you, from bitter experience, it's worse than hell. There are two guards you should be particularly careful of. One is the staff sergeant in charge of all the guards who carries a large walking stick, and the other is his second in command. When they want to move us quickly, they whack the nearest prisoner. These two are mean and cruel, and the other guards follow their example.

"Despite being in here, we are determined not to let the fascists win by making us less than human or like the walking dead. Most of us are resolved to keep our sanity by organising activities, such as lectures by other prisoners on all sorts of subjects. The big thing here is chess."

"I've never played that game."

"Now's your chance. A number of prisoners have been able to fashion chess sets out of bread, wood, and pebbles," Patrick said. "Also, two men from America publish a newspaper called *The San Pedro Jaily News*, which only has one handwritten copy and is circulated among the English-speaking prisoners. It's very funny and keeps us laughing for a short while. So you see, we try and occupy ourselves, keep our minds active and spirits up.

"Anyway, let's do one thing at a time. First, we must get you situated with the rest of the Irish contingent. Come on, follow me."

Patrick took Francis into a room, which had probably been a monks' dormitory. There were a number of men there who were either deep in conversation or playing chess.

"Listen up, lads. This here is Francis Reagan from Dublin who has been forced to join us," Patrick said with a grin. And he began to introduce Francis to a number of the men.

Then he turned to another group of six prisoners.

"These lads here are English. You'll have to forgive them for that though! They were captured with me. This is Nigel Ellis who I credit with saving my life, and I shall always be in his debt. By the way, he is an ace chess player. Francis wants to learn the game, Nigel."

"I'd be happy to teach him," said Nigel with a strong Yorkshire accent.

Just then, there was a clanging of a spoon on a saucepan. "That must be our gourmet dinner!" said Patrick.

They all went downstairs and lined up in the quadrangle. There were four large pots hung over fires that were heating the meal. Basque prisoners dished out their meagre meal of a small piece of bread and a watery bean gruel. Although he was hungry, Francis could hardly eat his meal. Seeing this, Patrick told him that after a few days, he would change his mind. When they had finished, they were ordered to go back to their floor.

That first night was a nightmare. The prisoners only had the bare stone floor to sleep on—no straw, no blankets, no bedding of any kind. They were crammed in so tightly together that they occupied about a two-foot-wide space each. It was cold and draughty, and however tightly Francis wrapped Peter's greatcoat around himself, he could not keep warm. He hardly slept, and instead, he listened to the noises of the night. There were cries and moans of men either asleep or painfully awake. Then there was the squeaking of rats as they foraged for food. The squeaks got more intense as they fought amongst themselves for a female's attention.

Francis was glad to see the dawn, which peered into their dormitory. After such a sleepless night, he was glad to get up and walk off the stiffness from his body. He looked out of the window and saw the sunlight sparkling on the rough terrain of the sierra, and it glittered as it hit the trees surrounding the monastery. Others now began to stir, and soon, everyone was up.

Breakfast was a piece of bread and a watery soup. When they had eaten, they were ordered out of the quadrangle for the morning parade on the forecourt of the monastery's church. They were helped on their way by the guards who wielded their sticks and hit prisoners as they passed. Once in the forecourt, they were formed up into three rows. The guards spent some time counting and then reported their numbers to the staff sergeant in charge. Then Spanish and Basque prisoners were led out, and the counting of them began. Half an hour passed before they were finished.

Finally, a priest appeared with an army major, who was the camp's commandant. The priest said a few prayers and handed over the proceedings to the major. He spoke only in Spanish, and one of the prisoners translated his words into English for the International Brigade prisoners. He told them of the great victories of the nationalists in stopping the Ebro offensive and how the fascists were going to build a stronger Spain. No one, of course, believed a word he was saying.

When the major had finished, he led the Spanish prisoners in singing the fascist anthem. It all ended with cries of "Viva Franco" three or four times, which was followed simultaneously by the fascist salute. The Spanish and Basque prisoners took part in this charade, but the International Brigade prisoners were silent in their disgust but did salute, although deliberately very sloppily. In fact, some of them, instead of calling out "Viva Franco," cried out "Viva fuck you" in defiance. None of the guards realised what they were saying because they couldn't understand colloquial English. Patrick told Francis that the prisoners' unofficial house committee had decided to conform to this order because the consequences would be beatings and other depravations. After the parade, they were marched back to their floor and left to their own devices.

And so began Francis's internment in one of Franco's notorious concentration camps. He joined in the life of the prisoners, learned how to play chess with Nigel Ellis, and became an avid player. He took classes in languages, mathematics, and other subjects, which were taught by other prisoners. Francis's sharp mind absorbed all these activities, and he was always full of questions, no matter what the subject. Because of the activities arranged by prisoners, he was able to fight off depression and, with it, that feeling of hopelessness.

After several weeks, Francis began to lose weight because of the appalling diet of white navy beans, which sometimes had a piece of pork fat in it, a bread roll, and a soup at breakfast made of water, olive oil, garlic, and bread crumbs.

He, like the rest of the prisoners, endured daily beatings by the guards for small infractions or for no reason at all. There were Catholic masses, and everyone was forced to attend. If the priest saw anyone not taking part in the service, he ordered the guards to beat the prisoner. They had to attend a compulsory six-week religious education class run by the local priest. Needless to say no one passed, so the course was repeated and repeated until the authorities got tired of it.

Life in the prison did have a lighter side, which helped improve morale a little, if not only momentarily. At the end of August, the International Brigade prisoners were subjected to a set of strange psychological tests. This was part of a study that set out to prove, among other things, that Marxism was caused by societal immorality and class resentment. As such, as the theory held, this had turned mentally troubled men into schizoids, paranoids, or psychopaths. Each prisoner was interviewed and had to answer some two hundred questions. Many were about their sex lives and activities. Also, they were stripped naked and subjected to measurements of body parts and had photographs of them taken. The whole episode created great amusement among the prisoners who competed with each other to give the most outlandish answers but, at the same time, being careful that their answers did not land them into trouble and, for some, reveal their true identities.

In September, the British prisoners, with their Irish colleagues (the Spanish authorities didn't know that Ireland was no longer part of Britain or did not care), were paraded for a visit from the British military representative to the Franco forces. When they were to give the fascist salute and shout out Franco's name and no one did, there was absolute silence. The result was brutal beatings every day for several days by the guards. When Lady Austen Chamberlain (sister-in-law of the British prime minister) came to the prison, the response of the prisoners and the guards was the same.

Cleanliness was a major problem because there was only one tap in the bathroom on each floor. Their clothes were dirty as well as their bodies. In September, they were marched down to a local river and were able to bathe and wash their clothes, which were dried by the sun. Also, one day, they had their heads and beards shaved by some of the Spanish prisoners who were barbers.

Soon, Francis developed sores on his arms and legs. These were infections caused by lice, which would suck prisoners' blood at night. There was very little that could be done for the sores, but Patrick showed him how to shake his blanket and clothes out of the window each morning to get rid of some of these pests.

After one morning parade, Francis and some others who were in his intake were summoned to the major's office. They lined up outside the office and were seen individually. When it was Francis's turn, he entered the room, and sitting behind the commandant's desk were two men in plain clothes.

Francis found out later that they were German gestapo officers on the hunt for leading communists. They were tall, in their thirties, and blond. On the desk in front of them was a file.

"Take a seat," one of them ordered.

Francis sat down and waited for the questioning to begin.

"You are Francis Reagan?" the senior of them finally asked.

"Yes."

"Well, Francis, why did you come to Spain? Are you a communist or anarchist?" he began gently.

"Neither. I believe in democracy, like a lot of people here, and wanted to stop the fascist rebels from taking over the country."

"Are you sure that was the reason?"

"Yes, definitely."

"Where did you come from, and how did you get here?"

"Look, why all the questions? I don't like fascists, and I will not betray anyone to you! I want to go back to my friends now," Francis said angrily.

"No! You haven't a choice. Now answer the question," he said threateningly, banging the table with his fists.

Francis sat in his chair silently.

"Right, you give us no choice! Guards!"

Four guards dragged him down the stairs and into the courtyard and started to beat him mercilessly with their sticks and rifle butts. He fell to the ground, and they began to kick him. One of the kicks hits him in his groin, and the pain was so excruciating it made him feel very nauseated. Mercifully, he eventually lost consciousness. He didn't feel the rifle butt that struck his ankle with a great deal of force.

When Francis started to regain his senses some hours later, he realised he was in what the prisoners called the black hole. This was a punishment cell that had no light and just a damp dirt floor. In the dark, Francis began to examine himself. His face was swollen, and he was bleeding from a large gash on his forehead. He had great difficulty just sitting up. When he tried to stand, his right foot gave way, and he collapsed on to the floor, writhing in agony. When the pain subsided, he thought his ankle was either broken or badly bruised. It was so enlarged that it was bulging out of his shoe and was hot to the touch. He sat back down again, and the ankle began to throb.

"Well, well, well, you look like death warmed up," said his father, as he looked down at the crumbled figure.

"What do you want?" replied Francis.

"Why don't you cooperate with them so you can get out of here? If you don't, they may well shoot you for being a troublemaker. Now wouldn't that be a shame? Don't forget this is a selfish world where you must fend for

yourself all the time. There are people out there who will take advantage of you and trample on you."

"That's not true. What about Mrs. Ritchie and Lady Alvin?"

"What about them? They are do-gooders who get their kicks out of helping people like you. Wake up! Who got you into this mess in the first place? Why don't you help yourself? Think about it."

Then he was gone wrapped in the red mist.

There was no way of telling time, and after what seemed like an eternity, the cell door opened, and the guards dragged him back upstairs. He had been in the cell for two days. His ankle was giving him a great deal of pain, so when they threw him into the chair in front of the desk, the room swirled around him. As the pain subsided, he was able to make out the two gestapo officers who had interviewed him two days before.

"Well, now you've seen what happens to people who don't cooperate. Don't make us do this all over again. Let's be civilised about this. We admire your stubbornness, but we have a way of dealing with people like you. Now are you willing to answer our questions?"

"How do I know you won't take me out and shoot me anyway?" asked Francis.

"Because, as gentlemen, we give you our word. Now tell us how you got here."

"I worked as a gardener in London," Francis responded through bouts of pain. "I was recruited by the Spanish Medical Aid Committee as an ambulance driver and went through Paris. When I got to Barcelona, I worked on helping civilian casualties of the fascist bombing and then was transferred to the Ebro front where I . . . God, I need to get splints on my ankle!" he screamed.

"First, you must answer our questions. According to the information you gave the Spanish authorities, you are Irish from Dublin. Now how come you went to London?"

Francis took in a deep breath and winced. "Work," he lied.

"Who was your contact in Paris?"

"We were met at the Paris rail station by an older man representing the International Brigade and taken to union hall in Montmartre. We went by train to a fishing village and took a boat to Barcelona."

"What were the names of your contacts in Paris?"

"We didn't get their full names. If I remember correctly, one was called Alec, and there was someone there from the International Comintern, and I don't know his name. What was strange was that nobody gave their names," Francis lied. He had decided to give them some information but not all.

He answered more questions about Barcelona and the International Brigade forces on the Ebro front. Then he was dismissed.

"All right, Francis, that's all. You may go. We'll get back to you if we need anything further."

Francis got up from the chair and slowly hobbled to the door and down the stairs. Climbing up to the third floor was long and arduous. When he finally reached the top floor, he was met by a concerned Patrick.

"We were all worried about you. My god, look at your face. You must have taken a big licking. And your leg. What did they do to you?"

Francis explained what had happened.

"So you got a taste of the black hole. Did you give them anything?"

"Not really. I was careful not to give them too much but just enough to stop them beating me. I didn't give them anything they couldn't find out for themselves," Francis replied.

Just then, the guards were screaming "Forma!" and they lined up for their nightly meal. Two of the bigger prisoners took Francis's arms over their shoulders and helped him down the stairs and into the quadrangle.

That night was the worse night he had ever spent. Whichever way he lay, there was a shooting pain up his leg from his ankle. One time, he passed out from the pain, which gave him some blessed relief, but when he regained consciousness, he was overcome with nausea as the acute throbbing started again. He began to sweat profusely, although it was a cool night, and then he shivered with cold. By morning, his delirium had reached fever pitch, and he was rolling over and moaning.

His friends called in a doctor who was a prisoner, and he examined his ankle. The doctor, with the help of other prisoners holding him down, pulled off Francis's shoe, which, after the initial pain, gave him a little relief. The doctor explained that he was going to first pierce the swelling in the ankle to reduce the pressure, but he had no medications or instruments with which to do this. Then Patrick remembered there was a Polish prisoner on the second floor who had a knife that he had fashioned out of one of the blades of a pair of scissors. How he got this, no one knew or cared to ask. The knife was priceless in the prison, and the prisoner guarded it very jealously. He used it to carve wood for chess pieces, and he had quite a business going.

At first, the prisoner was very reluctant to loan the knife but, after some forceful persuasion, agreed that they could use it so long as he was there to guard his prized asset. Now the problem was how they were going to sterilise the blade. There was no way that this could be done and the doctor reluctantly agreed to take the risk of infection and pierce the swelling, otherwise there was a chance of septicaemia spreading to Francis' whole body. The doctor tore off the tail of Francis's shirt, which, he explained, was the most sterile part of his clothing because it had been tucked into his trousers and less exposed to the grime they lived in.

With Francis's friends holding him down, the doctor made three small incisions on the swollen ankle. Almost immediately, puss flowed, and the swelling began to subside. The doctor began squeezing the wound to get as much of the infected fluid out. Francis writhed in agony, but he was held down well by his friends. When he got as much puss out of his incisions, the doctor wrapped Francis's shirt tail around the wound and then bound some large sticks on his ankle to hold it in place.

"The next forty-eight hours is going to be critical," said the doctor. "On no account is he to be moved. He has one thing going for him, and that's his age. Hopefully, he will pull through this." And with that, he left with the thanks of Francis's friends ringing in his ears.

Patrick, through an interpreter, explained to the staff sergeant in charge of the guards that Francis couldn't go down for meals and that he was willing to carry food up to him. After inspecting Francis, surprisingly, the staff sergeant agreed to the plan.

The next two days were fraught with concern for Francis's survival by the prisoners on his floor. They all took turns to nurse him. He just lay in a semiconscious state on some straw they'd been able to find. When he was awake, he was very lethargic and unresponsive. He started to hallucinate and called out strange names. No one understood what he was saying. By the fourth day, he began to improve and be more aware of where he was.

Very slowly, as the days and weeks passed, Francis began to gain his strength. His ankle hurt less because the wooden braces held it in position, and after a while, he found that he could stand up on it. One of the kinder guards brought in a crutch from the infirmary, which housed only sick Spanish prisoners, so that he could hobble around. Soon, he was able to go down for meals, take part in the morning parades, and resume his attendance at the lectures given by prisoners.

About six weeks after his interrogation and beating, the doctor visited him to take off the splints. He took some time looking at the ankle and manoeuvring it, much to Francis's concern as it hurt. Then he asked him to stand up and walk, which Francis did, and found that he could limp around unaided.

"I'm afraid it looks like you will have a permanent limp because we couldn't put your ankle in a plaster cast. You will be able to walk with it and maybe run a bit, but the limp will be always there," he said ruefully.

Francis took the news as if someone had hit him with a sledgehammer. "This can't be! I'll be a cripple for life! I can't play soccer! I can't do anything!"

He grabbed the doctor by his lapels and began to shake him, telling him it was his entire fault. Patrick and the other prisoners tore him away, and the doctor beat a hasty retreat. They begged him to calm down, but Francis collapsed on the floor in a foetal position and just cried. Finally, after a few minutes, he stopped and sat on the floor, and a glazed look came over his eyes. He did not talk to anyone, and this silence continued for several days, although his friends kept trying to get him to talk.

Francis was now facing a turning point in his life. He was suffering what is called nowadays as posttraumatic stress. It had begun when he arrived in Spain, with the sights of wounded and dying people he could do nothing for, the horrible deaths of his two friends, his interrogation in Vilalba dels Arcs, and his painful near-death experience at the hands of the guards in the San Pedro Monastery de Cardeña concentration camp. All the stress had built up inside. The problem with his ankle was the tipping point that set him off into a downward psychological spiral. His instinct now was for self-preservation at all costs, however irrational his actions might be. Maybe his father was right after all. He told himself that if he was going to be handicapped for life, so be it, but someone was going to pay for it.

In the days that followed, a serious change came over Francis. He was now very moody and would become very angry at the smallest slight, or one he perceived as. He was no longer the easy going man he once was. He picked fights with other prisoners, and although his friends often intervened before the guards did, he had spent some time in the black hole. Soon, his friends kept their distance from him, and he would often sit by himself or playing chess by himself. Even Patrick seemed to avoid him when he could.

By the beginning of November, harsh winter conditions began to bite, and the prisoners were continually cold. The guards did issue them with some blankets and some warmer clothes, but it did not block out the cold. The main problem was the open windows that had no glass. Some of the prisoners wrapped their thin blankets around the windows to cut down the cold blast from outside.

In the New Year, rumour had it that there would be another exchange of International Brigade prisoners for Italians who the republican forces had captured. Rumour was that the exchange would be made in February. A feeling of anticipation permeated the prison. Maybe, just maybe, they would be released from this hellhole.

One day in late January, Francis was summoned to the commandant's office. He was ushered into the warm room by a guard, and sitting behind the desk was a man in his late forties. He was athletic-looking, wore a well-tailored double-breasted suit, and on his lapel was a pin with the Nazi swastika. He was smoking a pipe, and there was a small fire in the grate.

"Come and sit down, Francis. I'm Helmut Dietrich, and I work for the German government," he said in a friendly tone in perfect English. "There are a few things I want to clear up with you, and I have a proposal that might be of interest to you that will get you out of this place."

Francis didn't respond. He looked a sight wrapped as he was in a filthy blanket. Francis stared at him through slits in his eyes with mounting suspicion. Why would this man want something from him? There must be a catch.

"You must be frozen in this horrible place. Why don't we sit by the fire?"

When Francis had settled, he turned to him and said, "Why did you join the republican side in this war?"

"They were looking for volunteer ambulance drivers, and I thought it might be a good opportunity to help people but not take part in the actual fighting," he replied reluctantly. The promise of a way out of San Pedro intrigued him. He decided to be as cooperative as possible so he could find out what this man's plans were for him.

"What I found was that many civilians were killed or maimed for life, and no one cared," he continued. "The in-fighting among the various groups of communists was disgusting, and I wanted to leave. Unfortunately, we were forced to the front or stood a good chance of being shot if we did not go. I am totally disillusioned by the Spanish government."

"Now tell me about your life in Dublin and don't lie like you did to the two gestapo officers."

This surprised Francis. This man must know a lot more about him, and he must be careful what he says. Finally, he told him about his life in the tenements of Dublin, how he was the result of a vicious rape by a British Black and Tan, and when he started work at the orphanage.

"Do you like the British?" Dietrich asked.

"I don't know. I hate my father because of what he did to my mother, but some of them I like."

"What do you think of the IRA?"

"They are heroes in my book. They kicked the British out of Ireland so we could rule ourselves and not be answering to a foreign power. I was too young to join them, but I wish I had been able to so that I could have helped free our country."

"But you said you liked some of the British."

"Yes, I do like the ordinary folk, but I have no time for most of the ruling class or their politicians. They're arrogant and unprincipled, especially, from what I've read, bloody Churchill. He was home secretary during our fight for freedom in Ireland, and his men committed some hideous crimes against our people."

"How about Lady Alvin, did you like her?"

Stunned by this revelation of his past, he said cautiously, "Yes, because she was honest and straightforward. She had no airs and graces, unlike her son."

"What do you think should happen to Northern Ireland?"

"It should be taken over by the Irish government, by force if necessary. It's despicable that those six counties in the North were never part of the deal with Britain."

"You seem to have done a lot of reading, how come?"

"I used to go down to the library near our street and spend a lot time there."

"Why did you leave Dublin?"

"I got in trouble with the police."

"You mean that they were after you for murdering a priest," he said matter-of-factly.

"How do you know that?"

"I think one thing you have to understand is that the German government is very thorough, and we have done some checking on you with our contacts in Dublin."

Francis fell silent. He was cornered, and he didn't know which way go. *Don't panic, let's see what this man wants.*

"I might know how you could help in a small way to get Britain out of Northern Ireland and help us at the same time. We need good Irishmen like you. That's all I'm going to say right now. I can get you out of here in a few days and take you to Germany, and we can talk more there. We can also take a look at that foot of yours and do what we can to mend it. What do you say?"

Francis thought about what his father had said about looking out for yourself in order to survive. It seemed a good way to get out of this hellhole of a country, make a new life for himself by putting everything behind him and starting afresh. But he had to be careful not to seem too enthusiastic.

"I don't know. A rumour has it that we are going to be released next month so we can go home."

"That's right. But you have a problem. They are sending people back to their home countries. If you get out of here, they'll return you to Ireland and the hangman. And of course, these pricks in here would like that. In their eyes, it would be poetic justice. Also, Mrs. Ritchie and Mr. Riordan would end up in jail for helping you. You don't want that, do you? Take your time and think about it. We would like you to work for us against the British."

He racked his brain for all the pros and cons of taking up the German's offer. Dietrich patiently let him think about his proposition. He went back to his desk and started to work on papers after he refilled and lit his pipe. After a few minutes, Francis finally agreed to go to Germany.

"Good. I'll arrange for you to be transported to Burgos, and from there, you will fly to Germany. Now one other thing, do not mention our conversation to anyone, not even the guards, because they might resent your good luck and take it out on you."

When he got back, other prisoners were curious about why he had been summoned but were satisfied when he told them that he had to clear up some information he had given the gestapo officers.

It was well over a week before he was ordered to the major's office again very early one morning. He had begun to think that the deal had fallen through. Behind the major's desk was not Dietrich but a much younger man in his middle thirties who introduced himself as Hans Gerhardt.

"I will be working with you in Germany and preparing you to return to Ireland. I've told the commandant here that we are taking you away for more interrogation, and I told him, confidentially, that we are then going to shoot you. I know he has a big mouth, and news of this will soon get around the guards and then the prisoners. You see, we have to make you disappear so that you can reappear with a completely new identity. Now turn around, I'm going to tie your hands behind your back, and we are going to march out of here," he said.

They went down the stairs, through the quadrangle, and out of the gate. Hans roughly pushed Francis, which was noticed by the prisoners. There was a small lorry waiting for them in the courtyard, and with a final flourish, Hans rough-handled him into the back, closing the tarpaulin flap. He got into the front with the driver, and as they drove off, Francis saw through the tarpaulin the monastery disappearing. He felt pleased with himself. So far, so good.

The lorry rolled into the airport at Burgos and stopped before some single-story wooden buildings. As he got out, he saw an airplane close up. It was a German Junkers Ju 52 transport plane. It had three engines, four machine guns mounted on the ninety-five-foot wide wings. Hans explained that the plane was to take them to Germany.

"But first, we need to give you a bath, shave, and haircut. We have a change of clothes inside for you. Please don't mention anything to anybody inside what you are doing here. Leave it to me," he ordered.

The bath was glorious, and he was glad to wash away the grime of the San Pedro concentration camp. After his bath, a barber gave him a shave and cut his hair. The man tried to ask him where he was going, but he only spoke Spanish, so Francis could not understand him. Hans supplied him with fresh clothes, shoes, and a suitcase.

When they left the building, there were a number of German officers waiting on the tarmac. Some ten minutes later, everyone was ordered to board the plane. Inside, it was very narrow, with just single seats on either side. Francis and Hans were the last to climb aboard the airplane and took seats at the back next to each other.

Then the engines thundered into life, and the plane began to shake. This did not disturb the other passengers as they continued to talk above the noise. But Francis was very disconcerted. As a first-time flier, he thought the plane was going to fall to pieces. Hans saw his white knuckles as he gripped his seat and smiled. Above the clatter, he assured him everything would be all right.

The plane began to taxi to the end of the runway. With a great roar from the engines, it picked up speed down the length of the runway and, soon, was climbing into the clouds.

CHAPTER 15

Berlin/Hamburg, March 1939

To say that Francis was scared was a gross understatement. He grabbed hold of his seat and closed his eyes, shutting out the frightening spectacle of the plane hurtling upward for what seemed to him like forever. He broke out in a cold sweat, and his body was rigid. The noise of the engines was deafening. When the plane levelled out at its cruising altitude of eighteen thousand feet, the noise level was reduced a little, although you couldn't carry on a conversation with the person next to you. By now, the plane had settled down to a speed of 130 miles an hour.

Finally, Francis opened his eyes to peak out of the window and saw that they were surrounded by a fairyland of clouds. He had never seen anything like this. His fascination for what was happening got the better of his fear until the plane, flying over the Pyrénées, hit a number of air pockets, causing it to drop down precipitously. Then his fear began again. There was shuddering as the wings hit the air pockets, and Francis thought that the plane would break apart. He looked across the aisle at Hans who seemed to be fast asleep. How could he be so nonchalant!

Then, as quickly as the shuddering began, it stopped as they had left Spanish air space and were starting to cross France. Then the plane broke free of the clouds, and Francis could see the ground. His curiosity returned, and he could make out fields, woods, roads, and towns. He began to feel more confident and was less anxious when they went through more clouds.

Four hours later, the plane began to drop altitude as it flew over a rain-soaked Berlin, turned to the west, and began to approach Berlin Tempelhof Airport. The undercarriage was lowered with a loud thud, which surprised an apprehensive Francis. A few minutes later, the plane bounced on the runway, reversed its engines, and finally came to a halt at one end of it. The plane taxied to a terminal building, which had a covered awning to shield disembarking passengers from the weather. When the engines were shut off, there was an eerie silence for a moment, and then everyone got up and began talking. Hans told Francis to stay in his seat as the other passengers began to deplane. When they had all left, Francis and Hans climbed down the ladder and collected their bags. Francis's ankle began to throb again.

"We need to get your leg seen to as soon as possible. We don't want it to get any worse. I'll talk to our doctors," said Hans, seeing Francis's discomfort.

A black Mercedes-Benz 170v drove up. The driver was in plain clothes and acknowledged Hans. He and Francis got into the back of the car, which drove out of a guarded gate at the west end of the airport.

Night was beginning to fall when they passed through the centre of Berlin. Bundled-up shoppers in their winter coats were scurrying between the shops, trying to avoid the rain as it laid a shimmering coat of water on the pavement. The shining lights in the shops were inviting, welcoming people into their warm ambience. Francis could see black-uniformed waiters with large white aprons in cafés and restaurants, serving families who were busily talking to one another and laughing. It was a joyous sight, and he wished with all his heart that he could be a part of it.

Leaving the city behind, they were soon in the country. There were lakes and rivers to the north, and much of the landscape was heavily wooded. They passed through Potsdam and then Werder. It was then that Hans turned to Francis and looked seriously at him.

"We are going to a special training facility near Brandenburg, which is about forty-five miles from here and is on Lake Quenze. We need to fatten you up and get you ready for your assignment in Ireland. You will be joining some other trainees who will be going into England and France. You all have false names to protect your identities. Yours will be Tom McClure," he said matter-of-factly.

About an hour later, they reached Brandenburg and crossed over a canal. In the rain, the woods on either side of the road looked dark and ominous. Some two miles out of the town, they turned off on to a dirt road, which led to a guardhouse. When the car stopped, Francis could see a tall barbwire fence. There were soldiers walking the perimeter of the fence with Alsatian dogs. A guard examined Hans's papers and then raised the barrier to let them pass.

"Welcome to Quenze Farm! As you can see, we have tight security here. We have the lake on one side, and the rest is fenced in by barbwire. This used to be the estate of a Jewish millionaire shoemaker, who has been removed and sent away. You will be in the old farmhouse with the rest of the group with whom you will be training," said Hans.

The car drove on, and deep in the woods, Francis saw the lights of the farmhouse and behind it Lake Quenze. They climbed out of the car and walked towards the house. The door opened, and a woman in her fifties greeted them.

"That is Elsa, and she is the housekeeper. She doesn't speak English, but she will look after you very well. She's a bit of a mother hen!"

"Hello, Elsa. This is Tom, and he needs fattening up," he said in German.

"Herr Gerhardt, nice to see you again. Don't worry I'll look after him."

"I know you will."

Turning to Francis, Hans said, "I'll leave you with Elsa, and I'll see you in the morning."

And he got back in the car, and it drove off.

"Come in, Tom. I'll show you to your room," Elsa said with a smile.

Francis followed her into the house and upstairs to a bedroom. In it were two beds—one was already occupied, and the other was for him. He put his suitcase on the bed and went downstairs to a large lounge. It had a fireplace, in which a fire was roaring. Seated around the fire were four men. Three of them rose to greet him. Francis couldn't see the fourth man. He was sitting in a high-backed wing chair in the shadows and had made no effort to acknowledge Francis's presence.

One of the other men stepped forward and shook Francis's hand. "You must be Tom McClure. I'm Raymond White. Let me introduce you to everyone. This is John Hoskins, Brian Caldecott, and François Poupart. That fellow in the chair is Frank Woodrow," he said. Everyone shook Francis's hand, except the man in the chair, who just sat there.

"Aren't you going to say hello, Frank?"

"I know who he is, and he is nothing but trouble!" said an angry Frank. Francis recognised the voice. It was his nemesis Barry Trevelyan from Lady Alvin's household who ran away to join the army, or so everybody had thought.

"Oh, don't pay attention to him, Tom. He is always grumpy. I don't know why he was selected for this training. He was one of Oswald Mosley's Blackshirts and was sent over here to train," said Raymond, ignoring Frank, née Barry. "Anyway, the rest of us were all students at Heidelberg University and have volunteered to help the Germans recover from the evils of the Versailles Treaty, which they were forced to sign by the allies after the Great War. It virtually crushed the life out of the people, and the depression added to their misery. Chancellor Hitler is beginning to rebuild his country.

"If you don't mind me saying, Tom, you look like death warmed up. How did you end up here?"

"That's a long story," said Francis, and he told them briefly about his life in Dublin and experiences in Spain.

"He's a commie and a Jew lover," commented an angry Frank, née Barry, getting up from his chair and approaching the surprised group. "He thinks Hitler's treatment of those vermin as inhuman."

"Frank and I know each other from London, and we don't get along," Francis explained to the group. "I don't know where he got the notion that I'm a communist. I never said anything to give him that idea," said Francis calmly.

"So why don't you tell them what you said in London," persisted Frank.

"Fine. We were talking about dictatorships, if I remember, and I pointed out that Stalin is a communist dictator in Russia, and there are right-wing dictators, such as Mussolini in Italy and Hitler here in Germany. I said that strongmen ruled in those countries, which is very similar to how kings or queens ruled in the Middle Ages. You accused me of being a communist just now, which was a silly thing to say because I'm certainly not one. I wouldn't be here if I were."

"Who are you calling silly?"

"What's really eating you?"

"You stole my girl!" Frank said after a pause.

"Ah, I see. The problem was she wasn't your girl, despite what you thought."

"Yes, she was. You turned her against me by your smooth talk."

"Look, I'm not interested in picking a fight with you. It's water under the bridge now. We have more important things to do than argue about this trivia."

"Too right. We have to focus on what we have to do. Cut it out, Frank," said Raymond White firmly, and the others voiced their agreement.

"Fuck you all!"

Everyone laughed at Barry who retreated back to his chair, sulking and mumbling to himself.

"Would you like a beer, Tom?" asked John Hoskins.

"That would be great."

He went over to a wooden barrel and filled a beer stein. He handed it to Francis and warned him that the beer was very strong and should be supped like a fine whiskey.

"What were you all studying at university?" asked Francis after taking a sip of beer.

"All of us were studying German literature. Three of us are from universities in England. John and I were at Cambridge, Brian was at London, and François was at the Sorbonne in Paris. We all got involved with a student club at Heidelberg that espoused conservative values and philosophy, which were in line with our own beliefs. That's why we volunteered for intelligence work," said Raymond.

As they were talking, Elsa came in and announced dinner. They all left for the dining room followed at some distance by Frank. The dining room had wood panelling and a large bay window that looked out on to Lake Quenze. A large, solid oak table that could seat at least twenty people was in the middle of the room. There were six places set at one end. On the sideboard was a large tureen from which Elsa was serving a mixed meat and vegetable casserole.

"Ah, Pichelsteiner Fleisch!" said Raymond with gusto. "You'll enjoy this, Tom. Elsa makes a very good, hearty casserole."

To Francis, who hadn't eaten properly for many months, it smelled delicious, and the taste was wonderful. He didn't speak as he hungrily ate his food, and it didn't take him long to finish his meal. The others were amused by his appetite, and when he eventually looked up, he saw everyone looking at him.

"Sorry, but this is the first real meal I've had in a year. You should have seen the slop we were served at the prison camp," he said apologetically and blushing.

"Don't apologise, Tom. We can only imagine what life was like for you. But be careful how much you eat at one time because your digestive system is not used to the richness of the food and the increased volume. You'll make yourself sick. Take it slowly, and over the next few days, you will build up your ability to cope with real food again," said Raymond.

After dinner, they sat by the fire in the lounge, drinking more beer and reading some magazines from the United States and Britain, which were banned from circulation in Germany. Francis was curious when he saw that they were stamped with "Property of OKW."

"What's the OKW?" he asked.

"It stands for *Oberkommando der Wehrmacht* or the German military high command," said François.

Eventually, they turned in, and Francis found that he was sharing a room with Brian Caldecott. Suddenly, his tiredness caught up with him, and after he had taken the three aspirins Elsa had given him, he settled down to sleep in a real bed for the first time in more than a year. He lay there wondering about Barry and what revenge he had planned for him. After a while, he drifted to sleep, but it was a light sleep because his instinct, developed in

Burgos, warned him of danger. Sure enough, he heard the door squeak as it was opened about an hour later, and when he opened his eyes, he saw Barry standing over him, ready to take swing at him.

"I wouldn't if I was you. You know what happened the last time you tried that! This time, I'll finish you off, you pathetic excuse for a man!" Francis said angrily in a loud whisper. "The last thing you want to do is to upset me or our hosts who have big plans for us. Get over your problem and stop acting like a real idiot."

Barry backed off and quickly left the bedroom.

Francis slept soundly for the rest of the night, his first since leaving Burgos earlier the day before. He was woken at six thirty the next morning by Brian. Having washed and dressed, they went down to the dining room for breakfast. They were the first to arrive, and the others came down shortly afterward, except Frank.

"How was your sleep, Tom?" asked Raymond.

"Fantastic!" replied Francis.

"I heard him mumbling to himself, and he was thrashing around, as if someone was attacking him!" Brian said jokingly.

"I'm sorry if I kept you awake, Brian. I dreamed that I was still in the concentration camp and was being beaten by the guards," said Francis.

"That's not a problem, old chap. I was only joking. I am sure you could tell us of some really horrific stories. Come on, let's have some breakfast."

They went to the sideboard and helped themselves to some cold meats, cheeses, and coffee. As they sat down to eat, Hans Gerhardt came in, helped himself to breakfast, and joined them.

"Where is Frank?" asked Hans.

"He's probably still in bed," said François. "At least he was when I left our room. He came in drunk very late last night and didn't even take his clothes off. I think he must have had too much beer to drink. I know he was down in the lounge when we left for bed."

"Would you go up and get him please, François. We're about to start your briefing and training."

Frank (née Barry) suddenly appeared at the doorway, looking dishevelled and unshaven. He grabbed some coffee and sat at the table smoking a Turkish cigarette, much to the disgust of everyone else.

Francis turned to Hans and asked him why they were being kept apart from the rest of the trainees in the camp.

"It's vital we keep you apart for security reasons. We don't want anybody to know what your missions will be, so secrecy is of paramount importance," replied Hans.

The door swung open, and in walked Helmut Dietrich. With him was a tall man in his late forties. He was balding and had a large girth, the result of too much beer over the years. He had intelligent eyes and a ready smile. They sat down at the table, and Dietrich looked at each trainee in turn without saying anything.

Finally, Dietrich spoke.

"Gentlemen, welcome to the Quenze training facility. You are now part of the Abwehr, which is the military intelligence arm of the German high command. The political situation in Europe is such that we expect to face opposition from Britain and France as we expand our territories. We have annexed Austria, and this morning, our troops marched in to Czechoslovakia. This, of course, will bring greater scrutiny of our intentions from the rest of Europe, and we need to know what actions the allies will take against us. The leaders of Britain and France are weak, and they are more likely to try appeasement rather than direct action. However, we have to be on our guard. This is where you come in.

"Each of you will be sent on missions to various countries. You will go in as 'sleeper' agents at first, and then when the time comes, you will be activated. We want you to get jobs and be part of the community. It's important that you fit in. If war comes, your activities will become very dangerous, but it is essential that we find out what we face.

"We will need you to report on things like harbour conditions, shipyard activity, munitions factories, oil refinery production, and information on other strategic sites. There are many more, and we will brief you individually before you leave here.

"Now let me introduce Kurt Bauer, who will be your main instructor here. Kurt."

"Thank you, Herr Dietrich. Gentlemen, we are going to teach you many things. Because of the urgency in making you operational as soon as possible, our course will be very condensed, and you will have to work hard in the next six weeks. There's a lot to learn. We will start right away. Come with me, and we'll get started on using a clandestine radio."

"Before you go, there are a couple of household points," said Dietrich. "First, Tom, we have arranged for a doctor to see you this afternoon about your foot. We will let you know when he is here. Second, Frank, I wonder if you would remain behind when the others leave. Thank you, gentlemen," he said, dismissing the group.

They followed Kurt Bauer out of the farmhouse, along a path through the woods to where three single-story wooden huts were in a clearing. They entered one of these and walked along a narrow corridor to a classroom, which was bristling with radio equipment.

"This will be your classroom for the next few weeks. You will start work here at eight in morning sharp. There is a half-hour break for lunch, and then you will work until dinner at eight in the evening. You will sometimes have homework to do on your own time.

"This is Julius Grebb, who will be your radio instructor. Pay attention to what he tells you because your life might depend on it one day. I will see you all at lunch," said Bauer as he left.

Julius Grebb was a small owlish man with glasses who made up for his size with a booming voice, which demanded everyone to pay attention to him. He spoke excellent English and turned out to be an excellent instructor as he infected everyone with his enthusiasm for radios. They were quickly absorbed by the operation of these small shortwave radios. To Francis, this was another eye-opener to the world beyond his limited experience. His natural curiosity enabled him to easily learn the intricacies of this fairly new communications media.

The morning passed quickly, and when they returned to the farmhouse for lunch, they all realised that Frank was no longer there. Francis asked Hans what had happened to him and was told that he had been recalled to Berlin by his gestapo handlers.

"Good riddance, I say," said Brian. "We won't have him around to put a damper on things." Everyone nodded in agreement.

Hans told Francis that a doctor would see him after lunch. There was a sick bay in the complex of buildings, and Francis reported there to a nurse. He was told to wait and took a seat in the small waiting room. About fifteen minutes later, he was ushered in to the doctor's office and ordered to take his trousers off and lie on the examination table. His temperature and blood pressure were taken by the nurse who duly noted them in her file. Then he was left alone again.

A few minutes later, the doctor came in. He was in his fifties, medium height, and had a muscular build. He wore the uniform of the Brandenburg regiment under his white coat. He examined Francis's ankle, twisting it this way and that. This gave Francis a great deal of pain, and it was all he could do to not cry out.

"There is nothing I can do about the ankle. It should have been set properly when you broke it. It is very swollen, and most of this is the infection. I will drain off the infected puss that has built up around the joint and give you some antibiotics to take. This should relieve the pain, but you will always have a limp," said the doctor.

"What I'm about to do is going to hurt a little, but we must get as much infected liquid out as we can. I'm going to give you a local anaesthetic to help dull the pain."

The nurse came in with two syringes. The doctor picked up the smaller of the two and injected a small amount of the anaesthetic just above his ankle.

"We'll let that take effect," he said.

The doctor went to his desk and began to work on papers.

After about three minutes, he came over to the examination table and pricked Francis's ankle with a needle. He seemed satisfied that the anaesthetics had taken effect properly, and he took out the bigger syringe and stuck its large needle into the swollen ankle. Francis felt very uncomfortable as the needle was inserted and when a quantity of puss was drawn. The liquid was emptied into a bowl, and the procedure was repeated two more times. The doctor finished, cleaned the three areas where he had made the incisions, and wrapped the ankle with a bandage.

"That does it. It will sore for a few days, but I think you will feel a lot more comfortable. The nurse will give you some tablets to take, which will take care of the infection," said the doctor, concluding his procedure on Francis.

He picked up his tablets from the nurse and returned to the radio classes. On his way back, his foot felt a lot better, and as the weeks passed, he was able to run, although he still limped, but it no longer hurt him.

The next six weeks were a whirl of lectures and practice. They were taught Morse code, elementary ciphers, construction of explosive devices, how to use invisible inks and spy craft, such as dead letter drops, silent killing, and shooting weapons. It turned out that Francis was a good shot and was top of the class on the shooting range. In the evenings, they had manuals to study and homework to do, but they always found time for a game of bridge and would sometimes play until after midnight. A close camaraderie was developed, and they often teased each other when one of them made a mistake. However, despite the jokes, each of them was nervous and apprehensive about what they faced in the future, particularly as their hurried course was coming to an end.

One day during the final week, Helmut Dietrich asked Francis to join him in a walk. They wore heavy overcoats and gloves against the cold wind that blew across the lake. They walked on a path that wound along the side of Lake Quenze and sat on a bench overlooking the water. It was the beginning of April and still cold, although the ice on the lake had melted.

"I understand from Herr Bauer that you have done well on this short course," said Dietrich, lighting his pipe. Francis enjoyed the sweet smell of the tobacco.

"Thank you, sir. I wish I had more time to fully learn some of the more challenging subjects," he said.

"Well, the problem is we haven't got the time to go so thoroughly into everything. Now here's the plan for you. We need you inside the Belfast shipyards so we can find out what warships are being built or repaired there and when they will see service. You are to get a job as a clerk in the purchasing office so that you can be close to what is going on."

"But I know nothing about purchasing," protested Francis. "I know the rudiments of clerking though."

"Ah, but you will. We have arranged for you to be taught the purchasing process at our Hamburg shipyards, and your cover story is that you worked in the purchasing office at a shipyard in Philadelphia in the United States. Your family moved there to escape the persecution of Protestants in Ireland following the civil war. You were homesick for Ireland, so you came back, but the rest of your family is still there. You will be supplied with American-made clothes, which will still have their labels in them.

"We will give you an Irish passport stamped with your entry into Liverpool, England, and from there, you travelled to Dublin. In actual fact, we will get you to Dublin from Hamburg, and from there, you will go by train to Belfast. We will also give you papers showing you worked at the Sun Shipbuilding Company in Chester, Pennsylvania. We know that the Belfast shipyard is looking for experienced office staff as the British government have started to ramp up shipbuilding, so you should have little trouble finding work. You will be given some United States and British currency as if you had come from America. However, the amount will just be enough to pay for two months' rent and for food. From then on, you are on your own, and you have to pay for everything out of your wages. Do you understand so far?"

"Yes. But what if I just didn't do as you asked and ran?"

"Then, my dear Tom, the authorities will be tipped off about your past, and your freedom will be short lived," Dietrich said tersely.

"Now you will report to us through a series of dead letter boxes. Hans will give you the details when you are due to leave Hamburg. If you have an emergency, and I stress an emergency, you can contact us through a Herr Stiegel at our embassy in Dublin. I think that's about it for the moment. You will be taken to Hamburg tomorrow to begin the second phase of your training."

Helmut Dietrich got up from the bench and turned to Francis. "Good luck. We probably won't meet again. Don't let us down and don't discuss with anybody here about your mission. Is that understood?"

"Yes, sir."

He walked away puffing on his pipe, leaving Francis staring out across the lake.

The next morning, Hans joined the group for breakfast. When the others had gone to classes, he and Francis left by the front door and climbed into a waiting car. The journey by car took some four hours, and it was the middle of the afternoon when they reached the Abwehr's Hamburg office in Sophienstrasse.

Hans asked Francis to wait in a room while he checked whether there were any messages for him. When he came back, he was with a man in his fifties who was in a cheap well-worn suit and was wearing a tie. He had thinning red hair, a fulsome moustache, and blue eyes that stared at Francis.

"Tom, I'd like to introduce you to John Steigler. He will be your instructor in the purchasing process for the next two weeks," said Hans.

"Nice to meet you, Tom. I hear you want to learn about how we order the supplies for building ships," said Steigler with a smile and with an American accent, which surprised Francis.

Hans handed Francis some papers and said that he was to show them if he were ever stopped. Also, he told him that he had a curfew of seven o'clock each evening and that if he missed it, he could be thrown in jail.

"John, I'll leave you two to it. You have a lot to cover in just two short weeks. You know where to find me if you want me," he said as he left the room.

When he had gone, John turned to Francis and laughed. "I guess you're surprised to hear an American accent here. Well, my parents were from Germany, and we emigrated when I was ten to Philadelphia. I grew up in the German part of the city and went to work in the shipyards there. When Chancellor Hitler called on all expatriate Germans throughout the world to come back to Germany and help the fatherland, I couldn't resist. You see, this country was crushed after the Great War and is now beginning to again take its rightful place in the world," he said with a seriousness that astonished Francis.

"Now I don't want to know anything about you. Hans has told me you are a fast-learner, and what I am going to teach you will need all your attention. First, I'll show you our digs. I've booked you into the same boarding house where I'm staying. The landlady is a bit of an old battle-axe, but she runs a clean house," he said.

When they left the Sophienstrasse office, darkness was falling. The buildings around them were large and richly decorated, and as they got into the dockland area, the scenery changed. The houses here were small and were built in terraces, which reminded Francis of the workman housing in Dublin. These weren't the tenements he grew up in but were the small homes of the dockworkers and tradesmen, which were very similar to those in cities across Europe. At the back of these houses, he could see the cranes and gantries of the dockyards, which loomed high above as if they were sleeping giants. People were coming home after a day's work, riding bicycles or on foot.

Finally, they reached their street and opened a door of a house at the end of a terrace. No sooner had they entered the house and were taking off their boots when a door opened. A very large woman with a bun on her head, sporting an angry scowl, came out of what was probably the kitchen.

"Ah, Mr. Steigler, you have brought the boy, good. Make sure he keeps his room tidy. I don't want any mess or trouble," she said in German.

"Mrs. Schütt, this is Mr. McClure. He doesn't speak German, but I have instructed him on how to behave in your house," John said.

"Good. What use is he to us if he can't speak German? Come and have your dinner," she responded.

They went into the kitchen, sat at the table, and ate their dinner of sauerkraut, sausage, and potatoes in silence. After dinner, John showed Francis his small room.

"I would get some sleep now. We start work tomorrow at six thirty, and I'll wake you at five fifteen," said John. "When you get up, make sure you make your bed and straighten your room, otherwise the battle-axe will be after you."

Francis slept well that night, and at five fifteen, John shook him awake. They ate their breakfast of bread and strong coffee, picked up their lunch boxes that Mrs. Schütt had prepared for them, and left the house by six.

It was still dark as they joined other men who were walking towards the shipyards. As they approached one of the gates, there was a policeman checking passes, and John told Francis to show him the papers Hans had given him. When it was their turn, the policeman, who looked very stern and humourless, took some time looking at Francis's papers and then looked him up and down. Then he handed them back and waved them on without saying anything.

Once through the gate, John led him to a building at the back of one of the enormous dry docks in which a naval ship was being worked on. They climbed some stairs and entered a large office which had desks for at least a hundred people. Other than to glance at Francis when he came in, the other clerks took no notice of them. They knew better than to be inquisitive in Hitler's Germany.

"This is where we are going to start your training," said John. "Getting the correct supplies to build ships at the right time has become a challenging part of shipbuilding here in Germany. After the Great War, we were limited to a certain tonnage for naval ships. The idea was to prevent us from building up our navy again with large warships. So we had to find a way to lighten ships without compromising their armaments. So for example, we couldn't build in the old way with rivets because they added to the weight of a ship. To save the weight, we weld the steel hulls. It's this department's job to scour the country and the world for raw materials that we can use to build ships."

* * *

By the end of the two weeks, Francis had become very knowledgeable about purchasing and accounting procedures. John was a very patient teacher and was impressed by the way his pupil was able to pick up the basics of his profession. He was able to give Hans positive reports on his progress.

When his two weeks were finished, Hans called Francis into the office.

"I think you are ready now to take on your mission, so please listen carefully to what I have to say. Herr Dietrich briefed you on your overall persona, but I want to give you more details. Because of the religious rift in Northern Ireland and the dominance of Protestants, you must pass yourself off as a member of the Church of Ireland, which is Protestant. This will give you good cover and enable you to get a job more easily in the shipyards. Go to church there so you can fit in and make Protestant friends. I know you were brought up Catholic—forget that. Don't do things like crossing yourself and genuflecting, which would be a dead giveaway. Your life will depend on this. Do you understand?"

"Yes. Most of the people I meet, on hearing my accent, will know I'm from the South and will assume I'm Catholic. I will have to work out a story that shows them I'm one of them. If I disparage Catholics too much, they will be suspicious. Perhaps if I just stick to the story of why my parents went to America, to avoid religious persecution from the Catholics, that would be enough," said Francis thoughtfully.

"You've got the idea!"

Hans spread a map of Belfast on the table and pointed out the areas populated by the Protestants and the Catholics. After a few minutes of studying the map and pointing out key sights, he turned to Francis.

"It's important that you find accommodation in this area of the city," he said, pointing to an area near the shipyards. "It's close to the docks and in a Protestant area.

"Now we come to communications. You will initially go to work at the yard. We will contact you when we need to activate you. We will communicate with you through three dead letter boxes. I will give you this city map with these marked. When you've located them, destroy the map. The first one is the Clifton Street Graveyard. Look for an old grave marked John Edwards who died in 1871. It will be along the west wall. Behind the headstone will be a brick. You will find messages or you can leave them there.

"The second dead letter drop is in Alexandra Park. By the lake, there is a large old elm that has a tree hollow at its base. You will find messages there. The final one is in St. Anne's Cathedral in Donegal Street. In the sixth pew from the back on the right-hand side, you will find a cardholder which normally has a welcome leaflet in it. Behind this will be a message for you.

"Lastly, we will contact you, and you us, by chalk marks. You will find these on the north side of the Albert Memorial Clock on the High Street. There is a wrought iron fence running around it and at its base is a three-brick-high wall. We will use crosses to indicate that we have a message for you. One cross means Clifton Street Graveyard, two means Alexandra Park, and three the cathedral. Once you've seen these, rub them out. You must check whether we need to contact you by going by the memorial every evening. You can contact us by using zeroes in the same way. Is all this clear?"

"Perfectly."

"Good. You leave by ship tonight. There is an Irish freighter leaving for Dublin. The master of the ship is a friend of ours, and he has agreed to see you safely ashore. You should keep out of sight on the ship during the day and only be on deck at night. You probably will not hear from us until Britain declares war, but don't be surprised if we contact you before this happens.

"Tom, I want you to fully understand that you are going to be doing dangerous work. Your survival is key to our success. Don't trust anyone. They could be a danger to you, and don't let anyone prevent you from completing your mission," said Hans.

Francis changed into his American clothes and put his other clothes in a suitcase. He noted that Hans had put a Philadelphia newspaper in his case as a way to authenticate his new identity. He collected his passport, other documents, and the money he would need and was ready to go.

At midnight, Hans drove him to the shipyard, and they boarded the freighter called *The Primrose*. They found the master in his cabin, looking the worst for wear and dishevelled. He had obviously been drinking, and by the look of him, this was a frequent occurrence.

"This is your passenger, Captain O'Reilly. I want him dropped off in Dublin with no funny business," said Hans sternly.

He took a large envelope out of his jacket pocket and handed it to the drunken master.

"This is a down payment, and you will get the rest when I know you have delivered him safely."

"Fine, Mr. Gerhardt, I understand. He will be delivered safe and sound. You have my word on that. Pat! Where the hell are you, Pat?" he screamed.

The door to the cabin was opened by a small elf-like man who was probably in his late fifties.

"Ah, Pat, show this gentleman to one of our passenger cabins. You will be eating with us in our galley, sir. It's going to take a few days to get to Dublin in this heap of steel."

"Tom, good luck!" said Hans as he shook Francis's hand and abruptly left.

CHAPTER 16

Dublin and Belfast, April 1939

The journey from Hamburg took four gruelling days at sea. As the ship passed through the North Sea, the English Channel, and into the Irish Sea, the conditions were extremely rough as the small freighter *Primrose* climbed the mountainous waves time and again. She rolled and pitched as she made her way slowly to Ireland. At last, Francis saw the Poolbeg Lighthouse at the southerly entrance of Dublin's harbour.

At five in the morning, the *Primrose* finally berthed at North Wall Quay, which was in the heart of the Dublin docklands. As dawn started to rise, the crew and several dockers were preparing to unload the ship's cargo.

Once he was satisfied that the work was being carried out properly, Captain O'Reilly asked Francis to join him on the ship's bridge.

"We will be visited by a customs official soon, and I have thought of a story to tell him," he said. "Your name appears on the ship's manifest as a member of the crew. Since you have a bad ankle and you need medical attention, I'm letting you go. This always happens when a crew member injures himself, so it's not unusual."

"I understand, Captain. I knew my injury would come in useful someday," Francis responded with a wry smile.

"Well, Tom, good luck on your endeavours. Now here comes the customs man."

Captain O'Reilly climbed down the stairway to the deck and greeted the customs officer like an old friend, and they both disappeared into the captain's cabin. Thirty minutes later, they emerged, and the officer asked to see Francis's passport. He looked at it and handed it back.

"How did you hurt yourself, boy?" he asked, breathing whiskey fumes all over Francis.

"I fell on the deck during a storm two nights ago. I bandaged it as tightly as I could, but it needs a doctor to look at it."

"The nearest hospital is on Jervis Street, about ten minutes' walk from here. All right, you're clear to go," he said as he began to walk down the ship's gangplank.

Francis watched him disappear into the custom house and then walked towards Amiens Street Station. He bought a ticket for Belfast and was told that a train would leave in two hours. He decided to go to the station buffet for a cheese sandwich and a cup of tea. He sat at a table and started to read *The Irish Times*, which he had also bought.

It was the peak of the morning rush hour, and people, by the hundreds, were making their way from arriving trains to their places of work. Suddenly, a voice from outside the buffet boomed out, "Good lord, Francis, how nice to see you after all this time!"

Francis was completely taken by surprise, and when he looked up, he saw the grinning face of Dermot Williams, his friend from Dun Laoghaire, entering the buffet.

"Dermot, how have you been? How's Margery?"

"She's very well. She'll be excited to hear that I've seen you. What are you doing with yourself these days?" he asked, sitting down at the table.

"I went to Spain as an ambulance driver, and I've just got back after being released from a prisoner-of-war camp." Francis then told him of his harrowing experiences in Spain up to his survival in the Burgos concentration camp. He mentioned nothing about Germany.

"So what do you plan to do now then?" Dermot asked.

"I'm on my way to Belfast to try and get an office job in the shipyards. I can't get one here because of the Irish government's disapproval and hostility towards people who went to Spain. It is encouraging employers not to hire anyone who served the legitimate government there. As a result, I've had to change my name. I am now Tom McClure and will have to use that name until things change," Francis lied to his friend.

"That sounds truly awful. You've seen things I hope I never will. Although when I look at what is happening in Europe today, with Hitler and Mussolini, I shudder to think what is going to happen to the world. And now to the present, it so happens I know someone who works in the accounting department at Harland & Wolf in Belfast," said Dermot.

He got a piece of paper out of his briefcase and wrote a short note of recommendation and handed it to Francis. "That should give you an entrée. I don't know what positions they have available, but this should help.

"Oh, by the way, we saw Rachel a few weeks ago. She was visiting her aunt. She has two kids now and has separated from her husband. He beat her and came home drunk a lot of the time. Needless to say her family is livid with her, so she has come to live with her aunt while things are sorted out. I suppose that's what can happen in these arranged marriages. If we see her again, can I send your regards?"

"Yes, please do, but don't give her my new name or tell her where I am, at least not for the moment."

"That's fine. You must come to see us. We are in the same place. I must rush to a client meeting now," he said, getting up.

They shook hands, and Dermot disappeared into the throng of other commuters heading to their work.

After several cups of tea, his train was finally announced over the loudspeaker. He went to the platform and climbed into a third-class compartment. He put his case in the overhead rack, settled in his seat, and casually glanced at his fellow travellers. They were a mixed bag, and he began to evaluate them and their lives. There was a fat woman whose hair was very greasy and who seemingly hadn't washed it for some time. It was done up in careless bun on her head, and she was so large that she took up two seats. Francis put her down as a farmer's wife returning from market.

Then there was the harassed mother of two boys trying her hardest to make them behave. She had that wild look in her eyes as if she would burst into tears at a moment's notice. She was dressed in a well-worn suit and had on very little makeup. Apart from a handbag, she was carrying a much-used paper bag, which had their sandwiches in it. The bag read "Roderick's of Dundalk." Francis guessed that she was married to a shop owner.

Rounding out his fellow travellers, probably the most interesting one was a suspicious-looking man in his fifties who was dressed in a three-piece old brown Worsted suit, which had seen better days. He was very thin, almost emaciated, and wore a studded collar on his shirt with a tie that had grease spots all over it. Francis thought this was very likely the only tie he had. The man also wore glasses and was pretending to read a book but, every so often, would furtively look around, as if expecting someone to join him. Francis wondered to himself what the man's story was. Was he a murderer on the run, just a clerk in an office with no hope of advancement, a henpecked son on his way to see his mother, or a civil servant?

He was jolted back from his musings as the whistle blew, and with a shudder, the train began to slowly pull out of the station. The journey was to take about four hours as the train was to stop at over twenty stations. As the train climbed north out of Dublin, it ran along the coast, and Francis was fascinated by the picturesque scenery as he looked out on to the Irish Sea and the small towns through which they passed. He reminisced about his harrowing journey the night before on the *Primrose*. The sea seemed so calm, the sun was shining, and it all looked so peaceful. When they reached Laytown, the train headed inland, so Francis settled down to nap as best he could, with people getting in and out of the carriage at the various stations.

Finally, the train pulled into Dundalk, the last stop before the border with Northern Ireland. By that time, everyone had left, except the strange man. While they were in the station, an Irish customs officer walked along the carriage, checking passports and tickets. After about thirty minutes, the train began to move again. It slowly crossed the border and then picked up speed before stopping at Goraghwood, where a British customs officer followed the same process and acknowledged the strange man as if he was a regular on the train.

When he turned to Francis, the customs officer appeared to be very suspicious, and Francis felt very uncomfortable under his stern gaze. He examined Francis's passport closely and then searched his case. Finding nothing, he then asked Francis why he was going to Belfast. Francis said he had worked in the shipyards in Philadelphia and wanted a similar position in Belfast. This seemed to satisfy the man, and he handed back Francis's documents without saying a word.

The train started off again, and Francis stared out of the window, wondering why the man had been so suspicious of him. Had he been tipped off by the Irish authorities? Maybe he was getting a little paranoid. He decided to put his concerns in the back of his mind and get on with what he had been sent to do. Soon, he was asleep again.

A sudden jolt of the train woke him. He looked out of the window and saw that they were just leaving Finaghy Station. The train was now beginning to enter Belfast suburbs, and everything seemed more built up. By three o'clock, the train pulled into Great Victoria Street Station, and everybody disembarked.

During his briefing with Hans Gerhardt in Hamburg, they had decided that he should find accommodation near the shipyards and possibly in a heavily Protestant area because he was more likely to find work if he was perceived as being one of them. From the map, they determined that he had to cross over the Queen's Bridge and walk down Newtownards Road.

That uneasy feeling of being watched came over him. He stopped several times and looked around, but all he could see were the trams and cars on the bridge. *God, you're getting very paranoid*, he thought to himself. Perhaps it's because the people here are so different from the friendly folk in Dublin. They seem suspicious of everyone. Maybe it was a guilty conscience about what he was about to do.

After a few minutes of walking, he saw a small general store and walked in. He asked the old woman behind the counter whether she knew of anyone looking to rent rooms. She pointed to a notice board, which had different personal advertisements written on cards. Francis spotted one and took down the information. He then asked his way to 17 Chatham Street.

He found number 17 easily enough and knocked on the door. The door opened, and a severe-looking tall woman with greying hair looked him up and down. She was very thin and had a large nose.

"Yes, what do you want?" she asked guardedly.

"Mrs. Thompson, I'm Tom McClure. I was looking for a room to rent."

"I don't take any Taigs here!"

"What's a Taig?"

"It's a Catholic."

"I'm not Catholic," Francis protested.

"I can tell by your accent that you are from the South, and they are all Catholics there," she said knowingly as she began close the door.

"Well, that's not entirely true, but I can understand your caution. My family attended the Church of Ireland, which is Protestant. We left Ireland for the United States when the Catholics started to make life difficult for us. My parents are still there. I came back to try and find work in the shipyards here," he said, looking her straight in the eyes.

After a moment's pause, she said, "I suppose your family have been through a lot. You seem to be a truthful lad, so I'll give you a chance. Lord knows I need the money. I'll provide you with full board, but I will need one week's rent in advance. Come on in, and I'll show you the room."

She led him into the back of the house and into the kitchen. Everything looked spotlessly clean. He entered the room which was just off the kitchen. It was small but comfortable with a window looking out on to the back garden.

"This will do fine, Mrs. Thompson. Thank you."

"Good. I'll leave you to settle in. Supper is at six. Don't be late."

Francis unpacked his few belongings. He decided to check the location of the dead letter boxes because he had two hours before his night-time meal. He left the house telling Mrs. Thompson he was going for a walk and headed across Queen's Bridge again. He walked along Ann Street to Victoria Street and found the Albert Memorial Clock. This tower was built in 1869 and was a constant reminder to the people of the loyalty most of the Northern Irish felt for Great Britain. Francis checked to see whether there were any signals. And once he was satisfied there weren't any, he took out his map and located the Clifton Street Graveyard. It took him some time to find the grave, but eventually, he found it and the loose brick in the wall. He had no trouble finding the tree in Alexandra Park, although it was a long walk up the Antrim Road.

Francis's last dead letter box was in St. Anne's Cathedral on Donegal Street. As he entered the vast nave, he looked in wonder at the sheer majesty of the place. This was the first time he had been in a cathedral, and what struck him most was the peaceful ambience of this sanctuary from the troubles of the world. He sat in a pew and looked in wonder at the vastness of the space and admired the stain glass windows, which cast an ethereal light on the altar.

He began to reflect on his life and the choices he had made. Most of them were forced on him by circumstance, like his current assignment with the Germans. He had to find a way to release himself from these burdens and be the arbiter of his own destiny. There must be a way out of the mess in which he found himself. He had to work on a plan to free himself from these bonds and do something really worthwhile with his life.

He was so deep in thought that he did not hear the approaching footsteps, which clattered loudly on the stone floor.

"It's magnificent, isn't it?" said a whispered voice behind him, which made Francis jump.

Francis turned around and saw a very tall priest, whom he thought was well over six feet. He was in his mid-fifties and had a red beard, and one of his ears was cauliflowered like a wrestler's.

"I've never seen anything like it, sir," Francis stammered in response.

"Well, this cathedral was consecrated in 1904, so it's fairly new as cathedrals go. It's what is called Romanesque in its design. By the way, I'm Canon McWilliams. Are you new to the area?"

"I'm Tom McClure. I just arrived here from Dublin," Francis said. He explained his background and that he was a Protestant from the Church of Ireland.

"Then you're in the right place. We're Anglicans here, and our teachings are very similar to the Church of Ireland. I hope you will find time to come and join in our services. I'll tell you what, our church youth group has a luncheon after our Sunday morning service this week. Why don't you come along and join us and meet some really nice people of your own age?"

"That sounds interesting. Maybe I will."

"Think it over, Tom, and we'll hope to see you. Now I'll leave you to your thoughts."

And with that, Canon McWilliams headed off down the nave towards the high altar.

After a few seconds, Francis got up and left. He was impressed with the friendly welcome the big priest had given him. He didn't feel at all apprehensive or uncomfortable talking to him. He thought he would attend the Sunday morning service and the meeting afterward. It wouldn't hurt to try it once. He felt better and more positive after the brief encounter with the priest. Perhaps things would not be so bad after all.

There was a definite spring in his step as he walked down Chatham Street. His heart sank, though, when he saw a B-Special police officer talking to Mrs. Thompson. B-Specials were armed reserve police officers in Northern Ireland who were overwhelmingly Protestant. They were organised to support the Royal Ulster Constabulary, but really, they were used to intimidate the Catholic minority and had been responsible for a number of murderous reprisals in the 1920s. In large cities, they usually patrolled their own neighbourhoods and were the eyes and ears of the regular police and the British Army to watch for possible IRA subversion.

B-Special Brian Kerr was in his mid-forties and had been in the reserve force for ten years. He was of medium build, muscular, and had a bullet head with no neck. He was, by nature, a bully with a barroom brawler mentality. He was dressed in a dark green, almost black, uniform and cap. Around his waist was a leather belt, on which he had a .45 revolver in a holster and a truncheon.

As he saw Francis approaching, he stopped his conversation with Mrs. Thompson and stood there waiting for him.

"I understand from Mrs. Thompson here you are her new lodger. I need to take down some particulars so I can register you at the police station. Let's see your documents," he demanded.

Francis looked at him suspiciously and reluctantly showed him his Irish passport. The man wrote the details in his notebook and handed the passport back.

"Why did you come to Belfast?" he said aggressively.

Francis repeated his cover story.

"Are you a Fenian?"

"No."

"A member of the IRA?"

"No."

Then the police officer suddenly grabbed him with two hands by the lapels of his jacket and lifted him onto his toes. "I don't like you. You people are nothing but a problem. Don't give me any trouble, otherwise you'll feel my truncheon or worse. I know how to deal with the likes of you. There's a cold cell at the station with your name on it. Curfew is at midnight and don't let me catch you on the street after that hour. Do you understand?"

"Yes," said Francis, thinking better about answering back.

"Good! Then we shall get on, you and me." He let go, turned his back, almost daring Francis to do something, and walked off.

"I'm sorry about that, Tom, but everyone has to register. He is a bit brusque, but we've had no crime around here since he's been responsible for this area," Mrs. Thompson apologised.

"That's all right, Mrs. Thompson. I don't know why he picked on me," said Francis, although he was seething with anger inside.

After supper, Francis helped Mrs. Thompson with the dishes. When they were done, he went to his room and laid out his street map of Belfast on the bed. He looked for Bryanston Place and found it over the Queen's Bridge, just off Ann Street. He folded up the map and left the house, telling Mrs. Thompson that he was going for a walk. It was now dark, and the intermittent street lights helped him find his way. Fifteen minutes later, he reached Bryanston Place. This was obviously a better part of town, with somewhat larger houses, and it was clearly not a working-class area.

He knocked on the door of number 114 and a few seconds later, the outside lights went on. The door opened, and a man in his shirtsleeves looked down at Francis. He was a heavyset man with broad shoulders and probably in his thirties. His black hair was neatly combed, and he had a small moustache on his bespectacled face.

"Yes, can I help you?"

"Mr. Lynch?"

"Yes."

"A friend of mine, Dermot Williams, suggested I contact you when I got to Belfast," said Francis, handing him Dermot's note, which he read.

"Why don't you come in, Tom?"

Kevin Lynch ushered Francis into his front room and asked him to sit down.

"So how do you know old Dermot then? We were at Trinity together."

"He and Margery were good friends of mine in Dublin. I used to spend time with them in Dun Laoghaire before my family moved to America."

Francis then told him his cover story and how he'd worked in the purchasing department at a shipyard in Philadelphia. He said he was looking for a similar position at Harland & Wolf. Kevin was very interested in Francis's working experience and kindly peppered him with questions. Thanks to the role playing he had done with John Steigler in Hamburg, he was able to answer Kevin's questions.

Kevin then explained that he was a management accountant at Harland & Wolf and knew one of the personnel officers there. He would be willing to introduce Francis to him, although he didn't know what was available. He did know that the company was always looking for clerks with experience. He told Francis to meet him at seven thirty the next morning on the southwest end of the Queen's Bridge.

They talked a little longer, and then Francis got up and shook Kevin's hand. Thanking him, he stepped out into the street as a light drizzle was falling and made his way back to Chatham Street.

The next morning at seven thirty, Francis was standing on Queen's Bridge waiting for Kevin. At that hour, the roads and bridge were filled with thousands of bustling men and boys on foot and on bicycles heading to their jobs in the shipyards. (At that time, Harland & Wolf employed some twenty-thousand people.) Many trams full of people also passed him, with some men hanging on to the outside and standing on a tram's bumper. Everyone was moving fast because they had to be at their places of work by the eight-o-clock siren, which signalled the start of the day's work. There was a warning siren at ten to eight, and everyone knew where they had to be to make it to work on time. Lateness was not an option because they would be sent home and that meant docked pay.

Then Francis saw Kevin walking up Ann Street towards the bridge. He greeted Francis with a smile, and they hopped on a red tram, which had slowed because of the traffic congestion. The conductor took their fares, and they stood precariously on the tram's running board. The tram turned left once it was over the bridge and headed down Queen's Road, eventually stopping in front of a large imposing red-stoned building, which was the headquarters of Harland & Wolf in Belfast. Many of the office workers got off here, and so did Kevin and Francis.

A bell rang, and the tram took off again towards the docks and cranes that Francis could see in the distance. They entered the headquarters building through ornate green gates and walked to an office at the back of a courtyard. A sign on the door announced that this was the "Personnel Office." Kevin asked Francis to take a seat and approached a receptionist at a desk at the far end of the reception area. After a few moments of conversation with her, he disappeared through a door. Several minutes later, he reappeared.

"I've spoken to Mr. John Lyons, who told me that there was an opening in the purchasing department. You are to fill this form in and give it to the receptionist. He will see you when he has reviewed everything. Now I want you to come to dinner at seven tomorrow to let me know how you got on. I must go now, otherwise, I'll be late." And with that, he rushed out of the building before Francis could say anything. Just then, the warning siren sounded.

Francis took out the American fountain pen John Steigler had given him as a parting gift in Hamburg and began filling out the form. The first part was easy, but he had to be creative in others that dealt with his experience. When he was finished, he handed the papers and the forged letters of recommendation from Sun Shipbuilding in America to the receptionist who gave him a sour look as she disappeared through the door.

After about half an hour, John Lyons appeared and ushered him into a small office. He sat down behind a metal desk and told Francis to take the only other chair in the room. He reread the file and then looked directly at Francis.

"Why would you come back here from America? I understand the wages there are much better."

Francis gave him his cover story, and Mr. Lyons listened intently, looking through steepled hands.

"What ships did you work on there?"

Francis was ready for this question. "We built mainly tankers for Standard Oil and other oil companies."

"What area of the purchasing department did you work in?"

"I was clerking mainly for the purchasing agent who looked after the buying of steel, and then I switched to the agent responsible for wood for the joiners."

And so the questions continued for another ten minutes. Finally, Mr. Lyons closed his file and told Francis about the opening he had in the large purchasing department.

"You will be reporting to Mr. Albert Wiggins who is the purchasing manager. You will have a trial period of two weeks, and if Mr. Wiggins is happy with your performance, you will be made permanent. Your salary for your trial period will be three pounds a week, and we will increase this to four pounds if you are accepted. Now when can you start?"

"As soon as you want me, say tomorrow."

"Good. Report here tomorrow morning at seven thirty, and we'll get you started."

And then the interview was over, and he quickly found himself out again in the courtyard. He walked up the Queen's Road, taking in the sights of the shipyard, and back towards his lodgings.

At six forty-five the next morning, and after a good breakfast, Francis was ready for work. He told Mrs. Thompson that he would not be in for dinner and left with his lunch pail. As he was early, he decided to walk down Queen's Road.

He arrived back at the personnel department where he was acknowledged by the sullen receptionist. She handed him a gate pass and told him to take a seat. After a wait of nearly an hour, a young man, about his age, came in and, with a smile, asked him to follow. They walked across the courtyard and out on to Queen's Road again. They went through a gate, showed their passes to the guard, and entered a building near a large pumping station. After climbing one flight of stairs, they entered an open-spaced office. There were about six desks in it, with clerks working on ship plans so they could estimate the supplies needed by the shipbuilders. At one end of the room was a glass-walled office so that the occupant could watch the clerks' activities in the department. On the door, the name of the occupant was announced—Mr. Albert R. Wiggins.

The clerk knocked on the door and was waved in by Mr. Wiggins, without taking his eyes off some papers he was reading. He indicated to Francis to sit in a chair and carried on studying the papers. Albert Wiggins was a pompous little man in his mid-fifties with a decided Napoleon complex. He was just over five feet and was about as fat as he was tall. He had beady little eyes that were constantly flitting from one subject to another through his horn-rimmed glasses. He wore an off-the-peg brown suit, which looked as though it was worn every day. A fob hung from his waistcoat, and at one end was a half-hunter pocket watch.

To show his importance, he kept Francis waiting a few minutes. Then he called out a name, and a man came scurrying in.

"This will do. See that it gets ordered today," he said very gruffly and dismissed the man with a wave of his hand.

Then he turned to Francis and eyed him suspiciously.

"I understand you've come from America and you are going to show us how purchasing should be been done, eh?"

Francis didn't respond. The man obviously liked the sound of his own voice and opinions.

"Frankly, I was reluctant to hire you, but we are short of clerks that have experience in accounts and purchasing. It looks more and more like there's going to be a war, and no one is going to catch me trying to play catch up with staffing. Just like the Great War, we're likely to be very busy around here. What do you think?"

Before Francis could answer, he carried on talking. "I run a tight ship here. I will not stand for any mischief, and I certainly don't want any Fenian talk."

"I think you better understand, Mr. Wiggins, that I am neither a Catholic nor an Irish nationalist. The reason my family moved to America in the first place was because we were persecuted by the Catholics in the South! I want you to judge me by the work I do, not who I am," replied a visibly angry Francis.

Mr. Wiggins looked a bit flustered at this outburst and looked around to see if anyone had heard. The fact that most of the department had heard Francis made him blush.

"All right, lad, I didn't mean to cast aspersions on you, but I try not to let politics be discussed during work," he whispered to Francis and then continued in a normal voice.

"I want you to team up with Billy Hunter who is responsible for buying wood for the joinery department. I understand from your application form you've had some experience in that work."

"Yes."

"Come on, I'll take you over to meet Billy," he said, getting up.

Billy was a man of about forty with an athletic build. He wore a well-creased suit and highly polished shoes. His hair was neatly cut, although it was receding. He shook Francis's hand with a strong grip. He had a friendly jovial manner, which made people take to him immediately. It turned out that he had been in the Coldstream Guards in the Great War as a supply sergeant, which meant he hadn't seen a lot of action. He hadn't lost the self-discipline that the Household Brigade instils in its proud soldiers, despite the anguishes of the trenches.

"Welcome, Tom. It's good to have you on board," he said, meaning it.

"I'll leave you two to it then," said Mr. Wiggins and turned and left.

Billy turned to Francis and, in a whisper, said, "Don't worry about him. His bark is worse than his bite. Try not to let him get you worked up. I don't. I just ignore his tirades. Now let me show you what we will be working on."

Billy showed Francis the plans for several ships and explained that they work very closely with the foreman of the joinery department in deciding what wood to order. He explained the system that they worked with, and Francis asked several questions. They spent the rest of the morning reviewing orders for the various ships that were being built and checked invoices against the shipping documents to ensure they were in order.

At noon, a whistle sounded for lunch. Billy introduced Francis to the other clerks in the department. Although Billy was a purchasing agent and therefore had management status, he preferred to spend his lunchtime with the clerks. They did not mind his presence, and they often complained to him about Mr. Wiggins's behaviour or used him as a sounding board for any ideas they had. He often agreed with their complaints but told them that Mr. Wiggins was the boss, and they had to do whatever he told them, even if they disagreed with his decisions. They all spent the next half hour eating their lunch and talking. Francis found out that the purchasing department had a soccer team, and he was invited to join them.

After lunch, Billy and Francis toured the various dry dock sites and checked off the deliveries against the orders. Billy introduced Francis to the foreman of the joinery shop who wore a bowler hat and had on a cheap suit with a tie. In fact, everyone in the joinery department was wearing a tie, which was a status symbol that set them apart from the unskilled workers in the yard.

The whistle blew at five thirty for the end of day, and they all clambered on trams that headed back along Queen's Road and over Queen's Bridge. Francis got off at Victoria Street and walked to the Albert Memorial Clock. He looked for any chalk marks, and there were none, so he walked back to Chatham Street. This was to be his daily routine for the next six months.

Francis knocked on the door of 114 Bryanston Place promptly at seven. Kevin opened the door and warmly welcomed him in. He introduced him to his wife, Patricia, and a teenage son, Raymond.

"Come on through to the sitting room. You'll have to excuse Raymond, he has homework to do. He will join us for dinner later," said Kevin, dismissing his son.

The room was clearly used a lot. There were two armchairs on either side of a fireplace and an overstuffed sofa facing it. A fire crackled in the grate and radiated cosy warmth to the rest of the room. The door to the room had a heavy curtain over it to protect everyone from drafts as did the long window curtains. The room was lit by two lamps on tables at opposite ends of the sofa, and there was a third lamp on a desk by the windows.

They sat down in the two armchairs, and Patricia came in with two beers on a tray. After serving the two men, she left to attend to the cooking.

"Tell me about your first day," Kevin said as they sipped their beers.

"I'm working with a very nice man called Billy Hunter. He is very patient with my questions and seems to do an excellent job. The head of the department, Mr. Wiggins, is the opposite of Billy. From what I gathered from the other clerks, he likes to control everything and gives them no opportunity to make even small decisions themselves."

"Yes, I've heard of Wiggins. He is good at what he does, but he needs to brush up on his people management skills. Learn what you can from him though. It will help you become more skillful at what you do."

They talked for a few minutes longer, and then Patricia joined them from the kitchen, carrying a sherry.

"So how's Margery and Dermot?" she asked.

Francis explained that he only saw Dermot in Dublin as he passed through. He then reiterated his cover story.

"I have an open invitation to stay with them, which I want to do one of these days."

Changing the subject, Kevin asked, "Do you fish, Tom?"

"No, I never have."

"Raymond and I go every Sunday afternoon, if the weather cooperates. Would you like to come with us sometime?"

"That would be fine so long as we aren't in a boat because I get easily seasick."

"No. We are just going to the Lagan River at Stranmills Weir, and we fish from the bank. We usually leave here about noon. No need to let us know, just turn up."

After a dinner of delicious stew with potatoes, he took his leave of his new friends, the Lynches, and walked back to his lodgings at about ten. As he turned the corner, he saw B-Special Kerr.

"Where you been tonight?" he demanded of Francis.

"Out with friends."

"Don't give me any lip."

"It's none of your business.

"I make it my business."

With some reluctance, Francis told him, and the officer let him go.

On Sunday morning, Francis attended the ten-o-clock service at St. Anne's Cathedral. When he entered the cathedral, Canon McWilliams saw him and smiled.

"Welcome. I'll see you after the service," he said.

The cathedral was so full with people that Francis had to sit on a back pew between two families. A number of times, he had to stop himself from genuflecting at certain parts of the service. The service, in many ways, was eerily like the Catholic services he had been used to, although there were a few differences. The main variance was that the service was in English, not Latin, so he could easily follow what was happening.

At the end of the service, as everyone was filing out and being thanked by the dean and Canon McWilliams, Francis sat in his pew so that everyone could leave before him. When they had gone, the canon approached with a young man about Francis's age.

"Tom, I'd like you to meet Rory Mitchell the chairman of the youth group."

They shook hands. Rory was dressed smartly in a suit and was wearing a tie on his crisp white shirt. He was small, thin, and had short brushed-back black hair. He made up for his waiflike appearance by his high energy and enthusiasm for everything he did.

"It's very nice to meet you, Tom. I hear you hail from Dublin and from Philadelphia. That's quite a combination!" said Rory.

"Well, I have this split personality you see." And they all laughed. Only Francis knew the irony of the remark.

"Come on, let me introduce you to the others in our group who are now busily gorging themselves on lunch in the parish hall."

Francis and Rory left the cathedral and crossed the courtyard to the parish hall. There were about twenty-five young people sitting at the tables, eating their lunches of roast beef sandwiches and potato crisps, which they had served themselves from a buffet set up at one end of the room by the stage. Rory banged on a table with a spoon to get everyone's attention. Finally, when there was silence, he introduced Francis as a new member of the group. Everyone cheered, and Francis turned red.

Rory and Francis helped themselves to some food and sat down at a table with four other people. They soon were in deep conversation about the political situation in Europe. Francis was amazed by the depth of knowledge they had. He was dying to tell them about his experiences in Spain, but he knew he mustn't or his cover would be blown. However, he did talk in general terms about Spain and the fascists, as well as about America and his supposed experience in Philadelphia. What struck him most was the diversity of the members of the group, which was about equally made up of men as women. There were students from the city's universities, office workers, and skilled tradesmen. They all seemed to get on with one another, and there didn't seem to be any separate cliques.

When everyone had finished their lunch, Rory banged on the table again and began to review an agenda of activities the group was planning to do, including helping out in a soup kitchen at a mission in East Belfast, as well as the speakers and subjects at the free lectures at Queen's University. He then told everyone about the arrangements that had been made for them to go to the Plaza Ballroom on Chichester Street on the following Saturday. Tables had been booked for them, and they were to meet at the entrance at six.

As the group broke up, one of the women came over to Francis and introduced herself as Margaret Ashton. She was an attractive redhead who worked at a bank on Victoria Street. To Francis, she had the most attractive smile he had ever seen and a very slender figure. He had noticed her first when the group was in deep discussion about world affairs.

"Tom, are you coming to the dance?" she asked.

"I don't think so because I can't dance."

"That's no problem. We'll teach you, won't we girls?" she said to the other women who nodded. "Please come. We'll have such fun!"

"All right, but it will be a torturous evening for you trying to teach me."

"Nonsense. We'll see you at six next Saturday." With that, she left with two of the other women.

"It looks like you made an impression on someone," said Rory, smiling.

Francis said goodbye to his new friends and walked quickly to Bryanston Place to catch Kevin and Raymond. He knocked on the door, and Patricia answered.

"You've just missed them. If you hurry, you can catch them up on Oxford Street. They are going down to fish off the embankment at Ormeau Park."

"Thanks, ma'am."

"Tom, please call me Patricia. Now hurry up!"

Francis ran off down Tomb Street and caught up with Kevin and Raymond just as they were walking down Victoria Street.

"Tom, I'm glad you could join us," said Kevin. "We brought along a spare rod and tackle in case you could make it."

Once Kevin and Raymond settled on a place by the river to fish from, they showed Francis how to set up his rod and line, as well as attach the float and hook. He baited his hook with some worms and was ready to try his hand at fishing.

They sat by the river, talking and enjoying the May sunshine that lifted their spirits after the gloom and early darkness of winter. Spring had finally arrived, and with it was a new beginning to life and the promise of better times to come. You could see it in the faces of people as they walked by on the towpath by the river. They were smiling and excitedly talking to their companions because this was the first time in months that they were able to soak up the sun, however weak it was.

However, there hung in the air the prospect of war, which would shatter all their dreams. The harsh reality of life was to come to them and Francis sooner than later.

CHAPTER 17

Francis was rudely awakened the following Monday morning by Mrs. Thompson telling him he would be late for work if he didn't hurry. He jumped out of bed, climbed into his clothes, and rushed to the outhouse, thanking Mrs. Thompson on his way. He washed and shaved in a hurry and ate his breakfast as he walked up the street to catch the tram.

As Francis walked along the road, he rejoiced in having spent a wonderful weekend, particularly Sunday. It was probably the best weekend of his life. He looked forward to seeing Margaret again on Saturday, but he was concerned about the way he looked. His clothes were worn and dishevelled. He was sure she wouldn't look twice at him the way he was dressed. She would be kind to him like one is to an untrained puppy, but if he had any hope of a relationship with someone like Margaret, he had to spruce himself up. He had about fifty pounds left over from the amount the Germans had given him, but he wouldn't need it now that he had been able to find a job very quickly. He decided to spend it on a suit, shirts, a tie, and a pair of shoes, but where?

At lunch that day, he broached the subject of buying clothes with Billy.

"Ah, you decided to do something about your dowdy look, eh?" he teased. "The best place to go is to Spackmans Men's Shop, which is on the corner of Victoria Street and the High Street. It's opposite the Albert Memorial Clock tower. You can't miss it. Their prices are reasonable, and they have a good selection. Most of us go there."

After work that day, Francis took the tram to Victoria Street and walked to the Albert Memorial Clock tower. He checked, as usual, whether there were any messages and then crossed Victoria Street on to High Street. Spackmans was three buildings down on the right. Just as he was about to enter, he saw Rory coming out.

"Hello, Tom, getting some new togs then?" he said, grinning.

"I thought I better not appear as a tramp on Saturday," Francis said with a smile. "But I don't know what to buy. This will be quite an experience. I'm sure I'll buy the wrong thing. Ah well, I'll just try my best."

"Look, Tom, don't take this the wrong way, I can help you make a selection if it would help."

"Would you? I'd rather have someone there who knows what they're doing. Thanks."

They walked into the store and went upstairs to the first floor where the suits were.

"Back so soon, sir," said an elderly clerk to Rory, who had obviously just been in the department.

"No, John, this time, it's for my friend here."

The clerk looked Francis up and down and said, "I see," with a thin veneer of politeness that he had to exhibit. "And what are you looking for exactly, sir?"

"We're looking for a dark Sunday suit," said Rory with authority.

An hour later, they left the store. Francis had tried on a number of suits and, when Rory was satisfied, decided on a dark blue one. They went downstairs and purchased two shirts, a pair of shoes, and a tie to go with the suit. Parcels in hand, they walked south down Victoria Street, and at Ann Street, they took their leave of each other.

The week dragged by, and by Saturday night, Francis could not contain himself in the anticipation of seeing Margaret again, as well as his other new friends. He left his Chatham Street lodgings at five thirty dressed in his new clothes. It was only a short walk to Chichester Street and the Plaza Ballroom, but he wanted to get there early so he could see the lay of the land. When he turned the corner from Victoria Street, he could see the radiant lights of the Plaza glowing invitingly in the growing darkness of the evening. When he approached, there was already a queue of young people waiting to get in, and they were talking excitingly to each other. The doorman looked suspiciously at Francis as he passed by. He was a large thick-set man with a broken nose, a scar over one eye, and very large fists.

Francis went to the back of the queue and was soon joined by the others.

"My, Tom, you look very nice and smart," said a smiling Margaret Ashton as she joined the others. They got involved in small talk as they waited for the ballroom to open and, when it did, began to move forward to a kiosk where they bought tickets. When they entered the foyer, the men took the women's coats and deposited them with a cloakroom attendant.

As they entered the ballroom, a floor manager approached Rory.

"Welcome, Mr. Mitchell. The tables for you and your friends are just over here."

And he led them to the side of the dance floor to two large tables. The manager removed the "Reserved" signs, and Rory slipped him a tip. They all sat down and looked around at the other people milling about.

Francis was amazed at the scene. Some two hundred or so young people sat or stood as if in anticipation of something. Francis wondered of what. They were all dressed in their best clothes, and all the girls looked particularly beautiful, but no more beautiful than the women at his table. Then suddenly, a band struck up somewhere, and the stage revolved to reveal a twelve-piece orchestra playing "Begin the Beguine." Everybody seemed to get up at once, and the floor was full. Some couples were dancing cheek to cheek and seemed oblivious of everyone else.

"Come on, Tom, time for your first lesson," said Margaret. She grabbed his hand and led him on to the floor. After a few false starts, he began to get the hang of the steps. The band then began playing a foxtrot, and the floor began to thin out a little. At the end of the set, they sat down and drank some lemonade one of their group members had bought.

"Not bad for a beginner!" Margaret told him.

"I have a very good teacher!" he responded with a smile.

As the evening wore on, Francis and Margaret danced a great deal together, and he became very adept at this new experience. Also, she danced with Rory, who was an accomplished ballroom dancer, as well as other men in their group, and Francis partnered with the other women. At the break, Francis and Margaret were deep in conversation about what each did and their backgrounds. She laughed at his jokes, and he was very complimentary about her dancing.

The evening progressed happily until nine o'clock, when a group of men came in from drinking in the pubs and were obviously the worse for wear. It started with a scuffle and an argument over one of the women at a table across the dance floor from them. Then the fight began. Several of the ballroom floor managers were quickly on the spot and were able to separate the men and took one out.

"That's one of the problems we have. These drunks are just looking for trouble and are out to ruin everyone's evening," Margaret said.

"What about the bouncer at the door?" Francis asked.

"He's worse than useless, and he's not too bright. That's what happens when you employ a punch-drunk ex-boxer. Unless they are really inebriated, he lets them in. It wouldn't surprise me if they gave him a few bob to turn a blind eye. The manager is not strong enough to keep them out," said Margaret.

The music started again, and they got up to dance, and no other thought was given to the altercation they had witnessed. Sitting down again, they took a sip of the lemonade and talked. Just then, a man walked up.

"How about a nice dance with me, sweetheart, and maybe we can play a little footsie later?"

"Go away, you silly little man," said Margaret.

"Who are you calling silly, you bitch!"

He made a grab for her wrist. From his six-foot-one height, Francis stood up and looked down at the five-foot-eight man with disgust.

"You heard the lady! Now scram!"

"Oh yes, you're going to make me, of course," he said threateningly, clenching his fists.

All the other men at Francis's table got up and stared at him. After what seemed like a long time, the man smiled a drunken smile and said to Francis, "You'd better watch out, my friend, because nobody—not nobody—crosses Archie Boyle!" And with that, he beat a hasty retreat to the back of the hall.

Archie was in his late twenties. He was as a thin rake of a man, but his lean frame disguised his vicious nature. Unbeknownst to Francis and his friends, he led a small gang of some six equally cruel men. He had a reputation on the street for being brutal to those he saw as a challenge to his authority, and rumour had it that he had murdered his best friend to become the leader of his gang. However, he didn't do his own dirty work but left that to his thugs. He had an odd hold over these men because he was their supervisor at the docks where they all worked, and they depended on him for work. The gang, if it can be called that, was responsible for petty crimes and some shake downs of shop owners in their neighbourhood.

"Tom, I'm sorry you got caught up in this, but that's what we have to deal every time we come here," said Margaret.

"Don't worry about it, Margaret. He'll probably remember nothing when he sobers up. Now, madam, may I have the next dance, please?"

At ten, several of the women said they had to be home by ten thirty, so they all left together. They collected their coats from the cloakroom and made their way out of the front doors. Nobody saw a figure watching them intently in the press of people in the lobby.

Francis started to walk Margaret home along Victoria Street. They reached Gloucester Street when Archie Boyle jumped out of the shadows and faced them.

"Now let's see how good you are without your friends around to help. Put 'em up!" he roared aggressively.

"Hello, Archie, lost your way home?" replied Francis.

"Don't take the piss out of me, you bloody Popehead! Come on are you frightened then?"

"I'm no more a Popehead or a Taig than you are. Anyway, I don't fight drunks. It wouldn't be fair."

Francis's calm demeanour seemed to infuriate Archie further.

"Right, you've asked for it," he said and took a wild swing that missed, and Francis, in turn, landed a blow to Archie's face. He staggered back, holding his face with a look of surprise written all over it.

"You'll regret this, you mark my words," he slurred.

Francis grabbed him by his lapels and lifted him off the ground.

"Archie, understand this, if I have any more trouble from you, I will be your worst nightmare, and that's a promise." He butted him with his head, bloodying his nose. Archie ran off, yelling about revenge in between sobbing with pain.

"Margaret, I'm sorry about what you just witnessed. I did give him a chance to back down."

"Serves him right, if you ask me. Mind you, you'll have to be careful. He could be trouble."

They walked down Cromac Street and into Ormslow Drive where Margaret lived. They said good night. She pecked him on the cheek and disappeared into her parents' house. Francis walked home via the Albert Bridge instead of retracing his footsteps in case Archie was lying in wait.

He saw Margaret at church the next day, and she introduced him to her parents. They were cautious of him at first but warmed to him more after the service when his friendliness shined through. He was invited to tea with them the following Sunday and looked forward to the opportunity of getting to know them properly. Little did he know that events would take a turn for the worst and prevent him from keeping his appointment.

As the weeks passed, Mrs. Thompson had warmed to the young Irishman, and they both got on well together. She was no longer the crusty, unforgiving person she seemed when they first met. Francis did small chores around the house, such as filling up the coal scuttle each morning and evening, running errands for her, and helping her paint the living room. They often played cards in the kitchen at night, and he would make the cocoa for them both before bed.

*   *   *

Each Wednesday evening, after work, Francis spent time playing soccer with his friends from the shipyard. This particular Wednesday was no different. At about seven, he was making his way home when four men jumped out of an alley.

"You Tom McClure?" asked a burly docker.

"Who wants to know?" Francis said cautiously.

"We have a mutual friend who wants to give you this," he said, ignoring Francis's question and hitting him hard in the solar plexus. Francis doubled up in pain, and the other men in the group started to pummel him without mercy. He collapsed on the ground, and they began to kick him in his body and head. Eventually, he lost consciousness and was not aware of a small man coming out of the shadows with high-pitched, excited laugh.

"That will teach you to cross me, you bastard," sneered Archie Boyle. And with that, he slammed a brick on to Francis's head.

*　　*　　*

Francis woke up two days later in the Royal Victoria Hospital. As he began to take in his surroundings through a drug-induced haze, he was aware that he was seeing out of just one eye and that the other was covered. Likewise, his head was wrapped in a bandage, and one of his legs was in a sling. He could not feel anything because of the morphine he had been given. He could see white curtains surrounding his bed, and it was then that he guessed that he was in a hospital. He was frightened and tried in vain to move.

After a while, a nurse came in to check on him and saw that he was conscious.

"Take it easy. Try not to move around," she recommended. "You're in hospital and you need to rest so you can get better. You've a number of injuries that will take time to heal."

"What happened?" Francis groaned.

"We don't know exactly. The police found you face down on the pavement. What's your name?"

"I don't know," he mumbled incoherently after thinking for a while.

"That's all right if you can't remember just now. I'm going to get the doctor who can explain your injuries." She disappeared behind the curtain.

Francis suddenly felt very tired and dropped off into an uneasy sleep. He woke conscious that he was being watched. He opened his good eye and saw the large figure looking down at him.

"Welcome back to the world of the living. I'm Dr. Robert Boothroyd. You gave us quite a surprise by the extent of your injuries. It's a marvel you're still alive. Do you remember what happened to you?"

"No, I don't. Where am I?"

"You're in a hospital in Belfast."

"What am I doing here?"

"Well, that's what we are trying to work out, as well as your name and where you live. By your accent, you are from the South, and that's all we know. Don't worry, short-term memory loss is typical with the injuries you received. It'll come back to you soon."

Dr. Boothroyd explained to Francis that he had broken ribs, had a fractured leg, and had severe lacerations on his face. Worst of all, he had a fractured skull and maybe the loss of sight in one eye. The doctor had operated to relieve the pressure on his brain by removing some skull fragments and had repaired part of his eye socket.

As the doctor talked, Francis drifted off to sleep again.

The next few days, Francis slept most of time, and every time he dreamed, he heard a high-pitched laugh of glee. When he was awake, he tried to remember who he was. The nurse took away the curtains around his bed, and he was able to see the rest of the ward of some twenty beds. There were families gathered around patients, eagerly talking about their lives. Nobody came to see him at visiting time.

"It's like he doesn't exist," Dr. Boothroyd said one day to the ward sister. "Maybe we should contact the police and see whether there is a missing person's report on him?"

As the days passed, there still wasn't any success in identifying Francis. The doctor had removed the bandages off his head and was satisfied by the progress he had made. He had a large scar down the right side of his face, which had needed twenty stitches. He was sitting now comfortably in bed and sometimes was able to sit in a chair, despite the cast on his leg, but he got very tired when he did so. Then the day came when they removed the cotton patch over his eye. Francis was nervous as they started to remove it because he didn't know what to expect. He opened his eye and saw the doctor, but his vision was out of focus.

"I want you to wear a patch and only expose the eye to light a little bit each day. We don't want to stress the optic nerve too much. It looks like you were lucky," said a pleased Dr. Boothroyd.

One day, he was reading a magazine article about the beauty and peacefulness of English Lake District when a priest came into the ward to visit one of the other patients. As he was leaving, the ward sister asked him to come into her small office off the ward.

"We are very worried about that patient over there." She pointed to Francis through the glass window of her office. "He was brought in about three weeks ago in a real mess. We've been able to patch him up, but he has no memory recall. We don't know who he is or where he's from. He's had no visitors and is all on his own. Could you talk to him? He'll be leaving here soon, and I don't know where he'll go."

"Certainly. Let me see what I can do to help," said Canon McWilliams.

He walked back into the ward and over to where Francis was sitting in his chair. Francis looked up as the priest approached.

"Oh my goodness, Tom McClure, we wondered what on earth had happened to you!" said the delighted priest.

"Tom McClure?"

"Yes, that's who you are. You work in the shipyards. What happened to you?"

"That's what I don't know, sir. I've been trying to figure this out."

Canon McWilliams told him about his friends and what they were doing. He stayed with Francis for half an hour and then reported who he was to a delighted ward sister.

When visiting time came around that day, Rory and Margaret came to see him. They had been warned that he had no memory. Margaret was teary-eyed and held his hand. She was shocked at the scar on his face but relieved to see him alive.

"We are all so glad we've found you," said a cheerful Rory. "The place hasn't been the same without your ugly mug."

"I'm sorry, but I don't know who you are."

"I'm Rory, and this is Margaret. You two were getting on like a house on fire. Do you remember going to a dance with us?" said a surprised Rory.

"No."

Margaret burst into tears.

They discussed their friends and what was going on with their group, but nothing came back to Francis.

Every day for the next week, Margaret visited Francis and talked of everyday things. They took the cast off his leg, and he spent time walking through the corridors with the support of a walking stick, sometimes with Margaret. At first, it was agony, and eventually, the stiffness and the pain began to ease.

Then his memory began to slowly return. It started with a dream one night about the concentration camp in Spain and his bitter experiences there. Now he remembered what he was doing in Belfast and about Margaret. She told him about his altercation with Archie Boyle, and it all came tumbling back.

Apart from Rory and Margaret, Kevin and Patricia Lynch visited him, and they talked about the world situation, the shipyards, and fishing. Kevin said he had found a new spot for fishing on the river that Francis should try.

He said he caught a two-pound perch there, although Francis thought he was exaggerating.

The ward sister, Dr. Boothroyd, and the nurses were amazed at the number of visitors Francis had.

"My, it's wonderful to have so many friends," said ward sister one day.

Francis had a surprise visitor one day—Mrs. Thompson.

"I am so glad to see you, Tom. Now when they release you from here, you are to come straight home, and we'll get you well. Miss Ashton told me all about what has happened. I thought you had done a bunk, but I always wondered why you didn't take your clothes. Now I know."

"Thank you, Mrs. Thompson. There's only one problem, I probably don't have a job. How am I going to pay you rent?"

"Now don't you worry about that. We'll sort it out when the time comes. I understand that Mr. Lynch is talking to the people at the shipyard, so we'll see what happens."

Two days later, he was released from the hospital, and Kevin drove him to Chatham Street in a borrowed car. Mrs. Thompson was waiting by her front door for him and took him into the kitchen where he sat in her comfortable chair, and she served him tea and biscuits. He was glad to be back in the environment he knew.

He was keen to get his strength back by taking long walks, but Margaret had urged him to take it easy and not to push it too hard. At first, he didn't take any notice and, as a result, had fainted several times and had run a temperature. Finally, he listened to her advice, and they would go on short walks, increasing the length of them as time went by. At last, he was able to dispose of the walking stick and, little by little, was beginning to feel his old self again.

He was lying in bed one night when the red mist filled the room, and his father stood at the end of his bed, taunting him.

"It's time you did something about that wretch Archie Boyle. His mates really did a number on you, serves you right for being so cocky, but he has to pay for the trouble he's caused. Not handling it properly will only lead to problems down the road. Your mission for the Germans is too important to risk. Also, don't get close to this new girl of yours. Women have a reputation for leading men astray. They are only good for one thing—screwing! Mark my words, nothing good will ever come of it!"

"Go to hell!" Francis shouted.

And then he disappeared, leaving Francis to contemplate his future and how he needed to be free of the shackles of his past. He fell into a troubled sleep. He dreamed that he was being pursued by the police with the help of Archie Boyle. When they eventually caught him, they dragged him to a gibbet on a windswept moor to hang him. Just before they kicked away the stool he was standing on, he woke in a cold sweat to Mrs. Thompson knocking on his door, asking whether he was all right. He assured her he was fine, and it was just a bad dream, but in truth, he was panic stricken.

The next day, he was visited by the police. Det. Sgt. Rodney Lamb was an old hand and was due to retire in just under a year.

"Mr. McClure, I'm looking into the vicious attack on you and would like to take a statement, if I may," he said in a bored voice. "But first, tell me about what you remember."

"Not too much. I was coming home from soccer that night at about seven thirty, and at least three men jumped out at me in the dark and started to beat me."

"Did they say anything?"

"No," lied Francis.

"Could you describe them?"

"No, it was pitch black."

"Did they steal anything?"

"Come to think of it, no."

The sergeant wrote in his notebook.

"I understand there was a confrontation at the Plaza the Saturday before you were attacked. Tell me about it."

"Oh, it was silly, really. A drunk tried to force one of our girls to dance with him, and when she said no, he got angry. He was by himself, and when he saw me and the other men at the table, he thought better than pushing his luck."

"What was his name?"

"I have no idea."

"Was it Archie Boyle? He works at the docks."

"I'm not sure."

"What happened after you left the Plaza?"

"My girlfriend and I were walking home when this same drunk challenged me to a fight. He took a swing and missed. I jabbed him on the chin, and he ran away. That's all that happened. Why? Do you think there is a connection between this and my beating?"

"We don't know for sure, but it's a possibility. Now, sir, could you write this down for me?"

After Francis had written and signed his statement, the sergeant asked whether he would be willing to look at some photographs.

"Certainly, if that would help," said Francis, knowing full well that if he identified Archie, it would lead to more trouble. Apart from the thug himself and his friends, a trial would invite further scrutiny. He decided it was time he took things into his own hands.

That weekend, Margaret and he had a picnic in Ormeau Park. The late July sun blazed down on them and many other couples who were walking arm in arm or picnicking. It was a wonderful, fulfilling Sunday afternoon. Kevin had arranged for him to meet Mr. Wiggins the next day to see whether he could get his job back.

"Penny for your thoughts," said Margaret.

"Oh, I was just thinking how lucky I was having the company of a beautiful woman and having such great friends. You've no idea what this means to me."

"Well, if it's any consolation, we're happy that you came back into our lives." Then she kissed him on the lips, and he responded with intensity. After that, they kissed again, and Francis massaged her breasts through her dress, which sent her into further spasms of ecstasy as her nipples hardened. Then suddenly, she stopped and looked at her watch.

"Come on, Tom, we've got to go. We have dinner with my parents at six and its five thirty now."

The next morning, he walked into the purchasing department, where he had worked, and everyone there clapped and cheered him, including Mr. Wiggins.

"Our wounded hero has returned then!" he said sternly. "I suppose you want your job back. Well, it just so happens we have an opening, and if you're willing to get started right now, it's all yours."

"Thank you, Mr. Wiggins. I can't thank you enough," said Francis.

"Don't make a habit of getting beaten up. Pick on someone your own size," he added, smiling.

The others in the department gathered around Francis, peppering him with questions until Mr. Wiggins reminded everyone they had work to do.

Francis decided to take his revenge on Archie but was determined to make a fool proof plan of action that didn't throw suspicion on to himself. If anything happened to Archie, he would be the first person the police would suspect. He had to be careful.

He waited outside several dock entrances until, one night, he spotted Archie coming out of the Clarendon Dock entrance. After work each day, he waited in the shelter of the Sinclair Seaman's Presbyterian Church and followed him. Archie was certainly a creature of habits. He seemed to spend a lot of time in one particular bar with his work friends. Then the breakthrough came. Often, on Saturday nights, he would go to a bar on Donegall Quay opposite the Queen's Bridge.

Francis watched from a distance, and eventually, about eleven in the evening, Archie would cross the road with a prostitute, and they would go into a workman's shed near the water's edge. Some minutes later, the woman would emerge and go back to the bar. Then Archie would appear and walk back towards his home. This pattern was repeated the next Saturday, and Francis knew that this was his opportunity.

Margaret and her parents were going to be away for the weekend to visit her aunt in Larne, so Francis decided that this was his best time to deal with Archie. That Saturday evening, at about eight o'clock, he put down the book he was reading. Mrs. Thompson had her usual card group in the living room, and they were busy concentrating on their game when Francis popped his head around the door.

"Is there anything you want me to do, Mrs. Thompson? Because I want to turn in. I've got this great book that I want to finish it."

"No, dear, just make sure the stove is working so I can make a pot of tea later. Good night."

"Good night, everyone."

Back in his room, Francis read his book and waited until nine thirty. At that time, he put his pillow and spare clothes under his sheet and blanket to make it look like he was in bed. He opened the window, climbed out, and slipped out through the back gate into the alley, carefully making sure that the latch and door didn't creak.

It took him twenty minutes to reach Donegall Quay. Nearer home, he had to stop and hide several times when he saw people coming. It was important that he not be recognised. When he reached the quayside and the shed, he hid behind a pile of rubble and selected a large lump of concrete and waited. Several courting couples passed by, stopped and kissed, and walked on.

Finally, he saw a man and a woman leave the bar together, laughing. As if on cue, Archie and his prostitute crossed the road and went into the shed. Francis heard giggling and then groaning noises that came to a climax with a muffled scream and a grunt of satisfaction.

After a few minutes, the girl left counting some money and headed off to the bar. Once she was out of earshot, Francis, with his piece of concrete, entered the shed, and there was Archie with his back to him, pulling up his trousers.

"What's wrong, Abigail, forget something?"

"No. Your worst nightmare is about to happen!" Francis said angrily.

Archie turned around fast and, in so doing, tripped over his half-mast trousers and fell on the ground. His face was ashen with fear when he realised who it was.

"No, no, please don't. I'll make it up to you somehow. How about a cut in our business?"

"You make me sick. You are nothing but a snivelling coward. It's time I put you out of your misery."

And with that, Francis brought the concrete down on Archie's head three times. Once he was satisfied that Archie was dead, he looked outside the shed. No one was coming, so he manhandled the body to the edge of the quay and eased it into the water. He then threw the concrete in after it, looked around, and calmly climbed the steps up to the Queen's Bridge. He was back in his bed in Chatham Street half an hour later.

It was strange he felt no regrets for killing Archie Boyle. He was a mad dog who needed putting down. He wondered why he felt this way. Was it because of what he had seen in Spain had hardened his conscience? Had he become immune to any human feelings when it came to dealing with the likes of Archie? He didn't know, but he regretted this new Francis. He knew it was wrong.

Weeks passed without incident until, returning from work one day, he met Detective Sergeant Lamb who was waiting for him outside his home in his car.

"Mr. McClure, if you've got minute, we can talk in my car."

Francis climbed in to the front seat.

"We have found the body of Archie Boyle, or what's left of it, downstream in the Victoria Channel."

He let this piece of news sink in. Francis didn't say anything or react.

"I say what's left of it because it had probably been hit by a boat's propeller. One side of its head was missing, and the fish had eaten away at his eyes and other parts. Strangely enough, his trousers were down around his ankles. We know it's him because his wallet was still on the body. We believe he was murdered and then thrown into the Lagan. There was no water in his lungs, which otherwise would indicate suicide.

"We've been able to trace his whereabouts. He was seen last on a Saturday three weeks ago at a bar on Donegall Quay. After that, he never turned up for work, and nobody had seen him."

"Why are you telling me all this, Sergeant?" asked Francis.

"Because you had it in for him after his people gave you such a beating. Naturally, I want to know where you were on a Saturday three weeks ago."

"First, I don't know this Archie Boyle and couldn't tell him from Adam. But if you want an alibi, I was at home that Saturday because my girlfriend was away."

"Have you got any witnesses who can verify this?"

"Yes, my landlady, Mrs. Thompson, and her card friends. I went to bed about eight that night with a book," said Francis.

"All right, sir, that's all for now. We'll check this out. Thank you for your help."

In the next few days, Sergeant Lamb interviewed Mrs. Thompson and her friends, but his heart wasn't in the job. He felt that this Tom McClure had something to do with the crime, but there was not a shred of evidence. People like Archie Boyle were so pernicious toward other people that it was good riddance and nobody should care. He was not going to waste time on finding out who killed scum like that.

The next month passed uneventfully. Francis's relationship with Margaret grew stronger, and they spent time walking and talking in the hot August sun. In addition, he and Rory had become firm friends. Often, the threesome would spend time in pubs, discussing many subjects from their work to the current state of European politics. One day, Rory raised the question of where they would go if they could get out of Belfast. He chose London and going to university there. Margaret said she would like to go the America, maybe New York.

"What about you, Tom?" asked Rory.

"I'd opt for the quiet life. Perhaps I would go to the English Lake District."

"Wow, that's off the wall! Where did you get that idea?"

"When I was in hospital, I read a lot of magazines, and there was a long article on this beautiful part of the country. I would like to go there someday."

The friends laughed, and the subject changed to whether Neville Chamberlain was right to negotiate with Hitler.

This quiet idyll and camaraderie was going to be shattered by the war that September, which would affect each of them in different ways.

CHAPTER 18

Belfast, Sunday, September 3, 1939

"It is to this high purpose that I now call on my people at home and my peoples across the seas, who will make our cause their own. I ask them to stand calm and firm and united in this time of trial. The task will be hard. There may be dark days ahead, and war can no longer be confined to the battlefield, but we can only do the right as we see the right and reverently commit our cause to God. If one and all keep resolutely faithful to it, ready for whatever service or sacrifice it may demand, then with God's help, we shall prevail. May he bless and keep us all."

After King George VI finished his faltering speech to the nation that evening, a deadly hush fell over everybody who had gathered around the Lynches' radio in their sitting room. Earlier in the day, the prime minister, Neville Chamberlain, had announced that Britain was at war with Germany, and this was a rallying cry from the king. It was an attempt to boost people's nationalism and support for what would be a hard road ahead. They all knew this news was coming, especially after Chamberlain's ludicrous so-called negotiations with Hitler. Already, the authorities had started to evacuate children from the cities to the countryside.

Also, work had started in earnest, installing antiaircraft guns, searchlights, air-raid shelters, and sandbagging buildings in the major cities, except, strangely enough, in Belfast. One would think the city would have been a priority as it was one of the most important shipbuilding and ship repair centres in the country, as well as its aircraft manufacturing factory. In addition, it had important linen manufacturers which supplied military uniforms and equipment, such as parachutes. But this was not to be.

No one spoke for a long time. Finally, Kevin said, "We've got our work cut out for us now." There was nervous laughter from the group. Each person was deep in thought about what this news would mean to them. None was more nervous about what the future held than Francis, who expected to be contacted by the Germans with a detailed brief of what they wanted to know.

"It looks like the shipyards will be very busy. I've noticed that work began to increase six months ago. This will be good for our people. God knows, we need the work," Kevin added.

"I heard that the war will be over before Christmas," said Patricia Lynch as she got up and left the room.

"I wouldn't bank on it," said Rory. "The Germans easily took over Czechoslovakia and Austria, and now look what's happening in Poland. Who is next, I wonder."

"I am sure the British Army will stop them with help from the French," said Margaret. "Like Patricia, I expect we'll turn back the Hun easily."

Patricia came back into the room. "Well, let's all sit down and eat supper. It's going to get cold otherwise," she said as she ushered everyone into the dining room.

The next morning at work, Mr. Wiggins summoned everyone to attend a departmental meeting. He got up on a desk and looked down at his expectant staff. He was full of his own importance as he stood there and preened. Then he began to address everyone.

"I have just come from an important senior management meeting, at which we discussed yesterday's announcement by the king and Mr. Chamberlain of war with Germany. As a fervent student of current affairs, I must say this is something I have been anticipating for some time, as many of you know. We have a lot of work to do. Our managing director told me today in very clear terms that he was relying on this department to ensure the materials the yard needs are there and on time. To achieve this, we will have to work harder than we have ever done. As a result, there will be no holidays, and some of you will be expected to work on weekends. This is a national emergency, and we have all got to do our bit."

He continued talking for another ten minutes about particular projects and then asked for questions. Someone asked what was being done to protect the yard from air raids.

"There will be no need to worry about that. The prime minister of Northern Ireland said that adequate preparations will be made. Unlike London or Birmingham, Belfast, thankfully, is out of the range of German bombers, so we can operate with immunity. Anyway, it is very likely that our army will stop them in their tracks.

"Now let's get to work!" And with that, he dismissed everyone.

After work that day, Francis went home via the Albert Memorial Clock, expecting to see a signal. But there was nothing. A feeling of relief surprisingly came over him, and he began walking along Victoria Street, passing shops as he went. He saw a man out of the corner of his eye in a shop's doorway who was dressed in a workman's overalls, a worn jacket, and a peaked cap. As he passed by, the man called out to him.

"Hello, Tom. Are you ready for some work?" he whispered.

Francis swung around, expecting to see one of Archie's men come to confront him. He was surprised to see instead Hans Gerhardt of the Abwehr. Hans put a finger up to his lips, signaling silence.

"My name is Dennis Freeman these days. Is there somewhere we can talk quietly?"

Francis led him to a small pub on Ann Street, and after he had got two beers, they sat down in a quiet corner.

"I see you still walk with that limp. It has not healed completely then. How does it feel?"

"It doesn't seem to bother me that much."

"I understand you have settled in here very well and have a number of friends, especially a very beautiful girlfriend," Hans said. The threat in his voice was ominously clear to Francis, but it was said in a friendly non-confrontational way.

"How do you know that?"

"As I told you before, we have eyes and ears all over the place and especially in Ireland, with its porous border with the North. Do you remember that frail dyspeptic-looking man in the carriage on the train when you travelled to Belfast? He's one of us. He checks on our agents and is one of our couriers."

The reality of his position hit Francis like a sledgehammer. *Oh my god, I thought I was free, but I'm tied to these people forever. Their tentacles are everywhere*, thought a panicked Francis.

"Now, Tom, there are several reports we want you to make in the next few weeks. First, we need to know about the defences that have been set up to protect the shipyard—where are the antiaircraft batteries and searchlights. We need to know how many of them there are. This is your immediate task. We need updates on a regular basis, even if there is no change."

Hans took a long sip of his beer and then continued.

"We want you to report on what is being built at Short and Harland's aircraft factory on Sydenham Aerodrome. They are building bombers there, and we need to know what type, how many, and at what capacity they have reached. The same goes for the shipyards. We want to know what is being built and refitted. And finally, we know that there are plans to convert some of the factories in West Belfast into munitions and armament manufacturing. We want to know what is being made and where."

Francis was staggered at the amount of information the Germans wanted.

"This is a tall order. I'll do my best to get it," he responded.

"Tom, your best is not good enough. We want you to go beyond that. This is war, and we all have to overachieve. You'll have to take some risks, but we need these reports in a hurry. You took a risk in dealing with Archie Boyle easy enough, so you can take an equal chance for us. Now when can you get us the first information?" Hans responded harshly.

This piece of new information again caused Francis to stop in his tracks. How did they know? He had been so careful. Come to think of it, he had had the feeling of being watched. But it was only a feeling, and he had put it down to nerves. Now he knew his gut instincts were right.

"Tom?"

"I'm sorry. I think the fastest way to find out what's going on is if I join the air-raid wardens. They were asking for volunteers at work, so I think I'll sign up. It will give me access to information on some sensitive areas. I can certainly get information on the shipyard in the meantime."

"Fine. Use the same dead letter boxes and signals we discussed in Hamburg. I'm going to leave now. Stay here for at least thirty minutes before you go. And don't let us down, or we'll be forced to let the authorities know about you!"

Hans got up and walked out, leaving Francis in a state of apoplexy. He was trapped. He couldn't move. He had to find a way of escaping from this nightmare.

When Francis returned home from work that evening, he found Mrs. Thompson at the kitchen table filling out a form.

"A man was 'round today with this form. Apparently, today is National Registration Day when everyone in a household has to register with the government. He said he would collect the form from me on Sunday or Monday and give us each an identity card. I'm supposed to register with the butcher and greengrocer I use because they are also issuing us with ration cards. Apparently, we will start using these in January. It seems a lot of trouble to go to for a war that isn't going to last long."

"I suppose they have got to be prepared just in case," Francis responded.

*   *   *

Francis submitted his first report to the Germans through the dead letter box in the graveyard two weeks after his meeting with Hans. It took him a long time to get the ciphers correct because he hadn't practiced since he left Hamburg. Even to his untrained eye, he was surprised at the lack of any real defences in the city. He counted only seven antiaircraft batteries being set up, and there were no searchlights anywhere to be found. There were a number of air-raid barrage balloons, but they were too few to be effective, and they were being flown too low to snag any potential aircraft.

Francis found that he was working long hours playing catch up with the demands of the shipyards. He was not seeing Margaret as much as he would like, but they cherished the small amount of time they had together.

The only break from the daily grind was his fishing trips with Kevin Lynch. He had become a very adept fisherman and took to the sport like a natural. Kevin showed him how to fish for pike, and a number of their catches made it to the table, which was a relief from the stark rations with which they, like everyone else, were forced to consume.

There seemed to be an added urgency to the pace of life in Belfast that spring and summer. It was as if the whole city realised that the country depended on them, and they weren't just this outpost of Great Britain separated by the Irish Sea. They mattered to the war effort as only a city with such a deep engineering tradition could. If good could come out of evil, the war meant that the city's chronic unemployment was at least partly assuaged. Despite this positive feeling, there was an underlying complacency among political leaders that Northern Ireland would not be involved physically in the war. This misplaced notion permeated down to the working men and women, and as a result, scant attention was paid to safety or security.

True to his word, Francis joined the Air Raid Precautions (ARP) service and attended a number of courses given at night over a six-week period. The training consisted of damage assessment and the reports that were needed by the civil defence headquarters, stirrup pump drills, how to extinguish firebombs, ensuring the blackout was adhered to, and rudimentary first aid. He was issued with blue denim overalls, an armband with ARP written in red on it, a gas mask, and a helmet. This was an unpaid part-time job, but through it, he was able to glean a wealth of information.

He was assigned to Region E, which looked after East Belfast, and he was only a few streets away from his home. His wardens' post was on the Newtownards Road, which happened to be in the local police station. His normal duty hours were from seven in the evening until midnight. He and his ten other colleagues were responsible for patrolling roughly a mile square section, which was a maze of terraced houses tightly packed together. The streets backed on to each other and bordered the shipyards and the aircraft manufacturing factory.

The other wardens were a mixed bag. Some took their responsibilities very seriously and wouldn't brook any contravention of the rules, others were comedians who saw the funny side of just about everything, and there were men, like Francis, who were pragmatic about what needed to be done. Francis also got to know B-Special Brian Kerr better. They had a polite regard for each other after the Archie Boyle incident as the policeman realised that Francis wasn't a threat to the neighbourhood. Mrs. Thompson was also full of praise for Francis, telling the officer what a good tenant he was. Now that he had joined the ARP, he garnered a grudging respect from the officer.

Events moved along at a fast pace. There was a whiff of positive news in the media when the much-lauded British Expeditionary Force arrived in France in October 1939, and many of Francis's friends really believed that the Germans would back down. But this was not to be. Nothing happened immediately, and the so-called Phoney War lasted six months. This gave Britain a chance to continue with its preparations for the coming conflict.

The Phoney War, in fact, had a negative effect on the civilian population, especially the people in Belfast. Francis and the other wardens were initially tasked with distributing gas masks because the authorities believed strongly that Hitler would use gas on civilians. Trying to encourage people to carry them at all times, along with their ID cards, was an uphill battle. Also, it was important that the wardens carry out a census of their designated areas so they knew who lived where and how many people were in each house. They met a great deal of resistance from a normally reticent population, and this attitude did not change until it was too late. However, the wardens, by observation and constant street patrols, were able to get around this lack of help and developed their own lists.

Francis got easily bored patrolling his sector, particularly towards the end of an evening when the streets were empty and there was nothing going on. He often thought about his predicament—spying for the Germans against the very people he was living among. He sometimes had a great pang of conscience about that but rationalised his actions as being harmless because, like everyone else, he believed there was no likelihood of the Germans attacking Belfast. What he was doing was keeping the Germans off his back and preventing them from revealing his true identity. To him, it was all a question of survival. He gave no thought to Margaret or his other friends in this context. Maybe he was getting more like his father, where self was more important than the consequences.

On some nights, one of the other wardens patrolled with him. To pass the time, they would talk to him about their work and often revealed a lot of what was going on, particularly at Short's aircraft manufacturing company. Around the table at their post's duty room, they talked over cups of tea before going out on patrol. Some talked of how there had been an increase in aircraft production and how they were building Stirling bombers and flying boats, and others would tell him about what ships had come in for repair at the shipyards.

Apart from the information given to him by his warden colleagues, Francis spent a lot of time listening to conversations among groups of men in pubs around the city, and he found they became very vociferous, particularly around closing time. As he had become a regular at the various pubs, many of these men were very friendly and often answered his carefully put questions without suspicion. They were often complaining about their schedules and changes in their shifts to accommodate production of war materials.

Many factories were being converted to manufacture munitions like James Mackie & Sons on Springfield Road and its subsidiary, the Albert Foundry on Albert Street, which produced gun mountings. The York Street Flax Spinning Company was now making parachutes and canvas coverings for aircraft. Workers at these companies were a great source of intelligence for him which he was able to pass on to the Germans.

When the gathering war storm finally broke, the unbelievable happened. The Germans suddenly attacked the Low Countries of Holland and Belgium and invaded France, and within a month, the allied armies were crushed and began their retreat towards Dunkirk. A massive evacuation was ordered, and about three hundred forty thousand British and French troops were rescued from the Dunkirk beaches by a flotilla of small craft which were captained by civilians. They had left behind not only all their equipment in France but also their dignity. Many of their colleagues were either dead or captured.

The effects on morale in Britain were devastating. The likelihood of invasion gave new urgency in preparing defences. But the ensuing fight would show the world the bloody-mindedness and toughness of the British people. The Battle of Britain began in earnest in July 1940 when the Germans were able to use recently captured air bases in France to strike at the British mainland. The fight was for air dominance before an invasion took place, and by autumn, the anticipated German victory was thwarted by the Royal Air Force. The Luftwaffe bombed industrial areas as well as firebombed the civilian population. By the spring of 1941, some forty thousand people had been killed.

Francis watched these developments from the relative safety of Belfast. He, like others, read the newspaper accounts and saw the newsreels in the cinemas of the devastation of London, Coventry, Clydebank, Birmingham, and other cities. The sheer might the Germans were using was mind-numbing and reminded him of the utter devastation he had seen in Barcelona. Despite his growing unease about the evil that was being visited upon innocent people, he continued to send reports to the Germans, although there was not much new information to give them.

As the weeks passed, Margaret was the first to notice it, and then his friends mentioned it to her. Francis had become very moody. His happy-go-lucky demeanour had been replaced with sullenness, quiet introspection, and unresponsiveness to other people, which was totally the opposite of his normal personality. No one knew, but his secret predicament was getting to him, and he had no one to talk to about it. He was on his own.

One evening, he had a flaming row with Margaret when she tried to raise his behavior with him. As a result, they hadn't seen each other for several weeks. Francis heard that she was going out with someone else. Just as well, he thought, she wouldn't want to be around him if she knew the truth. His depression worsened, and apart from going to work, he kept to himself either in his room or at a pub when he could afford to buy a beer or two.

One evening in December, when he checked for signs at the Albert Memorial Clock tower, he found an instruction to retrieve a message from the dead letter box at Alexandra Park. He picked up an envelope in the elm tree and took it home. When he had deciphered it, and it read, "RAF building base at Lough Erne at Castle Archdale. Need report on progress."

The battle of the Atlantic was in full swing at this time. The convoys coming from North America were a key target for the German U-boats because if Britain was brought to her knees for lack of food and munitions, the war would be soon won by Germany. The convoys were afforded limited protection from the air from Canadian flying boats and then, when they were close enough to Europe, by British aircraft. However, there was a black hole in mid-Atlantic, where there was no protection, and this was having a devastating consequence as U-boat packs preyed on the convoys in this area. If the RAF were to establish a flying boat base at the most westerly point in Northern Ireland, they could close this gap a little and, thus, give better protection to convoys. So it had been decided to set up a base in Lough Erne, known as RAF Castle Archdale, where number 15 group with Stranraer Flying Boats was to start operations in February 1941 after most of the construction was hurriedly completed by the beginning of the year.

Francis took out his map of Northern Ireland and located Lough Erne and Castle Archdale. There was a railway that ran between Belfast and Enniskillen, and then there was a local line that would take him to Irvinestown. He decided that he would pay a visit to the Castle Archdale area the following weekend. On that Monday, he told Mr. Wiggins he wouldn't be in on Friday because the doctors wanted to give him a final check-up, and of course, he was not at all pleased. That night, he told Mrs. Thompson he was leaving Friday for a fishing weekend in Antrim on Lough Neagh, and he would be back on Sunday.

On Friday morning, with fishing equipment and an overnight bag in hand, he walked to Great Victoria Street Station. It was about three in the afternoon by the time he reached Irvinestown. He left the station and walked down Mill Street to the town centre. He visited a nearby pub and was able to secure a room. He told the landlord that a friend had told him that there was good fishing to be had in Lough Erne and asked where the best place was.

"A lot of our fisherman guests reckon that the best place is off Rossmore. You can get there by taking a bus to Lisnarrick and then walk to the lough. There are only two buses a day from here. They leave at six in the morning and three in the afternoon," said the landlord. "What sort of fish are you after?"

"Pike," said Francis.

"Yes, Rossmore is your best bet."

That night, he spent some time visiting a number of bars before he found a group of British airman in uniform relaxing over a few beers. Listening to their conversation with the locals, he was able to find out that the construction of the air base was almost complete and that they expected their supplies and aircraft to arrive in January.

The next morning, he boarded a local bus and was in Lisnarrick by seven. It was one of those days when you froze to your bones. It was cold, dank, and raw. No one in their right mind would have chosen that day to fish, but he thought this would give him the best cover. Even with his heavy coat, Francis felt miserable, and he hadn't started fishing yet.

As he walked along the Killadeas Road, there was a bustle of military vehicles, even at that hour, leaving and arriving at the camp. No one took much notice of Francis as he trudged up the lane past the main gate as the guards were too busy keeping warm inside. He had studied his map the previous evening and decided to fish from the peninsula just north of Castle Archdale since this would give him a good view of the construction. He found his way along a lane that ran parallel with the lough. When he decided he had gone far enough, he climbed a fence and walked towards the lough and on to the peninsula.

At first, he fished for small fish at the water's edge, and after a while, he was able to catch about six small ones which he put in his "keep net." He then changed his line and took out his live bait tackle and cast it with one of the fish further out in the lough. All this time, he was noting the activity on the other bank. Vast slipways were in place, and what looked like fuel tanks were being filled from camouflaged tankers. There was a lot of activity on the lough itself. Marker buoys were being put out as well as buoys for tethering the flying boats. Francis counted twenty and made a mental note of the channels that were being laid out for arriving and departing aircraft.

He was too busy keeping warm to hear the approach of a four-man military patrol. He was startled by the sound of man's raised voice.

"Now what the hell are you doing here in a restricted area? I thought we told you local Paddies that this area is off limits to civilians!" said an officious sergeant, pointing his rifle at Francis.

"I . . . er . . . I didn't know that. I'm not from around here, and there were no signs."

Two of the patrol searched his fishing kit and his pockets.

"Let's see your ID card."

The sergeant snatched it from Francis and examined it closely. He got out his notebook and wrote down its number and Francis's name and address and handed the book back to him.

"You're from Belfast, I see. What do you do there?"

"I work in the shipyards, and I'm an air-raid warden," said Francis, hoping this last bit of information would give him some leeway with the sergeant.

"Well, you of all people should know the need for security. You can't fish here though."

"Can you suggest where I can?"

"If you go north of here, you can fish at Drumbarna. Tell me, why do you need to fish at this time of year and in this weather?"

"We don't get much time off at the yards, and I had to take the time off when it was offered. A friend told me that this lough had large pike in it. It would be nice to take back a pike for my landlady. Our rations are so terrible, and that would make a nice present for her."

"All right, lad. Pack your stuff up and move on. And good luck catching your whopper!" he said with a grin.

The patrol watched Francis pack up his rod and tackle and escorted him back to the road.

"If you take this road, you'll come to Drumbarna where you can fish to your heart's content," said the sergeant.

Francis set off again and spent the rest of the day fishing near Drumbarna. At about four o'clock, he headed back to Lisnarrick to catch the bus back to Irvinestown. He was thankful to be out of the wind and the rain and was glad of a pint by the fire in the pub. He soon warmed up and thought about his near miss with the authorities, but he had the information he wanted and planned to return to Belfast in the morning.

He didn't know it, but a noose around his neck was beginning to tighten.

CHAPTER 19

Belfast, April 1941

Hell was about to break loose, and nobody in Belfast knew it. Life went on with no thought given to the possibility of air raids. At that time, Belfast's unemployment rate was more than 20 percent, and over one third of the city's residents lived below the poverty line. Those lucky enough to find work were focused on earning as much as they could to feed their families while the work lasted. Air raids were something furthermost from their minds.

This lack of concern was endemic among the province's leadership, and the attitude filtered down to the general populace, except for a small minority of officials and some air-raid wardens. There had been half-hearted attempts to prepare for air raids, such as the building of a small number of public air-raid shelters, but these were to prove to be death traps.

There had been some excitement when the air-raid sirens sounded the arrival of enemy reconnaissance planes. No one took cover, and they had just looked up as the pilots took their aerial photographs. What people were thinking nobody really knew, but they were about to find out what their unpreparedness would cost as a holocaust was about to visit them in just a few days.

Francis had given a lot of thought about the danger. He realised, of course, that the Abwehr's interest in information about Belfast's defences and its industries was not idle curiosity. At first, he thought they were interested in what was being supplied from there for the British war effort, but then he realised this was just naïve thinking. He read in the papers about the bombings of industrial areas on the British mainland, such as Manchester, Clydebank, and Liverpool, and knew the German's attention would soon be turned their way. It was only a matter of time.

He resolved to leave the city as soon as possible and find a refuge where he could start a new life, but where? He could go back to Ireland, but that was like walking into a minefield not knowing what or who would give him away. He remembered when he was in hospital, he had read a magazine article about the English Lake District and how quiet and serene it was. He went to the Belfast Central Library on Royal Avenue and looked up the reference material about the area. After more than an hour of studying the books and the maps, he decided that Keswick would be an ideal small town to which to escape.

But how was he going to get there? There were, of course, the ferries that ran from Belfast to the British mainland, but he didn't want to attract too much attention, particularly from his German masters. Hearing that he had suddenly gone, they would be on the lookout for him at the ferry terminals and trains going south to Ireland. Also, they probably could trace him, and his luck would run out. No, it had to be some unconventional way. Perhaps he was deluding himself into thinking that he was too important to the Abwehr. Nonetheless, he couldn't take a chance. Then he remembered that one of the old hands from work had told him of his first job on a coal boat that plied between Belfast and Whitehaven in England, bringing much-needed coal that powered the linen and other industries in Northern Ireland.

The other burning question was his identification. He needed a new identity card and ration book to use on the mainland. This was going to be a difficult hurdle, and he would have to give it more thought.

On the evening of April 7, Francis reported for duty and began his usual patrol of his area in East Belfast. The evening turned out to be uneventful, and he returned to the wardens' post at midnight. He was just signing out in the roster book before leaving for home when the shrill air-raid sirens went off, and he and the rest of the wardens scrambled to their patrol areas.

The raid was small and primarily damaged part of the Shorts Aircraft Factory, Rank's Flour Mill, and had caused fires at a large lumberyard as well as at some houses. One of these houses was in Francis's area, and he managed to get the occupants out. It was about thirty minutes before the overstretched fire brigade arrived and doused the flames, but at least, everyone was safe. He made his report, and the Civil Defence volunteers looked after the family.

Six German Heinkels had dropped both incendiary and high explosive bombs, and one of the attackers had been shot down by a British Hurricane night fighter. Despite the fires, the damage was relatively light, although some fifteen people were killed.

However, the effect on the population in the aftermath of the raid was one mixed with fear, anger, and astonishment. Why had this happened?

They were supposed to be out of range of their bombers. Why hadn't the government been more prepared for what happened? But this was only the beginning.

People were gripped by fear, and an exodus out of the city was started, particularly by the children. Francis and his colleagues saw much more cooperation by households in their areas, and it was easier to ensure the blackout. Also, there had been some damage at the shipyards, but it hadn't stopped the work of Francis's department.

Despite the jarring to people's psyche that this experience had been, this religious city was preparing to celebrate Easter which followed eight days after the raid. On that Easter Tuesday, April 15, the weather was sunny and bright, and many had taken time off to picnic and relax. Spectators at a soccer match that afternoon saw a Junkers Ju 88 passing overhead. Many thought it was a British plane and went back to watching the game. This was just a prelude of what was to come.

Late in the afternoon, Francis and the other wardens were called in to their post. They gathered in the duty room, and a very serious warden in charge of the post briefed them.

"We are very concerned that there may be an air raid tonight. This afternoon, a reconnaissance plane was spotted flying over the city, and that usually means an air raid will follow," he said. "We took a hit here last week, and we may be in for it again. Communications are important, so get back to me as soon as possible with damage reports."

After a few more minutes, the briefing finished, and the wardens sat around, waiting for darkness. There was a palpable tension among everyone in the room that comes from the expectation of danger. There was very little talking, and the usual card game had been abandoned. Finally, when the time came, they all left in silence with buckets of sand and water and their stirrup pumps to position themselves in their areas.

Francis left his equipment in the entrance to a local grocery store and walked his area. He had to remind some households about their blackout, and for once, they paid attention to him. Then it was time to wait again. People were beginning to go to their beds for the night, whereas he was standing there, waiting for what the wardens believed would be a raid.

Just after ten thirty, the sirens began to wail. About fifteen minutes later, parachute flares drifted down and lit the night sky. It was daylight again. Then the rumbling sound of aircraft engines grew louder and louder as hell was unleashed. The vanguard of some two hundred enemy aircraft started to drop their deadly cargoes. This time, the raid was spread over Belfast, with the shipyards and factories on the north and west side of the city taking the brunt of the bombing. The small workers' houses surrounding the factories, which were the scenes of joyous celebrations just a few hours before, were set ablaze.

Francis was blown off his feet when a parachute mine exploded on a nearby house. Picking himself up, he ran towards the burning building and began to shout out for the occupants. There was no answer. He began to use his stirrup pump in vain attempt to put out the fire. And still, the bombs fell, crushing homes and setting wild uncontrollable fires. People were rushing out into the street, screaming, crying, and hugging their children. Francis directed them to the nearest air-raid shelter. Then suddenly, there was silence from the sky above. The first wave had finished.

Francis ran around the streets in his area, checking on families. A whole street was flattened, and what was left of the houses was just a pile of rubble, with the wooden beams burning. There were no signs of life. As he walked around, he called out, hoping against hope for a response. Then he heard a cry. He started to dig, throwing aside the pile of bricks that was all that remained of a house.

"Keep shouting so I can find you!" he screamed.

He listened, and there, again, was this muffled cry. He started to dig more furiously. He then saw the bodies of a man and a woman lying underneath a beam. He examined them, and they were both dead. He saw the stairs of the house and cupboard below the stairs and started his furious digging again. Eventually, the door gave way, and huddled together were a boy and a girl. They couldn't have been more than seven or eight. They were covered in dust, had saucer eyes of sheer fear, and were crying uncontrollably. Miraculously, they had no broken bones.

"Let's get you out of here," he said encouragingly.

Francis carried them each to the street, and they walked together to the wardens' post and the police station. He left the children with a civil defence volunteer and reported to the senior warden. Then the drone of aircraft engines began again, and another wave of aircraft began dropping their bombs. Francis ran back to his area, not knowing what he would find.

As he rounded a corner, the sight of utter devastation took his breath away. Streets had been flattened, fires were burning out of control, and shell-shocked people were wandering around, despite the still falling bombs. The level of devastation was hard to comprehend. The scene captured the almost incomprehensible brutal power of man.

The survivors walked unsteadily over piles of rubble in the hopes of finding some memento and keepsakes that told a story of their lives. Francis knew these people. Some had lived in their homes for thirty or more years, and the home had been their parents' before them.

And the bombs kept falling.

Francis continued to work hard, digging out survivors and giving first aid to those people that were wounded. The grimmest task of all was the collection of bodies found in the rubble. With the help of men from the neighbourhood, he carried these often burned corpses to the corner of each street. The bodies would be picked up by the Civil Defence teams in lorries and taken to the city mortuary.

For the umpteenth time that night, Francis combed the streets for survivors. In an alley between rows of houses, he found a headless body of a man. He had obviously been hiding there when a parachute mine had exploded nearby and had taken his head off. Remarkably, the rest of him was untouched. Francis searched his pockets, looking for some identity, and found his identification card and ration book. Then a thought suddenly occurred to him: Here was a chance to create a new identity so that he could escape the city without leaving any trace of Tom McClure. He grabbed the documents and stuffed them in his overalls as well as the fifty pounds he found in the man's pocket.

He went to the corner of the street and found one of the men who had been helping him. Between them, they carried the body to the collection point.

By the end of the raid at five in the morning, more than one thousand people were dead in the city and about one hundred thousand were homeless. The hospitals and the city mortuary were so full with bodies that temporary mortuaries were set up at the emptied Falls Road and at Peter's Hill swimming pools and at the St. George's Market, a large fruit market.

As dawn crept up into the sky. it revealed a dirty and exhausted Francis. He was so desperately tired. He just stopped and stared at the scene of absolute carnage. There were no buildings standing, and fires continued to burn in many of the streets. There were still people trapped alive in their homes who the wardens were unable to extricate. Finally, a rescue team arrived, and Francis directed them to buildings, in which people were trapped. With their heavy equipment, they were able to pull people out. Others had to have limbs amputated before they could be pulled to safety.

Francis returned to the wardens' post. The mood in the duty room was sombre. Tired and wasted men sat around, not saying anything. Sometime later, information about emergency services arrived and was posted on walls for all to see. Also, reports of the damage and deaths in West Belfast came in, and Francis was shocked to learn that Margaret's street had been obliterated.

He ran as fast as he could to Margaret's address, only to find that there were no buildings left on her street. Rory was there, searching through the wreckage.

"Tom, the whole family is gone," he said through tears when he saw Francis approaching. "They received a direct hit and just didn't stand a chance. I'm trying to gather up some possessions so that I can give them to Margaret's brother, who was away in Larne.

"I've some more bad news. The Lynches' home was also destroyed. Patricia made it out alive, but Kevin and Raymond bought it. She was taken away this morning in an ambulance, and I'm not sure to which hospital. God, what an awful mess!" He started to sob.

"I can't believe all these good people are gone! What did we do to deserve this?" said a distraught Francis. Then he let out an anguished scream and sank on his knees, sobbing.

"Nothing!" said Rory and put his arm around Francis in a comforting gesture.

"There's nothing we can do but grieve and then press on with our lives. I will never forget them though. What a terrible waste of human life was visited upon us last night! I wish I could get my hands on those responsible for this butchery!"

Francis helped Rory search for personal items, and they took them to the nearest police station for collection by Margaret's brother.

"I've decided to leave the city and go to my mother's in Bangor. What are you going to do, Tom?"

"I haven't given it much thought. I'll probably stick around for a bit and help out. I might go back to Dublin. At least, they're not bombing there. But who knows? At this point, I have no idea."

They shook hands and parted. This was the last time they would see each other.

Francis went home to Chatham Street to see what damage had been done there. The whole front of number 17 had been demolished, and the room that had been the kitchen had partly collapsed. He called frantically for Mrs. Thompson, but there was no answer.

"I'm afraid she was killed last night, lad," said a tired, gravelly voice behind him. It was the dishevelled B-Special Brian Kerr. "We took her body away this morning. I've arranged to contact her sister in Derry so that funeral arrangements can be made."

"Not her as well!" cried a hysterical Francis.

"Why don't you come back to the police station? We can discuss what needs to be done."

"I just want to be left alone!" shouted Francis.

"All right, Tom, all right. You know where to come if you need me."

Francis climbed through the kitchen to the back of the house where his room had been. He was able to find his bag and some clothes, and strangely, his bed was almost untouched.

Then the whole world seemed to collapse on him. He began to sob loudly and collapsed in a foetal position on his bed. He felt so useless. There was nothing he could do to help these people. Then a realisation hit him: What had happened was entirely his fault. If he hadn't spied and worked with the Germans, this would never have happened.

Then his father stood before him, swathed in that red mist, emblematic of the blood that had been spilled that night.

"It's about time you pulled yourself together and thought about how you are going to get out of this city. The Germans will be back because they haven't finished what they set out to do. Your friends were just collateral damage to the bigger picture of my master's plans for dominance of this world. You need to pull yourself together, boy, and get out of your self-pitying mind-set. There's too much to do! Now think! It's time to go!"

Francis just lay there, letting the words wash over him, getting angrier and angrier, but feeling too impotent to fight back. When his father was gone, he sat up and just stared ahead. Maybe his father was right. He should leave Belfast as soon as possible. He was so exhausted that he soon fell into a deep sleep.

He woke five hours later when the night chill started to creep into his bones. He got up, took a final look around at what had been his home for the last three years, and walked down the wrecked street, bag in hand. When he reached the wardens' post, he found the others sitting around, talking about their experiences the previous night, and drinking tea.

"Hello, Tom, it's nice to see you," said the senior warden. "We were worried that you had become a casualty."

"I was visiting my old home, which has been destroyed. I was able to find some of my things, and I now have to find somewhere to live."

"Don't worry about that, Tom, you're more than welcome to stay with us until you find something permanent," said one of the other wardens, Richard McKinney. "We were lucky. The bombs didn't do any damage in our street, although all around us, it was another story. We have no water or electricity, but we have our house."

"Thanks, Richard, I'd like to take you up on your offer."

"There's some water you can use to clean yourself up. A water truck came by this afternoon and gave us a filled water barrel," Richard said.

He went outside with a basin of cold water and washed himself and shaved. Even that simple procedure felt like pure luxury.

The next day, Francis checked in at his work and found out there wouldn't be any that day. The shipyard was in absolute chaos, with men working to clear the damage caused by the attack. However, the Germans had missed most of the docks, except for a couple of damaged ships. The aircraft carrier HMS *Formidable*, which was in for repairs, was miraculously unscathed. He was told that they were hoping to start work again the next day.

He walked to nearby Station Street to the offices of Murphy Coal and inquired about work on one of their coal boats. He filled out a form with his new identity as Patrick Duggan and was told to check back in two days to see whether they had anything for him.

On Saturday morning, he reported back to the offices and was told there was a job of assistant cook on one of the boats. He said he would take it and was told that because of the bombing, none of their boats had made it up the Lagan River to the coal quay. They were unloading, for the time being, in Whiteabbey, which was some eight miles from the city on the western side of Belfast Lough, and he would have to meet the ship, *The Kinnear*, there on that Monday at noon. He was given some paperwork for the ship's captain and was wished good luck.

Sunday night, he told the McKinneys he found a place and was moving after work on Monday. He left as usual for work on that Monday and walked towards the shipyards. People were arriving for the early morning shift and leaving their bicycles propped up against the shipyard wall. He selected one and started to ride across the Queen's Bridge for the last time against the press of people going to work.

The manager at Murphy Coal had said he would have to take the Belfast Road towards Carrickfergus. He found the road after asking several people and was soon in the country with the lough on his right. Two hours later, he entered Whiteabbey and found the harbour area. There was no sign of *The Kinnear*, so he bought a cheese sandwich and a cup of tea from a nearby café and sat there, eating and waiting.

The coal boat eventually docked at about eleven, and by that time, there several lorries lined up, ready to off-load the coal. There was a small crane on railroad tracks which was pulled alongside the boat and was lifting the coal onto the lorries.

Francis walked up the gangplank and asked a seaman where he could find Captain Doyle. The man pointed to the bridge, and Francis climbed up.

Captain Doyle was a thin man, standing at more than six feet tall. He had a red beard and a scar down the left side of his face. His uniform, if you could call it that, was in desperate need of cleaning and repair. Both its master and the uniform itself had seen better days.

"What the hell do you want?" Captain Doyle growled at Francis.

"I'm Patrick Duggan, your new assistant cook," Francis responded, handing him the envelope with the papers in it.

Captain Doyle examined them and looked sternly at Francis.

"Why would anyone in their right mind want to work on a tin can like this? It's dangerous work, especially with the war on. We are forever watching out for mines laid by both the Germans and our lot. Last week, one of our sister boats was lost with all hands after hitting a mine."

"I need the work. Since the air raids in Belfast blew up the place where I worked, I am desperate to find something."

"God, you must be desperate. All right, go and report to our cook, Mat Riley."

Francis found the cook in the galley. He looked Francis up and down with a jaundice eye.

"I suppose you'll do," said the unshaven man, as if he had any option in the matter. "Your job is washing the dishes and keeping the galley clean, understood?"

Francis nodded.

"Now stow your things in the crew's cabin and put on this apron. Then we'll get started on your education."

Francis worked hard on cleaning the dingy galley, and at five in the late-afternoon, the crew came in for their supper. Shortly after this, the boat pulled away from the dock and started its dangerous journey to Whitehaven.

After he had finished his chores in the galley, Francis went out on deck just as the boat passed Whitehead and entered the Irish Sea. Francis pulled out the passport and identification and ration cards for Tom McClure and threw them overboard.

"So long, Tom," he said to himself.

CHAPTER 20

Frith Street, Soho, London, April 15, 1941

Barry Trevelyan had had a very good night. He was feeling very pleased with himself as he closed the street door that led to the flats above a strip club. He paused in the street and lit a cigarette. After taking a long satisfied drag, he let out the smoke, slowly savouring the taste. He enjoyed his weekly visits to Soho, where the girls seemed to be very accommodating and met his needs famously. He liked the twosome idea that Doris had suggested and had made it a regular tryst.

He always started the evening with dinner at the very private Sunset Club on Greek Street, where rationing played no part in what was available so long as you were willing to pay. Having eaten well and drunk a lot of Scotch whiskey, he visited the girls. Doris was the lead player in their robust romps, encouraging Louise, who couldn't have been more than seventeen, to do things to him that sent him into a wild ecstasy. Each time, it got better and better, and he looked forward to his visits as they came up with different ways to satisfy his cravings. The girls were worth the five pounds he paid them.

Since he had returned from Germany in 1939, the gestapo had kept him busy with reports they needed on various sites in England. They paid him well, and he could easily afford his little jaunts to Soho. He had taken a job as traveling salesman for a brush company, and this gave him the excuse to travel by train around the country. He wasn't a very good salesman and had to buy some brushes himself to make it look like he was meeting his monthly quota. The truth was he hated the job. The people he met on the doorsteps were rude, demanding, and flat out ignorant. He was always glad when Friday came, and he could return to his small flat in Clapham.

From his point of view, the war was going well, and soon, the Germans would invade the country. He thought that once that happened, Sir Oswald Mosley would be freed from interment and elevated to his rightful place as leader of the Britain. In turn, Barry, and others like him, would be given positions of prominence, and he hoped that this would be with the British version of the gestapo. He couldn't wait to take his revenge on the likes of Lady Alvin, her family and friends, and that bloody butler of theirs. *My betters? I'll show them.* For the moment, though, he, like most Londoners, spent many nights in nearby underground stations. They would emerge each morning hoping that the bombs hadn't destroyed their homes.

There were no underground trains at this time, so he had to walk home. A light drizzle was falling, and he cursed to himself about the bloody British climate. So far tonight, there had been no sirens warning of air raids, and he reckoned some other poor bastards were getting it—he was right. At that moment, bombs were falling on poorly defended Belfast.

He walked down Frith Street to Charing Cross Road. As he went to cross the street, a black Austin 10 car pulled up alongside him. Three men got out, and the first, who was obviously in charge, ordered him to get into the car.

"No, I won't!" said Barry, and he tried to make a run for it. But the man was too quick. He grabbed him by the arm and forcefully pushed him into the backseat of the car. Two men sat one on either side of him while the other drove.

"You can't do this to me! Where are you taking me? Let me out!"

"Shut up!" said one of the men seated beside him.

The car drove slowly because of the hooded headlights that gave only limited light so that the driver could only follow the curb. Everywhere else was in darkness, and the rain made driving more difficult. They headed south across the Thames and then west along the A3 main road.

When they reached Wandsworth, they were stopped by a police car. Barry tried to scream that he was being kidnapped, but one of the men punched him viciously in the kidneys. This took his breath away. So when the officer approached, he could not utter a sound. The driver produced an identity card. The policeman examined it and then saluted.

"Right you are, sir." And they drove off.

Barry realised then that these men were either from the police or some government department. He kept his mouth shut, but fear replaced his aggression. He was trapped.

The car passed through a darkened Kingston-on-Thames and then north to Ham Common. Eventually, they turned into a large house, and Barry could see from a sign at the gate that this was called Latchmere House. He was dragged out and pushed through front door.

Another man met the group in the front hall.

"Put him in number 6."

They dragged him along a corridor to a room and shoved him in. The room was bare, except for a metal bed at one end, a slop bucket and a table and two chairs in the middle. It had a small window some fifteen feet up, but that was the only connection a prisoner had to the outside world. The door slammed shut, and a key was turned in the lock. Footsteps were heard walking away, and then there was silence.

By nature, Barry was a coward, and he had to find a way of weaseling out of his present predicament. He sat on the bed, and thoughts began to cascade through his mind. If these were special branch or MI5, someone must have ratted on him. What's the best way to face his interrogators? They must have some evidence against him. Maybe silence or denial was the best thing to do. No, they would just torture him, and he couldn't stand pain. Maybe he would give them some harmless information and then go to a prisoner-of-war camp and wait until the Germans rescue him when they take over the country. First, though, he must find out what they knew.

The whiskey and the exertions of the evening were having their effect on him. After an hour of sitting on the bed, he began to feel drowsy. He lay down and eventually fell into a troubled sleep. Several times in the night, he was awoken by slamming doors and screams. Each time, he jumped like a scared rabbit and lay on his bed trembling with fear, wanting this mess to go away. He sat up and cradled his knees, willing himself not to fall asleep in case they came for him.

Several hours later, a key in the lock on his door turned, and the door was opened. There before him was a young man of about twenty-five with a muscular build. He had brown hair cropped short, army style, and was smartly dressed in a dark blue suit and was wearing a regimental tie. He was carrying two cups on a tray, which was balanced on a large brown file.

"I thought you might like to have a cup of tea," he said with a friendly smile. "Come and sit down at the table so we can have a talk."

With some reluctance, Barry walked over and sat down.

"My name is Capt. Mark Bennett, and I'm with military intelligence. And you're Barry Trevelyan. Tell me about yourself, Barry," he said kindly.

On hearing the captain's accent, Barry jumped to the conclusion that he was another one of *them*, a supercilious bastard who grew up with a silver spoon in his mouth. His type disgusted him. He decided to be as difficult and aggressive as he could be.

"I don't want talk about myself."

"Why not? We all have something we are proud of. What about you?"

"What I want to know is what am I doing here? Why was I, a law-abiding citizen, snatched off the street and brought here by three thugs? I want my brief!" he demanded.

"It doesn't work that way in this place, I'm afraid. Lawyers are out of the question until we bring you to trial."

"Trial, what trial? For what?"

"Treason."

This bit of news struck Barry like a thunderbolt. Treason—that means hanging. *God, I must think of a way out of this.*

"Let's start again, now that I've got your attention," he spoke quietly but firmly.

"All right. There's not much to say. My parents were in service, but it was something I didn't want to do after working for a Lady Alvin. It just wasn't me. I did a few odd jobs and then found work as a traveling salesman."

"Why did you join Sir Oswald Mosley's British Union of Fascists and become one of his Blackshirts?"

"Your lot wouldn't understand."

"Try me."

"People like me are fed up with the Jewish-led conspiracy going on in this country and the growing communist threat. The Jews control everything. We can't get jobs because of them. All we want is what's rightfully ours. They aren't British. They're not one of us. Mosley has the right ideas for this country, and it seemed a good idea at the time. He gave me a good job in a movement that will make this country proud again."

"Why did you go Germany in 1938?"

"I'm not answering any more questions. Either charge me or let me go!" He got up and went to his bed and turned his back on Captain Bennett.

"So you don't deny going to Germany. From what we understand from our sources inside the BUF, you were one of Mosley's golden boys. In fact, he selected you to have some training there by the gestapo. Isn't that true?"

Barry didn't say anything.

"You are in a very precarious position, my friend, and it looks like it's going to end sadly for you. That's a shame because you could help yourself."

With that thought left dangling without explanation, Captain Bennett got up and left.

The night was a sleepless one for Barry. His guards brought him some food, which was a stew of an indiscernible origin with some bread. He ate a little of it and then lay back down on his bed, trying to figure out how he should get out of the jam he found himself in. Captain Bennett had left the door open a little, but he didn't want to seem too keen on jumping through it that quickly. *Don't be a fool, take the offer, and to hell with the consequences.* When the Germans invade and free him, he'll have to come up with some excuse why he had betrayed them.

The next day, Captain Bennett entered Barry's cell, and this time, there was no tea or friendly smile.

"Are you willing to talk about what you did in Germany?"

"There's nothing wrong with me joining Sir Oswald's party and then going to Germany. I didn't break the law," Barry said in a monotone.

"True. But you did break the law when you worked for the Germans after war was declared. Some days ago, we did a search of your flat, and apart from the pornographic pictures, we found cipher books. Also, there were notes you had made about our munitions works near Coventry, our spitfire bases in Southern England, and our port facilities in Bristol. You've been a little eager beaver for your masters, haven't you? Do I have to go on?"

Barry was stunned. He had had no idea that anyone had been through his flat.

"Oh, one other thing, we followed you for several days and caught the woman radio operator you used to contact the Germans. Why didn't they give you a radio? Perhaps they didn't trust you to operate it properly. Anyway, your radio operator has agreed to send messages to the Germans for us rather than be hanged."

Just then, a short stubby man in his fifties walked in. Captain Bennett handed him his thick file, and after reading some of the pages, he stopped and stared at Barry.

"So this one of the Aryan agents for the SS Security Service, is it? God, they must be hard up if they recruited him. Look at him. He has as much intelligence as a chicken and a sexual appetite of a randy dog!" He burst out, laughing. "That animal Reinhard Heydrich must be desperate in his effort in finding recruits to outclass the Abwehr. This miserable wretch has nothing to offer us. I would let the hangman take care of him." He left the room, laughing.

Barry began to snivel and let out a low moan.

"I suppose the colonel is right. We have all we need," said Captain Bennett as he gathered up his file.

"What if I gave you some names, what can you do for me?" Barry asked peevishly.

"That depends how useful the information is. If it enables us to catch other agents, we might be able to get the court to reduce your sentence to life with hard labour."

Barry thought for a moment. What option had he? He didn't believe that fervently in the Nazi cause, certainly not when his life was on the line.

"All right. When I was in Germany, I was sent to the Abwehr's training facility at Quenze Farm. There, I met some Englishmen who were going to be sent to Britain. I don't know their real names, but they went under Raymond White, John Hoskins, and Brian Caldecott."

"Yes, we know about them, and we have them in custody. There's nothing new here."

"Ah, there was one name I'm pretty sure you don't have—Tom McClure. His real name is Francis Reagan from Dublin. He was being sent to Belfast to spy on the shipyards and other industrial factories there. I met him first at Lady Alvin's house."

This last name was new to Captain Bennett, but he didn't let on to Barry. He was disgusted by this man who was willing to rat on his friends to save his wretched neck, but he didn't show his revulsion.

"How do you know he was to go to Belfast?"

"I overheard the trainers talking one day," said a confident Barry.

Captain Bennett stood up and began to leave.

"Well, is the information I gave you helpful? Will it get me off the hook?"

"We'll see."

Captain Bennett knocked on Colonel Thomas's office door and entered.

"I think we may have something, sir. He gave me a name of an agent in Belfast who I haven't come across before."

"I've just been reading the reports of the bloodbath in that city two days ago," the colonel said grimly. "The Germans were able to bomb there with ease. There wasn't even a night fighter to be seen. It seems they knew what they were after. Apart from the shipyards and Shorts Aircraft Factory, they hit the waterworks and gas works as well as our munitions factories and the Victoria Barracks. My god, what a mess! About a thousand people died.

"Whoever their agent was, he was able to pass important information over to them. We need to stop him quickly. Mark, contact special branch in Belfast and go there to try to find this man. Your time there is limited, though, to just a few days because we have other serious cases to follow up."

And so the pursuit began.

THE CHAMELEON

False face must hide what the false heart doth know.
  —The Tragedy of Macbeth, *William Shakespeare, 1564–1616*

CHAPTER 21

Whitehaven, England, April 1941

It had been a long hard night of diversions and near misses. Because the *The Kinnear*'s holds were empty, she had bobbed and weaved her way across the Irish Sea, like a spinning top on an uneven surface. With special charts given to him by the Royal Navy, Captain Doyle had to manoeuvre around mine fields, and so the journey, which normally took about twelve hours, was much longer.

Also, ships were not allowed to show lights, which made the journey slower and more treacherous because of the fear of collisions. At one point, the coal boat, which was only 480 tons, very nearly ran into a Royal Navy destroyer, which was four times its size. It was only because of the captain's alertness and skill that he was able to turn the boat 360 degrees to avoid disaster.

Francis had felt bilious the whole time and had spent most of the voyage outside in the stern. He didn't feel better until the boat came into the calmer waters of the Solway Firth. *The Kinnear* made land fall at nine o'clock in the morning and anchored offshore with other coal boats waiting for the high tide at eleven o'clock. Whitehaven Harbour was tidal, so no boats were able to enter it at low tide. At the innermost part of the harbour was Queen's Dock, which had lock gates that, when closed, would hold the water at low tide, and in this way, there would be little delay in loading the ships.

Because *The Kinnear* was the last in a line of some half dozen coal boats, she didn't enter Queen's Dock until two o'clock, and at that time, the gates closed behind them as the tide began to ebb. Much to Captain Doyle's annoyance, this would mean that the boat would not leave until midnight, when the next high tide was expected. However, the crew on the other hand was pleased because they could spend time ashore once they had finished loading the coal.

The quayside of Queen's Dock was lined with railway tracks so that the coal was brought directly from the mines on trains to the dockside and the waiting boats. The coal was tipped into special chutes that delivered it straight into a boat's hold. It was quick and very efficient, except that it created a great deal of stifling coal dust that was layered on just about everything and everybody.

The Kinnear was loaded and ready to go by three thirty. Captain Doyle had his crew working on a number of tasks around the boat until five in the evening. He eventually let his men go and told them to make sure that they were back by ten thirty that evening so they could sail at eleven thirty. He told Francis that, since he was the new member of the crew, he was to remain on board with an older seaman to watch over the boat.

Darkness was falling when Captain Doyle left the boat at six to visit a captain in another coal boat nearby in the dock. The old seaman, by this time, had gone to his bunk and was sound asleep. Francis gathered his bag, walked unseen down the gangplank on to the quay, and headed for the town.

He walked around the town centre, getting his bearings. The town was in total darkness because of the enforced air-raid blackout, although there were still people out and about. He asked a passing air raid warden where the railway station was. As he walked along Strand Street towards the station, he saw a public bath house and decided that, in the morning, he would wash away the coal dust and the smell of death that was on him from Belfast. He found the station and walked back into town.

Francis went to a pub that was on the east side of the town, well away from the harbour area. He didn't want to run into the members of *The Kinnear*'s crew. At closing time, he went to nearby Castle Park and started to look for a bench on which to sleep. Much to his annoyance, most of the benches were taken up by courting couples who were taking advantage of the total darkness.

Francis walked around the park looking for a place to sleep, and then he saw a gardener's shed hidden behind some trees. The door was unlocked, and he went in. At the back of the shed were gardening tools and some empty sacks. Francis lay down on these, resting his head on his bag. He was exhausted, having not slept on the boat the night before, and was soon asleep.

He was awoken the next morning by daylight streaming in through the dirty shed window and the creaking of the door as it opened. He jumped up and looked for a hiding place but could find none. An elderly man stood facing him with a look of surprise and then anger on his face.

"Who the hell are you, and what are you doing here?"

"I am sorry, sir, I got off a boat late and couldn't find anywhere to sleep, so I ended up here."

"This isn't a bloody hotel, you know."

"I'm on my way to Keswick, and I will be catching a train this morning. I'm sorry for any trouble I caused."

"Be off with you. You're lucky I'm not twenty years younger otherwise, you'd get a whopping. Now go before I call the police."

Francis gathered his things together and ran out of the shed. He didn't stop running until he was in the street, heading back to the town centre.

According to a clock in a church tower that he passed, it was seven in the morning, and he walked down to the public baths on Strand Street. He paid an attendant two shillings and sixpence and received in return a minute bar of soap and a towel. The attendant ran a small amount of hot water in a bath from a small boiler on the wall.

Francis stripped and lowered himself slowly into the hot water in the bath. He lay there for several minutes, luxuriating. He took great pleasure in being able to wash away the grime of the past few weeks and looked forward to starting a new life away from death and destruction. When he had washed, he sat in the bath until the water went cold, and then he dried himself. While he was getting dressed, he looked in the mirror, which was on the changing room wall, and was surprised at the gaunt figure who stared back at him. The injury to his face had healed but had left a permanent scar on his lower jaw. He badly needed a shave and determined he must buy a razor the next opportunity he had.

Instead of putting on his dirty clothes again, he dressed in his suit, put on a clean shirt, and his shoes. He packed his work clothes in his bag. When he left the public bath, he looked and felt like a new person. As he climbed the hill out of the town towards the station, he glanced at Queen's Dock one more time and saw no coal boats.

He walked into the station and went up to the ticket counter.

"I would like to go to Keswick, please."

"Single or return?"

"Single."

"That will be four bob. You'll have to change at Workington and ask which platform for the Penrith train," the man said.

Francis handed him the money and thanked him.

The train journey to Workington followed the picturesque route north along the coast. When Francis changed on to the Penrith line, the train headed east, and the scenery changed to a mountainous landscape with crystal clear lakes and rivers. Everything seemed so green and lush, with sheep and cattle grazing peacefully. They took no notice of the steam engine as it chugged its way up the ever-increasing gradient. It was like nothing Francis had ever seen before. He thought that the magazine article hadn't done justice to the scene before him.

The train reached Keswick at about eleven, and Francis walked down Station Road to St. John's Street. He was able to get a room at a small hotel and decided to explore the town. A light rain began to fall as he left the hotel, and it wasn't long before he was thoroughly soaked. He saw a small café and walked in.

"My, look at you, love. Do you want a nice cup of tea?" said the friendly lady behind the counter. "You need a raincoat and hat. You can't go about like that. You'll catch your death."

She poured him a cup of tea, and Francis drank it thankfully. The café was almost empty, except for an old couple by the window. The lady busied herself cleaning tables.

"Are you new around here then?"

"Yes. I'm from Belfast, and I am looking for work. My home was bombed, and I lost everything. I decided to try and get some work around here because I need peace and quiet after the bombing. I can't volunteer for the army on account of my leg."

"With many of the men away in the military, we are always looking for help. What sort work do you want?"

"Office work. I was a purchasing clerk in the Belfast shipyards."

"You should see Miss Biddle then. She has a secretarial agency on Southey Street, and she often knows about local openings. But before you go to see her, buy a rain coat and hat. The Co-Op is near here.

"By the way, I'm Nancy Lambert. I own this place. Would you like another cup of tea?"

"Yes, please. I'm Patrick Duggan."

Nancy and Francis talked for at least half an hour. It turned out that she was locally born and bred. She had married a sheep farmer who had been killed in France in the Great War. She had two sons who were in the army. The eldest boy was wounded at Dunkirk, and the youngest was still in training in Aldershot. Her daughter was in the Auxiliary Territorial Service and was a driver for a general in London. For his part, Francis listened to the kindly woman, wishing that she had been his mother. He told her about life in Belfast and about the blitz that had occurred only a week previously.

Francis took her advice and bought a raincoat, cap, and some walking boots, which he had read he needed for cross-country walking. He also went to a chemist's shop and bought toiletries. He returned to his hotel that evening and, after a satisfying dinner, turned in. He fell asleep almost immediately and didn't wake until late the next morning.

He walked out of the hotel at about eleven that morning. It was a clear day, and with satisfaction, he breathed in the clean crisp air. He followed the directions that Mrs. Lambert had given him and soon found the entrance to Miss Biddle's secretarial agency, which was on the second floor above a grocery store. As he climbed the stairs, he heard the clatter of a typewriter. When he reached the top landing, he stopped to catch his breath and then knocked on the door of the Biddle Secretarial Agency. The typewriter stopped, and a few seconds later, a very pretty young woman of about twenty opened the door. She blushed on seeing Francis.

"Can I help you?"

"I would like to see Miss Biddle. Is she in?"

"She's not here right now, but I'm expecting her at any moment. Come in and take a seat."

Francis was ushered into a small reception area. It had two chairs, a small table with old magazines on it, and a desk with a typewriter. There was a door led to an inner office and another to a storage cupboard.

"I'm Margery Adams," said the woman as she sat back down behind the desk.

"Patrick Duggan. Nice to meet you."

"If you'll excuse me, I have to finish these letters by noon." And she continued to type.

Ten minutes later, after he had exhausted the reading material, Francis heard loud footsteps on the stairs, and Miss Biddle bounded through the door. She was a very athletic-looking woman in her late forties dressed in tweed skirt and jacket and wearing "sensible" shoes.

"Right, Margery, we've got some more work from Jackson's. We'll have to get Pamela in to help. Give her a call. Hello, who are you?" she asked when she saw Francis.

"Patrick Duggan, ma'am. Mrs. Lambert suggested I see you. She thought you might know about an office job."

"Did she now? You better come in and tell me about your background, although there isn't much available just now."

Francis followed her into her office. He wasn't prepared for the sight that met his eyes when he went through the door. Apart from being in desperate need of painting, there was clutter everywhere—files piled high one on top of another on the floor, filing cabinets were open with other files on the drawers, as if someone had been searching for something and then had been distracted. A large oak desk was in the front of a bay window, and like everywhere else, it was piled high with books and files. There was a small work space on the desk, which had a telephone and a large ashtray piled high with cigarette ends. Behind the desk was a captain's chair, where Miss Biddle plonked herself down.

But what struck Francis was the putrid smell, and he soon saw the reason for it—a large Persian cat jumped up on the desk and was caressed by Miss Biddle as it purred loudly.

"Now tell me about yourself," she said as she put a cigarette in a holder and lit it with a silver lighter which was on her desk.

"I had a desk job in Belfast, clerking in an accounting firm. When they were looking for volunteers, I joined up as an ambulance driver to fight the fascists in the Spanish Civil War," he partly lied. "I was wounded in the leg and captured. When I got back to Belfast, I worked in the shipyards as a purchasing clerk. When the war was declared with Germany, I became an ARP warden, which was a very stressful job. As you probably know, the city was bombed heavily just over a week ago, and I was lucky to get out of there alive. My friends were all killed, and the place where I worked was destroyed. I just had to get out of there. I had read about this part of the country, so I came here to escape the devastation and the strain of living under constant danger. It was as if my experiences in Spain were repeating themselves."

Miss Biddle listened intently, and Francis could see that she was impressed with his story. She then peppered him with questions about his work in Belfast and seemed satisfied with answers.

After an hour interview, Miss Biddle got up and went to shake Francis's hand.

"Let me make some inquiries and see what I can do. Where are you staying?"

Francis told her.

"Why don't you come and see me again at four tomorrow, and I'll tell you what I've found out."

Francis went to see Mrs. Lambert to tell her what had happened with his interview. When he entered the café, he sensed an ominous air of foreboding. The customers were speaking to each other in hushed tones, and they were surreptitiously looking towards the kitchen.

Mrs. Lambert was not in her usual place behind the counter. Then he heard a whimper coming from the kitchen. He knocked on the door and peered in. There was Mrs. Lambert, sitting at the table and crying. Before her was a small official-looking piece of brown paper.

"Mrs. Lambert, what on earth is the matter?"

"My eldest boy has died. He got out of Dunkirk, but he was wounded and was in a hospital in Brighton. He must have died from his wounds. I was going to see him next week. Oh god!" she sobbed as she handed him the telegram. He read it and lay it back down on the table.

"What can I do to help you?"

"There's nothing you can do. I need to contact my other son in Aldershot and my daughter, as well as to talk to the vicar. I have to make arrangements with the undertakers to have his body brought here. I suppose I will have to close this place for the rest of the day, though I will lose business as a result, and God knows I need the money."

"No, you won't, Mrs. Lambert. I'll keep it open for you. Tell me what I need to know, and I'll keep things running for you. You've been so kind to me. Now it's my turn to return the favour."

"I couldn't expect you to do this. You're so kind but no. Our baker comes in at five thirty in the morning. Then a friend of mine, Mrs. Jericho, will come in tomorrow at seven and look after things."

"Please let me help you today. You've got so much to do, and the last thing you want to worry about is this place."

She hesitated. "Well, are you sure you don't mind?"

"Of course not."

Mrs. Lambert briefed Francis on prices and how to work the till. She then left. It was fairly quiet all afternoon. The lunch crowd had gone before Francis had come back to the café, so he had only to deal with customers looking for afternoon teas. At six, he closed up the café, locked the front door, and put the key through the letter box.

The next morning, he walked by the café and saw Mrs. Jericho working behind the counter. He walked on to a bookshop that he had seen the previous day. He bought a map of the area and took it to the library. He spread it out on a table, and with the help of tourist books, he was able to locate several places of interest on the fells. He was particularly interested in the Newlands Valley, which boasted of a sixteenth-century lead and copper mine. He determined that when he got the time, he would visit all these places.

Promptly at four, he was back in Miss Biddle's office.

"The government has taken over a large house which is owned by a friend of mine. Sally now lives in one of the cottages on the estate until she gets her home back. It's called Derwent Hall and is on the Borrowdale Road just out of town. It has a very picturesque view of the fells and of Derwent Water. They have converted it into a convalescent home for wounded soldiers. Many of the men are recovering from operations they have had elsewhere, and this is just the place to help them rest and recuperate.

"I talked to the medical director there, a Dr. Robert Morrison, about you this morning. They are looking for someone to organise their office and run their medical store. I've arranged for you to see him at ten tomorrow morning. Have you got a bike?"

"No," he replied. Francis thought that this was a strange question.

"Well, you'll need one around here. Petrol is not available to the likes of you and me. To get anywhere, especially in the countryside like this, you need to either walk or cycle. You can buy a good second-hand bike at Latimers on Station Road, and you can tell them I sent you so you will get a good price. Now have you any questions?"

"No, not really."

"Good. I'll draw you a map of how to get there."

Francis left Miss Biddle's office elated. If all goes well, he'd have a job in this peaceful part of the country. He found Latimers and was able to buy a bike for a pound.

The next morning, he set off early on his bicycle at nine because he didn't know how long it would take. He followed Miss Biddle's instructions and found himself at the entrance to the grounds at what used to be the gatekeeper's lodge. The long driveway wound through a wood, and eventually, the woodlands gave way to a stunning vista.

The large house was perched on the edge of Derwent Water, and the morning sunlight reflected off the water so that the lake seemed to shimmer. The design of the large Victorian house was simple yet imposing. It was made from locally quarried stone and slate. It had two levels where the family lived, which was obvious from the large picture windows on the first two floors. At the top of the house, on the third floor, there were smaller windows which signified the servants' quarters. The front entrance had a carriage portico which protected visitors and the family from the cold winter wind and rain when they entered or left the house. To the left of the house were other buildings which were the former stables. On the lake, Francis could see a wooden dock with several boats moored.

As he cycled towards the house, he noted that there was a military ambulance, two lorries, and several motor cars. He leaned his bike against the wall of the entrance and walked inside.

The front hall had a wooden floor and panelling. Portraits of various ladies and gentlemen, who were probably relatives of the current owner, lined the walls. A uniformed nurse in a well-starched cap and apron was sitting at a desk, reviewing files and writing notes. She looked up when Francis entered the house.

"Can I help you?" she asked kindly.

"I'm Patrick Duggan, and I have an appointment with Dr. Morrison."

"If you'd just take a seat, I'll see if he is available."

Francis took a seat and waited. As he was sitting there, an ambulance arrived, and nurses and porters appeared from nowhere and rushed out to help bring in the patients. Several of the men were on crutches and, with some difficulty, negotiated the steps that led to the front door. One patient was on a stretcher, and two others walked in under their own steam, but as Francis observed, they had arms missing.

An efficient-looking woman in a dark blue uniform, who seemed to be in charge, began checking names against her list and assigning rooms. One thing that Francis noted was that they were all officers. He wondered where the other soldiers went.

"Mr. Duggan?"

"Yes."

"I'm Dr. Morrison. I see you've seen our latest intake of wounded. Most of those poor fellows were whisked from the beaches of Dunkirk. They've had operations in various hospitals, and it's now our job to get them back on their feet. Why don't you come on through to my office?"

Francis followed Dr. Morrison along a narrow corridor and into a room that was his office.

He went over to a table where there was a tray with two cups, a teapot, a milk jug, and sugar.

"Would like some tea?"

"Yes, please."

"Help yourself then."

He sat down behind his desk and ushered Francis to take a chair.

"I need to see your ID card. This is a formality the government is insisting on."

Francis handed over Patrick Duggan's ID card. The doctor took a quick look at it and handed it back with thanks. He took a sip of tea and looked around the striking wood-panelled room.

"This used to be the study. It's very grand, isn't it? It's something that I'm not used to, I can tell you. Growing up in a mining village in Yorkshire with six siblings, I didn't have a very privileged beginning to life. What about you?"

Francis told Dr. Morrison his cover story of being brought up in Limerick, moving to Philadelphia, and then coming back to Belfast. He explained how he went as an ambulance driver to Spain, was captured, and then, when he came home, worked in the Belfast shipyards. He told him about the blitz and what he had seen.

"That's a lifetime of experience you've squeezed into just a few short years. I see you have quite a limp, how did you get that?"

"I was badly beaten one day by the guards at the concentration camp in Spain. They broke my ankle, and I could not get it set properly, so I ended up with this limp."

"We'll have to take a look at it. Let me tell you about what we do here. We have been only open a few months, and we're still getting organised. Although we are all civilians, we report to the Royal Army Medical Corps. They're pretty good at leaving us to our own devices.

"Many of these chaps who come here need pretty intensive physiotherapy and some we have to fit with artificial legs or arms. These men have to learn how to use these new limbs. It takes a long time, and patience is the name of the game. Many of them also come with significant psychological problems. We can often fix their physical wounds, but it's not so easy to mend their minds. This often presents itself as anger, deep introspection, or self-loathing. Some of our worst cases are referred to special psychological clinics for treatment.

"What we need is someone to take the paperwork out of our hands, or at least minimise it, so we can get on with the business of healing these poor fellows. There are all these government forms to fill in, accounts to be kept, and supplies to be ordered. There isn't enough time in the day for this. Do you think you would be able to help us?"

"I've certainly got a good business background for this. Also, my war experiences make me very keen to help in my own way with these men. I've seen enough to understand a lot of where they are coming from. Yes, I would like the opportunity to do my bit."

"Good. Do you have anywhere to live?"

"No. I'm staying in a hotel right now."

"We can provide you with a room here, and of course, the meals would be free. I'm afraid the salary isn't the greatest at three pounds a week, but you are getting board and lodging. When can you start?"

"Tomorrow, if you would like."

"Tomorrow it is then, say nine in the morning. Now let me show you around."

Dr. Morrison walked Francis around the large house. They had converted the ballroom into a gymnasium, which had all kinds of physiotherapy equipment in it, and the patients were using the equipment with the help of the staff. The library had been made into a common room for the patients and was filled with newspapers and books. Several of the rooms on the ground and first floors had been converted into dormitories for the patients. One of the rooms on the first floor had been made into an operating theatre, and the room next to it was the pre- and post-operating area.

At the back of the house was the kitchen and what had been the servant's dining room. This had now become the staff room. Here, Francis met Mrs. Jackson, the housekeeper. She was a gaunt woman in her fifties who always looked serious. Despite her solemn demeanour, she cracked a welcoming smile and wished him well.

"Mr. Duggan is starting here tomorrow, Mrs. Jackson. He'll be reporting to you here before nine in the morning, so you can get him settled in the staff accommodations."

"Right you are, doctor. Patrick, I'll need your ration card."

Francis gave this to her.

Dr. Morrison took Francis out to the stables where the medical stores were kept. He told Francis that he would be responsible for this area but that it didn't include the dispensary.

"This is matron's domain, and she is in charge of ordering the medicines we need. Also, I look after the patient files which are locked in my office, so you don't have to worry about them," he said.

As they were walking back into the house, they met the same woman who had been organising the intake of patients, which Francis had witnessed in the front hall.

"Matron, may I introduce Patrick Duggan who has agreed to help us out with the stack of paperwork the government requires. Patrick, this is Miss Royston, our matron."

"How do you do, ma'am."

"I hope you are efficient because you'll need to keep up with it all. Just one word of warning, keep away from my nurses. They have a lot to concentrate on. Is that all, doctor?" And she walked off before Dr. Morrison could reply.

"Matron is very old-fashioned, but she really knows her work. This place couldn't work without her. Now come on, I'll show you where your office will be. It used to be the butler's office, and it's next to the kitchen," said Dr. Morrison.

When they walked into the room off the kitchen, it reminded Francis of Miss Biddle's office, except there wasn't the smell.

"As you can see, it's a bit chaotic, but I'm sure you'll get it sorted out. This week, I've arranged for one of the administrators at the Royal Army Medical Corps based in the Catterick Garrison to come in and go through what paperwork we need to file. They are coming in two days."

Just then, a young doctor in a white coat peered around the door.

"Dr. Morrison, we have a problem with one of the new patients. It seems that septicaemia is setting in on one of his wounds. We should probably operate."

"Right, Dr. Abelson, I'll be right with you. Patrick, I'm going to have to leave you. See you tomorrow."

After Dr. Morrison left, Francis sat down in a chair behind his desk and just looked at the devastation of papers before him. Where to start? He began by trying to understand the filing system and then creating files on key subjects such as equipment, Ministry of Defence, the local health board, etc. He came across some official papers he didn't understand and put them to one side to ask about in the morning. After about three hours, he had got most of the files sorted. He made a list of questions for Dr. Morrison, particularly the priority of the government forms. In the morning, he would have to do an inventory of the stores to see what was needed.

He left Derwent Hall at two and cycled into Keswick. He wondered how Mrs. Lambert was doing but decided not to trouble her. Instead, he continued cycling out of Keswick and headed west towards Portinscale. He followed the signposts for Newlands, and the road began a steep climb. As he pedalled hard, the road took him through woods, and he finally reached open country and saw Barrow Fell in front of him. He cycled on to a small village called Stair.

He left his bicycle by a gate and walked up towards the top of the fell. It was hard going, and he realised he was not as fit as he thought he was. Halfway up, he stopped to get his breath back. He was amazed at the sight that lay before him. Derwent Water was in front of him. Off to his left, he could see Keswick, and to his right in the distance, he could just make out Derwent Hall. The whole area was surrounded by what he thought were small mountains, or what the locals called fells. He spent a good half hour taking in the beauty of the magnificent scenery. Then it began to rain.

The ride back to Keswick, thankfully, was all downhill, and he reached the town as dusk was falling. He had his last meal at the hotel and packed his bag, ready for the morning. He wrote a letter to Miss Biddle, telling her that he got the job and thanked her for all her help. He put the letter through her letter box at her office that night before going to bed.

He arrived the next morning at Derwent Hall at nine, and Mrs. Jackson showed him to his room. He then went to his office and began to work on the mound of papers. At ten, other staff members were gathering in the staff room next to his office, and he joined them. Mrs. Jackson had made a large pot of tea, and everyone was helping themselves to it. Francis introduced himself to the nurses who were there and to Dr. Abelson and a much older Dr. Mackie.

Dr. Robert Mackie was in his late sixties and had been called out of retirement at the outbreak of the war. He had been a consultant orthopaedic surgeon at St. Thomas's Hospital in London and had had wide experience in artificial limb replacement surgery during and after the Great War. Despite his celebrity status, he was friendly and interested in other members of the staff. He took instantly to Francis and peppered him with questions, particularly about the Spanish Civil War. He knew several of the doctors that had volunteered there.

The door opened, and Dr. Morrison and the matron entered. A hush fell over the assembled staff.

"I think just about everyone has met Patrick Duggan. His background in administration will help us make sense of the government paperwork and hopefully keep them off our backs so we can do what we are best trained to do.

"Because there is a big demand for our services, the Ministry of Defence plans to build a temporary wing on the side of the house. The structure is called a Nissen hut and will enable us to have an additional twenty beds. We will be going over the designs on Wednesday with people from the ministry, so I'll keep you apprised of when they plan to begin construction. This will mean that we will have to increase our nursing and physiotherapy staff, so I will be looking into this."

He then changed the subject to the care of current patients. He went over each patient's file and care plan. During this dialogue, a number of staff asked questions or made suggestions. This open type of meeting was unheard of in the 1940s, particularly within the status-conscious medical profession, and Francis suspected that this was Dr. Morrison's own style of management. It certainly didn't go down well with matron, and you could read the disapproval on her face.

For Francis, it was interesting to be able to size up the members of the staff by their questions, or lack thereof, as well as their personas at the meeting. Often, Dr. Morrison would defer to Dr. Mackie who gave succinct answers. He was particularly good at sizing up a patient's mental state, which would make at an important contribution to his recovery.

After an hour, the meeting finished, and the staff made their way back to their respective stations.

"Patrick, have you got any questions for me?" Dr. Morrison asked as he was leaving.

"A few."

"Why don't you come in, and I'll try to answer them."

That night after dinner, Dr. Mackie asked Francis if he played chess.

"Yes, sir. I learned to play in the prison camp."

"Great. I'll give you a game before I head home."

"You'll have to show me each piece because we just used dried bread and pebbles."

Dr. Mackie went to a cupboard and got out a board and a box of chess pieces. He explained each piece to Francis, and they set up the game. It was a half hour before Dr. Mackie checkmated Francis.

"Not bad, Patrick. Here, let me show you some better moves."

They spent time going over each move, and Dr. Mackie explained that, like in life, you have to think many moves ahead.

"Now I must go. Mrs. Mackie will be after me if I don't go home," he said with a laugh.

Francis's room, although sparse, was the most comfortable he had ever had, except for the hotel. He lay in bed reading a book he had got from the library and was soon drowsy. He turned off the light and drifted off to sleep.

At one in the morning, he was jarred awake by a scream.

CHAPTER 22

Francis sat up in bed. He heard another scream, and it seemed to come from downstairs. He quickly got up and snatched his dressing gown as he ran out of the door. He went down the stairs two at a time to the second floor where there was a gaggle of people talking among themselves on the landing.

"What's going on?" he asked anyone in the group.

"A patient has grabbed one of the nurses and is threatening her with a knife. He's already slashed one of our porters who tried to take the knife away from him and is threatening to kill her," said an excited nurse.

"How did he get the knife?"

"He must have taken it when he was given his dinner. It's not that sharp but could cause a lot of damage," replied a porter.

Dr. Abelson joined the group.

"It's too dangerous to approach him. He would only harm Nurse Stevens. He is totally delusional. He thinks he has caught a German and won't let go. We'll have to wait until he tires and then rush him. I'll get a sedative ready to inject into him," said Dr. Abelson.

"Doctor, I have seen this type deliriousness before in the prison-of-war camp in Spain. Let me try and speak with him and see what I can do. He might do something stupid and hurt the nurse before we could get to him," said Francis.

"I don't think that would be a good idea. You haven't had the training in psychology to know what you are doing," said Dr. Abelson patronisingly, and he began to turn away. This infuriated Francis.

"I don't need any training because I have had experience of dealing with people with this type of illness. I have more training in this sort of thing than you have!" said an exasperated Francis. "Now tell me about him," he demanded of the shocked doctor, and the hushed crowd of people gathered around him.

After a few seconds, and seeing the earnestness in Francis's face, he said, "Well, be it in your own head. We haven't many options. His name is Lt. John Edwards of the East Surrey Regiment, and he lost a leg during the retreat to Dunkirk. He was carried by members of his platoon some thirty miles on a makeshift stretcher to the beaches. Eventually, he and his men were able to get out on a small fishing boat. His ankle was badly damaged, and it had to be amputated. Then gangrene set in, and his leg was amputated above the knee. When he recovered from his various operations, he was sent to us for convalescence and the fitting of a prosthesis."

Francis walked into the dormitory where Lieutenant Edwards lay in his bed with a very frightened Nurse Stevens gripped around the neck by his strong, unyielding arm. Her eyes were enormous, and she was whimpering uncontrollably. The other patients in the dormitory looked apprehensive as they lay in their beds not moving. The lieutenant's eyes warily looked around him, and as Francis came into the room, he drew the knife closer to the nurse's throat so that a small amount of blood flowed.

"Who the hell are you?" demanded the lieutenant.

"Private O'Reilly, sir. You don't remember me?" Francis pretended.

"No, I don't."

"I was in three section with Corporal Williams, sir."

"Where's your rifle, man?"

"Oh that, sir, I'm a Bren gunner, if you remember, sir. I left my Bren with the corporal since he'll need it if Gerry should attack. Sergeant Adams ordered me to come to you and take the prisoner back to the company HQ for interrogation. One of the IOs from battalion has turned up and wants to put the screws on the prisoner."

"I'll take him there myself. He's a very slippery character, but I have the better of him."

"But, sir, you're wounded, and besides that, we need you here if Gerry should come calling."

"True. But you haven't got a weapon."

"I can use your knife, sir. I'll get one of other men to make some tea. You need your rest because we don't know what will happen next. We have a long way to go to Dunkirk."

"How do I know you're not a German? How do I know . . . ?" he said as his voice tapered off. And then he began to cry, although, much to Francis's consternation, his grip on Nurse Stevens didn't loosen.

"Come on, sir, do I look like a Gerry?"

"No, but you have a funny accent."

"Oh that. I'm Irish. I joined the regiment in Woking."

"I thought I heard an accent."

"Now, sir, let me take the prisoner and you get some well-earned kip."

"I am tired, that's true. I need to rest."

With that, Lieutenant Edwards released the nurse and calmly handed the knife to Francis.

Francis whispered to the nurse to walk slowly out of the dormitory with him. As they did so, the lieutenant fell asleep. Two porters rushed in and held him down while Dr. Abelson injected him with the sedative.

Now there was a flurry of activity as soon as the lieutenant fell asleep. Matron took charge of moving him on a trolley to a small room, where they strapped him to a bed, and a porter stood guard outside the door to the room. The nurses were checking on the other occupants of the ward and were settling them down again for the night. With all the fuss, no one saw Francis leave and quietly go back to bed without saying a word to anyone.

He came down to breakfast the next morning at his usual time and entered the staff room. There was spontaneous applause and singing of "For he's a jolly good fellow and so say all of us" from everyone in the room, including Dr. Abelson. Francis turned bright red and sheepishly thanked everyone. He helped himself to some food off the buffet and sat down. Jane Stevens got up from her table and sat next to him.

"I just want to say a big thank for what you did last night," she said warmly.

"Oh, you're welcome. It was a bit of a risk, but it was the only option we had to resolve the situation."

"When did you learn how to handle a patient who was obviously mentally sick? Was it in a mental hospital?"

"No, it was purely a reaction to what I had learned in Spain." Then Francis told her briefly about his experiences as a prisoner of war.

As they were talking matron came in.

"Stevens, you were due on your ward five minutes ago!"

With that, Jane Stevens jumped up and left in a hurry, silently mouthing thank you to Francis as she went.

"I suppose I need to thank you for saving Jane Stevens's life. It was a big chance you took with someone else's life, and I hope you won't make a habit of it."

"No, matron."

Matron cracked a small smile and left.

Breakfast finished, Francis went to his office and started work. About an hour later, Dr. Morrison came into his office.

"I hear we had a bit of excitement last night. I just wanted to add my thanks for a job well done."

"Thank you, sir. How is Lieutenant Edwards doing?"

"I'm afraid he's had a total mental breakdown, poor chap. We are sending him off to a mental hospital in Manchester. They will be able to help him."

After dinner that night, he sat by the lake, thinking how his new life was turning out to be better than he had expected. Then the red mist heralded the arrival of his father.

"Well, well, well, the conquering hero! I don't understand why you didn't let him kill her. You had to interfere, didn't you? It would have been amusing to see those supercilious bastards' faces if he had slit her throat.

"Anyway, I just wanted to let you know that you should enjoy your respite now while you can because your past will soon be here to haunt you. A ghost of San Pedro will visit you and ruin the tranquillity of this place for you! Also, the police will soon know where to find you. So you better make plans to leave as soon as possible otherwise the hangman will get you. The police will blame you for the destruction of Belfast and for the murder of your friends there. Now let's see how you get out of this problem! Use your wiles. Remember, my master expects total loyalty to his cause and won't appreciate any distractions from our main mission."

"Who is your master? Whoever he is, he's not mine!" Francis shouted.

"Oh, but he is. We are both the devil's disciples now. You're my seed. That's why he has taken an interest in you. Once you had killed that priest, he saw your revulsion with the church, and he was pleased with the way you fulfilled your task. Keep it up and we will help him conquer the world."

"I will not follow him! That priest deserved what he got because he was an evil man who preyed on children—nothing more, nothing less! I am going stay here!"

"We'll see!"

"I won't, I won't," Francis cried as his father disappeared.

"Won't what?" said a female voice behind him.

Francis turned around and saw Jane Stevens and another nurse approaching. They sat down on the bench next to him, and Jane got out a packet of cigarettes. She offered him one, but Francis declined. They both lit up and took a drag on their cigarettes.

"What won't you do?" Jane pressed.

"Oh, I was just thinking aloud. I often do that when I'm alone. Do you think that's strange?"

"Not really. We all have different ways of thinking and working out our problems," she said with a smile. "You haven't met my friend, Patricia Sullivan. She's Irish like you and comes from Cork. We were in nursing school together in London and came here. She was off last night, so she didn't see or hear the kerfuffle. We share a small flat in town, and it's nice to get away from this place once our shift finishes."

"Tell me, Patrick, where do you come from?" asked Patricia.

"I'm from Dublin."

They spent the next half hour talking about their work and what they will do after the war. The two girls said they planned to study midwifery so they could travel the world as nurses on passenger ships.

"What are your plans, Patrick?" Patricia asked.

"I don't know, maybe I'll study to be an accountant, but nothing as exotic as your plans," said Francis. They all laughed, and then the girls said they had to get back for night duty.

That night, he lay in bed thinking about what his father had told him. There was no doubt the police would be after him, although he had covered his tracks pretty well. His new identity as Patrick Duggan was untraceable. Patrick Duggan was just a corpse buried without any identity, or was he? Maybe they had a way of identify him. Perhaps one of his friends recognised him by the clothes he was wearing or something else, like a ring. *My god, I didn't check whether he was wearing a ring or a watch. How could I be so careless? I'll have to watch myself in future. I need to change my identity again when I see an opportunity.*

Just then, he heard a familiar roar of aircraft engines. The noise was getting closer and closer. He dived under his bed for cover, fearing the worse, as painful memories of Belfast began to flash before him. Some five minutes later, the noise had subsided and the country quiet returned.

Francis put on his dressing gown and went down to the kitchen. He had been so rattled by the aircraft he could not sleep and had decided to make a cup of tea. Mrs. Jackson was there, getting ready for the following morning before she went to bed.

"Hello, Patrick, you still up?"

"The aircraft noise woke me. Who were they?"

"Every few days, on clear nights, the Germans fly over here using the string of lakes in the Lake District as landmarks on their way to bomb Glasgow or Manchester. We're used to it, but I always pray for those souls in that city. A lot of people are going to die tonight."

"It reminded me of the bombing in Belfast. It brought back some painful memories."

"Sit down, lad. I've got just the thing to help you sleep."

Mrs. Jackson went to a cupboard and brought out a bottle of Scotch. She took two glasses from the counter and poured two large amounts.

"Here, get that inside you," she said, passing him a glass.

"Thank you. Where did you get this?" Francis asked as he took a sip.

"Ah, that's my secret. Don't ask and I won't lie" was all she would say with a wicked grin.

The next day, a staff sergeant from the Royal Army Medical Corps arrived, and he and Francis spent a good deal of time reviewing the paperwork that was needed by the government to keep the clinic running. By six that evening, they had finished, and the staff sergeant had left.

The following week, Francis decided to visit Mrs. Lambert. Keswick seemed much busier than when he had first arrived three weeks before. There were army lorries passing through the streets, and the pavements were busy with soldiers who had been billeted in the town. The streets were also abuzz with schoolgirls in their uniforms from Roedean School, a girls' boarding school. The school had been evacuated from Brighton in Southern England and was using the Keswick Hotel as its temporary school. He was passed by other young children who were evacuees from Newcastle. They had labels, with their name and address, attached to their clothes. They were being taken from the railway station to the evacuee centre where they would each be sent to homes in the area.

Francis walked up to the café on Victoria Street, anticipating a warm welcome and looking forward to talking to Mrs. Lambert. There was a young man about his age behind the counter who Francis thought was probably her younger son. He walked in and introduced himself and asked for Mrs. Lambert. The man looked at Francis with cold eyes, and a vicious scowl came over his face.

"How dare you come in here as if nothing was wrong, you thief! Get out before I call the police and never darken this door again."

"Why? What's wrong?" stammered Francis, at a loss for words.

"Don't tell me you don't know. You took advantage of my mother when she needed your help. You stole from her, and she trusted you. She even helped find you a job."

"What do you mean?"

"You took ten pounds from the till after you closed up for her. My mother doesn't want to prosecute you, but I do. Now that you've turned up again, looking to con her once more, I am going to tell the police that you were here. Now get out!"

Francis hurriedly left the café. There was no point in arguing with the man. He sat on a bench in Fitz Park by the river and tried to puzzle who could have stolen the money. Was it possible she was mistaken because she was very upset at the time about the death of her eldest son? No, he remembered there was a lot of cash in the till, and it was something he was going to mention to her. He had to find the truth because the last thing he wanted was police scrutiny.

The next day, Francis was sitting in his office at work when there was a knock on the door. He went to the door, and there was a rather rotund middle-aged man in a raincoat and wearing a trilby. His face was drawn, and he had doleful eyes that gave him a bloodhound look.

"Patrick Duggan?" he asked.

"Yes."

"I'm Sgt. Robert James from the Keswick police. Can I come in?"

"Of course, please take a seat."

"Thank you. I've come to see you about a theft at Mrs. Lambert's café. Although she doesn't want to press charges against you, I want to warn you about going to the café or contacting the Lambert family again."

"The first I heard about the theft was yesterday when I called in to see Mrs. Lambert and I was falsely accused of stealing from her. Why do you think I'm the culprit?"

"Access and opportunity."

"I'm not that stupid. Let's suppose for a moment I wanted to steal from her, it would be too obvious if a lot of money went missing all at once and I'm still in town. I can think of two other people that fit your description though—her friend, Mrs. Jericho, and the baker who comes in early and is by himself until seven. Apart from this one occasion, has any more money been missing, ten bob here and five shillings there?"

"We don't know."

"Well, I think you need to find out before coming here and accusing me. I wasn't the only person with access to the till. I wouldn't be surprised if someone took advantage of my presence though. No one would believe a stranger and a Mick at that!" said an annoyed Francis.

The sergeant was taken aback by Francis's aggressiveness. "I hear what you say, and it does make a lot of sense. Let me look into the other possibilities. I'll let you know but don't leave town without seeing me first."

"I just want to clear my name."

The police sergeant left, and Francis sat at his desk, mulling over these new developments.

That evening, he took his usual walk by the lake after dinner and was surprised to see Jane Stevens sitting by herself on a bench, smoking a cigarette.

"It's very peaceful here, isn't it?" she said to him.

"Yes, it is. You hardly know that there is a war going on. Tell me about Jane Stevens. I'm interested in hearing about why you became a nurse."

"My father was a dockworker in the East End of London, and we had very little money. I have two brothers and one sister. My mum died in childbirth when I was ten, and I helped bring up some of my siblings. I didn't want to get on the same treadmill that my mother and many other women were on. You get married very young, have a lot of kids, suffer abuse from a drunken husband, and die young. It wasn't for me. So I crammed at school and passed my School Certificate. I was lucky to have a teacher who wanted to help me. Although I had to work at night when everyone else was asleep, it was worth it."

Francis warmed to Jane and found they had a lot in common. They spoke for another fifteen minutes, and he found that she was very easy to talk to. He broke his own rule about not revealing his real background by telling her about his life in the Dublin tenements.

"How about going for a row on the lake?" Francis suggested. "We can take one of those boats tied to the jetty."

"I'd love to, but I have to go back to work in a few minutes."

"Would you like to come out for a drink on Saturday?"

"That would be great. You can pick me up at my flat, say at seven. Here's the address," she said, handing him a piece of paper.

On Saturday, he cycled into Keswick and picked up Jane. They walked to the Pack Horse Inn. He was just getting their drinks when he spotted Sergeant James at the bar.

"Any luck yet?" Francis asked.

"Not yet. We had a problem with one of the soldiers killing another, so I've been busy with the military police. What checking I've done has been a dead end. I suspect the baker was involved because he's been throwing his money around, but I can't prove anything that would hold up in court. But I'm still working on the case."

Francis thanked him and rejoined Jane.

On Monday, at lunchtime, Francis waited at the back of the café hidden from the sight of the baker, Albert Blackwell, who was about to leave for the day. He followed him to his lodgings and then cycled back to work. That night, he skipped dinner and rode his bicycle to the baker's address and then went into a nearby pub. Sure enough, sometime later, Albert Blackwell and another man entered the pub and ordered drinks. The baker did not see Francis who was hidden from view by the high-backed bench seat, on which he is sitting.

The baker left at nine thirty, telling his friend he had to be up early in the morning. When he had gone, Francis went to the bar where the other man was drinking and smoking. The man looked at Francis up and down and then took a swig of his beer.

"How come a healthy lad like you has not signed up to fight the Germans?" he asked, slurring his speech and looking at him through red shot eyes.

"Unfortunately, no one will have me on account of my wound."

Silence.

"Wound?"

"Yes, I was a prisoner of war in Spain. They tortured me and broke my ankle. Franco's prisons are the worst in the world."

Francis then told him of some of the things the guards did and about the black hole.

"You poor sod! What are you doing now?"

"I'm doing nothing at the moment. I've just got out of hospital, and I'm staying with an aunt. No one seems to understand what's like to be in prison."

"You had it bad, mate. It makes a British prison sound like a cushy number."

"I wouldn't know."

"I do 'cause me and my mate were in one."

"Buy you a drink?"

"I wouldn't say no."

"What were you in for?" Francis asked casually.

"Oh burglary—me and Albert got caught in a house in Newcastle."

"What do you do now?"

"I'm a plumber, and me mate's a baker. We're out on probation and live in a house nearby. They taught us a trade inside to keep us on the straight and narrow," he said with a laugh.

Francis changed the subject to the war, rationing, and whether the Germans would invade. At closing time, he helped the drunk back to his lodgings and then rode back home.

At four thirty the next morning, Francis cycled back into Keswick and rode up the very narrow path that ran behind the café where the back entrance led to the kitchen. He hid behind some dustbins and waited. At five, Albert Blackwell rode his bicycle down the path towards the back of the shop. He was a man in his early fifties with greying hair and a large stomach that hung over his trousers.

The baker unlocked the back door, and as he turned the handle, he felt a hard push from behind and went flying into the kitchen.

"What the hell!" he shouted.

Without saying anything, Francis closed the door behind them. The baker grabbed a large metal ladle that was hanging near the oven. Francis was too fast and wrestled it away from him. He managed to wrap the ladle across the baker's throat, and he began to choke.

"Now listen very carefully to what I'm going to say. The money you stole, I want it put back."

"I didn't steal anything. You can kill me if you like, but I didn't do it!" he remonstrated.

"I don't plan to do it right now. How did you like it in prison?"

"How did you know that?"

"Let me say a little birdie told me. I have a letter in my pocket that tells the police about you. If you don't return the ten pounds to Mrs. Lambert, I will post it to Sergeant James, and your goose will be cooked. I am sure, with your record, you'll do hard time, and maybe, at your age, you will die in prison."

"All right, all right, I'll return the money if you keep your mouth shut."

"I'll keep my end of the bargain, and if you do what I want, you'll never hear from me again."

Francis released the baker and quietly left before the man could recover from his choking fit.

The next few days passed with nothing out of the ordinary happening, except for an intake of new patients. The home was at full capacity now, and the building of the extension had begun.

Francis returned to the Pack Horse Inn to see Sergeant James. The sergeant reported that, miraculously, the money had reappeared, and he had urged Mrs. Lambert to keep better daily records in the future. When Francis went to his room that night, he tore up the letter. The next day, he received a note from Mrs. Lambert, apologizing for ever suspecting him and inviting him to visit her at the café.

Soon after, Jane and her friend, Patricia Sullivan, left for their midwifery course at Guy's Hospital in London.

Sitting in his usual place by the lake one evening, he heard someone come up behind him and, imagining it was Jane returning, turned with a welcoming smile on his face.

"Hello, Francis, I thought it was you. How's the chess game? Have you played much since San Pedro?"

CHAPTER 23

Belfast, May 9, 1941

Captain Bennett sat in a jump seat of a Bristol Blenheim light bomber, which was making a supply run to RAF Aldergrove, an RAF station just outside Belfast. He had read the reports of the devastation the city had sustained but was not prepared for what he saw as the airplane circled to land. The path of destruction was mainly in the east, and there was a clear south to north corridor swathe of severe damage. The Luftwaffe had carried out two raids in April, and the final coup de grace was on May 4, which was a firestorm that set the docks and the surrounding areas on fire. What he saw below reminded him of the blitz in the East End of London.

He was met at the RAF base by Special Branch Inspector Alan Downing. (MI5 has no police powers and rely on special branch to conduct most legal searches and arrests.) The inspector was a dour man at the best of times, and the recent travails of his city were written clearly on his face as he greeted Captain Bennett. After shaking hands and exchanging a few solemn words, they got into an old car and rode into the city in silence.

Captain Bennett took in the scene as they drove through the centre of Belfast. Parts of the city had been totally demolished, and there were still smouldering fires, even four days after the last raid. He could see people collecting what they could of their belongings, putting them on carts, as they trudged zombie-like out of the city.

"Where are all these people going?" asked a pensive Captain Bennett.

"The lucky ones are going to relatives in other cities in Northern Ireland or in Ireland. The train service is still operating, so those with money are getting out of town. The poorer people are heading to the safety of the open fields outside the city. They hide in ditches at night out of fear of other air raids. It's called ditching.

"On top of all that misery, we have a real problem here now with racketeers taking advantage of people and charging high rental rates for shanty buildings. This sort of disaster really brings out the very worst in people!"

They arrived at an office building in Lisburn, which is a town southwest of Belfast. They sat down in Inspector Downing's makeshift office since his office on Belfast's Victoria Street had been destroyed.

"As I told you on the telephone, all we have to go on is a name, a Tom McClure née Francis Reagan," said Captain Bennett. "We think he might have left Belfast and gone to mainland Britain, although none of our people in any of the ports have anything on him coming over."

"I hope you catch the bastard. Someone has to pay for the havoc that has been wrought on innocent people. This city will probably never really recover. The shipyards and the aircraft factory will reopen, but many of the skilled workers have left or have been killed, along with their families," said the angry inspector.

"Trouble is he's probably not the only agent reporting to the Germans. We've had a lot of whispers that the IRA are trying to curry favour with the Germans so they can claim Northern Ireland when they invade Britain. Maybe he was part of that campaign," Captain Bennett added.

"I've been doing some checking after you phoned, and there was a Tom McClure living on Chatham Street, according to his identity card registration. He seems to have fit into the community well as he worked at Harland & Wolf and was an air-raid warden."

"Very clever. He had many opportunities to report on the layout of the yard, on what ships were there for repair, and on the damage the first raid caused," commented the captain.

"Chatham Street was wiped out in the raid on April 15 and 16. I've checked with the wardens, and he was based at a post on the Newtownards Road. It seems he disappeared shortly after the second raid. He was staying temporarily with one of the other wardens. After a couple of days, he announced that he had found a place and then just vanished.

"We've checked with the personnel department at Harland & Wolf, but their records were mostly destroyed in the raid. A Mr. Lyons remembers him only because he had come from America, which was very unusual. He was introduced to the company by a Kevin Lynch, one of the financial managers who was killed in the main raid in April. His wife, Patricia, survived and is convalescing with her sister here in Lisburn. I've arranged for us to visit her this afternoon.

"Also, a police detective sergeant told me that he was their prime suspect in the killing of a thug that was shaking down various businesses in the city. He's sending me the file on the case," Inspector Downing concluded.

That afternoon, their car pulled into a quiet cul-de-sac in Lisburn. The neat and well-maintained houses stood out in stark contrast to the desolate streets of Belfast. A number of curtains were seen to move as they got out of the car and walked to 20 Sheldon Close. They knocked on the door, which was answered by a small pale woman with her grey hair fastened in the back by a ponytail. She had dark sunken eyes which gave the impression she hadn't slept at night for a long time. The inspector showed her his warrant card.

"Mrs. Sheridan, I'm Inspector Downing, and I arranged to meet with your sister, Mrs. Patricia Lynch, today."

"Ah yes, inspector, do come in, gentlemen. She is in the front room, but before you go in there, I would ask you to be gentle and considerate of her. She is still in a fragile state of mind and gets upset very easily. The loss of her entire family has devastated her, and I don't think she will fully recover."

"We promise to be gentle."

They were shown to the front room, and sitting on one of the armchairs was Mrs. Lynch. Her head was covered with bandages, with only one eye showing. She was in a dressing gown and was wrapped in blankets. She just stared ahead without acknowledging their presence. The inspector introduced them, which drew no reaction from her. He apologised for bothering her, particularly so recently after her loss.

"We've come to ask you about a man called Tom McClure," he said gently. When she heard the name, she turned slowly and looked at them.

"Nice boy, our Tom. He came to see me in hospital. Is he all right?" she whispered in a hoarse voice.

"As far as we know, he is fine."

"Good."

"My Kevin got him a job in the shipyard."

"Oh, why did he do that?"

"His friend from university in Dublin, Dermot Williams, recommended him."

"Mrs. Lynch, do you know where we can find Tom?"

"He lives on Chatham Street with Mrs. Thompson."

"He has moved from there, and we need to talk to him urgently."

Mrs. Lynch thought for a moment. "Perhaps Rory Mitchell could tell you. I know they are friends."

"Where do I find Rory?"

"He's probably at his home on Duke Street or at his mother's in Bangor."

"Thank you, you've been very helpful."

They quietly left the room, leaving the shattered woman to her thoughts and to again stare into the distance.

"Duke Street was flattened in the raid," said the inspector as they walked up the path from the house. "We'll have to find his mother in Bangor and check whether he is still alive. Bangor is about fifteen miles from Belfast and is a seaside resort town. I'll get one of my lads to check the registrations for Bangor, and I hope there won't be many Mitchells there."

It was about four in the afternoon when one of the detective constables reported back that there were three Mitchells listed in the town. It took them about an hour and a half to reach the outskirts of Bangor. With a street map in hand, they found the first address easily, but there was no son called Rory living in the house. It was the same with second address. The last one was that of a widow, a Mrs. Andrea Mitchell, and this time, they were in luck. After identifying himself, the inspector asked whether she had a son called Rory.

"Yes," she replied cautiously. "He's in the kitchen, having his supper."

"We need to talk with him," said the inspector.

"What's he done?"

"Nothing, as far as we know. We are looking for a friend of his."

Just then, Rory came out of the kitchen.

"What's up, Mum?" he asked, seeing the two men in the front hall.

"These police officers need to ask you a few questions. Why don't you take them into the front room?"

They entered the room and sat in two wing chairs. Rory remained standing.

"How can I help you, gentlemen?"

"We are looking for a man called Tom McClure. Do you know where we can find him?"

"Hmm. The last time I saw him was the day after the big air raid in April. I was going through the rubble of a house his girlfriend lived in when he came looking for her. He was very distraught, especially when I told him that his girlfriend and her family had all been killed. I was here in Bangor, thank goodness, when the raid happened otherwise I would have been killed along with everyone else in my street. Since then, I moved back in with my mother."

"Did Tom say where he was going?"

"Not really, he was very vague about that, although he did say he might go back to Dublin."

"Is their anywhere else he would go?"

"I don't remember him mentioning anywhere else. What's he done?"

"We believe he may have been working for the Germans."

"Tom? You must be joking. He was doing his bit to help the war effort."

"We have irrefutable evidence that he did. Was there anything else that struck you about his behaviour?"

Rory thought for a moment. "Not that I can think of—no, wait a minute, he was always going for walks to the Albert Memorial Clock pretty much every day after work. I don't know why. Maybe he wanted to get some exercise."

They thanked Rory, and Inspector Downing handed him a card. "If you should think of anything else call us," he said.

When they got back in the car, they reviewed their interview with Rory.

"Why was he going to the Albert Memorial Clock? Let's check it out," said Inspector Downing.

They drove back to Belfast and parked the car on Skipper Street near the monument. They walked around it, looking for any signs. The inspector stopped when he saw two crosses in chalk on the brickwork under the wrought iron fence surrounding the tower.

"Ah, I bet these are some sort of signal, but what it means, I can't tell. I'll get one of my men to stake out this spot just in case anyone comes by and tries to contact him."

"Can we go to his old address on Chatham Street? I'm interested in taking a look at what's left of the house in case he left something behind that may help us," said Captain Bennett.

They had difficulty finding the right house because the whole street was nothing but piles of rubble. As they walked along the street, they were approached by Brian Kerr, the B-Special, who demanded to know what they were doing. Inspector Downing produced his warrant card, and the B-special blanched.

"Sorry, sir. We've had a problem with looters since the raid."

"That's fine, constable. You were right to ask us. We're looking for what remains of number 17."

"Over here, sir." The B-Special led them to what was left of the house.

"Did you know a Tom McClure who lived here?"

"Yes, sir. He came from Dublin and was one of us, if you know what I mean. He was friendly and outgoing and was one of the wardens for this area. That's all I know about him."

"Thank you, constable, we'll take it from here," the inspector said, dismissing the man.

When the B-Special was out of earshot, Captain Bennett asked, "What did he mean by 'one of us'?"

"Oh, it's a euphemism for saying he was a Protestant. In other words, he was not Catholic. That's very important in this city, which is overwhelmingly

Protestant. People here see the Catholic minority as enemies that want to unite Northern Ireland with Éire. Now let's take a look at what is left of the house."

There wasn't much to see, except the chimney and part of a wall supporting it. They found a bed at the back of the house and what remained of a man's burned suit. Underneath this were two scorched magazines. Captain Bennett picked these up and looked through them, expecting to find nothing of importance. What struck him about the magazines, though, was that they both featured holidaying in the Lake District, and he wondered why there were two magazines on the same subject. *Here's something that might be important,* he thought. They carried on their search, and on lifting the bed frame, they found the charred remains of a notebook. The inspector looked through it and could just make out a simple code book.

"Well, we have the evidence now to hang him. Now we have to find him," he said bluntly.

That evening, Captain Bennett, in his room at Thiepval Barracks in Lisburn, which was the headquarters of the British Army in Northern Ireland, began to mull over the investigation. So far, they had established that Tom McClure or Francis Reagan was an Irish national probably from Dublin. He was trained by the Abwehr at their Quenze training facility near Brandenburg. He and some British nationals had left for various British cities before the war. It was clear, from their interview with Rory Mitchell, that he was very upset with the destruction of Belfast and the deaths of so many of his friends. Had he run away from the city and from the clutches of the Abwehr in disgust at what he had been part of, or had he been sent elsewhere by the Germans?

The two magazines they had found may be a clue to his whereabouts, but he knew it was a long shot. There were many other cases pending in his in tray in London, and the colonel had only given him a few days to make progress and then wanted him to move on.

The next morning, Inspector Downing's opposite number in the Irish special branch, Insp. Peter O'Donovan, called. Captain Bennett picked up the extension to listen in to the conversation.

"Alan, I've done some checking as you asked me to do. Francis Reagan was brought up by a single mother in the tenements here in Dublin. She committed suicide after losing her job as a housekeeper for the local priest. Reagan worked at an orphanage as a clerk and, apparently, was well liked by the people there.

"However, he is wanted for the murder of that same local priest. Apparently, this priest had a predilection for young boys. The garda were warned off pursuing the case by the church because of the embarrassment it would cause if it came to trial. It looks as though they gave him a free pass on murder. He ran away after the garda interviewed him and is thought to have gone to Spain to fight in the civil war. After that, there has been nothing heard from him.

"I've checked with border control, and they have no record of a Francis Reagan or Tom McClure entering the country. That's all I've found out for now. I will let you know if find anything else. What's your interest in him?"

"We think he had something to do with spying for the Germans in Belfast and was feeding them information about targets here."

"I'll check with my IRA contacts to see whether they know anything of him. Please remember we never had this conversation because we are supposed to be a neutral country. However, I can't just stand by after the devastation that was visited on you two weeks ago without helping out."

"Thanks, Peter, we never talked."

Captain Bennett and Inspector Downing spent the rest of the day interviewing people at Harland & Wolf and the air-raid wardens who knew Francis. A picture of him emerged of a polite gracious man with an outgoing personality. He was hardworking, would help other people out, and was always willing to go that extra mile in his work. It didn't seem that he was the stereotype of a spy—secretive personality and a loner—or maybe he was just good at hiding his true traits.

Captain Bennett called Colonel Thomas. "The bird seems to have flown the coop, sir. There's not much I can do here now. It seems he might have gone to ground in Britain somewhere, and we'll just have to wait for him to pop his head up."

"Right, Mark, why don't you head home? It seems that you have hit a dead end for the moment. I need you back here because there has been some movement on the Bloemfontein case. I'll brief you when you get back."

Mark Bennett caught the next RAF flight out to the mainland. He took with him the two magazines and the notebook he had found on Chatham Street. In the back of his mind was the notion that they were important to the case, but he didn't know why.

CHAPTER 24

Derwent Hall, Keswick

Francis froze when he saw Nigel Ellis standing there. He was shocked at the sudden appearance of this man from his past. His past was something he only wanted to forget. His father was correct; he was being visited by someone from San Pedro.

His nemesis from San Pedro hobbled on crutches over to the bench and sat down. He took out a cigarette and lit it. Nigel Ellis had put on some weight since Francis had last seen him in Spain. He was still thin and stood at about the same height as Francis. In Burgos, he had always seemed distant to Francis, and although he had taught him to play chess, Francis was never comfortable around him.

Nigel liked to control situations, and when he couldn't, he would fly into a white hot rage. He always had a cruel streak and made malicious comments about some of the other prisoners. He had his favourites, especially among the younger prisoners. Francis had refused to be dragged into the man's circle of friends, and as a result, he believed that one of his beatings by the guards was the result of a deliberate petulant comment Nigel had made about him to them. He couldn't be certain, but he was pretty sure. So now he was at Derwent Hall.

"I gave you quite a shock, didn't I?" Nigel said, smiling maliciously.

"What are you doing here?" asked Francis when he had recovered from his surprise.

"I have been here for about a week, and I thought I recognised you on the couple of occasions I saw you."

"How did you get out of Spain?"

"Most of the international prisoners were eventually repatriated, and after I put some meat on my bones and recuperated, I joined the army to fight fascism again. I was posted to Egypt with the Durham Light Infantry. When the Italians started their invasion of the country, we were able to push them back, but I was wounded and shipped back to England. They had to take part of my leg off, and that's how I ended up here."

"What are your plans for the future when you get out of here?" Francis asked politely and trying to be as casual as possible.

"I applied and was accepted at St. Michael's College in Durham to study theology. I intend to become an Anglican priest. I've seen enough cruelty and man-made horror to be able to serve poor people who have no hope. Anyway, that's what I'm going to do. I was interviewed while in hospital in London and was accepted, so I start next month. Since I am a free man with no incumbents, like relatives to visit, I will spend a week in Blackpool before I go to the college."

"That sounds great, Nigel. I wish you the best of luck, and I'm sure you'll make a fine priest."

"Enough about me, how did you end up here? We all thought you were dead, at least that was what the guards told us."

Francis thought fast.

"The gestapo tried to recruit me to spy for them because I was Irish. They thought I would have an axe to grind with the British, and when I refused, they beat me up. When I woke up, I was in a dirty cell, and I thought I was going to be shot. They threw me into a cart, and I was forced, with republican prisoners, to work on a road. I was only there for a short while because, thankfully, there was an amnesty for foreign prisoners. We were put on a train to the French border.

"I ended up back in Dublin, but I couldn't find a job because of my Spanish Civil War service, which the Catholic Church herald as the defeat of the anti-Christ. So I changed my name to Patrick Duggan, and a friend of mine found me work in Belfast. Trouble was, the city was badly bombed, and my job just evaporated. I came here because I had read about the beauty of the Lake District, and I wanted peace and quiet after all that chaos and death. I'm quite happy here, and I like my job, which is, in a roundabout way, helping the war effort."

"That's interesting. After you left, we asked the camp's commandant what happened to you. He was being friendly to us because he knew we were leaving and didn't want us talking negatively about him. Turns out, those men weren't gestapo but were from the Abwehr. Also, I find it very difficult to believe you weren't shot. They were gruesome times, and the Germans didn't care about anyone who wasn't helpful to them.

"I have been in touch with Patrick Tierney and others in the Irish contingent because I was curious about what really happened to you. I asked about you and whether they heard anything. Patrick wrote back to me that he had made some inquiries and found out that you were wanted for murder in Dublin. This was news to me. So I suspected you weren't in Dublin that long, if at all.

"So you see, we were all suspicious of what happened to you. If you had told them you weren't interested in helping them at the prison, they would have put you back with us. That's what they did with Patrick when he refused to help them. Your story about being put in a labour camp doesn't make sense. Why are you lying? Did the Germans threaten you with the murder charge in Dublin?"

Francis's face reddened. He was stunned and angry that his past was catching up with him in such an unexpected and potentially lethal way.

"I don't care what other people or you think about me. What I told you was the truth," he blustered. "Yes, I had some trouble with police before I went to Spain. I won't talk about it."

He got up and began to storm off, barely able to control his anger.

"Still got the limp from Spain, I see," Nigel called after him. "Don't worry, your secret is safe with me, at least for now," he said ominously.

Francis went to his room, ignoring the greetings from other people in the halls. As he lay there on the bed, his mind was in a whirl. He knew he had to think logically and systematically. His first reaction was to run and get away before the authorities arrested him.

Then the red mist appeared, and his father was at the foot of his bed.

"Well, I was right, wasn't I? This man is no good and needs to be disposed of before he can do you any harm. He seems the blackmailing type, so you'd better be careful, but he has to be dealt with. I don't like the implied threat in his voice. If I was you, I'd play along with him until you've devised some sort of plan of action."

His father left, and Francis lay on his bed, still thinking about what action he needed to take. Was his father right? Maybe he should just play along until he came up with a solution.

The next morning, Francis was eating his breakfast and looking through the day's issue of *The Manchester Guardian*. He had almost finished the paper and was on page six when a headline screamed at him—THE DEFENCE OF BELFAST, A REALISTIC EXERCISE: WERE NAZI AGENTS WATCHING? It quoted an army major saying that they knew that they were spied upon all the time by German agents who had the freedom to come across the Irish border.

"Patrick, you look like you've seen a ghost, lad," said Mrs. Jackson as she poured him another cup of tea.

"No, no. I just realised I have forgotten to do something," he said absentmindedly as he took his cup from her and rushed into his office, leaving a startled Mrs. Jackson in his wake.

"I don't know what has gotten into the boy," she tut-tutted as she cleared the table.

Francis sat in his office and couldn't believe what he had just read. They were all closing in on him, and he didn't know what to do as his paranoia grew. After a few minutes of panic, he told himself to get control and to logically go through what he knew. Apart from Nigel Ellis, they didn't know where he was. Dealing with Nigel must be the first priority.

Francis was on his way to a staff meeting that afternoon with Dr. Morrison and others when he saw Nigel Ellis shuffling along on his crutches. "I thought today's *Guardian* article on Belfast was interesting," he said as he passed, smiling. "Let's meet after dinner at your usual spot and discuss it." With that, he was gone. It was all Francis could do to concentrate on the meeting.

After the meeting was over, Dr. Morrison pulled Francis to one side. "Patrick, you don't seem to be with us today. Is there anything wrong?"

"No, sir, I'm sorry, I have something on mind."

"If you want to talk about it, you know you can always come to me. Incidentally, one our patients, Nigel Ellis, says he knew you from your days in Spain."

"Yes, we've talked."

"I bet you spent a lot of time talking about your adventures there, eh? Try and cheer him up. Losing a leg is no easy thing to cope with."

"Yes, sir."

That evening by the lakeside, Francis sat still, wondering how he was going to solve his problem. He heard Nigel approaching, and when he settled on the bench, he turned to face Francis.

"We both know you worked for the Germans."

"That's not true."

"Don't waste time protesting your innocence with me because it won't work," he said, sneering at Francis's protest. Then there was a long silence, as if Nigel was letting his accusation sink in.

"In exchange for my silence with the authorities, I want you to make my life more bearable here. The first thing is that I expect you to give me twenty pounds so that I can fund my little trip to Blackpool and give me some spending money when I'm in college."

"But I haven't got that sort of money!" Francis protested.

"I am sure the Germans gave you some money. I bet you squirreled it away somewhere. Also, what about the wages you earn here? You're not the big-spender type, so I expect you've got some on the side.

"The second thing I want is for you to get me bottle of Scotch whiskey. This place is driving me mad, and I need a diversion.

"Where am I going to get that?"

"I am sure you will use your agent's guile to locate a source. Let me know when you have the money and the whiskey." And he left.

It was all Francis could do to control his anger. He told himself just to play along. But this situation couldn't go on. He had to find a solution.

The next morning, he deliberately came down early and sat with Mrs. Jackson, drinking tea. "You know, some weeks ago, you were very kind to me and gave me a drink of whiskey," he started to say.

"It never happened," she responded firmly.

"Quite. But is it possible to get a bottle of it as a present for a friend?" he persisted.

She looked at him and thought for a long time. "Seeing it's you, I might be able to get you some, but it will cost you."

"How much?"

"At least a fiver."

"All right. I'll give you the money at lunchtime."

"This friend must be very special," she said, fishing around for information.

"See you at lunchtime," he said, blowing her a kiss.

Two days later, Francis gave Nigel Ellis his money and the bottle of whiskey.

"I told you, you could do it. Now my next request is more difficult. I leave here in two weeks, but I want some female companionship. Do you think you can arrange that?"

"I wouldn't know where to start," said Francis cautiously.

"Think about it and let me know what you find out. Maybe one of the nurses would be interested, or would that be too close to home?"

"You leave the nurses out of this, you pervert."

"Now, now have I hit a nerve? Remember, I can spoil your little bolt hole. Find a woman for me soon, or you'll regret it!" he shouted.

Francis remembered that he had visited a run-down pub called The Crown in the poorer part of town. He had been there once when he was looking for a friendly place to frequent as his "local." However, the beer in this pub was cheap and tasted as though it had been watered down. He had mentally crossed it off his list but remembered that its customers were mostly workmen and seedy-looking men in dirty suits looking for cheap beer and companionship. Their female companions seemed very loud and dressed provocatively in ill-fitting dresses. He decided to try his luck in finding a prostitute there for Nigel Ellis.

He entered The Crown at about nine o'clock. This was the time he thought people might be more friendly and animated by the drink. He got himself a beer and sat on bench in a corner away from the other patrons and studied them. The landlord was busy reading a newspaper and took no interest in the noisy groups of customers who were laughing and telling their bawdy jokes. He only paid attention when a fight broke out and easily silenced the offenders by a pugnacious profanity-laced growl.

The work of serving customers was left to the barmaid who was, Francis thought, probably in her early thirties. She was heavy-set with large melon-shaped breasts. Her redeeming features were her long brown hair, doe-like eyes, and ready smile. He noticed that she had been eyeing him when he first came in and then, when her services were not required at the bar, came over ostensibly to wipe down his table.

"On your own then?"

He smiled. "Yes."

"Are you a copper?"

"No, far from it. I work at the convalescent home on Borrowdale Road."

"What do you do there?"

"I'm the accountant and look after the books."

"So what are doing here then? You don't look the type who usually comes in here."

"I just stumbled in here on my way back from the cinema here in town. It was a pretty boring film, and I left early. I wish there was more excitement going on. I'm tired of being cooped up all the time with sick people, and I just wanted to get away for a night. What about you?"

"Me husband was killed in the war, so I'm trying to make ends meet any way I can. Do you really want a fun time?"

"Yes."

"It'll cost you a quid, but it will be money well spent. My name, by the way, is Sara. Meet me at quarter to eleven after the pub closes, and we'll have some fun together."

After the pub closed and Sara had cleaned up, they walked a short distance out of town and along a path leading to a small cottage nestled in the side of a hill. They went to the back of the cottage and entered a large kitchen, and Sara lit a large oil lamp that cast its light over the whole room. It was a mess with unwashed dishes in the sink and on the stove. On the large kitchen table was part of a leftover meal, and next to this were some bills.

Sara went into the living room and came back with a bottle of Scotch whiskey and took two clean glasses from a Welsh Dresser.

"Here, this will loosen us up," she said with a smile as she poured two large helpings. They sat there drinking for about half an hour. "Sara, do you need extra cash to make ends meet?"

"Yes. But I don't just do it with anyone. I had a feeling you were all right the moment I set eyes on you."

Francis put a pound note on to the table. Sara smiled.

"You stay here, and I'll go and get changed," she said.

About five minutes later, she reappeared and was dressed in only a light dressing gown, which showed off her voluminous breasts, and the sight didn't leave much to the imagination. She lifted Francis to his feet and started to undress him. When he was totally naked, she slipped off her dressing gown and led him into her bedroom.

An hour later, Francis got up and slowly began to dress. Sara lay naked on her bed, watching him.

"Sara, I was wondering about helping you make money—whether you might consider having some of the patients at the home as clients that are in dire need of female company. I would only select those who I know to be honourable and treat you with honesty."

After a moment's thought, she said, "Yes, I would be willing to service them so long as you're involved in their selection. I enjoy sex with the right people, and if I make a few bob at the same time, I don't mind."

"That's great, Sara. When would be the best time to bring them to you? I have someone in mind."

"My night off is Monday, so why don't we make it then, say eight?"

"Fine, I'll see you then."

Cycling back to the hospital, Francis couldn't believe what he had just done. It was bad enough paying for sex, but he had just arranged to pimp for her. He rationalised it by telling himself that it was all in a good cause to keep Nigel Ellis at bay until he had worked out how he was going to deal with his threats. He only had two more weeks before Nigel was to leave.

Maybe that would be the best time to move on again. It was only a matter of time before the intelligence service caught up with him. That article in the newspaper clearly said that they knew there were spies in Belfast, so soon enough, they will check on all Irishmen from Belfast living on the mainland of Britain. The national registration cards would give them the information they wanted. He had to get a new ID somehow.

The next day, he told Nigel Ellis that he had found a woman he could visit. He explained that she was available on Monday nights, and Francis would drive him there in the Austin van the hospital owned. Francis had often run errands for Dr. Morrison and had ferried patients to the railway station in Keswick when they had finished their treatment. On that Monday, he arranged to pick Nigel up in the mews so that their movements wouldn't attract attention.

They drove to the cottage, and Francis knocked on the front door. Sara answered the door, and Francis introduced Nigel Ellis. "I'll call back at nine thirty for you," he told Nigel. He smiled at Sara and walked back to the car. He drove into Keswick and went to the Pack Horse Inn.

At nine fifteen, he set off for Sara's cottage. When he got there, he honked the car horn and waited. Ten minutes later, Nigel Ellis appeared, and they drove back to the hospital.

"I must say Sara is quite a woman. She taught me things I didn't know. It was a great evening," he said with a wry smile.

Francis just drove in silence.

The evening repeated itself several more times before the day finally dawned when Nigel was to leave.

During the intervening two weeks, Francis had formulated a plan of escape from Keswick. The idea had come to him suddenly one evening. It was so simple but involved some risk. He had reconnoitred the locations from which he was about to put his plan into action.

Francis drove up to the front of the convalescent home at seven thirty the next morning. He put Nigel's cases in the back of the van. As they drove off, Nigel turned to Francis, "I promised Sara that I would drop in to say goodbye to her."

"But you have a train to catch," said a worried Francis.

"There's always the next one," Nigel replied. "Just do as you are told."

They reached the cottage, and Nigel disappeared inside. Very soon afterwards, he came hobbling back as fast as he could down the path with a welt over one eye and a bleeding nose.

"Her husband isn't dead. He came back on leave!"

Francis laughed to himself as they drove away. He reckoned that Sara had pulled the wool over all their eyes and good luck to her.

"You knew her husband wasn't dead, didn't you, you bastard?" said an angry Nigel. "I'm going to get my own back on you. You'll regret ever being born."

They drove on in silence.

As they passed some woods, Francis said he had to relieve himself and drove up a lane that was hidden from the road. Nigel decided to join him, and when his back was turned, Francis picked up a heavy stone and brought it down several times hard on his head.

Francis looked around to make sure there was nobody in sight. Apart from a distant cry of a pheasant, everything was quiet. The mist off the fells was settling on the lower valleys and hid from view the mischief that was unfolding in the woods.

Francis showed no emotion, knowing exactly what he had to do. He went to the van and put on a workman's overalls so that he would not get blood on his clothes. At first, he went through Nigel's pockets and retrieved his identification card and his wallet and in its place put Patrick Duggan's card. He lay out an old blanket on the ground and wrapped the body in it. He tied off the bundle with some telephone wire he had found in the storeroom at the home using pliers to twist and cut the wire. Once he was satisfied that the body was well wrapped and would not leak any blood, he dragged the corpse to the van and manhandled it into the back.

He picked up the blood-soaked rock he had used and also put it in the back of the van. He closed the van's rear doors and checked for anything left behind. He knew the rain would wash away any blood on the ground, so he was not concerned about that. Once he was satisfied there was nothing left to indicate that this was a place of violence, he got into the van and drove off.

Francis drove through Keswick and headed for the small village of Newlands. The journey was uneventful, except when he had to stop to enable a farmer to drive his sheep along the road to a new pasture. Although this was frustrating and nerve-racking, Francis was ice cold and focused on what he had to do. After he had passed through Newlands, he found the small track he had reconnoitered earlier. It ran upwards for about a mile through some woods, and when this was cleared, the track levelled out on a ridge which overlooked the valley below.

Alongside the track, there was a dilapidated building. This had been the wheelhouse for an old copper mine, which had been long since abandoned. The forty-five-foot wheel had been used to lift the copper and miners from the mine floor which was a hundred feet or so below. Although the wheel was no longer there, the remains of the building protected people from falling down the mine shaft, which had since partly filled with water. This was an ideal hiding place for a body.

Francis backed the van as close to the building as he could. He pushed open the building's door and made sure nothing had been disturbed from when he was there two days before. He had moved the old timbers that had been laid across the shaft. He threw the body over one shoulder and took it into the building. He went out to the van again and, with difficulty, lifted a heavy iron vice, which he had found on the floor in the convalescent home's storeroom in the stables, and placed it on floor next to the body. He then strapped it to body with some more wire so that the weight would help sink the corpse once it hit the water.

As soon as these preparations were complete, he carried out a last-minute check to make sure everything was in place. Then he pushed the swaddled corpse over the edge of the shaft, and after a few seconds, he heard a satisfactory splash. He took off his workman's overalls, bundled them around the stone he had used to kill Nigel Ellis, and also threw them down the shaft. He put the timbers back in place across the shaft and closed the door.

When he got back to the van, Francis then opened the suitcase and found two large envelopes full of papers in the top of it. He quickly went through them. A third envelope included instructions on when and how to report to St. Michael's College in Durham and a military travel warrant. There was also a letter from a hotel in Blackpool, confirming a reservation addressed to Nigel Ellis at the convalescent home. He took the envelopes and closed up the case.

Francis drove the van back again into Keswick and to the railway station. He put the bag in the left luggage office and, using the travel warrant, purchased a single ticket to Blackpool, which would indicate to the authorities that Nigel Ellis had left Keswick that day. Finally, he drove back to the convalescent home and continued with his work for the rest of the day. It had been barely three hours since he had left, and no one had missed him.

That evening, he wrote a letter to the hotel in Blackpool, cancelling his reservation, saying that his plans had changed, and enclosed five pounds as compensation. He went over all the printed materials about St. Michael's College he found in the suitcase. He committed to memory the details of Nigel's life from his birth certificate, as well the adoption papers listing his home, and the death certificates of his adopted parents, who had been killed in a car accident in 1938. He studied their family photographs and letters. Also, there were a school certificate and higher school certificate from the Durham University Examinations Board.

After dinner that night, he went to his usual spot by the lake where he did most of his thinking. Overall, his plan had gone well. He had decided to take Nigel Ellis's position at the divinity school. This plan would finally shake off any pursuit from the authorities, and he could really disappear. He had covered his tracks well, and this was the opportunity he was looking for. Nigel Ellis was supposed to report to the college at the end of the following week, and this would give him a chance to plan his departure.

He didn't mind becoming an Anglican priest; in fact, he relished the thought. He had admired Canon McWilliams in Belfast and knew that he could be of help to people who were in need of advice and guidance. He had met the canon's wife when he had dinner with them one night and found them to be dedicated people enthusiastically tackling their calling. He believed that by becoming an Anglican priest, he would be able to hide successfully forever from his pursuers.

The following week was uneventful. He had his office working like clockwork, and everything had become routine. In fact, he had become bored, although he enjoyed the people.

* * *

The telephone on Captain Bennett's desk in London gave a shrill ring. He was just finishing a report on the interrogation of some German agents caught in Coventry.

"Yes?"

"Captain Bennett, this is Inspector Downing from Belfast."

"Hello, Inspector, any new developments in the McClure case?"

"Maybe. You remember that friend of his Rory Mitchell? Well, he came to see me today. He remembered something that might help us track down him down, but it's a long shot. Apparently, McClure was in hospital after a vicious beating he received from a thug and his gang. Anyway, he did a lot of reading there and was particularly taken with the Lake District and told Mitchell that he would like to go there someday. Maybe that's where he's hanging out."

"I'll get this checked out. Thanks."

"I hope you get the sod!"

* * *

One evening, Francis was in the Pack Horse, having a drink, when Sergeant James came up to him and sat down. Francis had become quite friendly with the older man, and they had spent time talking.

"What's new?" Francis asked.

"We got word my son is coming home on leave next week, and the missus is running around like a broody hen. I'm glad to get out of the house."

"That'll be fun for you both," said Francis.

"Patrick, there is something you can help me with. We got teletype from London, asking the police in the Lake District to locate a Tom McClure from Belfast. Have you ever come across this man?"

Francis's stomach churned, although, outwardly, he didn't show his shock at the news.

"No, I haven't. What's he done?"

"I have no idea, but it must be pretty big for them to contact us. We're pretty much of backwater as far as serious crime is concerned. A Capt. Mark Bennett of military intelligence wants us to interview all Irishmen in our area in case he's here. I doubt he's here myself, but we have to conduct these interviews."

"I'll keep my eye out for him," said a panicked Francis.

When he got to his room that evening, he started to pack his things in his rucksack, ready for an early start in the morning. The first train to Penrith left at six in the morning, and from there, he could travel to Carlisle and then on to Durham.

*   *   *

Superintendent Bradbury was a typically impatient man, and he didn't like pressure from his superiors, so he made everyone under him suffer from his angst. He was in charge of South Cumbria Police Division based in Kendal, which included Keswick. He was going to make sure this German agent wasn't on his patch, and so he had visited all police stations in his division, going through their files with the inspectors in the hope of not finding anything. His division had located six and had broadly cleared them. However, the superintendent was not happy and insisted that each of them be interviewed again, so Sergeant James called in to the convalescent home several days later to talk to Francis.

Dr. Morrison met him in the reception and told him that Patrick Duggan had vanished several days before without leaving a note about where he was going. The sergeant searched Francis's room, uncovering nothing.

In London, Captain Bennett received the news of Patrick Duggan's flight with a great deal of frustration. The police superintendent said that one of his sergeants had become friendly with the man and had mistakenly tipped him off that the search was on. He had a description and arranged for a general alert to put out, but he knew the trail was cold.

Three days previously, Francis had gotten off the train in Durham and walked up the hill towards its magnificent cathedral. After asking directions twice, he found the entrance to St. Michael's College, and the gatekeeper directed him to the student reception area. Here, he was asked to take a seat, and after a while, a tall priest who was in his sixties bounded into the reception.

"I'm glad to see you, Nigel," a jovial Rev. John Prentice, the college's warden, greeted Francis. "Now let's get you started. Come and meet the other fellows you'll be studying with."

And with that, he strode off again, with Francis following behind.

CHAPTER 25

Notting Dale, London, October 1956

A damp cold was creeping into the drab and menacing streets of Notting Dale as October was nearly at an end and winter proper would emerge to hold everyone in its icy grip until the end of April. This added to the already bleak and ashen landscape in this forgotten corner of London.

The frigid weather would soon usher in smogs caused by coal burning in fireplaces of homes throughout the city when windless conditions prevailed. Londoners called these "pea soupers."

Thirty-five-year-old Rev. Nigel Ellis (née Francis Reagan) sat behind his large oak desk in his study in the vicarage, which was next to the church. It was eight fifteen in the evening, and a coal fire gave out welcoming warmth as he prepared his Sunday sermon.

His church was named St. Hubert's and was on Latimer Road. Being a priest secretly amused him in an ironic way, especially when he was in a mellow mood with a Scotch whiskey in hand. Francis had successfully hidden away from the authorities by becoming a priest, and this disguise made him feel safe, particularly as the years went by. What amazed him was that he really enjoyed his work.

This was his first parish. It had a small congregation, and its parishioners were drawn from both Notting Dale and North Kensington, although he hadn't had many service attendees from the former. North Kensington was a middle-class neighbourhood of neat homes. The residents there were made up of mainly skilled tradesmen, as well as shop and clerical workers. His duties in this part of his parish were more straightforward and traditional in comparison to the needs of his parishioners in Notting Dale.

The contrast between North Kensington and Notting Dale, which were just streets apart, couldn't have been more striking. Francis had spent a lot of time visiting parishioners in Notting Dale where the need was more critical for his guidance. He had had some success counselling some families. He had married some of the young people, baptised their children, and buried many of their old.

Notting Dale was a working-class slum area made up of terraced houses and tenements which had seen better days. Many of them were in disrepair, with windows that were broken and roofs that leaked. There was no indoor plumbing. Residents had to use outdoor privies and collected water from standpipes in the street. The area had been famous for brick making and piggeries in the in the eighteenth and nineteenth centuries, but these industries had long gone. The people who were there now were mostly the ancestors of poor Irish and English workers who helped build Britain's railways.

Notting Dale reminded Francis of the Dublin tenements of his youth. The depressing colourless streets were similar to those of his boyhood. There was outright poverty, crime, drunkenness, gangs, and fights. But even with all this, there was a sense of community, with people helping each other whenever they could. It was a closed society in that the residents always kept to themselves, watched out for each other, and hated strangers.

It had taken about five years or so for him to be accepted in the neighbourhood. He was known in the community for his sound advice, ready jokes, and easy-going personality. But everyone knew that they could not pull the wool over the eyes of the vicar, and those who tried had been easily found wanting. This shrewdness had commanded respect and street creditability.

For his part, Francis knew that to proselytise to these desperate people was a useless exercise and would cause untold resentment. He knew that the Christian religion was not about just going to church on Sundays; it was about living as best you could by following the teachings of Christ. He understood that Christianity and morals have to come from within a person and could not be forced on anyone. He had to accept the mores of the community. He began to slowly chip away at the more egregious parts of their lives so that, in this way, he could help them be more meaningful Christians. He realised that his role was mainly as a social worker, and he was determined to help relieve some of the poverty and the conditions that had a depressing downtrodden effect on its residents.

Francis had cajoled the diocese into funding a soup kitchen once a week. This had been a great success after a slow beginning because there was a strong hostility to anything that was seen as charity. By force of his own personality, he had overcome the residents' resistance by presenting these occasions as parish dinners and asking them to pay a penny. As a result, they had become the focal point of the area's weekly social calendar. In just sitting down to a meal with people, he heard about some of the issues that bothered them the most and was able to give advice.

Harking back to his Dublin youth, he had also started a youth soccer team, which played in Avondale Park, and he ran a youth programme in the basement of the church. Many of the children in Notting Dale came to these activities as it was an outlet for them from their austere and poverty-stricken lives.

However, the racial makeup of the residents of Notting Dale and parts of Notting Hill had changed considerably since he had arrived eight years before. The area had slowly become a cauldron of racial resentment and hate waiting for the inevitable fuse to be lit.

Great Britain had seen a great influx of immigrants after the Second World War, particularly from the West Indies. These people had been encouraged to come to the country by the British government because of a large labour shortage following the war. They were poor and had settled in parts of the country where they could afford the rents. In London, this meant places like Brixton and Notting Dale. They took on menial and low-paid work, despite many of them being professionally qualified or skilled tradesmen.

There was a general animosity towards West Indians by white working-class people. Many believed that they were taking jobs from white people, and this anger was particularly evident when it came to housing. Because of the bombing during the war, there was a vast shortage of housing in London, and this resulted in great competition for affordable housing. The racial prejudice faced by West Indians from landlords made finding accommodation almost impossible for them. As a result, they were forced into very substandard houses owned by slum landlords, such as Peter Rachmen, himself a Polish immigrant. These slum landlords were the only people to offer immigrants a place to live, although at exorbitant rents.

Underlying this was the perceived sexual prowess of West Indian men by white men. This sexual jealousy was aggravated when a number of white women started to date coloured men, and some of them had married. The Caribbean flamboyance and happy-go-lucky attitude compared favorably with the dour demeanour of their often drunk white counterparts. Most pubs in the area would not serve coloured men, and they had resorted to having their own illicit drinking clubs where the music parties would last all night. This also attracted white women who were out for a good time. And thus, the white community regarded any white woman who consorted with a coloured man a prostitute.

On the seamier side, it was true that some of the more disreputable members of the Caribbean community were pimps for white prostitutes.

A number of these women had flats in the neighbourhood where they entertained their clients.

All these factors were a recipe for a dangerous mix in such a small area of London. White anger was evident in the growing number of beatings by gangs of Teddy Boys, who often attacked or harassed coloured people. The Teddy Boys were the new teenage subculture in many poor areas of the country, and they had a growing reputation for their antisocial behaviour. They were so called because of their distinctive clothes of long jackets in the Edwardian style, drainpipe trousers, string ties, brocaded waistcoats, creped-soled shoes, and their quaffed hairstyles. They usually roamed in gangs and took out their angst on anyone who got in their way. West Indians were an easy target.

This was the societal background Francis had to deal with on a daily basis. It worried him that there could be an explosion of racial violence as had happened in the south of the United States of America. Despite the challenges in his parish, he had worked hard to defuse the growing friction that was developing. But he was a lone voice. The diocese turned a deaf ear to his protests, and he was regarded by them as a radical.

Francis sat back in his chair and reflected on his good fortune. He had come a long way from the Dublin tenements of his childhood, escaping the police, through two wars, and ended up in divinity school. He was naturally intelligent and had relished the academic challenges it had presented. Now in his spare time, he had begun to study the history of the Celts at the British Museum in London. He was very happy with his progress. When he had finished his divinity studies, he became a curate for four years at a church in Hammersmith, which was also a poor area of London with mainly an Irish population. After his curacy period, he asked for a parish in a poor area of London and was assigned to St. Hubert's.

Francis had never married, and he told anyone who questioned him about it that he was too busy helping his parish family. The truth was he had not met anyone who interested him since Jane Stevens, the nurse in the Lake District. Also, he knew he had too many secrets to hide from a spouse who would question his moods and want to dig too deeply into his past. There had been women in Durham, and again in Hammersmith, but they had not matched up to Jane, whom he truly loved. Jane had been different. She had accepted who he was and was not judgmental. They had discussed many things, but she had never delved into his past. Maybe it was her upbringing in the East End of London where people took you on face value for who you were.

He still had the limp in his right leg and had put on some weight. He had grown a beard which had turned out to be red. He had now completely lost his Irish accent, and it only came out these days when he got very excited or lost his temper, which were both very infrequent. He hadn't been haunted by his father since his last few days in Keswick, when he was stressed out by the appearance of the real Nigel Ellis. No, he was happy in himself and was truly satisfied with his life.

He was brought out of his thoughts by several desperate rings of the front doorbell. He reluctantly left the warmth of his study and walked down the cold corridor to the front door. When he opened it, he saw John Williams, one of his West Indian parishioners, covered in blood from cuts on his face.

"John, what happened to you?"

He caught the man as he staggered through the door. He sat him down in the chair in the front hall. Francis quickly looked at him and then went out of the front door, carrying a cricket bat he picked up from the umbrella stand. He peered into the darkness. After his eyes adjusted to the dark, he made out six teenagers at the corner of the street. He marched up to them, and his large size and weapon frightened the group who backed off to a safe distance.

"Now what the hell's going on?" he demanded.

"That nigger got what he deserved," said the bravest of the group. "They come here and steal our jobs, take our homes, and fuck our women. It's about time these spades were sent back to where they came from!"

The rest of group nervously sniggered.

"That's a load of rubbish! You're just cowards!" said the angry priest. "You pretend that's the reason, but the truth is you don't get off your lazy backsides and look for work! I recognise some of you, and unless you go home right now, I'm going to call the police and then see your parents. Now go!"

As he said that, he began to march towards them with his bat ready to swing in their direction. The boys ran, calling out racial slurs as they went, and threatened to beat up the priest.

Francis went back to the vicarage.

"They've gone. Let's take a look at you," he said to the frightened man.

He helped John into his study and sat him down by the fire. He fetched a bowl of water and a cloth from the kitchen and began to clean off the blood from the cuts. All this time, John Williams was whimpering uncontrollably.

"Now sit here a while, get warm and try to calm down," he said gently.

John Williams was a young man in his mid-twenties. He was slight and wore glasses, which gave him a studious look. He was dressed in workman's overalls and was a cleaner at Hammersmith Hospital.

When Francis returned from taking the bowl back to the kitchen, he poured two Scotch whiskeys from a decanter on the sideboard.

"I think you need this. Tell me what happened."

John took a gulp from his whiskey glass and let the liquid burn his throat as he swallowed it. He felt a little better but just stared into the fire. After a little while, he turned and looked at the vicar.

"I was coming out of Latimer Road tube station and walking home on Bramley Road when these lads surrounded me and started to pummel me. I tried to fight back, but it was no good. There were too many of them. Then I saw my chance, and I ran as fast as I could. They were catching up with me, and your church was the nearest place I could reach," the frightened man sobbed.

"John, just calm down. I suggest you stay here for the night because they may be waiting for you to come out of here. You can sleep on my sofa. Have you eaten yet?"

"No."

"Neither have I. What do you say to some shepherd's pie?"

Francis went into the kitchen and checked the pie in oven. He laid the kitchen table.

When they sat down to eat, Francis turned to John and said, "Tell me more about yourself. How did you end up here in London? Where are you from?"

John didn't reply. He just looked at his plate.

Then reluctantly, he began, "I was born and lived in Antigua. I came here three years ago, vicar. I am a trained accountant, and I lost my job in my country when the sugar mill there closed. I couldn't find any work, so I thought I might come to London and get a job in my profession.

"Many of us thought that, and the British government encouraged us to come because there was a shortage of workers. We were in for a shock. People here hated us because of our colour. We couldn't get jobs in the professions for which we had the qualifications. I'm now just a janitor, and others have jobs the white man doesn't want," he said.

"Where do you live now?"

Silence.

"Come on, John, tell me more. You know what you tell me won't be told to another person. Your private thoughts are safe with me. How can I help you if you won't say?"

"You can't help me, Vicar. If you get involved, it would only mean trouble."

"I promise I won't make trouble for you. But I can't just let you leave here without you giving me some clue as to what's going on. You're a bright man, so what you say is important to me so that I can understand some of the problems coloured people have here," he said earnestly.

Silence.

"All right. I know you are someone I can trust. When we arrived in London full of hope, we couldn't rent a flat for love nor money. There were signs in the windows of houses which often said 'No Irish, No Blacks, No Dogs' or simply 'No Coloureds.' I spent my first year here living on the streets or going to homeless shelters. Those were tough times. Eventually, I found a landlord in Notting Hill who would rent a flat to me, although it was in a basement. It was damp, and I had to share it with six other men. Still, it was a roof over my head and a start.

"I moved last year to my place on Morgan Road and share it with four other West Indian men. The rents are high, and they are very strict about payments. Miss one payment and you're out!"

"Yes, I have heard similar accounts," said Francis. "Have you ever thought about complaining to one of the rent tribunals, which could help set your rent at a reasonable level?"

"With all due respect, Vicar, that would be the kiss of death for us because we would be out on our ear. The bully boys would make sure we were kicked out and we wouldn't be able to find another place to live in the area."

"But the law wouldn't allow this!"

"Maybe not, but these landlords take no notice of the law. They have a way of making sure you toe the line or else. We're stuck."

It was Francis's turn to remain silent. After a bit, he said, "What can be done to stop this kind of behaviour?"

"There's a long list of things, really. But I suppose number one is getting more houses for poor people, black or white, and, therefore, reduce the number of us living in these squalid conditions. People's attitudes towards coloured people need changing. I don't know how you do this. When was the last time you saw a policeman down here? The police also hate coloured people. They should protect us from the hooligans you saw tonight. The only time we see them is when they raid one of our clubs," said John angrily.

"I think the first thing you have to do is to arrange for at least three of you to meet at the tube station and walk home together," suggested the vicar. "These wretches are cowards and will not attack you when there are several of you. I know it's not right because you should be able to walk down the street alone without the fear of attack, but it's a practical solution for your own safety."

"But how long do we need to do this? We should make a stand and not be bullied!" John responded.

"Let me talk to the police and see what they will do."

They continued to discuss and argue about the rotting state of Notting Dale until eleven. John helped clear the dinner table and dry the washed dishes. The vicar fetched a pillow and blankets from the upstairs hall cupboard and set them on the sofa in his study. He wished John good night and went to his room.

Francis came down at seven the next morning and found that John Williams had already left. The blankets were neatly folded and left on the sofa.

As he prepared his breakfast, he thought about the worsening situation in Notting Dale and Notting Hill. It was clear that the current social unrest had been primarily caused by a housing situation which was getting worse, not better. The government had promised to build new homes, but there was no evidence of this. It left people like him who were in the trenches, so to speak, little room to manoeuvre to try and keep a lid on the situation. Even if there was no housing problem, there was that underlying racial tension which would be difficult to diffuse. The one truth was he and others had no control over the situation. He saw that it was only time before the Caribbean community would hit back, and there would be mayhem on the streets, which would lead to even more victims.

He decided to make reconciliation and learning to live with one another the subjects of his Sunday sermons. He should talk to other ministers and social workers in the area to get some more ideas on how to deal with the mounting tensions. Perhaps they should all see their local member of parliament and voice their concerns. And what about the police?

Later that morning, he walked down Silchester Road on his way to serve communion to a bedridden parishioner. The three-story houses in this road were mostly of brick that had seen better days. This was a white working-class neighbourhood which hadn't yet been integrated with West Indian immigrants. Seventy-year-old Mrs. Welden had lived in her flat for more than forty years and had outlived three husbands. She had three children and four grandchildren. All the grandchildren had been baptised by Francis.

She was a stalwart of the St. Hubert parish until a stroke had crippled her. She had been responsible for supporting the vicar in his outreach to this neighbourhood when he had first arrived, and it was thanks to her introductions to her neighbours that he was able to make some headway with the community. He had a lot to be thankful to her for. He always enjoyed seeing her because she always regaled him of stories from the London Blitz.

As he walked down the road, he was conscious of being watched by unseen faces behind ragged curtains. Every so often, he would hear the rumble of the tube line which was above ground in this section of the line. When he reached Mrs. Welden's building, he saw a young man whom he recognised sitting on the stoop at the front door.

"Hello, Raymond. What are you doing here? Shouldn't you be at work?"

"Nah, Vicar. The missus went into labour, and I had to get the midwife. She's up there now. She told me to leave and wait downstairs. She's a real bossy boots, I can tell you!"

"The baby is going to be your third, right?"

"Our fourth. Although I've done this before, I still get nervous."

"Well, good luck. I am going to see Mrs. Welden right now."

He entered the house and climbed the stairs to the first floor and knocked on one of the doors to a flat. Without waiting for a reply, he went in and called out to Mrs. Welden. She replied, and he went to her bedroom.

"Hello, dear, how are you?"

"I'm fine. I just saw Raymond Jones downstairs. It seems he will be a father again today."

"Yes. Sally went into labour early this morning. Please put the kettle on before we start."

About ten minutes later, they heard a healthy cry of a baby from the flat upstairs.

"There we go. Sounds like all's well!" said Mrs. Welden.

Francis stayed talking to Mrs. Welden for another thirty minutes and then told her he must go to visit someone else.

As he closed the flat door behind him, a woman with a medicine bag was coming down the stairs. He looked up and smiled. He was surprised at who he saw.

"Jane, is that you?" he asked when he got his breath back.

"Patrick!"

CHAPTER 26

Francis just stared at Jane. She looked older, and there were wisps of grey in her hair. She was just as slim as he remembered, but her face had a careworn look. She was dressed in a nurse's uniform, and her overcoat was regulation navy blue. He saw that she wore no wedding ring, and this gave him great relief.

"Well, are you going to just stand there and not say anything?" she teased as she smiled broadly.

Francis grabbed and hugged her.

"I never thought I'd ever see you again. This is wonderful" was all he could say.

"What's with you and the dog collar?" she said as she held him at arm's length, looking him up and down.

"That's a long story. Have you got time for a cup of tea? My vicarage is just a few streets away."

"Of course. I'll have to make it quick, though, because I need to get back to the hospital."

When they reached the vicarage, they went to the kitchen, and Francis put on the kettle.

"Now tell me, Patrick, what has happened to you in the last thirteen years?"

"Quite a lot. It's so great to see you after all these years. My name is really Nigel Ellis. I used the name Patrick Duggan as a cover because I was in trouble with the police in Belfast," he reluctantly lied. "I left the convalescent home in Keswick about a year after you did to go to a divinity college in Durham," he said.

"I hope it wasn't serious trouble with the police."

"They were looking to blame me for the murder of a gang leader there. It wasn't me, but I had to disappear for a while. Later, I heard that they had arrested and convicted another man for the crime. So I was off the hook.

"When I left college, I was posted to Hammersmith as a curate and then here as the vicar."

Francis picked up the tray of teacups, milk, sugar, and the teapot with a large cosy on it. They went into the study and sat down. He poured two cups and handed one to Jane.

"Now what about you? What have you been doing all these years?"

"After I finished my midwifery course, I got a job on the ocean liner *Queen Elizabeth* as a nurse. We did go to some exotic places, and it was exciting at first, but I was bored with the work and fed up with many of the patients I saw who had ridiculous requests and more money than sense. They were spoiled and very demanding. After taking this abuse for two years, I left and got a job as a midwife in the gynaecological department at Hammersmith Hospital. This is more my line of work, helping people who really need and appreciate what you can do for them. It's very tiring but very fulfilling."

"I'm surprised we haven't bumped into each until now."

"I don't usually cover this area. Acton is the neighbourhood I'm responsible for. I'm covering Notting Hill because the midwife for this area has left, and they haven't yet filled her position."

Jane finished her tea and got up to go.

"I must go back to the hospital," she said.

"Perhaps we could meet for dinner and have a longer chat. How about this Friday?" Francis asked.

"I'm on duty until Sunday night. Could we make it Monday night?"

"That's fine. When and where should I pick you up?"

"Seven is fine. I live in a small flat near the hospital." She wrote the address on a piece of paper she retrieved from her pocket and handed it to Francis.

For the rest of that week, Francis was on top of the world, and he went about his work with renewed vigour. On Sunday, at his eleven-o-clock service, he gave the sermon of his life, and many of his parishioners commented on how the vicar seemed very happy and more enthusiastic than ever. Some of the older women said that he had found a girlfriend. After all, he was seen walking and talking to that new midwife earlier the previous week. They nodded knowingly to each other.

Monday evening finally came, and he rang the bell at Jane's flat precisely at seven. She greeted him with a warm smile. She was attractively dressed in a dark skirt, a long-sleeved pink sweater, and high-heeled shoes. The little makeup she was wearing enhanced her most alluring features, her mouth and her large brown eyes.

"I'm glad to see that you are not wearing your dog collar for our date!" she teased.

They walked down to the White City underground station and caught a Central Line train to the Holland Park station. From there, they walked towards Clarendon Road, and on the corner of that street and Holland Park Avenue was a small French bistro. The maître d' showed them to a small table by the window. The waiter brought them a carafe of white wine, and then in the very relaxed atmosphere, they started to catch up with each other.

Jane had had a few boyfriends and, in fact, nearly married one. It seemed that just as she was getting close to someone, they were torn apart by her erratic schedule, which made great demands on her time and energy.

"When you met me the other day, it was my first time in Notting Dale," Jane said during a lull in their conversation. "I must say it is the most derelict neighbourhood I have ever seen. I was brought up in the East End, and I thought parts of Brixton and Bermondsey were bad, but this section takes the cake. It's as if the world has forgotten about it. How do you help people who live in such abject poverty with no hope of improving their lot in life?"

"It is hard going, and you take tiny steps at a time. Many of the people have hearts of gold once you get to know them. The biggest problem we have is the growing number of Caribbean people who have come to live in the neighbourhood because they can't afford to live elsewhere. They have become victims of unscrupulous slum landlords, such as Peter Rachman and André Baudin. There is a built-in resentment by whites of coloured people, and one day, it's going to result in violence on a large scale. They are wonderful people, but in the societal mix with white people, it's like oil and water."

"But what do the authorities do to help?"

"Nothing. These landlords tread a legally fine line, and when they can't get their way, they use muscle to intimidate recalcitrant tenants. There are these rent tribunals, but no one yet has complained to them out of fear of retribution. It's a vicious cycle."

They talked about their work and got into a deep discussion about the government's housing policy and its serious deficiencies. Francis was thrilled that he could talk with someone who shared the same ideas and kept up with current affairs.

After dinner, they caught the underground back to the White City and walked to Jane's flat. At her door, she turned to him. "Thank you for a wonderful evening. I would invite you in, but this is a one-room flat, and my flatmate has an early call in the morning. She is going to her family's home this weekend, so why don't you come over, say Friday, and I'll make us some dinner."

"That would be great. I'll bring some wine, and we'll make an evening of it."

Jane put her arms around Francis and said, "Thank you so much. I'm thrilled we met again. I missed you." And with that, she kissed him on his lips, and he responded.

A passing policeman surprised them. "Now, now, you two, it's time to move on."

Jane blushed and pushed him away. She unlocked her door and disappeared, blowing a kiss as she went.

That Friday, they spent the evening in bed, making up for lost time, or so they joked. Jane was a thoughtful lover and knew how to slowly and gently guide them both to raptures of pure ecstasy as they came together. In between bouts of lovemaking, they would sit exhausted on the bed and drink the wine Francis had brought. He didn't leave the flat until early next morning.

The next six months were a whirl of excitement and frustration. Jane would spend some evenings at the vicarage when she could. Her schedule was so intense, and Francis soon knew what her other boyfriends must have felt. His schedule was almost as bad. He would be called out at all times of the night and day. They just enjoyed each other when they could, and it worked out for both of them because they understood the other's passion for their work.

Jane had managed to get assigned to Notting Dale and parts of Notting Hill so they were able to meet more often. When she was in the area, she would often call in for a quick cup of tea and then fly out to another assignment.

One day, Francis was sitting in his study at the vicarage, thinking about his relationship with Jane. It had been truly breath-taking. When they were apart, he sorely missed her and was elated when she called in unexpectedly. It wasn't just the sex that attracted him to her but her company, even in the most trivial events, like the time she had helped with the parish jumble sale. She had spent time helping him and the volunteers price the sale items. He felt that their relationship had gone far as it was going to go, and he was determined to take it one step farther and ask Jane to marry him.

They were in their favourite restaurant one late summer evening, and after dinner, he suggested they go for a walk. As they strolled arm in arm in Holland Park, she was laughing about some of the antics her patients' husbands got up to when their wives were giving birth. He found the stories amusing, but his thoughts were elsewhere. She stopped.

"All right, Nigel, what's the matter?"

"I've been thinking for a long time about our relationship."

"What about it?" she asked cautiously. "What's wrong with it?"

"Absolutely nothing. Jane, I love you deeply, and I want to marry you."
She looked stunned.

"I'm in love with you too, but I think marriage would be out of the question. I don't want to hurt you because I know you will get tired of me and my lifestyle, and I wouldn't blame you. What, with our work, we see little of each other as it is. I can't give up my profession. People need me."

"I'm not suggesting that you should, just in the same way I cannot. I don't expect you to be a housewife and stay at home, far from it. You should do what you want. We have a very strong relationship, and I just want to seal it by marrying you. At least we will see more of each other if we lived under the same roof and certainly more than we do now. What do say, Jane?"

"I'll have to think about it, Nigel."

Now it was his turn to be stunned. They walked on in silence.

When Francis saw her to her door that evening, he said, "I am sorry to upset you. Maybe it is a bad idea, but please give it some thought."

"I will." She kissed him on the cheek, smiled, and went in.

Francis felt distraught over his marriage proposal. Maybe he was pushing her too hard and had been too premature in his proposal. In truth, he had expected her to accept but was shocked at her reluctance. He desperately wanted to put back the clock and go on as before. But he knew this was dreaming, and he had to deal with the reality of what he had done.

The following week was a living hell of uncertainty. He had morosely gone about his work—taking communion classes, visiting the sick, and conducting services—but his heart wasn't in it. What made it worse was that Jane never came by for her usual tea and had not contacted him. Clearly, she was upset and taking her time to reach a decision, but it was killing him.

That Friday, he threw all caution to the wind and knocked on her flat door. Her flatmate answered, and he found out that she had gone home for the weekend. Now he was in a state. Had he driven her away by his foolishness? Would he ever see her again?

Monday morning came and still no word from Jane. He was beside himself with anxiety now. Then the front door bell rang. Shit! Who was that? Had he forgotten a meeting, or was that one of his parishioners wanting something? He was not in the mood to face whoever it was. The bell rang again.

He slowly opened the door, and there was Jane.

"You sure know how to keep a girl waiting," she said with a smile as she stepped in. "You look like hell!"

Francis was surprised to see her.

"It's good to see you. Would you like some tea?" he asked nervously. This was it. His whole world would be soaring or come crashing down.

They went into the kitchen. He put the kettle on. She grabbed both of his hands and looked into his eyes.

"I've been giving a lot of thought to our relationship and your proposal. Anyone that has put up with me these six months or so will likely put up with me for the rest of my life. Yes, I will marry you so long as I can continue with my work." And she kissed him, and he hugged her with sheer joy.

The following Saturday, Jane took Nigel to meet her father and her siblings. On their underground train journey to Mile End, Jane briefed him on the members of her family. Her father was a widower and was now a retired docker. He had been an air-raid warden during the London Blitz and had survived, with other East Enders, seventy-six consecutive nights of bombing which had devastated the dockland area. Her father had been awarded the George Medal for civilian bravery for rescuing disabled residents one awful night. He had helped them find shelter in an underground train station where the rest of their family had taken refuge. He had been badly burned when he tried to pull an old lady from her house which had been set on fire by an incendiary bomb.

Jane was the eldest by five years. Her brother, Edward, was next, and he was in the police force. Her other brother, Charlie, was an apprentice plumber, and her younger sister, Alison, was in nursing school. Her mother had died shortly after Alison's birth.

Nigel and Jane emerged from the tube at Mile End and caught a red London bus. They were seated on the top deck of the bus, which gave them a good view of the areas they passed through. Parts of the dockland area were still dotted with piles of rubble even more than a decade after the war, although there were a number of new buildings going up.

I wish they were tearing down the slums in Notting Dale and building homes for our people like this, Francis thought to himself. *I suppose they do have a roof over the heads, whereas the people here do not.*

The bus went down Burdett Road to East India Dock Road, and they got off a Chrisp Street. Jane's family had been given a council flat on the new Lansbury Estate. Their house near the docks had been completely destroyed in the bombing. Her siblings had been evacuated to town in Devon, and she had completed her nurse training in London. Her father went to live with relatives whose house had survived the raids.

With a key she took from her handbag, Jane opened the front door of her family's flat. Her sister, Alison, heard the door opening and came out of the kitchen into the hall and greeted them. She was a vivacious woman of twenty-two; she was petite with a quick smile and curvaceous figure.

"So this is your knight in shining armour," she said impishly. "Not bad-looking either."

"Now, Alison, stop teasing!" Jane reprimanded her as she blushed. "Nigel, this, as you might have guessed, is my terrible sister."

"Nice to meet you, Alison. I hope you are not as bad as Jane said you were," he said, smiling.

"What have you been telling him?" she asked Jane.

"Nothing. Can't you tell when your leg is being pulled, little sister? Where is everyone?"

"Charlie and Edward went to watch West Ham play and will be back soon. Dad's in the living room. I've put the kettle on, and I'll bring some tea in."

"How is he?"

"Grumpy. He won't take his blood pressure medicine like he should. He occupies himself with reading and going to union meetings. Go on in and introduce Nigel."

When they entered the room, Mr. Stevens was sitting in one of the soft armchairs near a gas fire. When he saw them, he put down the paper he was reading and stood up.

"Father, I want to introduce you to Nigel, my fiancé."

Francis extended his hand to shake hands, but the gesture was not reciprocated. Mr. Stevens looked him up and down and then grunted.

"I suppose I should welcome you here," he said reluctantly.

"Not unless you want to, sir," said Nigel, who decided he was not going to be intimidated.

Ignoring the remark, Mr. Stevens continued, "Take a seat. So you've come here to take our Jane from us, have you? I can tell you she has been the mainstay of this family since her mother died. Since she became a nurse, we don't see her as often as we would like, and now when she marries you, we will see her even less."

Francis did not respond but let him talk.

Mr. Stevens began to fill a pipe with tobacco. As he did so, he continued, "This is a working-class family. Me, my father, and his father before him were stevedores and proud of it. It's a tough life with layoffs, piece work, and dock closures. I didn't want my kids to follow me into the docks. I wanted them to better themselves, and they have all done so."

He lit his pipe and began to draw on it.

"Nigel was an air-raid warden just like you, Da," Jane interjected. "He was in Belfast working in the shipyards during the day and was warden at night."

The old man showed interest in this. "Why didn't you join up? Both my boys did."

"I was a prisoner of war in Spain during the civil war there in the late thirties. I was beaten up one day by the guards who broke my leg. Other prisoners put splints on it, which saved the leg, but it didn't set properly. I was left with a limp. As a result, I couldn't join up, so I did the next best thing."

"Oh, you were in Spain, were you? Hmmm. Which side were you on?" he said suspiciously.

"I was an ambulance driver for the government side."

"One of my childhood friends, Fred Tanner, went to Spain. He was in the British Communist Party and volunteered to go there when the call came. He died somewhere near Valencia. I miss Fred terribly," he mused. "Now tell me all about it and your work in Belfast."

For the next hour, Francis discussed his experiences in Spain and Belfast. They only stopped once when Alison came in with the tea. Jane slipped away to the kitchen with Alison, and the men were left in deep conversation. He also spoke about his work in Notting Dale and some of the social injustices he had seen.

Jane's brothers, Edward and Charlie, came home from their soccer match and joined Francis and Mr. Stevens in the front room. They were soon talking about the West Ham game and were peppered with questions by Francis who wanted to know the result. He told them he was trying to organise games in his parish for the youths who had nothing to do.

On their way home, Jane said she was pleased that the meeting with her family had gone well. Francis said he liked her father once the ice had been broken. He thought to himself that Mr. Stevens was a proud man who knew he no longer counted for much anymore. This was a sad fact of life which affected many retired people. Jane's brothers were very interested in Francis's upbringing and his soccer plans. They had promised to take him to a West Ham match.

Francis had written a letter to the dean of the diocese, informing him of his engagement. A week later, he had a call from an aide to the dean who told him very snootily that the protocol was to ask permission to get married and not simply to inform the diocese of his intention. Francis was about to give the man a piece of his mind when the aide abruptly changed the subject and invited him and his fiancée to join the dean for dinner at his club in St. James's the following week.

Jane was very nervous about the meeting.

"I know we are going to get a grilling. I don't like being put in the hot seat like this," she said. "What happens if he doesn't like me? What will we do then?"

"You'll be fine. He only wants to get to know you," Francis reassured her. "Now have you decided on an engagement ring yet?"

"Yes. There's one I like at Samuel's in Oxford Street."

"Right. Let's go to West End this afternoon and get it."

When the appointed day and time came for their dinner with the dean, they entered his club, and a porter took their coats. He ushered them into a dining room where the dean, the Very Rev. Marcus Dixon, greeted them warmly and held a chair for Jane to sit down. When they had ordered drinks, he turned to Jane.

"How on earth did you meet this rogue, Jane?"

"It was during the war. I was a nurse at a rehabilitation centre in Keswick for our wounded troops, and Nigel was its accountant. He rescued me from one of my patients when I was threatened with a knife. The poor man was delusional. We lost touch because I went to midwifery school and he went to divinity college. We met up again last year."

Jane was surprised at how friendly the dean was and how easy he was to talk to. She told him her life story, and he was very interested in the work she was doing. His jokes were funny and his grasp of current affairs outstanding.

"What is the one thing you would like to see changed in Notting Hill?" he asked earnestly.

She didn't hesitate. "There is a lack of good affordable housing in the area. The situation is out of control, with slum landlords reaping big profits off the backs of poor whites and West Indians. It's setting these groups against each other, and there will be trouble. The government has to rein in the abuses and protect renters from unscrupulous landlords."

"Do you think the government's rent act this year helps?" he asked.

"Frankly, it's a disgrace. It has done away with rent controls and other rights tenants had on unfurnished flats. What we've seen is a rise in rents and a decline in the number of these flats available to rent with a rise in the number of furnished ones. This plays into the hands of people like Peter Rachman."

The dean was a little taken aback by Jane's forthrightness but wondered at the depth of her knowledge on the subject.

"Do you think that you will make a good vicar's wife?" he asked, changing the subject. "It's a difficult job."

"I will naturally support Nigel and his demanding parish work, but I have my own work as well. Nigel and I are in the same profession in a sense. We both help people with their needs. With me, it's birth and childcare. With him, it's practical and spiritual guidance. I think we will complement each other very well," she responded.

Just then, a well-dressed man in his forties greeted the dean as he walked into the dining room. They shook hands, and the dean introduced his two guests.

"Nigel and Jane, let me present Col. Mark Bennett who is an old friend of mine. We go back many, many years. I was a vicar at his parish church which he and his parents attended."

Francis froze when he heard the man's name. Where had he heard it before?

"It's very nice to meet you both. Nigel, do you run a parish here in London."

"Er . . . yes, in Notting Hill," he replied nervously.

"I hear it's a pretty rough area."

"Yes, that's true, but there are some really wonderful people there who make up for the more unseemly residents."

Just then, two other men came in.

"Ah, there are my guests. You will have to excuse me."

He said goodbye and walked off.

"Mark is a very interesting man," the dean remarked when he was out of earshot. "He worked for military intelligence during the war and was one of our top spy catchers. He now works for some secret department in Whitehall."

Then it came to Francis, and it was like a dagger through his heart. Yes, he was the officer who was hunting him down in Belfast and Keswick. Sergeant James had mentioned him in connection with the manhunt they were carrying out in the Lake District. *Get a grip on yourself*, he quietly told himself. *This was just a chance meeting and the man had shown no interest in your background.*

"Penney for your thoughts, Nigel," the dean said, breaking into his racing thoughts.

"I'm sorry, I was just reflecting on Colonel Bennett's responsibilities. It must have been a tough job."

"Yes, it was. He told me he caught almost all the spies, especially a group of English students. He trapped most of them in this group, except one man who was Irish and had given the authorities the slip on a number of occasions."

Francis swallowed hard and was determined to avoid Colonel Bennett at all costs.

CHAPTER 27

East London, May 1957

Francis and Jane were married in May at All Saints Church in Poplar. The small congregation at their wedding was made up of Jane's relatives and friends. His best man was Jane's brother, Edward. They spent a week honeymooning in Keswick, the place where they first met. After this brief interlude, they found themselves suddenly back in the harsh reality of life in Notting Dale and Notting Hill.

Jane's work hours were unpredictable as usual. It was governed often by the ring of the telephone or a knock at the door, mostly in the middle of the night. They savoured what time they had together, and on her days off, they would take trips to the cinema or just go out to dinner.

As the months passed, social conditions in Notting Dale and Notting Hill continued to deteriorate. Housing and racism remained the main issues. Slum landlords continued to buy up houses to add to their inventory of derelict properties, and a blind eye was turned to the situation by the local authority, the Royal Borough of Kensington. The Conservative councillors, who had the majority of votes in the council and lived in the affluent Kensington or South Kensington sections, did nothing to curb the abuses of the slum landlords who were free to profiteer from the desolation of their coloured tenants.

Racial tensions mounted, and there were numerous instances of West Indians being beaten up by gangs of Teddy Boys. The local Member of Parliament for North Kensington, George Rogers, avoided involvement in the problems of his coloured constituents. He sided with the white residents; after all, they were the people who could vote for him in elections. Instead of tackling the urgent need for satisfactory housing for all, he urged government ministers to stop immigration and to reverse its flow.

Also, what angered Nigel most was the ambivalence of the church authorities to the growing racial tension in his and other parishes in the area. He had voiced his feelings at a number of diocesan meetings he had attended, but nobody seemed worried. Their main concerns had been purely administrative and were not about current issues. A number of other nearby parish vicars had even discouraged coloured people from attending their services. Francis was appalled and had vociferously condemned these actions, calling it a moral issue that should be championed by the church. His protests fell on deaf ears.

Francis had had visits from a senior clergy in the diocese who explained that what was happening was a political issue and therefore not in the church's purview. Their main concern was the encouragement of parishioners to seek solace and guidance from the teachings of Christ. Although they didn't say it, it was clear that they were referring to the white residents. His outspokenness had made him a pariah, and he was not invited to many social functions the diocese ran.

One evening at a regular meeting between Francis and his two white church wardens, racial prejudice raised its ugly head. The two wardens were Elizabeth Riding, a large woman who ran a laundry from her house, and Joseph Jones, a thin wisp of a man who worked as a porter for British Railways at Paddington Station. Towards the end of a routine meeting, Francis asked innocently, "As we are getting a number of Caribbean parishioners coming to our services, I thought it might be a good idea if we had another warden who could represent them. What do you think?"

There was a long silence. Then Elizabeth Riding spoke up.

"We have been losing a lot of our people because there are too many darkies in the congregation. They have been going to other churches where Caribbeans are banned. They don't feel comfortable around these people and go where their own kind is," she responded after looking at Joseph Jones.

"A number of people have come to us to complain about the fact that there are too many of them at the services, and they wonder why we can't be like other parishes and keep them out," Joseph said nervously. "Of course, Elizabeth and I don't feel this way. We believe that we should live and let live."

Francis went red in the face and tried to control the anger he felt, but he couldn't.

"Keep them out of God's church?" Francis said in an exasperated angry outburst. "What the other churches near here are doing is totally wrong and un-Christian! These are God's people who want to worship in God's house. I understand that we all don't agree with a lot of their way of life, but I can assure you there are many white people who I don't agree with either. You have to ask the people who complain to you 'What would Jesus do?'"

"Now, now, Vicar, don't go on so. We are just telling you what a lot of people have been saying," said Elizabeth. "Many people think they should form their own church and not bother us, like the Russian Orthodox or Methodists do."

"Well, it's not going to happen in this parish!"

After they had gone, Francis went into the kitchen where Jane was making dinner and told her about their conversation.

"It is true that the number of white parishioners has been dwindling. We are known as the only Church of England parish in this area that accepts everyone, white or black, and I think it would be wrong of us to change," Jane said firmly. "Why don't you talk to some of the Caribbean parishioners about the problem and see what they suggest.

"The problem is that you can't change people's attitudes overnight. You need to get both groups together socially, and over time, they would recognise they have nothing to fear from each other. In the meantime, perhaps you should hold two services on Sundays. This would quell a lot of the concerns by white people, and then you could eventually revert back to one service," she suggested.

"That might take years to change. Your suggestion is really worth considering," said Francis. "I still don't like dividing the parish in this way."

"What option do you have? If we go on like this, we won't have any white parishioners at all. Now to change the subject," she continued, "I have an announcement to make of my own—I'm pregnant!"

Francis just stared at her, at first in disbelief, and then smiled happily. He grabbed her in a bear hug and lifted her off her feet, kissing her wildly.

"I'm so happy. I can't explain how much this means to me. How far along are you?"

"About two months. I wanted to make sure before I told you."

"Well, that's the best news I've ever had! When should we tell your family?"

"We plan to see them next Saturday, so we might as well tell them then."

"What should we name him?"

"Don't jump the gun. Anyway, what happens if it's a girl?"

"It doesn't matter. I'm still the happiest man in the world!" he said jubilantly.

When Jane had gone to bed that night, Francis poured himself a large Scotch and sat down on the sofa in his study and beamed with satisfaction. His life now had meaning. Gone were the doubts of whether he had lost the shackles of his past. Gone was the fear of retribution for his previous actions.

Gone was his father's malevolent advice. He was free and looked forward to the future with pride. He decided that he would seek a living elsewhere, somewhere where Jane and he could bring up their child properly and not in the hellhole that was Notting Dale. He owed that to his child.

Over the next two months, Jane's stomach grew bigger, and she was more evidently pregnant. She had tried to hide the fact for as long as possible from her patients and friends at the hospital but eventually told everyone. She was beginning to find it hard to climb the stairs to her patients' flats and had to stop often to catch her breath.

Francis had applied for a number of vacant parishes without success. His negative relationship with the diocese was now a telling factor in these rejections. Of course, verbally, his rebuffs were sugar-coated by senior priests responsible for selecting candidates, telling him that he was doing such good work where he was and it would be a shame to move him when he was doing so well. Francis didn't buy this and was becoming more frustrated.

In addition, his white parishioners had boycotted his services when he appointed John Williams as the first Caribbean church warden. Shortly after this, Elizabeth Riding and Joseph Jones both resigned as church wardens, and Francis never saw them again in his church. He heard that they had joined another parish. He now ran one of the first black parishes in the area. This did not worry him as, by now, the area was mostly West Indian.

Francis's church wardens' meetings were now pretty lively affairs because his wardens were suggesting many changes and events. They had introduced more Caribbean music into the services, and in the after-service social events, West Indian foods were served. Francis had fought to no avail for the right of children in his parish to be confirmed with white children from other parishes in Notting Hill. Usually, a combined service was held at one of the churches, but parents threatened to boycott the ceremony if West Indian children were included. As a compromise, the bishop of Kensington had confirmed twelve children at his church in a separate ceremony.

At one of the warden meetings, he heard complaints that rents had risen considerably and that people were finding it difficult to pay for their mean lodgings. Rents were particularly high in buildings owned by Peter Rachman and a John Ramos.

"I think a group of tenants from one building should appeal to the West London Rent Tribunal," suggested Francis. "I know I've suggested this before, but it's the only way to stop the abuse."

"It is very dangerous for us to do it. We'd have to think about it. The situation is getting worse and worse, particularly in buildings owned by a Spaniard by the name of John Ramos. Suppose we decide to go ahead, how do we go about an appeal?" asked John Williams.

They then discussed how the application was made. Francis offered to work on the wording of the appeal but stressed that they would have to find someone willing to use their name on documents. Then the meeting broke up.

The following week, Francis saw John Williams in the street coming from work.

"Hello, John, any news about your rent appeal?"

"We can forget about that, Vicar. It won't happen. Someone let Ramos know what we were doing, and his heavies convinced everyone, including me, to drop our plan. We can't afford to lose our homes, even if you can hardly call them that."

"That's too bad. We'll have to think of something else."

He was determined to do something about the intolerable situation, but he did not know what.

At dinner that night with Jane, he told her of his conversation with John Williams.

"I don't know what else to do to help them," he said.

"Why don't you talk to Donald Chesworth, the Labour Party member of the London County Council for North Kensington? I met him once at a hospital Christmas party. He seems a very approachable man," Jane suggested.

"That's a good idea. Maybe he can suggest something."

The next morning, Francis telephoned Donald Chesworth's office and arranged to see him the following day at his Ladbroke Grove office.

Donald Chesworth was a slim man in his thirties and was smartly dressed in a double-breasted suit. He ushered Francis into an office and offered him some tea. He listened very intently to Francis's description of the housing conditions in Notting Dale and how landlords had taken over many buildings to turn them into high-priced slums. He also told him of the threats that had been made when some of them planned to go to the rent tribunal.

"We know about some of the egregious things that have been happening in your area and in Notting Hill in general. I'd like to see these conditions for myself. Would you be my guide? Have you got time to show me now?"

"Yes, I would be delighted."

They spent the next hour walking around the streets of Notting Dale. Francis took him to John Williams's flat on Morgan Road and showed him the conditions the tenants were living in and told him about the rents that were being paid. Councillor Chesworth was appalled.

They walked back to the Latimer Road tube station, and Councillor Chesworth turned to Francis as he was paying his fare.

"Thank you for the tour, Nigel. It's been very educational. There are a number of us that will be taking action to stop this, but it's going to take time. I will keep in touch with you and let you know what progress is being made."

That evening, Nigel was making his way back home from visiting a sick parishioner. The street was dark because the street lights did not work, and the only light was from the windows of some of houses along the street. As he walked along Silchester Road, a car pulled up alongside him. Three men got out, and he was dragged to a nearby alley by two of them. A large man with a scar down the side of his face grabbed him by the throat and lifted him until only his toes touched the ground.

"I understand you are causing trouble with my tenants, trying to get them to go to a rent tribunal," he said in a thick foreign accent. "And then this morning, you were seen with that interfering busybody Chesworth, going into one of my buildings without permission. This is just a friendly warning this time—back off or there will be hell to pay! Do you understand?"

"Of course, I understand. The days are numbered for you and people like you. You're just scum who prey on poor people. I won't be bullied by you or anyone!" said a nervous but defiant Francis.

"Well, that's a real shame. I am sure your pretty and pregnant wife will regret your interference."

"Leave my wife out of this!"

The man just laughed. Turning to the other men, he said, "I think he needs a lesson in manners, boys."

He released Francis, and the other two men started to pummel him in the face and stomach. When he fell to the ground, they started to kick him.

"Mr. Ramos don't like interference in his business, so back off," said one of the thugs as he put in a final kick into Francis's rib cage.

They left as quickly as when they came. Francis was sitting on the ground, hurting too much to get up. He was bleeding from his nose, from a cut above his left eye, and from his swollen lip. His breathing was laboured and painful because of the bruising around his ribs. He tried to get up by grabbing a railing to pull himself up, but he had to give up when his legs finally gave way. He sat there for a few minutes, hoping that, soon, he would have the strength to get up.

Then he heard a whispered voice, "Vicar, is that you?" He wheezed a yes. Two men gathered around him and looked at him. Then they lifted him painfully to his feet. Francis then realised who his rescuers were. They were Martin Davis and his brother, James, who were members of his congregation.

"Let's get you home. We heard a commotion and came to see who it was the three men were beating," said Martin.

With the brothers taking hold of him under each arm, they made their way slowly to the vicarage which was two streets over. On their journey, Francis lost consciousness several times, and he was relieved when they made it to his front door and sat him down in the hall chair.

Jane came out of the kitchen when she heard the front door open and the voices. She looked horrified when she saw Francis, and then her professionalism kicked in.

"Martin and James, get him upstairs and take him to the spare room which is the first on the right. When you've done that, take his clothes off so I can take a look at him."

Jane ran into the kitchen, poured hot water from the tap into a bowl, and took some clean flannels from a drawer. She went upstairs and sat on the bed next to Francis and started to clean his wounds.

"Boys, thanks for bringing him home. I'll take care of him now."

When the Davis brothers had gone, she asked Francis, "My poor darling, who did this to you?"

"John Ramos and his thugs," he said slowly through his swollen mouth. "They were warning me not to interfere with their business."

She felt around his ribs, and he winced a couple of times.

"Hmm . . . It looks as though you've got two broken ribs, and you'll need stitches over your eye and on your lip. I'll have to get a doctor in to take care of this and to give you something for the pain."

Francis was too exhausted to argue with her, and he just closed his eyes and tried to rest. After she had telephoned the hospital, she came back and started to bandage his rib cage and then put on his pyjamas. When she had finished, he was grateful that it was all over because to do anything was a painful effort.

An hour later, a young doctor who Jane knew arrived and stitched up Francis's face. He gave him some codeine tablets for the pain, and Francis heard him talking to Jane as they went down the stairs to the front door. She was soon back and gave him two tablets.

"You're to stay in bed and rest. Those pills should help you sleep. Now get some rest, and we'll talk in the morning."

He soon fell asleep.

Francis woke at five the next morning, feeling as though he had been driven over by a steam roller. Every part of him ached. When he had found a position to lie in that was less painful, he began thinking about what had happened the night before. He thought he recognised John Ramos from somewhere because the scar on his face was too memorable. But he could not remember where. Obviously, he had rattled the man's cage, otherwise he wouldn't have taken such a foolish step, or perhaps he thought he was beyond the law and he could do what he liked. He decided to keep a diary of events so that if anything happened to him, the authorities would know where to start looking.

His thoughts went back to where he had seen John Ramos before. As he lay there for the next hour, it gnawed at him. Where had he seen the man before? He remembered that someone had told him that Ramos was a Spaniard. Perhaps he saw him during his time in Spain. Then it came to him: This man was the cruel sergeant that had tortured him after he was captured. He was the man who had summarily executed his friend, Jimmy, when they had been stopped by the patrol Ramos had led. What was his name? Suddenly, it came to him.

"Sergeant Farina!" he exclaimed out loud.

"Who is Sergeant Farina?" said Jane as she walked in with his breakfast on a tray.

"Oh, some bastard I knew in Spain." Then Francis explained to Jane the circumstances of his capture and how he recognised the man called Ramos again after all the years that had passed.

"Did he recognise you?"

"No. Even if I didn't have this beard, he would not remember me."

"It seems to me that you should avoid him. I've seen the same thing happen in the East End, where the Kray brothers and their gang have terrorised people. Some just disappeared. I don't want the same to happen to you. You've too much to live for now that the baby's coming."

"I can't let him get away with what he's doing though. Perhaps I should quietly feed information to Mr. Chatsworth and not be seen to be involved outwardly in the movement to bring Ramos down."

"That's probably the best way to protect us from any more repercussions," she agreed.

It took a week before Francis was able walk again and another to move around without hurting. His ribs were still very sore, but he was able to go about his normal routine, albeit slowly. He had had a visit from a Detective Sergeant Haig who had been alerted to his beating by some anonymous tipster. Francis told him he didn't know who attacked him and couldn't give a reason for this happening. He could tell the policeman didn't believe him, but he left to file his report at the police station.

One evening, about a month later, Jane came back from a confinement very late. She was physically exhausted and lay on the sofa with her eyes closed. She had not touched the supper Francis had prepared for her which was on a tray on a coffee table. When she heard him come in, she opened her eyes.

"I don't know how long I can go like this. Tonight's delivery was very hard, as the baby was a breech birth, and I had to call in a doctor from the hospital to help. We managed to deliver the baby and unwrap his umbilical cord from around his neck so he could breath. The mother, poor thing, was totally exhausted from her efforts. I have to go back in the morning and check on them."

"In the meantime, our mother-to-be must eat something and drink this cocoa I made," said Francis soothingly.

"You are very kind to me, Nigel. I love you so much."

"I love you too."

Jane slept in the next morning, and it wasn't until ten she appeared in the kitchen in her dressing gown.

"One egg or two, madam?" Francis said as she came in.

"One boiled egg and some toast Jeeves," she replied, smiling.

Francis gave her a cup of tea and then busied himself making her breakfast. Jane sat down at the kitchen table and took a drink of her tea. She savoured the hot sweet drink.

"I need to go and visit Mrs. Barton this morning. I hope she and the baby are all right," she said.

"I'm sure you would have heard if she wasn't."

"What are you doing today?"

"I've got one of those wretched quarterly deanery meetings at a hotel in Kensington this afternoon. I'll expect they'll argue about minutiae of church administration. It is a waste of time. There's a cocktail party afterward, but I won't be staying for it. I'm persona non grata at the moment because of the fuss I have made about conditions here, and they have chosen to stick their heads in the sand like ostriches."

Jane left the vicarage at eleven and walked to Stoneleigh Street where Mrs. Barton lived. When she reached the Georgian building where the Barton's rented a flat, she started laboriously to climb the stairs to the third floor. As she ascended, she heard voices arguing and saw clothes being thrown out on to the landing. She reached the landing of the third floor and stopped to catch her breath.

She heard a woman pleading, and then she screamed. Jane hurried through the front door where she saw three large men grabbing Mrs. Barton's things, throwing them out of the door. Mrs. Barton cradled her new-born baby in her arms.

"You don't pay your rent, so you're out!"

"Please, please, let me have another week. My husband lost his job, but he will get another one," she pleaded.

"It doesn't work like that. We have someone who wants to move in right away, and they'll pay rent on time. It's time for you to go!" he said roughly.

Then he saw Jane standing there.

"What do you want?" he demanded.

"Do you realise that Mrs. Barton just had a baby last night, and she is in no condition to move anywhere?" said an angry Jane.

"So what? These niggers have babies all the time, that's not our problem. Now get out of the way and let me do my job."

"This woman should be in bed!" Jane persisted.

The man rounded on Jane.

"Now I'm going to ask you only once nicely to go or we'll throw you out."

"I'm not going to stand here and let you rough up one my patients. Now get out of the way so I can examine her," she said as she tried to push past him.

Without warning, the man pushed her very hard out of the front door on to the landing where she tripped over some of Mrs. Barton's belongings and fell head long against the rickety balustrade. As she grabbed it to pull herself up, it gave way. She desperately tried to stop herself from falling, clawing at anything to stop her forward momentum. To the onlookers of the tragedy, everything they witnessed was in slow motion. Jane fell three flights and hit the stone floor of the front hall with a sickening thud and blood started to ooze out of her head.

CHAPTER 28

Francis returned home that evening at about six o'clock. As he rounded the corner, he saw a police car outside the rectory. *Not more bloody questions*, he thought. As he approached, Detective Sergeant Haig, who had interviewed him when he got beaten up, got out of the car.

"Hello, Sergeant, have you got more questions for me?" he said with a smile.

The sergeant didn't smile back. "I'm afraid I've got some bad news for you, sir. Your wife has had an accident, and in fact, she is dead."

Francis was stunned and began to faint. Sergeant Haig caught him and guided him into the rectory and into the living room where he sat him down in a chair. The sergeant saw the whiskey decanter and poured a drink into a glass and gave it to him. Francis took a sip.

"What about the baby?" he asked as tears began to well up in his eyes.

"I'm afraid he's gone as well. By the time the ambulance got there, it was too late for both of them. They tried to save the baby at the hospital, but it was no good.

"One of the doctors who knew Mrs. Ellis at the hospital made the official identification so you won't have to do that. Have you anyone I can call, sir?"

"No, I have no one. Jane was my life and my best friend," he murmured, and then he began to wail. "What am I going to do now? We were going to move out of here once the baby was born," he cried.

"Should I call someone at the bishop's office to let them know what has happened, sir?"

"No. They don't care!" he said savagely. "I'll have to call her family and let them know what has happened. Oh my god!"

There was silence for a long time, and he took sips of his drink. Slowly, Francis began to pull himself together.

"Tell me how this happened," he said to the sergeant.

"We interviewed some witnesses who saw what happened. Apparently, she was going to visit a Mrs. Barton, and when she got there, her patient was being evicted. After a heated exchange with three men, she tripped over some of the woman's belongings and fell against a balustrade, which gave way, and she fell three floors."

"Who were the three men?"

"We haven't caught up with them yet. They scarpered after she fell. We know the building belongs to a John Ramos, and they were probably working for him."

"So they killed my wife!"

"Now, sir, we have no evidence to prove that. All we can tell is that it was a terrible accident."

Nigel kept his own counsel.

When Sergeant Haig had gone, he rang the nurses' home at the hospital where Jane's sister, Alison, had a room. He left a message for her to call him urgently. He then called the police station where her brother was based. Fortunately, Edward was at the station, and Francis let him know what had happened. He could hear the heartbreak in Edward's trembling voice.

"Dad will be devastated. I'll tell him tonight. It'll kill him."

Later that night, Alison called back after her shift had finished at seven. "Oh no, no!" she wailed when she heard the news and sobbed inconsolably. "She was such a wonderful sister. I can't believe this has happen to our Jane. I'm going to miss her. You must be so upset. What are you going to do? Who's looking after you?"

Francis explained that he had told Edward and that he was going to tell their father. When Alison had gathered her thoughts, she said she would be coming to stay for a while to help him. Despite his protests, she insisted and turned up on his doorstep at midnight, suitcase in hand.

"How did you get here?" Francis asked astonished.

"I got one of my boy friends to drop me off."

The funeral for Jane and their baby was held the following week in the same church in Poplar where they were married just six months previously. They buried them together in the Tower Hamlets Cemetery and hosted a reception in the saloon bar of a local pub.

After the funeral, Alison left the rectory and went back to work at the hospital. Francis was left on his own with his thoughts for the first time since Jane's death. The silence was eerie, and a feeling of emptiness came over him.

The cold dank night air made him shiver. He built a fire in his study and poured himself a large Scotch. Once the fire took hold, he felt comforted by its warmth and by his drink. He had to take stock of his future. Where does he go from here? As he sat there, a red mist started to creep in from under the door, and his father appeared.

"Well, what a mess you have made of your life. Your woman was killed by that Spaniard's thugs, and you are just going to sit there and take it. And what about your promise to your friend, Jimmy, that you would avenge his death? Obviously, you're not man enough to deal with it. Perhaps you don't care. You're a real disappointment. You're not living up to your potential, boy."

"Just leave me alone, will you!" Francis said angrily.

"What amused me the most was that the priest killer has become a priest," continued his father, laughing and ignoring Francis's outburst. *"Maybe you did the right thing by becoming a spy in the enemy's camp. That was quite a subtle move on your part. You did well getting rid of Nigel Ellis, but you've turned soft since then. It's about time you bucked up and did something meaningful. You have the makings of a faithful disciple."*

His father's comments were interrupted by the ring of the front door bell. When Francis opened the door, he was surprised to see John Williams and his wife, Tessa, and the Davis brothers. They were all carrying dishes of food.

"We thought you might need some dinner and company," said a smiling John Williams. "You are always there for us, so we're here for you."

This generosity amongst the wasteland that was Notting Dale brought tears to Francis's eyes. He was always astonished by the munificent spirit of people who have very little themselves.

"This is a wonderful surprise. Please come in."

The evening turned out to be a fun occasion and helped lift Francis's spirits. However, when they had left his, depression returned.

Two days later, he had another surprise visitor, Dean Dixon. When they had sat down in Francis's study, Dean Dixon turned to him.

"This is my first time in Notting Dale, and I must say it's a very grim place. I've never seen poverty like this. And that impression comes only from walking up the street. Heaven knows what is happening behind those curtains."

"It has been made worse by the new Rent Act. Many more poor people are being evicted from their homes and now live on the streets," Francis responded. "Coupled with the racial tension here, this area is powder keg of resentment which will one day explode."

"I understand you've been working with Donald Chatsworth. He's a good man, but be careful of getting too openly involved with him. I understand you were the victim of a severe beating because of your association with him."

"Yes. I've decided to keep a low profile to avoid any more trouble. I've been passing along information to him on the quiet."

"Good. Now how are you personally coping with your loss of Jane and the baby?"

"I suppose I'm learning to deal with Jane's death, although being surrounded here by memories of her doesn't help the healing process. My moods swing back and forth. One day, I'm up. The next day, I'm down."

"I understand how you feel," he paused. "When my wife died, I was very morose like you. I questioned my faith even and couldn't seem to function properly for many months. After a while, I accepted the cards I'd been dealt and again found my enthusiasm for my work. This will happen to you."

"I hope so, sir. To be honest, I feel very tired. I have been feeling this way long before Jane's death. This parish has been a tough assignment, and I have found my enthusiasm waning. I really need new challenges."

"I know. You've been here now for, what, almost ten years? I can see how this place could wear you down. Your situation coincides with some parish consolidation moves we've been thinking about. I've got a proposal you might be interested in which would take you away from this place.

"The bishop of Exeter, who is an old chum of mine from university, is looking for a young priest for a living in the Devon village of Branton. It's a different sort of parish from your current assignment. It's in the country far away from the urban jungle you're used to, but don't be deceived, it still has its country poor who have to be helped."

"That sounds very intriguing, sir. It certainly presents me with new challenges. Can I let you know once I have given it more thought?"

"Of course, you can, Nigel. Here's some information on the parish which the bishop sent me." He reached into his briefcase and handed a file to Nigel. "Let me know whether you're interested by the end of the week."

"When do you anticipate my making this move?"

"If you decide you want to go ahead and they like you, I expect you can move down there at the beginning of the year, once we have celebrated Christmas. We'll install another vicar as a stopgap until we make the final arrangements for the amalgamation of parishes."

When the dean had gone, Francis sat at his desk contemplating his options. He was under no illusion that this offer was the diocese's way of ridding themselves of a "turbulent priest." He looked through the file. Maybe this was the change he needed as it would be a complete break from the stress of Notting Dale. And then there was his Celtic history hobby which he could pursue now that the pace of his professional life would be slower. With Cornwall nearby, he had an opportunity to study the Cornish Celts. Yes, this would be a good move for him.

The next day, he contacted Dean Dixon to say he was very interested in the position. Two weeks later, he found himself in Exeter, being interviewed by the diocesan dean. He then visited Branton and met the church council there. They were a very friendly group led by a retired businessman from London who owned a large estate in the area. Francis, with his natural charm, hit it off with them almost immediately. He listened to their concerns and hopes for the future and told them about some plans he had thought about. He asked probing questions about the parish which impressed them. He left with the impression that the job was his.

When he got back from his weeklong trip to the West Country, he found a note pushed under his front door informing him that Martin Davis was in a coma in Hammersmith Hospital. Francis rushed to the hospital to see him and was met by an anguished group of his parishioners. Martin had died that day without regaining consciousness. Apparently, he had tried to intervene when some of Ramos's men were evicting a family in his building. After being cornered by them, he was able to get away but was hit by a passing car as he ran across the street.

When he got home after helping make funeral arrangements for Martin's distraught brother, James, Francis began to think about the futility of this tragic episode. These beautiful engaging people had come all that way from their homes in the Caribbean for a better life in the mother country, only to find a hell on earth here. What astounded him was that the authorities didn't care. In this instance, the police weren't involved in any investigation. The Caribbean community had closed ranks and, out of fear of retribution, did not complain to the police who they knew would not take any action against the perpetrators.

The more Francis thought about this shockingly cruel treatment of human beings, the angrier he got. First of all, his wife and child were victims, then poor Martin, and there was his treatment in Spain by Sergeant Farina née Ramos, and the execution of his friend, Jimmy. His long-hidden white anger began to smoulder in his thoughts. Something had to be done to stop this cruel man from inflicting any more pain on these people. He had to develop a plan to eliminate John Ramos. He couldn't wait for the long-drawn-out machinations of the well-meaning Donald Chatsworth and his cohorts. What was needed was action now.

On his journey back to London, Francis had had many conflicting thoughts. On one hand, he felt like a Judas leaving his parishioners in the lurch, but on the other hand, he knew that it was time for him to move on to achieve some tranquillity in his life. He must do something decisive for his parishioners' sake before he left them. The one act he had in mind would mitigate his guilty conscience a little and satisfy his burning desire for revenge against a man who had perpetrated so much evil in his life. The fact that he was planning to act as a vigilante never crossed his mind.

He had to think the plan through, particularly the consequences of his actions on others. If he was able to deal with Ramos, the police would naturally suspect James Davis. But Francis knew he was planning to move in with a cousin in Nottingham after the funeral, so he would be out of the picture and less likely to come up on their radar.

The funeral service for Martin Davis was a joyous occasion with celebratory music and songs. Francis's small church was full of mourners with some who couldn't find seats standing around the sides. As the body was loaded into the hearse for its journey to the Kensal Green Cemetery, there were boos and catcalls from a group of Teddy Boys who were across the street. When they saw the scowls on the faces of a large congregation spilling out of the church, they left.

Two weeks later, Francis received word that he had been accepted as the priest in Branton and would start his new appointment at the first of the year. He had a sense of relief at the news and looked forward to new challenges and a new beginning. But there was some unfinished business here in Notting Dale.

Francis spent some time observing the movements of John Ramos. He found that the man liked to gamble virtually every Saturday night at an illegal club near Notting Hill Gate just off the Bayswater Road. His habit was to park his car in a mews at the back of the club which had a number of car repair garages in what had been stables and carriage houses. Ramos, a bit worse for wear from drink, would emerge from the back door of the club by himself at about one or two in the morning. Francis saw this as his opportunity because none of his goons were ever around.

On a Saturday night in mid-December, he walked to the mews just after midnight, armed with the cricket bat that was in his hall hat stand. He hid the bat under his raincoat so that no one would see him with it. He was also wearing a trilby hat which covered his face, and he wore his leather gloves. He was carrying a duffel bag which had items in it, including a coil of rope he had bought at a hardware store in Acton. There weren't many people around on this cold and rainy night, which meant that he wouldn't be easily recognised.

It took him about thirty minutes to walk down to the mews, and he was pleased to see Ramos's large ostentatious Austin Princess car parked in its usual place. Behind the car were some dustbins and a large storage bin. Francis pushed the latch button on the boot, and to his delight, the lid came open. He raised it just enough to attract Ramos's attention and then hid behind the bin. He had managed to find a wooden box that had been put out with the rubbish and sat on it well hidden from anyone coming into the mews.

After about thirty minutes, Francis, who had been sitting in his hidden position, getting colder and colder, decided to get up to walk around to warm himself up. He was just about to stand up when he saw a man walking into the mews from the street. The man was weaving from side to side as he walked and mumbled to himself. The tramp started to go through the dustbins when he saw that the car boot was open. He made a beeline for it but, after rummaging around for a few minutes, decided that there was nothing of value in the boot and weaved his way out of the mews cursing. Francis resumed his wait.

Finally, at about one thirty, the back door of the club opened, and a large figure stumbled out. John Ramos had had a good evening and had won for a change. He was smoking a Havana cigar and staggered towards his car when he spotted the boot partly open.

"What the fuck!" he slurred and went to the back of the car.

As he reached out to close the lid, he was felled by a blow from Nigel's cricket bat. Nigel quickly tied the unconscious man's wrists and gagged him with a rag he brought along for that purpose. When he was satisfied that Ramos could not get free, he went through his pockets and found the keys to his car and a revolver tucked in the belt of his trousers. He then heaved the unconscious Ramos into the boot and closed the lid.

He got into the car, and after much fiddling in the dark with the controls, he finally was able to start the engine. Nigel was apprehensive about driving because he hadn't done so since he was in Spain. After a few false starts, he was able to drive and was surprised how smooth it was compared to the rickety lorries on which he had learned to drive.

Francis turned out of the mews on to Princedale Road and drove north to Walmer Road. He turned into Avondale Park and followed the dirt path to a large shed that was used by his soccer side when they had games in the park. He took out of his duffel bag the large pry bar he had bought and wrenched off the padlock hinges on the door.

Once inside the shed, he threw the rope over a beam and was ready to bring in his prisoner. He had chosen this location because it was far from the nearest houses, very secluded, and an ideal structure for him to execute his plan. Occasionally, on summer nights, you'd see courting couples here or prostitutes with their customers, but tonight it was pouring with rain, which would keep everyone away.

Francis went to the boot of the car, ready for trouble. He knew that this would be the tricky bit. He opened the lid to the boot and jumped back as two feet came flying towards him from the seemingly wild animal inside who was behaving like a wounded bull. Francis cocked the revolver and pointed it at Ramos.

"Now you can make this easy or I'll kill you here and now. Now get out of the boot and do exactly as I say."

Reluctantly, Ramos climbed out as Francis grabbed him by his collar and pulled him out.

"Now walk to that shed door very slowly."

When they entered the shed, Francis tied one end of the rope around the bindings on Ramos's wrists, which were behind his back, and pulled the man up in a stress position so that just his toes were on the ground. He tied the rope back on some machinery at the back of the shed. He closed the door so that sound would not carry so far.

"Sergeant Farina, how do you feel? Our positions have been reversed since the war in Spain. Last time, I was in your position, do you remember?"

Francis punched the man hard in his stomach.

"You and I have some reckoning to do. You see, apart from torturing me, you killed a friend of mine when your patrol stopped our ambulance. If it were not for Captain Estrada, you'd have killed me too. More recently, you are responsible for the atrocious living conditions of the people in Notting Dale, and no end of excuses could make up for the pitiless way you treated them just to make yourself rich off their despair."

With that, he spat in Ramos's face.

"What is worse to me personally is that your men killed my wife and child and were responsible for the death of Martin Davis two weeks ago. So what do you have to say for yourself? Oh, I forgot you can't talk because of the rag in your mouth," he said sarcastically. He untied the gag, and Ramos spat out blood on the ground.

"You bastard, I should have killed you when I had the chance, but that softy Estrada wouldn't let me. You're not a vicar but a devil. You'll pay for this, I promise you!"

"What makes you think I'll let you go? Your time is up. You'll not get a chance to reap any more profits from the people."

Francis put the gag back and picked up his cricket bat. He went back to Ramos whose eyes were now as big as saucers, and they showed absolute fear. Francis gave him a villainous smile, and the man began to urinate down one leg.

"Now this is for Jimmy." He hit one of Ramos's knees with the cricket bat which smashed his kneecap. The man violently twisted in pain. He went purple in the face.

"This is for my wife and child." And he hit him on the other knee.

"And finally, this is for the people of Notting Dale." He hit his crotch.

Ramos writhed around on the rope in great agony.

"Well, it's time I went."

Francis aimed the revolver at the man's forehead.

"Goodbye, Sergeant Farina." And he shot him.

Francis gathered up his equipment and left. He walked to Walmer Road and took off his shoes and put others on. He didn't want to leave any incriminating footprints that might be traced back to him. He threw the shoes into some bushes. He had worn gloves all the time so that there would be no fingerprints.

On his way back to the rectory, he didn't see anyone. When he got there, he burned the cricket bat in the fireplace. He made some cocoa and went to bed satisfied that he had put part of his life behind. Now he could move on.

THE RECKONING

And the devil did grin, for his darling sin is pride that apes humility . . .
—Samuel Taylor Coleridge, "The Devil's Thoughts," 1799

CHAPTER 29

Stair, Lake District, September 1982

Twenty-one-year-olds Brian Fenton and Iain Hilton had been best friends since their first year at Manchester Grammar School, and both were now at the University of Durham. When they were seventeen, they had attended an Outward Bound course near Ullswater in the Lake District. They were taught, among other outdoor activities, climbing and fell walking across the open, hilly, and windswept spaces of the Cumbrian hills and mountains. Climbing and fell walking had become their passion, and when they could, they would spend weekends on the fells.

One particular adventure they enjoyed was exploring abandoned mines by using their climbing skills to abseil down old shafts, exploring and then climbing back out again. The Lake District is dotted with disused copper, graphite, slate, and lead mines, and this particular weekend, they had planned to explore an old mine on the Above Derwent Fell near Stair.

They had parked their car in a lane leading to the mine and had camped near the mine's old wheelhouse the previous night. They were up at seven the next morning and had enjoyed a fried breakfast over a propane stove they had brought with them. By eight, they were ready to go.

Brian was to be the first down the mine's shaft. He secured their climbing rope around a sturdy outcrop of rock and put on his climbing helmet, harness, and gloves. He secured the rope around the harness and through his carabiner. He switched on the light on his helmet and positioned himself straddled over the shaft entrance. Then he began to slowly climb down, dropping a few feet at a time and making sure he didn't disturb any loose rocks or any rotting wood which lined the shaft.

It took him almost ten minutes to drop down the shaft's eighty feet. As he looked around with the powerful torch he had taken from his rucksack, he could see by the markings on the wooden trusses of the shaft where water had risen. Now it had receded so that all that was left was a small shallow pond along a wide tunnel. He heard Iain shout "below" as he began to make his descent. Brian ducked into one of the four tunnels that led away from the shaft in case any debris fell.

While he was waiting for Iain to join him, he scanned the bottom of the shaft with his torch. He saw in one corner what looked like a small pile of clothes. Sometimes they had found miners' belongings but usually nothing of value since the mine owners, before they left, had stripped the mines of anything salvageable.

When Iain joined him at the bottom of the shaft, Brian pointed to the clothes, and they walked over to examine them.

"My god, it's part of a skeleton," cried Brian. "Look, there is a skull and some bones. We better get the police."

Their climb up the shaft was painstakingly slow, but within an hour, they were on the surface again. They sat down exhausted from their climb.

"I'll take the car to the police station in Keswick if you would stand guard here," said Brian.

*   *   *

Insp. Ray Kidner sat back in his chair in his small office at New Scotland Yard on Broadway in London. He had just returned from the trial of a man accused of murder at the Norwich Crown Court. The trial had taken longer than expected, but eventually, there was a guilty verdict. His week away from the Yard had resulted in a backlog of paperwork that he knew he would find on his desk when he got back. He had come in at six in the morning, bought a coffee at a small café on Victoria Street, and had begun to plough through the paper mountain. Other inspectors had taken on his outstanding cases, and he knew he would have to take them back later that morning.

Thirty-five-year-old Ray Kidner had not come into the police through the usual channels. He was a graduate of the University of London where he had read law. When he joined the police force after training at the Metropolitan Police College at Hendon in North London, he was assigned to the East Ham police station in the East End of London. After serving several years as a beat officer, he became a detective. He was promoted to sergeant and, eventually, to inspector. His success rate in investigating crime had come to the notice of his superiors in the Met, and he was transferred to Commander Moore's squad at New Scotland Yard. He was part of a team of four inspectors who investigated serious crimes.

At ten, Inspector Kidner was coming to the end of the paperwork and had begun writing reports on his desktop computer when his phone rang. It was the commander's secretary summoning him to his superior's office. He picked up a notebook and pen and walked along the corridor to the commander's office.

"Come in, Ray. Glad to have you back from your holiday in Norwich," Commander Moore said with a smile.

Why was it that the old man always pulled your leg? It's good not to take the bait as it will encourage him to continue.

"Well, we got the right result, and he's been put away for life. It's his son and daughter I worry about because they have to go into a foster home. With a murdered mother and a father in jail, it's a rough start to life," Raymond commented.

They discussed the trial further as well as some of the cases he had left behind when he went to Norwich.

"We have been asked by the chief constable of Cumbria to help out in an unusual murder case," said the commander, changing the subject. "They are a small force, manpower wise, and haven't got people to devote to the investigation or, I suspect, the experience because murder is very rare in their neck of the woods. They have found a skeleton with its skull bashed in and some clothing in an old mine shaft. Go and take a look at what's there, and if you cannot fathom out anything in a week, we can hand it over to the Cold Case Squad to deal with."

"Fine, sir," said the inspector unenthusiastically. "I need to take Sergeant Lockhart with me."

"That's OK. You have to report to a Superintendent Davis."

Inspector Kidner and Sgt. Brenda Lockhart arrived in Penrith late the next afternoon. They had left London in the early morning and had driven north on the A1. They had joined the A66 at Scotch Corner which took them directly to Penrith and Carlton Hall, the Cumbria Police Headquarters. The driveway to this listed early 1800 building in the beautiful Cumbrian countryside was lined with trees. The drive then led to a car park in front of the hall.

"Quite impressive," said Brenda. "It beats Broadway any day."

They walked through glass-paned front doors to a reception desk and asked the officer on duty for Superintendent Davis. They sat down in some chairs in the reception area and took in their surroundings as they waited.

Superintendent Davis walked down the oak staircase. He was a tall lean man with a bald head and was smartly dressed in a well-pressed grey suit. He greeted them warmly as he ushered them up the stairs to his first-floor office. They all sat down at a conference table, and the superintendent passed

Inspector Kidner files which contained autopsy reports and pictures of the crime scene. The inspector quickly read the file and passed it to Sergeant Lockhart.

"This is a rum affair. It seems as though the body had been in the mine shaft for years," said the superintendent. "We recovered World War II identity card that was in a large leather wallet, which was in a plastic sleeve. Despite the water damage, we could just make out the name Patrick Duggan and Belfast. All the rest was ruined. The other unusual thing was that he had a wooden leg."

"Have any fingerprints turned up in the wheelhouse, sir?"

"None were taken because our crime scene people reckoned, after so many years, they couldn't lift any."

The laziness of some of these provincial crime scene units irritated Inspector Kidner.

"We'll have to get them to go over the site again," he said calmly. "Fingerprints sometimes last more than forty years on unfinished wood which has not been exposed to the elements. I presume this structure is still intact enough to preserve anything inside."

"That's a good point," said the chastened superintendent. "I'll get them working on it first thing tomorrow."

"We'd like to start in the morning by taking a look at the body and the remains of the clothes that were found at the scene," said Inspector Kidner.

"Fine. They are in the mortuary at Cumberland Infirmary in Carlisle. We kept them together until you arrived. A Dr. Bayat is the pathologist, and I'll call him to let him know you're coming. I'll tell him you'll be there about nine. We've booked you into a local hotel, and I'll get one of my staff to show you where it is."

The next day, Inspector Kidner and Sergeant Lockhart met Dr. Bayat at the mortuary. The skeletal remains were laid out on an examination table, and they examined them very closely.

"The cause of death was probably blunt force trauma to the head," reported Dr. Bayat.

"He didn't hit his head on the ground when he fell or was thrown down the shaft?"

"No, his head was crushed by some sort of blunt weapon, maybe a rock. A fall wouldn't have made the same impact on his skull. I said probably because we haven't got the complete body to check. He was submerged in water for many years so that any tissue has rotted away, and we are only left with the bones and some clothing. The very dry weather we have had in the last two years caused the water table to recede in the mine, so his remains were revealed. We found a heavy old vice near the body which was probably used to weigh it down."

"Can you tell how long he's been down there?"

"It's very difficult to say. That prosthesis he was wearing probably dates back to the 1940s. It would have had leather straps on it that secured it to his stump, but as you see, they are missing. That helps us give you a rough date. Another interesting thing is what remains of the waistband of his underwear. The label says 'Government Property' which indicates that he was likely in the armed forces. But that's all I can tell you."

Inspector Kidner picked up the prosthetic leg and started to examine it closely, wiping away some of the grime that had accumulated on it.

"Dr. Bayat, could you get someone with a scrubbing brush to wash this leg thoroughly," asked the inspector. "It could be an important clue in this murder, and I want to make sure that we aren't missing anything."

A few minutes later, a laboratory technician brought back the scrubbed leg which the inspector pored over. He asked Dr. Bayat for a magnifying glass and wrote down some numbers in his notebook.

"Brenda, I can just make out some numbers in the instep. Take a look and see if you agree with those I have written down."

"The last number is a three, not an eight, and there's a slash mark before the two last numbers," she said after a careful look.

"I wonder if that number relates to the individual limb which was different for each patient or whether it was a product number. Anyway, it will give us a start in tracing who it belonged to."

They thanked Dr. Bayat and left. As they walked through the hospital corridors to the car park, they discussed their findings.

"If he was in the armed forces, what's he doing carrying a civilian ID and ration book and not a military pay book which would have been his ID?" said Inspector Kidner. "It doesn't make sense."

"Unless someone stole his identity and disposed of his body where no one would come across it. Thanks to Mother Nature's drought, his body was eventually found," said Brenda.

"That's a good theory, Brenda, and that's what I'm thinking. Now let's go and visit the scene of the crime."

It took them fifty minutes to make the journey to Keswick. They stopped at the police station on Bank Street and asked for the duty sergeant. Sergeant Bader came out of the inner office.

"How can I help you?"

"I'm Detective Inspector Kidner, and this is Detective Sergeant Lockhart," he said as he showed his warrant card. "We're here from London looking into the corpse that was found in an old mine near here."

"Yes, sir. Superintendent Davis said you might be calling in. The lab boys have been up there this morning checking for the fingerprints that you wanted."

"Could you get someone to show us where to go?"

"I will take you there myself, sir. Before we go, we need to find you some wellington boots because it's very muddy up there."

They drove out of town with Sergeant Bader sitting in the backseat. They passed through Stair and reached the track that led on to the Above Derwent Fell. They changed into their wellington boots and started the long climb up the fell to the old mine's wheelhouse. Sergeant Bader led the way inside.

"Those timbers over there were covering the shaft opening, and the techs found several different prints."

Inspector Kidner and Sergeant Lockhart spent a lot of time examining the wheelhouse but found nothing new.

"Sergeant Bader, if you were going to throw a body down this shaft how would you get it here?" asked the inspector.

"I'd want to bring it in a car and drive it as close as possible the wheelhouse so that I didn't have to carry it far. The path here is very overgrown now, but I bet, years ago, it would have been easy to drive a car up here."

"Precisely. Petrol during the war was in short supply unless you had a vehicle for official business or were in the armed services. Now tell me, was there any army camp or unit in Keswick during the war?"

"Oh, I wouldn't know, sir, long before my time. Perhaps you'd better talk to old George Lambert. He was in the war and runs a café on Market Street. Failing him, there is the Keswick Museum or the library that may have the records."

They dropped Sergeant Bader off at the police station. They parked the car in a public car park and walked up Market Street. As it was the beginning of the holiday season, the street was bustling with tourists and hikers. After trying a number of cafés, they eventually found the one they were looking for and sat down at a table. They ordered some tea and asked the waitress whether George Lambert was there. A large man with a mane of grey hair came up to them.

"Mary said you were looking for me," he said suspiciously. "Are you county inspectors?"

"No. We're from the police," said the inspector. "We are looking into the body that was found in that old mine on the Above Derwent Fell. We wonder if you could help us."

"I don't know anything about a body," a shocked George Lambert said.

"We know you don't. Can you tell us whether there was an army unit based here during the war?"

"Um. There was a driver and maintenance school here, and the Yanks had something outside of town."

"Was there a military hospital here?"

"No. But there was a convalescent home at Derwent Hall on Borrowdale Road run by the army. They used to fit wooden limbs to the poor sods that had theirs blown off. It closed down after the war, though, and is now a hotel."

"Does the name Patrick Duggan ring any bells with you?" Brenda asked impulsively.

"Sure, I remember him. He was a nice Irish lad that helped my mum out when my eldest brother died in 1941. He worked at Derwent Hall doing office work for them, if I remember. Was it his body that was found?"

"We don't know. His name came up, and I wondered," said Brenda, showing no sign of interest.

"He left Keswick in 1942, or was it 1943? I know that everybody that knew him was surprised by the suddenness of his disappearance. My mum was particularly upset because she had become very fond of him."

"Mr. Lambert, do you happen to have a photograph of Patrick Duggan?" Inspector Kidner asked. "Perhaps one was taken with your mother?"

"I don't know. There were a lot old photographs in a box in our loft that was left by her when she died. I've never been through them."

"Would you be willing to do so tonight when you get home? It would help us very much if you could find one."

"Right you are. If I find anything, I'll bring it with me to the café tomorrow and ring you."

"Here's the number where we can be reached. Thank you, Mr. Lambert, you have been very helpful," said Inspector Kidner, closing the interview.

Inspector Kidner and Sergeant Lockhart drove back to Penrith that evening, and in their hotel's empty lounge bar, they reviewed what they had found out that day.

"I think we need to follow up with the Royal Army Medical Corps at the Catterick Garrison in Yorkshire and see whether they have any records of the Derwent Hall convalescent home. I'll give Commander Moore a call tonight and see whether he can help us gain access to their records. Hopefully, the number we found on the wooden leg relates to a specific patient. It seems this Patrick Duggan is the key to unravelling this case."

"We know that Duggan was at the home in 1941, 1942, and, possibly, 1943," said Brenda. "If we can't get information from the number on the leg, we could look at all the patients that received prosthetic legs and follow up with them or their relatives and, thus, eliminate them from our search. I know it's a long shot, but we might have to do that. I hope Mr. Lambert can find a photograph because it would help us narrow down the field.

"Also, it would be helpful to have a list of the staff at that time and follow up with them, if we can find them."

The next morning, Brenda joined Inspector Kidner for breakfast.

"I called the commander last night and briefed him on the case so far. He has agreed to contact someone he knows at the Ministry of Defence. I'll call him again tonight. In the meantime, Brenda, would you go to the museum and library in Keswick and see if there are any press clippings from this time period about Derwent Hall."

Sergeant Lockhart didn't get back to the hotel until sometime after three in the afternoon, bearing photocopies of press clippings in a large envelope.

"After a lot of searching, sir, I found some press stories about Derwent Hall. The first one was about its opening as a military convalescent home which is interesting background. It does mention a Dr. Robert Morrison, who was the director of the home, and his second in command, a Dr. Roger Abelson. There are pictures of them and the sour-looking matron, Annabelle Royston.

"My pièce de résistance is a blurry picture of Patrick Duggan. A group photograph of the staff was taken for a story in 1941 about the good work the home was doing, rehabilitating wounded soldiers."

Inspector Kidner read both articles several times. "Good work, Brenda. You can now follow up by calling the General Medical Council and asking them about registration status of those two doctors."

"I did, sir. Dr. Morrison died in 1963, and Dr. Abelson is retired and lives with his daughter in Ambleside which is just thirty minutes or so from here."

Inspector Kidner chuckled. "I should have known better. Of course, you followed up. What time are we seeing him tomorrow?"

"Ten."

The very narrow road to Ambleside was treacherously windy, and they were slowed by hikers who were walking in the road. Also, they met several oncoming delivery lorries which took up most of the very narrow road, and often, they had to back up the car into passing spots to let them pass. Following the instructions Dr. Abelson's daughter had given them, they finally reached the large Victorian house, which was set back off the road and was approached by tree-lined drive.

They rang a bell at the front door, and after a few seconds, it was opened by a well-dressed woman in her forties.

"Good morning, madam, I'm Sergeant Lockhart, and this is Inspector Kidner. We talked yesterday about seeing your father."

"Oh yes. Come in, come in."

She took them through the hall into a large and spacious living room. Sitting at a desk doing a *Times* crossword puzzle was the robust-looking seventy-two-year-old Dr. Abelson. He turned as they came in and greeted them with a broad smile.

"Please sit down. Mary, can we get some coffee for our guests?"

When they had sat down, he asked, "What can I do for the constabulary today?"

"We're from Scotland Yard, sir, and we are looking into a murder that took place probably over forty years ago," the inspector said.

"Ah, the body in the mine case. I read about it in the paper. So they've brought in the big guns then."

"That's right, sir. We understand that, during the war, you were a doctor at the Derwent Hall convalescent home run by the army in Keswick," said Inspector Kidner.

"Yes, that's right. I was a young doctor straight out of nappies, and I learned a lot there under Dr. Robert Morrison. After the war, I was at the Manchester Royal Infirmary and became an orthopaedic surgeon there until I retired."

"We've found the skeletal remains of a man who had a prosthetic leg. It is evident he was murdered, and he had on him an identification card of a Patrick Duggan. Does his name ring any bells, sir?"

"It certainly does, Inspector. He was in charge of administration at the home and was a very friendly Irishman from Belfast, I think. He rescued one of our nurses from a patient who had gone off his rocker and was threatening her with a knife. I understand the nurse and he went out together. She went off to midwifery school in London, and he suddenly disappeared."

"You have a good memory, sir. Do you remember her name?"

"Yes. Her name was Jane Stevens. I fancied her myself, but she only had eyes for Duggan after his heroic rescue," he said, smiling wryly. "The war did some funny things to us back then. We were all thrown together in an intense environment where mistakes were costly to our patients. Of course, it wasn't as bad as the traumas being suffered by our frontline troops and our air force pilots, but it was a pressure cooker nonetheless."

Just then, Dr. Abelson's daughter came in with a tray of cups and saucers and a large coffee pot. She poured coffee for all of them and then left the room.

"I know it wasn't Duggan's remains you found, though, Inspector," the doctor continued.

"Oh, why is that, sir?" said a surprised Inspector Kidner.

"Well, he didn't have a prosthetic leg. He had a limp caused by a severe beating he received in a Spanish prisoner of war camp during the civil war there. His broken ankle wasn't treated properly, and therefore, it became deformed."

Sergeant Lockhart showed Dr. Abelson some photographs of the prosthetic leg they had found. "It had a number on it. What does that stand for, sir?" she asked, showing him a piece of paper with the number on it.

"Hmm, I haven't seen one of these legs since the war. We changed its design in 1943, or was it 1944? Anyway, the number is the model number, so we could trace it back to the manufacturer. After the slash, there was another number which refers to the patient. So looking at this number you have, this was the thirteenth patient to get this type of leg. We had to keep meticulous records for the army in a logbook of who got what, God knows why."

"Do you know where these records went after the war?"

"I think they went to the army barracks at Catterick, but I'm not certain."

"Are you still in touch with anybody from the home?"

"Not really. I haven't heard from anybody in years. We all went our different ways after the war. Wait a minute, though, I read somewhere that one of our patients, Robin Taylor, had taken over his father's transportation business in Workington just after the war. He and I had become quite friendly while he was with us, and that's why I remember him. He loved classical music as I do. He said that he was going to join his father's firm when he got out of the army."

"Thank you, sir, you've been really helpful," said Inspector Kidner as he got up to leave.

They got back to the Cumbria police headquarters in Penrith at about two that afternoon, and there was a message for them to call George Lambert. When Sergeant Lockhart reached him, he said he had two photographs of Patrick Duggan taken at a Christmas party which he found in his mother's box of belongings. Brenda arranged to pick them up from him that afternoon.

Inspector Kidner called Commander Moore and briefed him on the progress of the case. The commander said he had phoned his contact at the Ministry of Defence who suggested he call a Maj. James Jefferson at the Catterick Garrison. He apparently was in charge of a warehouse complex that stored army records for the north of England. When he spoke to the major, he briefed him on what he was looking for and was told it was unlikely that they would have kept such records that far back. He promised to get back to him if they found anything.

This news was a disappointment to the inspector because they had made such good progress and had now reached a dead end. At least, he had two names, and that was a good start. He took out the telephone directory for Workington and, in its Yellow Pages section, looked for a listing of transportation companies. There were four companies listed, and one was called Taylor Transportation. He called the company and found out that a Robin Taylor was the managing director. He wasn't in, but the inspector arranged with his secretary to meet him the following morning.

At precisely ten the next morning, Inspector Kidner and Sergeant Lockhart walked into Robin Taylor's office. As they sat in a conference room, waiting for him to join them, they inspected the certificates and plaques that adorned its walls. The door suddenly opened, and a man in his late sixties walked in. He had a prosthetic right arm and shook their hands with his left hand.

"Now, Inspector, what's all this about? My secretary didn't give me much information, except to say you wanted to see me as soon as possible."

Inspector Kidner told him briefly what they were investigating, and he was amazed that such an old case was being taken seriously.

"Sir, did you know an Irishman by the name of Patrick Duggan?" Brenda asked.

"No, I don't remember anyone of that name."

"He would have been at Derwent Hall at the same time you were. He worked there as an administrator," Brenda persisted. "This is a photograph of him at that time."

"Ah, now I remember him. A nice man."

"Did he have any particular friends among the patients?"

"Not that I recall. Wait a minute, there was someone he talked to a lot. I think they knew each other from the past. What was his name? He was a miserable sod who wasn't very friendly, and he told us he was going to be a priest. God help his congregation!"

"Do you remember what he was there for?"

"They gave him a wooden leg after he was wounded at Dunkirk—Ellis, that's it, Nigel Ellis."

The inspector and the sergeant were going over the day's findings in the hotel bar that evening when he was paged by the hotel's reception. The call was from Major Jefferson from the Catterick Garrison.

"You're lucky, Inspector. We've found papers and a logbook from Derwent Hall. It was part of a batch of old files that were due for incineration. Anyway, that number you gave me was, according to the logbook, a prosthetic limb was given to Lt. Nigel Ellis."

Gotcha, thought a relieved Inspector Kidner.

CHAPTER 30

Branton, Devon, December 1982

Rev. Nigel Ellis (née Francis Reagan) was now in his early sixties and had been the parish priest for Branton and surrounding villages for almost twenty-five years. This had been the most peaceful period of his troubled life.

Branton was a village of some nine hundred people who were a mix of farm families, retirees, and business people who commuted to nearby Exeter or Okehampton. The village was dominated by a sixteenth-century church, which was surrounded by cottages and farmhouses on narrow side streets as well as those in the main square. Some of these were medieval dwellings, but most were Victorian. In the centre of the village, there was the small general store and a pub called The Feathers. On the north side of the village, on a secondary road that led to Okehampton, was a council housing estate that was built in the 1960s where farmworkers lived, as well as some factory workers who worked in the nearby cities.

Francis was still a slim man with his red hair and beard, both of which had become mottled with grey over the years. He hadn't revealed much about his background to members of his parish and told them that his limp was the result of a motorbike accident when he was young. Other than this information, no one knew much about his past, except he had come to Branton from a small parish in London.

He never remarried and lived a bachelor's life, indulging his three biggest passions: historical research, fly fishing, and a good Scotch whiskey. Over the years, he had gained a well-earned reputation for his scholarly work on the Celtic peoples of the West Country. He was often a guest lecturer at the University of Exeter and had published two books on the subject.

Francis had been happy to move from his first parish which was in the hellhole that was Notting Dale, London, in the late fifties. The very next year, after he had left his parish, his dire warnings about racial trouble had come to pass. The Notting Hill race riots that happened in late August and early September 1958, and those in Nottingham that had preceded them, were Britain's wake-up call to the racial tensions which were boiling just below the surface of its post-war society.

His vicarage, which was next to his church, was a large draughty two-story Victorian house built when vicars had large families. It had three bedrooms on the upper floor, a large dining room, a library, and a lounge on the ground floor. It was far too big for one person, although sometimes the household had included a curate. Since attendance at his church had dropped off in recent years, the diocese had decided that the he didn't need the help, so he hadn't had an assistant for at least ten years. This suited him. Apart from occasional visits from the bishop or dean from Exeter, he was left to his own devices.

During his first year in Branton, Alison, Jane's sister, had invited herself down to Devon and stayed with Francis for a week. She still believed he needed cheering up and was very solicitous to his needs. Francis became very attracted to her and she to him. She had a habit of walking around the house just in her see-through underwear and thought nothing about going from her room to the bathroom naked. It was as if she deliberately enticed him to look at her. At her last night in Branton, they got very drunk and made love on the sofa in the living room.

After she left, Francis heard nothing from her. Some six months later, he got a wedding invitation in the post. She was marrying some doctor at the hospital where she worked. Francis sent her a gift but did not go to the wedding. He was puzzled at her behaviour. It was as if she wanted something or someone that belonged to her elder sister. Anyway, that was the last contact he had with anyone in Jane's family. Now he was well and truly on his own.

For Francis, the first fifteen years in Branton had been successful. He was able to rebuild the membership of his parish and his parishioners took to him in return. When the diocese amalgamated his parish with two others, he became even busier, holding services and other activities in three different churches.

An event in the village caused Francis to fear the discovery of his past. This only increased, and it began to fuel his paranoia.

He was taking the harvest festival which, apart from Christmas and Easter, was the third most important service here in the countryside. The church was full to the brim with his parishioners. As he entered behind the choir at the start of the ceremony, he looked around at the congregation smiling as he recognised many faces. Then his glance fell on an elderly man whom he had never seen before, or had he? The man had a military bearing and was smartly dressed. During the service, Francis tried to remember from where he knew him.

At the end of the service, he was at the door of the church, shaking hands with the parishioners. Towards the end of the line of people was the elderly gentleman. When he finally reached Francis, he shook hands with him with a firm grip.

"It was a very nice service, Vicar. I'm Mark Bennett, and I moved into Briar Cottage last week."

Francis was horrified. Now he knew where he had met this man before. Here in his village was the military intelligence officer who had been searching for him during the war and someone he must avoid at all costs.

Just calm down, he doesn't know who you are. I hope that my face hadn't given anything away.

"Welcome to our village. My name is Nigel Ellis, and I hope we will see you in our church on a regular basis."

"Thanks, Vicar. I retired here after working in Whitehall for more than thirty-five years. Now I plan to spend a lot of time in my garden and write my memoirs. Look, I'm having some people in for cocktails next Saturday evening. Would you like to join us?"

Oh god, what am I going to say? You've got to carry on as if nothing was wrong.

"That would be delightful."

"Say six o'clock then."

And then he was gone.

Francis went to the cocktail party, which was given for a mixture of members of the parish council and some of Mr. Bennett's friends. As the evening progressed, it became clear to Francis that Mark Bennett did not recognise him, and he relaxed more.

Mark Bennett soon became the heart and soul of the village. He was voted on to the parish council and soon became its chairman. He supported all church functions and was a cosponsor of the annual fete with Richard Jacobs, in whose garden the event was held each year.

True to his word, Mark Bennett's memoirs were published two years after his arrival. Francis bought a copy of the book and assiduously read it, frantic to find out whether he was mentioned. And there it was—in the final chapter, the author regretted not being able to solve several cases, particularly that of a German spy who had helped reconnoitre Belfast before the blitz started there. He had had a tip from Barry Trevelyan, a German agent, who they had caught. Before he went to the gallows, Trevelyan had told them that the man, a Francis Reagan, had been recruited to work in Belfast. Bennett had said that this spy always seemed one step ahead of them and appeared to have a sixth sense for danger when they were getting close.

This chapter in the book hit Francis like a thunderbolt.

What should I do? Run again? But where? Stop panicking! Think through the problem logically. I can't! Oh, but you can! Right! The man doesn't know who I am. Apart from a brief encounter twenty-five years ago, he has no clue who I really am. He's retired so will not be interested in pursuing me. Besides, the war was over almost forty years ago, so the likelihood of being caught is almost non-existent. I've still got to be vigilant, though, in case of trouble. I must keep close to him so I can be warned of any danger.

In the intervening years and despite his misgivings, Francis had become quite friendly with Mark Bennett. They both had an interest in fly fishing and had spent many days fishing in the nearby River Avon or Dart.

Despite this and his usual outward joie de vivre, there was in Francis a hidden desperate inner self. This grew worse as the years passed. He was a lonely man with no friends. He found it difficult to make friends and was always suspicious of anyone who tried to befriend him. He was cautious about talking about himself in case he gave anything away.

Alone in his empty vicarage, he always reminisced about his past. He missed Jane terribly and was haunted by thoughts of what his life would have been like if she had lived and they had had their child. He also regretted in many ways the killings for which he had been responsible, but he rationalised to himself that they were justified and that his victims were evil people who needed eliminating.

His biggest regret was his work for the Germans in Belfast which he was sure had led to the deaths of so many hundreds of innocent people. He often relived these past horrors. They always centred on the Belfast Blitz and his experience there as an air-raid warden—the bodies in the makeshift morgue in the empty swimming pools, his bombed-out street, and the deaths of his good friends. He believed it was his fault that they died, and his thoughts always reduced him to tears of melancholy.

These flashbacks did not happen just when he had too much whiskey to drink but also occurred in nightmares time and again. He kept his descent into ignominy from his parishioners. He was still the outgoing vicar they had known because of the façade he erected each time he interacted with them. The more astute villagers noticed that he increasingly appeared unkempt and dowdy, but they put this down to his old age and to his bachelor ways.

As the years passed, Francis's self-loathing grew. He dreaded going home at night and had, from time to time, visited prostitutes whom he would meet at Derry's Cross in Plymouth. He knew this was wrong and, on the way home from his assignations, regretted what he had done. And so the spiral downward continued.

Added to his growing melancholy was his physical health. In 1980, he had suffered a serious heart attack which had put him in hospital for three weeks. His recovery was slow and painful, but finally, he was able do light work and then ease back into his usual routine. At first, he took powerful medications and had to be closely monitored. He was told his cholesterol was much too high and was put on a strict diet.

However, the consultant at the hospital on one of Francis's visits told him some very disquieting news. Tests came back which showed he had a very serious heart defect for which there was no cure. The doctor estimated that he had about two or three years to live. Francis decided to carry on as best he could rather than retire and wait for the axe to fall.

This feeling of normality came to a sudden halt in September 1982. Francis was reading the *Daily Telegraph* newspaper with his breakfast when a small news story caught his attention and sent a cold shiver down his spine. Skeletal remains had been found in a disused mine near Keswick in the Lake District by two explorers. Apparently, the remains had been in the mine since the 1940s, and a Detective Superintendent Davis said the police were trying to identify them.

With this newspaper revelation, Francis felt that his whole world was crashing down on him.

I just don't believe this could happen. I heard the splash as his body dropped into the water. Could this lead back to me? Maybe. I've got to go before they find me. If it was his body, how long would it take for them to find me? It's just bones they found, so it would be very difficult to identify them. Nah, I'm safe. I must be vigilant though.

In the autumn of 1982, the main topic that was on everybody's minds and lips in Branton was a proposed retirement complex development near the village that had riled so many in the area. The two friends spent many evenings discussing the pros and cons of the project. Where Mark Bennett wanted to reject the plan because it would ruin the integrity of the village, as he saw it, Francis took the view that it would give people in the area desperately needed jobs.

The public meeting about the plan took place in November and had almost turned into a riot when agitators from an organisation called Protect the Countryside Now! or PCN whipped up the pent-up feelings of many of the villagers. The parish council was going to vote on the issue at its January meeting in the New Year. The members of the council had been inundated with literature from both sides and swamped with threatening phone calls.

In mid-December, Francis was glad to get away from the turmoil which had pitted neighbour against neighbour in Branton over the retirement home. He was to attend a seminar in London on historical research and was to be a guest panellist at one of the sessions. He drove his old MGB-GT out of the village and headed for Exeter St. Davids, which was the nearest station on the main line to London. Except for the good Scotch Whiskey, his car was the only luxury he allowed himself, and he had bought it several years previously.

When he reached the station, he bought a paper and settled down with a cup of coffee in the small snack bar on the platform where his train would arrive. He was there for only a few minutes when Mark Bennett came in.

"Hello, Nigel. What are you doing here?"

"I'm off to a seminar in London. And you?"

"Oh, I've got a dinner for my old regiment in the City's Goldsmith's Hall, and I have one or two things to do as well. To be honest with you, I'm glad for the break from Branton. People are getting pretty testy."

After a few minutes, their train pulled in to the station. Francis went to his reserved seat in the second-class compartment and Mark to his in first class. At Paddington Station in London, they shared a taxi. Mark dropped Francis off at St. Ermins Hotel on Caxton Street in Victoria and then went on to his club in St. James's.

It was four o'clock when Francis checked in to his hotel, and when he had unpacked his overnight bag in his room, he decided to take a walk. Although cold, it was not raining, so he decided to walk around St. James's Park.

He left his hotel and walked into Broadway from Caxton Street. On the opposite side of the street was a modern building that stood out from the other much older buildings nearby. A revolving sign announced it was New Scotland Yard, the headquarters of the Metropolitan Police. Nigel headed north along Broadway to Queen Anne's Gate and the park. On his way back, he bought an *Evening Standard* newspaper from a vendor at St. James's underground station and got back to his hotel just as it started to rain.

Francis went to the hotel bar, ordered himself a drink, and began to read the newspaper. On the page that dealt with nationwide news, he was horrified to see a piece reporting that police had been able to identify the remains in the Keswick mine. They didn't reveal the name but said that they were "making progress" in solving the forty-year-old murder case.

Francis went to his room and got out the bottle of malt whiskey he had brought with him. He had to think about what he was going to do. He was in a panic.

With Christmas coming next week, I have some time. The holidays, and the fact that it's an old case, will mean they won't be in a hurry to trace me until the New Year. They won't be able find me because I'm certain no one knows that Nigel was going to divinity school. He had no relatives, and he had no friends at the convalescent home. He told me that. They all hated him there. No, I should be all right if I keep my head.

That night, he fell into a fitful sleep and woke up several times in a cold sweat from his recurring nightmares. Dawn finally arrived, and he got up. He took a long shower, dressed, and went down for an early breakfast. His presentation at the conference went off well, and he was able to forget temporarily the danger he envisaged he was in.

At the close of the conference at five o'clock, he again decided to take a walk in St. James's Park. As he emerged from Caxton Street and turned left on to Broadway, he suddenly saw Mark Bennett coming out of New Scotland Yard. He was deep in conversation with a man in the police uniform of a deputy commissioner. When a chauffeured car pulled up, they got in and were whisked away.

Francis went back to his hotel room and took a stiff drink of his whiskey. He was puzzled why Mark was at New Scotland Yard. Had he found something out about Francis that connected him to his time in Belfast, or was it about the remains in the mine? His paranoia began to affect his rationality. The more he drank, the more morbid he felt, and the more he believed he was being hunted. The red mist began to waft under his door, and his father appeared.

"You're a big disappointment, you know. Making friends with that Bennett man was a big mistake. He's only going to shop you to the police. You saw him tonight. You'd better deal with him, otherwise they will come after you."

And then he was gone.

For once, Francis thought his father was right. He'll have to take care of Mark, and everything will be all right again.

CHAPTER 31

Branton, January 12, 1983

Little did the villagers in sleepy Branton know that on that winter night, their cosy world would come to a sudden halt by a series of killings.

It was one of those cold piercing January nights, and the darkness was foreboding, accentuated by a vicious storm that had brought down many power lines in the area. Yet eerily, power to some parts of the village was not affected.

The wind was blowing hard, picking up intensity from the Atlantic as it crossed Dartmoor and hit the village, which was nestled on the edge of the moor's great expanse. The wind was a hard taskmaster to the living. It cut like a sharp knife and, combined with the constant rain, was freezing a lone figure to his bones as he hurried up the street.

Sixty-eight-year-old Dr. Robert Galway, who was the local doctor, was rushing to a parish council meeting, and he was late as usual, mumbling to himself as he fought his way up the street. Dr Galway was a heavy-set man who was just under six feet tall. In his youth, he had been thin and handsome, but the years had taken their toll on his appearance. He was overweight and suffered from high blood pressure. His once fulsome brown hair had given way to baldness with wisps of grey around the lower part of his head.

The wind was so strong it was making the rain come at him sideways as he struggled to walk through the village. As he made his way, he wondered to himself why, after almost forty years, he lived in such a desolate and godforsaken spot. And it wasn't just the winters that made him so restless. There were growing pressures of urbanization that was now making an impact in the village. This was the subject of tonight's meeting.

Dr. Galway was late because of his last patient at his evening clinic. He was agitated by the foolishness of some people but supposed that having to deal with problem patients came with his profession. Their behaviour seemed to be getting to him more easily these days. He made a mental note to tell his secretary to schedule Mrs. Robertson earlier in the evening when he would have more time for her nonsense. What should have been a ten-minute visit turned into a thirty-minute discussion of the latest happenings in the village. A lot of what she said was pure gossip, but as always, there was a sliver of truth in it.

He wondered why he still lived in Branton. When he came to the village in 1946, it was a great solace after his turbulent World War II experience. Branton had been good to him. He had met his wife there, and they had a daughter on whom they doted. As the local GP he covered some three other villages, including Branton.

He knew he should have retired some years ago and moved to Southern Spain or maybe France, like many of his friends, but the fear of change and letting go of his practice made him procrastinate. He knew this was irrational. The truth was that he liked what he was doing. It gave his life purpose after his wife and daughter died in a car accident some twenty years before. As he made his way to the village hall, he decided to take the plunge and retire. He must do it this time.

What had awoken the sleepy villagers of Branton and nearby Crampton was a plan to develop a large retirement complex near the villages which would have about two hundred residents and would be on six acres of prime agricultural land. The issue had pitted older residents, who wanted no change to their way of life, and the more vocal younger generation saw it as a job opportunity for themselves and their children.

Dr. Galway was leaning towards voting for the project. He believed that many villages like Branton had to face the hard truth that many of the younger generation were moving out to the cities like Exeter or Plymouth for jobs and what they saw as a better life. Maybe this was one way to stop the people drain from villages in the area. On the other hand, many of the newer residents retired there for the peace the country environment offered.

The parish council had to make the initial decision on whether to approve the planned retirement home. If this plan was given the green light, it would then move on to the district council, and finally the county council, before it was implemented. The parish councils of Branton and Crampton had been combined some twenty years before in a move to make the legislative system more efficient and less fractious. There were seven parish councillors, four from Branton and three from the much smaller village of Crampton.

The council members making this key decision were a diverse group. Apart from Dr. Galway, there was sixty-eight-year-old Mark Bennett. A feisty member, Roxanne Stevens, who owned the general store in Branton, the council's chairman was a very rotund woman who was always seemed to be picking fights with other council members and giving her usually unwelcome opinions in a loud whining voice. One of her favourite targets was Richard Jacobs, a retired businessman, who had come to the village some ten years previously and had joined in with the community life with alacrity. He lived in a large mansion that had about twenty acres of land and was a keen sponsor of many village events, including the annual garden fete.

Representing Crampton were Martha Torren, the headmistress at the area school, and Peter Bryant, a local farmer whose family had been farming in the area for more than a century. Martha had a great eye for detail and often pointed to inconsistencies in their decisions, much to Roxanne Stevens's annoyance. Peter could always be counted on for sound practical advice. The seventh member of the council was Andrew Dwyer, the landlord of The Fox & Goose pub in Crampton.

They were meeting in executive session before the formal meeting at seven thirty to discuss issues that had been raised by someone in the community. Mark Bennett wouldn't say what it was or who it was from.

As he passed The Feathers pub, Dr. Galway envied the people inside who were relaxing in a warm and inviting environment around the fireplaces in each bar. With a sigh, he continued on to the village hall which was probably the newest building in the village, having been built in the 1960s. It was next to the oldest, the church, and next to this was the vicarage. Dr. Galway got on well with the vicar who had been in the parish for almost the same number of years as he had and was a soft-spoken man. The vicar was very supportive after the deaths of his family, and the doctor would always be grateful.

Mark Bennett was the first to arrive for the meeting. He was reviewing his notes and going over in his mind what he needed to tell the other members of the parish council of what he had found out. He had helped himself to some of the decaffeinated tea Mrs. Clarke, the janitor, had prepared for him, as well as other refreshments for the other participants at the meeting. Just then, Roxanne Stevens made her windswept appearance.

"I think we should protest to the county council about the drainage system here in our village. You should see the flooding in the main square. Mrs. Shelby told me that they aren't going to do anything because they haven't got the money. I suppose you know that we won't get much of a turn out tonight, with the weather being so bad. I don't know why you didn't call it off," she said.

"I called everyone, and they said they would be here," an exasperated Mark Bennett replied, not looking up.

"Oh look, Mrs. Clarke has given us a real treat tonight, biscuits with jam fillings," she cooed, scooping up four of them and helping herself to some of Mark Bennett's decaffeinated tea just to annoy him. It was second nature to her to agitate people.

Little did they know that a shadowy figure was watching them from behind the curtains on the stage.

*　　*　　*

I'm sorry, Mark, but you have to go. I can't risk you tracing me, not after all these years. You won't get me! I have to do this for my own survival. I've been free for fifty years, and I can't let you get me now. Drink the special tea I made for you. I'm watching! You can't get away!

Oh god, there's that wretched woman from the shop. Look at that fat piece of lard put away those biscuits. She wasn't supposed to drink the tea! It was for him. Oh well, serves the bitch right. She'll be well and truly sick.

I've seen enough, time to go. Out the back. Still raining. Up the path and through the car park. Shit! Headlights of a car turning into the car park. Did they see me? I better make sure. Ah, a woman struggling with an umbrella. I just know she saw me. I must deal with this, and oh, Lord, when will I be free? There is a rock I can use. Sorry, lady, you were in the wrong place at the wrong time.

If I creep up behind her, she will never hear me in this weather. Here she comes down the path that leads towards the front of the hall. Ah, she sees the emergency door open. Oh god, she's turning around. Maybe she senses something. She recognizes me. I bring the rock down on her face. It's over. I need to hide her. Oh god, I can't do this. I must. There are bushes to my right. I'll drag her there.

I must go!

*　　*　　*

Dr. Galway crossed the empty street and walked up the path leading to the front door of the village hall. The layout was very typical of these mass-produced buildings which are scattered all over England in towns and villages.

As he entered, he shook off the rain from his coat and hat. Then he heard loud groaning noises. He opened the doors to the main hall and stood aghast at the scene of human misery before him. Mark Bennett was lying on the floor, foaming at the mouth, with his body stiff as a rock. Roxanne

Stevens was slumped over the meeting table in a semiconscious state. She had vomited across the table and was grabbing at her throat as she lay there. Both were semiconscious. The other parish council members, who had come in just before the doctor, stood there dazed as if in state of shock.

Dr. Galway shouted at Peter Bryant to call for an ambulance and the police at the phone box in the entrance to the hall. This pulled Peter out of his trancelike state, and he rushed off to do what he was told.

Dr. Galway realized that there was nothing he could do medically until the ambulance came and got them to hospital. That would be at least an hour because they were deep in the country and the storm would slow things down. He went over to Mark Bennett because he was the nearest. His pupils were pinpointed, and he had an irregular heartbeat. He then went to Roxanne Stevens who was in a lot worst shape. He pulled her down to the ground and examined her. She had the same symptoms.

The fact that they were so sick at the same time with the same symptoms puzzled him. However, it was essential they get Mark and Roxanne to the hospital. Delay would contribute to their possible deaths.

Richard Jones and Andrew Dwyer were suddenly at his side, asking what they could do. "I think we have to make them comfortable and ensure their air passages are clear. I can do this if you would go to the front entrance and stop anyone from coming in. You'll have to say the meeting has been postponed. We need time to evaluate what we are dealing with here," Dr. Galway said in concerned tones.

Peter Bryant was soon back, saying that the emergency services were on their way. "I hope they get here in time to help Mark and Roxanne," Dr. Galway said grimly. "Now tell me, Peter, what went down here?"

"I'm not too sure, it all happened so fast. We just got here, and we were waiting for you and Martha to arrive before starting the meeting. Mark and Roxanne were here first and were drinking the tea prepared by Mrs. Clarke. It's odd that Martha hasn't arrived yet. I don't understand where she is. It's not like her to be late. Anyway, we were talking about the vote we were taking this evening. Suddenly, Roxanne collapsed and then Mark."

"Have you any idea why Mark called us together before the meeting?"

"No."

About ten minutes later, the first sign of help arrived in the form of Constable Frank MacFaden who was the local policeman. His first reaction was "Oh my god!"

"Frank, I think we have a crime scene here which we must preserve. But first, we need to get these two very sick people to hospital. We've already contacted the emergency services," said Dr. Galway.

"It might be some time before an ambulance arrives," Frank commented. "The weather has caused many trees to come down."

"You will need to contact your Okehampton headquarters and tell them what has happened," Dr. Galway instructed the constable. "They will have to get a senior detective and a forensic team here."

It was over an hour and a half before an ambulance arrived because of the violent weather which had made traveling treacherous. The paramedics started work with the victims immediately under instructions of the doctor, who wanted to stabilize them before they were taken away. Eventually, they were moved into the ambulance, each with IVs in their arms and oxygen masks covering their faces.

Despite the weather, the blue emergency lights of the ambulance had attracted a small crowd of villagers wanting to know what all the fuss was about. All they were told by Constable MacFaden was that two members of the parish council had been taken ill and that the meeting had been postponed.

As the ambulance pulled away, Nigel Ellis (née Francis Reagan) rushed up and inquired what was happening. Dr. Galway took him to one side and explained the events of the evening. Also, he told him of his suspicions that a crime had been committed.

"I must go to the hospital to be with them," Francis said. "Do you know which one?"

"Royal Devon and Exeter," said the doctor. "I'd join you, but I have to wait for the police team."

Francis limped off to find his car and get on his way. Dr. Galway returned to the crime scene and the survivors of the attack. He started going over everything in his mind. With his curiosity peaked, he decided to take another look around the village hall. He knew he shouldn't be doing this before the forensic team arrived, but there was something bothering him, and he didn't know what it was.

For the life of him, he couldn't think what was out of place. Then he remembered—Martha Torren wasn't there. She was late, and this never happened before, and there was a draft blowing up the corridor to the stage.

With his senses sharpened, he approached the door, which was partly open, and wet leaves had blown into the corridor. Someone had recently used that door. He knew that Mrs. Clarke brought the refreshments through the front door because the kitchen was near the main entrance. She had help from her husband who, as usual, had probably parked his car on the street in front of the building. No, this was someone else.

The storm was unrelenting in its ferocity as Dr. Galway put on his gloves again and carefully opened the door. There was a light above the door, which shone for about six feet, and he was able to see the path. What took his breath away was the body lying partially in the bushes. Despite the hard rain, he could tell it was a woman because she was wearing a skirt, but that was all he could see. He rushed out and quickly established that Martha Torren was dead.

CHAPTER 32

The demanding ring of the telephone startled Chief Inspector George Kaeley as he had just finished loading the dishwasher in his kitchen, had selected the music he wanted to relax to, poured himself a large Scotch, and sat down in his reclining chair by a roaring fire. *Oh shit, not tonight*, he thought.

He had told himself that he was going to do what he wanted tonight. *To hell with them all!* He was fed up with being the go-to guy in the department. It wasn't any inflated ego that made him think that was the case. Truth was that he had been too successful in solving the cases other officers were glad to hand over to him and he was too eager to take them on. He didn't know why, but he always got an adrenaline rush which was not satisfied until he got to the bottom of a case and solved it. It was an addiction. Each case was a mental challenge to him in his attempt at understanding what motivated the criminal behaviour. Often, he would put himself in the perpetrator's mind-set to solve the intricate puzzles of a case.

But tonight he rejoiced in the fact that he was not on call and not home to anybody. *Leave it! You are not here.* However, the ring seemed so shrill and had completely destroyed the warm atmosphere and expectations for the evening.

He picked up the receiver. "Yes," he said in the gruffest and most annoyed voice he could possibly muster. It was Chief Superintendent Mallory, telling him to get himself to Branton as fast as possible. So much for his precious night off.

"But, sir, this is my night off," he protested.

"Look, George, we have a likely attempted murder of the entire parish council in Branton. I want an experienced senior officer down there who has dealt with murder cases before. I've already asked for a complete forensic team from Plymouth, and I need you down there pronto to take charge."

When the chief superintendent finished his briefing, Kaeley's attention was riveted by the enormity of the crime. "OK, sir. I'm on my way."

There was no point in arguing. The old man knows how to get his own way. It was true that Kaeley was experienced in murder investigations. He had been involved in a number of them in London and had seen his fair share here in the West Country.

The chief inspector was big man and weighed about seventeen stone. Despite his fifty-two years, he was thin where it mattered and muscular. He put this down to his years as a top-class rugby player for London's Metropolitan Police.

Although his family was from Devon, he had begun his career in the Met, but after twenty years, he had put in for a transfer to Okehampton so he could take care of his elderly parents. The Devon and Cornwall Constabulary was glad to have him, and he rose quickly in rank. This had been the cause of some resentment by other officers as they saw him as an interloper. He didn't care. Getting a case solved was more important to him than the politics of who was in line for promotion or who was "in" with the chief superintendent.

He had never married because his career had always got in the way of any true relationships, although there had been a number of possibilities. The truth was that he was very shy around women and found it difficult to express his personal feelings. The same couldn't be said of his police work, just the opposite.

When he had got off the telephone with his chief superintendent, he called Sergeant Bill Evans who had been with him as his number two for about three years. The two had grown close and could anticipate the other's thoughts and actions. Where Kaeley was instinctive, Evans was pragmatic. They were a good team.

"Bill, I'm sorry to wake you from your beauty sleep," he said sarcastically to the very sleepy voice that answered on the other end, "but there's been an incident at Branton's village hall. It looks like there has been a poisoning of parish council members at a meeting. We need to get down there as soon as possible. There's a forensic team on its way. I'll pick you up in ten minutes"

"I'll see you in ten," he said with a heavy sigh. Sergeant Evans rolled out of bed and grabbed his clothes as he went to the bathroom to dress, trying not to wake his sleeping girlfriend, Susan. They had lived together for two years now, and the arrangement suited them fine because each had a job that made great demands on their lives. Susan was a casualty department nursing sister at the local hospital, and her hours, like his, were unpredictable.

They were both in their late thirties and dedicated to their careers. But they thoroughly enjoyed the limited time they had together and had become soul mates. They were devoted to each other in their own special way.

When he opened his front door, he could see Chief Inspector Kaeley waiting for him in his car. They both lived in Okehampton and were based there. The trip to Branton should have taken just under an hour, but instead, it was two hours before they were able to reach the village. Getting to these small villages was slow at the best of times, but it was made even worse that night. The fierce weather had caused flash flooding, and there were downed trees all over the area. It reminded Chief Inspector Kaeley of the storms that hit Britain's West Country in the 1970s. He mused to himself that the devil must be angry tonight.

What he knew about the situation was that the local constable had contacted central dispatch to report a possible poisoning. The constable had reported that a Dr. Galway had told him to contact a senior officer to let him know of his suspicions. As they were doubling back for the umpteenth time, trying to find a route to Branton that hadn't downed trees across the road, central dispatch contacted them on their car radio to report a body had been found outside the village hall.

Chief Inspector Kaeley and Dr. Galway were well acquainted. Dr. Galway was the police surgeon for the area, and Kaeley knew that if this no-nonsense Scot insisted on reporting a possible poisoning, this was not a fool's errand. He was glad Dr. Galway was on the spot because he would ensure the crime scene was preserved. In this role as police surgeon, the doctor was called in mainly to examine people who had been arrested and, when necessary, conduct tests, such as sobriety or drugs, or patch them up if they had been injured.

Chief Inspector Kaeley and Sergeant Evans arrived in Branton soon after midnight, and the inspector was very frustrated by the delay in getting started with the investigation. When they pulled up in front of Branton's village hall, they saw that the area had been efficiently taped off. There was nobody around. Chief Inspector Kaeley thought to himself that at least with the weather, the media would be slow to respond. This would give him a chance to get some work done and concentrate on the investigation. The downside was that the rain would have washed away a lot of evidence outside, especially near the body.

They grabbed their flashlights from the car and walked up the path to the village hall. Constable McFadden suddenly appeared from the shelter of a big oak tree at the side of the road. Instead of acting surprised, the inspector shot a question at him. "Has anyone, apart from Dr. Galway and yourself, been anywhere near the body?"

"No sir," he replied.

"Show me where it is."

"This way, sir."

They followed the constable along the path at the side of building. They knew they had to be careful where they trod because forensics hadn't been over the area, but it was important to take a look because the rain would wash away much of the evidence.

They reached Martha Torren's body and used their powerful flashlights to examine the area. The body lay partly hidden in the bushes beside the path that led to the car park at the back of the hall. Her face was grotesquely contorted, with her eyes bulging, as if in disbelief, and her tongue was hanging out of one side of her mouth. The blow to the side of her head had pulverized the left side of her face. She had been hit with such force that her ear was crushed into her eye socket. What was left was a pulpy bloody mess.

The side of the building near the back door was spattered with blood, which was being slowly washed away by the constant rain. There was more blood being washed away on the path and scrape marks where someone had dragged the body.

Kaeley turned to his sergeant. "Bill, what's your take on the evidence we've seen so far?"

"I've seen some really grisly murders in my time, but this one is beyond belief. She was hit with such force by someone who is either extremely strong or maniacal. I find it interesting that the perpetrator went to the trouble of trying to hide the body. Maybe he was ashamed at what he'd done or wanted to delay anyone finding her. She was not well hidden, though, which tells me that the murderer was in a hurry. If he had done a proper job of hiding the body, it wouldn't have been found until the morning," he said.

"You said 'he,' and I think you're right," Kaeley said. "Our perpetrator was a man because it is very unlikely that a woman would have the strength to cause such damage. I wonder what he used. We'll have to wait for forensics to tell us. We'd better not look around anymore in case we disturb something. Let's go and talk to Dr. Galway."

They found Dr. Galway sitting in the village hall's kitchen with the three remaining council members. He introduced Peter Bryant, Andrew Dyer, and Richard Jacobs.

"I'm sorry to keep you all waiting," Kaeley said. "I know it's late, but I want to understand exactly what went on tonight while it's fresh in your minds, and then we can perhaps talk again when you've had time to think about events. Every little bit of information is important to us, however seemingly irrelevant it might be. Perhaps, gentlemen, Mr. Dyer, Mr. Jacobs, and Mr. Bryant would go with Sergeant Evans, and he will go through what you know. We'll take statements in the morning."

When the others had left, he turned to Dr. Galway. "What has happened here? I've never seen anything like this before. Was this random, or was the whole council targeted?"

"Good question. I was wondering this myself. What I do know was that our chairman, Mark Bennett, had something on his mind and wanted to talk to us about it before the official meeting. He and Roxanne Stevens were the early arrivals and had helped themselves to refreshments. I know Mark had a decaffeinated tea which was prepared separately by Mrs. Clarke. Maybe Roxanne had some of his tea as well. Anyway, they were very sick and had to be taken to the hospital unconscious. Peter, Andrew, and Richard came together and I was late.

"I was busy trying to help Mark and Roxanne, and I forgot that Martha Torren was missing. When I had a chance to take stock of the situation, I remembered about Martha and thought it very unusual that she was not here. She is always punctual. So I went looking for her and discovered that the back door to the car park had been opened. When I looked out, I could see her body lying partly under some bushes. I felt for her pulse, and I was careful approaching the body."

"The forensic team will be here soon, and we can get started on examining the area. Was there anything unusual on the agenda tonight?"

"We were to give planning permission for a retirement home near here. The developer has bought some farmland and is ready to start building. The whole subject was very controversial, and there were a number of contentious public meetings. There were angry words exchanged on both sides," he said.

"Was there anybody who was particularly angry?" Kaeley asked.

"Well, there was an organization formed to oppose the plan called Protect the Countryside Now! It's part of a national group, and a chapter was formed here headed by two firebrands, John and Wendy Burgess. They managed to totally disrupt one of the meetings with the help of local members and some people from London," he replied.

"We thought we might have problem tonight, but we've not seen hide nor hair of the Burgesses. Maybe they are keeping their powder dry for the county council hearings, which are expected after our approval," the doctor continued.

"Or perhaps they are responsible for this crime and wanted to make themselves scarce with an alibi," Kaeley commented.

"I hope you are wrong because I don't believe they would do such a thing. They are somewhat intense maybe, but murderous no."

Some thirty minutes later, Sergeant Evans returned and briefed Kaeley on his interviews with the parish councillors.

"Bill, would you arrange for a mobile incident room to be set up here by the village hall so we can operate efficiently. Also, I want a team of officers to go house to house first thing in the morning. We'll see whether they turn up anything," said Kaeley to Sergeant Evans.

Just then, there were raised voices in the hallway. They opened the door and saw a very angry man being restrained by Constable MacFaden. His glasses were askew in the struggle, and he was shouting "I want to see my wife!"

"Please, sir, just calm down and tell me who you are," said Kaeley with authority in his voice, which made the man stop his tirade and look the chief inspector in the eye.

"Are you in charge here?" he demanded.

"Yes. I am Chief Inspector Kaeley, and you are?"

"I am George Torren. My wife, Martha, is missing. She went to a meeting here tonight and hasn't come home. I set off from home to find her because I am worried sick about her. Then I saw all the police tape and . . ." His voice trailed off.

"Perhaps you would like to come in here," Kaeley said. Reluctantly, George Torren followed him as if he suspected what the chief inspector was going to say. Kaeley closed the kitchen door behind him and turned to face him.

"I am sorry to have to tell you your wife is dead, and we believe she was murdered. We have a forensic team on its way, and a post-mortem will be carried out to verify our suspicions. Dr. Galway here identified her for us," Kaeley said.

George Torren was silent. Then, as if his grief was suddenly released, he began to moan, at first very quietly and then it grew louder as he rocked back and forth on his feet. Dr. Galway caught him as he began to fall to the ground, punching seemingly at nothing, except his disbelief. He sat on the chair where Dr. Galway had guided him, his hands covering his face, sobbing very loudly and painfully. Then as quick as it began, the crying stopped, and he looked up red-eyed with an angry look on his blotched face.

"I'll kill the bastards who did this! Mark my words," he said with such venom. "They are going to pay for this!"

"You said 'they,' sir," said Kaeley, ignoring the threat. "Who do you mean?"

"The organisers of Protect the Countryside Now! My wife had been getting a lot of calls from them, telling her to vote against the land development plan or else."

"Who made the calls? Did your wife say?"

"No. She did say, every time, the caller was a woman and that there was a lot of background noise, like a busy office. That's all. She didn't take them very seriously. I wish we had. I think we might have a recording of one of these calls on our answering machine at home."

"Doctor, did you receive any calls?"

"Yes, two or three. My secretary screens my calls, and I usually call back when I have time between seeing patients. She had taken two, and the caller had just rang off. Then I started getting calls at home, and I put the phone down when they started ranting. My caller was a man," he said.

"Right, here's what we will do," Kaeley said, "Mr. Torren, please go home with Sergeant Evans and give him the tape from your answering machine. If you would remain there, we will keep you informed of what we find so that when the time comes, you can make proper arrangements for your wife's funeral. We'll have to let you know when we can release her body."

"But I want to be here with my wife," he pleaded lamely. An oppressive tiredness had come over him as he sat slumped in the chair.

"You can help your wife best if you would go home and give us the evidence we need. Is there someone we can call who can come and stay with you?" he asked gently.

"Martha's mother lives in Plymstock. Oh my god, what am I going to tell her? Then there's our daughter who is at the University of Exeter. I'll have to call her first and get her to come home. Oh my god, why did this happen to us?" he said and began to sob again.

"I'll tell you what," said Dr. Galway kindly, "I'll call the district nurse and have her meet you at your home tonight, and she can stay with you until your daughter comes. She can give you something you can take to help you sleep."

Dr. Galway went to the pay phone in the entrance hall and called Linda Renton, the district nurse. He briefed her on what he wanted and returned to the kitchen. He guided George Torren outside to the waiting police car. During all this activity, nothing was heard from him, except low sobs.

"Probably it's best you get some rest," Kaeley told the doctor when he returned to the village hall. "There's not much going on right now. I will want to continue talking with you tomorrow."

"Fine, I'll take my leave then," he said and started down the front path to walk home. At least, he thought, the rain had let up for the time being, and he could get home dry.

Just then, a black van and a car came down the street. It was the crime scene investigative team. As the men got out, Dr. Galway recognized one of the figures and greeted him. "Bill Grainger, how nice to see you! I'm glad you have been assigned this case," he said to the pathologist.

"Bob, what are you doing here?" Dr. Grainger responded. Dr. Galway explained briefly what had happened and that Chief Inspector Kaeley was already on the scene.

Dr. Grainger then went into the hall in search of the chief inspector. The remainder of the forensic team led by Constable McFadden went to side of the building to start their grim task of examining the body and the crime scene.

Chief Inspector Kaeley came hurrying out of the village hall and called to Dr. Galway, "I'm glad I caught you. I've just heard from the hospital that Roxanne Stevens has died. So we have a double murder on our hands. We'll have to do a post-mortem on her to confirm the cause. I'll let you know the results. Take my advice, be careful because we seem to have a desperate murderer on our hands."

CHAPTER 33

It was eleven the next morning when Detective Chief Inspector Kaeley and Sergeant Evans walked down the path that led to Briar Cottage. It had been a long night, and by the time the forensic team had finished their preliminary investigation, they were able to get only four hours sleep.

The team had found nothing that the police hadn't already suspected and had sent samples of all the refreshments that were in the village hall to the police crime laboratory. The post-mortems on Martha Torren and Roxanne Stevens were being done that day. Mark Bennett was still in serious condition in the hospital, but at least, he had been taken off the critical list.

For the two policemen, it was back to basic police work of interviews and establishing where various people were at the time of the crimes.

Briar Cottage was picture-perfect even in winter. In summer, it would be an idealistic place you would see in *Country Life* magazine and to which city dwellers would give their eyeteeth to retire. It was clear that its owners were perfectionists because the flower beds had been geometrically laid out. Even the little fountain in the pond projected water precisely so that it hit the space between the lily pads and the rocks on the side. The garden, it seemed, had not suffered much damage from the storm the previous night.

As Kaeley and Evans walked down the path, they saw two figures bending over a flower bed deep in conversation. When they heard the approaching footsteps, John and Wendy Burgess looked up at their visitors with some annoyance.

Kaeley thought they were both in their early sixties, and he knew from the inquiries he had made that John Burgess was an engineer by training. He had retired early because the firm he worked for had run into financial difficulties, and although he had a pension, they were living off investments Mrs. Burgess had inherited from her parents.

"Who are you, and what do you want?" John Burgess demanded.

"We are police officers. I'm Chief Inspector Kaeley, and this is Sergeant Evans," Kaeley responded.

"Let me see your identification then," he said suspiciously. Bemused, Kaeley handed him his warrant card, and it was examined closely. When he was satisfied, he handed it back.

"What have you come to bother us about?" he demanded. "If it's about those phone calls, we had nothing to do with them!"

"We are here about the murders of two parish councillors at the village hall last night," Kaeley said simply. This seemed to stun John and Wendy Burgess, who looked at each other.

"Who was killed?" a chastened John Burgess asked.

"Martha Torren and Roxanne Stevens," said Kaeley.

"Oh no!" Wendy Burgess uttered with genuine surprise.

"We wanted to know where you were last night so we can eliminate you both from our inquiries," Kaeley continued after noting their reactions.

"Why do you think we had anything to do with it?" Wendy Burgess asked defensively.

"Because you and your husband have been harassing parish councillors at meetings, as well as with abusive phone calls, over planning permission for the new retirement home. Now don't waste our time, tell us where you were last night," said Kaeley tetchily.

His aggressive response seemed to deflate the Burgesses. "We were at our daughter's in Tavistock for dinner. We got there about six and left after nine. It took us about two hours to get home because of the storm," John Burgess replied.

"OK. What is her telephone number so we can confirm this?" asked the chief inspector. Wendy Burgess reached into the pocket of the jeans she was wearing and handed Kaeley a card. "This her business card with her home telephone number on it," she said. Kaeley looked at the card and saw that Ruth Burgess was an investment advisor in Plymouth.

"Can you tell us why you were not at the meeting last night since it was something important to you?" asked Sergeant Evans.

"Well, it was foregone conclusion that the resolution about the retirement home would pass because a number of the councillors had interests in seeing this happen," said John Burgess. "Anyway, London told us to stay away because they were going to make their stand at the county council level where they hoped they would have some success."

"London? Who in London?" he said.

"Well, we can't really say. It has nothing to do with the murders. We want to keep that information confidential," she stammered.

Kaeley rolled his eyes and said threateningly, "This is a murder inquiry, and any information you have may be crucial. It is for us to decide what is important, do you understand me? This not a *Boys Own* magazine adventure where you pick and choose the information you give us," he growled.

"Chief Inspector, we will not be bullied by you or anyone else. Now kindly leave our garden!" John Burgess blurted out, momentarily finding his courage.

Kaeley turned to Sergeant Evans and said, "Put the cuffs on them and take them down to the station and charge them with obstruction and wasting police time!" With this, he turned and started to walk up the path.

The Burgesses were shell-shocked at this and looked at each other, wondering what to do. Then Wendy Burgess decided and said to Kaeley's back, "Oh, all right then, it's an organisation called Protect the Countryside Now! or PCN. They enlisted our help in fighting the retirement home proposal. We've been acting as informants for them and helping out where we could," she said.

"How did they find you?" Kaeley asked, turning back to face them.

"Well, the truth is we found them. You see, when we heard that this retirement home was planned, we knew we had to act and oppose it. It stood for what we were trying to get away from when we moved here from Manchester. We are looking for peace and quiet, and this project would bring with it more people and higher crime," said John Burgess. "We knew we needed to get people in the area riled up enough to put pressure on the parish council to stop the plans. But we didn't have the experience or resources to take on the local government machine.

"After a bit of research, we found PCN, and when we called and explained to them what the problem was, they invited us to meet with them in London. After our meeting, they invited us to a one-day seminar to learn the techniques we and they could use to stop the urbanisation of the countryside. That's how it began. They insisted that they must control the campaign and that we help as directed. Success, you see, was only achievable if things were coordinated," he explained.

"Who was the person you were in contact with?"

"A Randal McGuire."

"Well, thank you both. We'll get back in touch with you if we have any more questions," Kaeley said, bringing the interview to a close.

As they walked back up the path, something was worrying Detective Chief Inspector Kaeley.

"Why does the name Randal McGuire ring a bell?" Kaeley said to Sergeant Evans.

"Maybe you ran into him while you were in the Met all those years ago."

"I think I'll make a few calls when I get back to the office and arrange to see him in London."

Their next stop was to visit Dr. Galway. They found him finishing his morning clinic. "Gentlemen, please come in," said Dr. Galway as he ushered them into his office.

"Thanks. I just want to go over our conversation last night and then put it into a statement for you to sign," Kaeley said.

Dr. Galway quietly and patiently went through his observations at the village hall the previous evening.

"Is there something you might have thought about overnight that you might want to add, however seemingly unimportant?" Kaeley asked.

"It seems to me that one of the parish councillors was targeted. Because Mark Bennett and Roxanne Stevens were taken so ill, one of them could have been the intended victim. My guess is that the poison was in the decaffeinated tea carafe because both drank from it. The other thought I had was that the killer is probably local because he or she would know that at our meeting's refreshments were provided, particularly the decaffeinated tea that Mark always insisted on being supplied."

"What about Martha Torren, doctor?" Sergeant Evans asked. "Could she have been the intended victim?"

"I think poor Martha was in the wrong place at the wrong time. She was probably a witness to the killer's identity as he made his escape."

"What was it Mr. Bennett wanted to tell you all before the official meeting started?"

"That is a mystery. I know he was up in London last month. As far as I know, he was at a regimental dinner at Goldsmiths' Hall in the City of London. Other than that, I don't know what his movements were," he replied.

"Tell me about the opposition to the retirement home proposal," Kaeley said.

"Well, it all started about six months ago. First, it was stories appearing in the local press, giving one side of the argument. It was not only press coverage but also letters to the editor. We got a visit from two of the national papers as well. Then there were the local radio discussions on the issue. Most of the commentators opposed the proposal. The coverage for the next month or so became progressively angrier, mainly on the part of the opposition.

"Then there were the telephone calls to members of the parish council, berating them for supporting the plan. Mind you, no one had made their thoughts public. It was just assumed that they would be for it," Dr. Galway said.

"What action did the council take to counter this, sir?" Sergeant Evans asked.

"Well, we decided to have a public meeting to calmly discuss the proposal. That was a mistake! The developer of the site was there to brief residents and so were about a hundred people. Unfortunately, so were the Burgesses with a group of locals who clearly were against the plan. Also, there were a couple of men I have never seen before who seemed to be egging on the opposition. I'm afraid the meeting got very heated, with insults being thrown around, and ended up in a fight. Mark closed the meeting and called the police," the doctor replied.

"Can you describe the men you saw?" said Kaeley.

"Well, I thought they looked like Laurel and Hardy. They were dressed badly and seemed uncomfortable in suits. The tall one was about six-foot-two, dark brown hair, and he had a moustache. The other was quite short with red hair. He seemed to have a temper as well, but I noticed he was using one of those small inhalers, so he probably suffered from asthma."

Just then, the telephone on Dr. Galway's desk rang, and he picked up the receiver. He turned to Kaeley and said, "It's for you."

Kaeley listened as the others watched him. "I'll be over right away."

He turned to them and said, "It seems that we have a possible suspect or a witness. A tramp by the name of Ned Russet was stopped and questioned. It turns out he was sheltering from the storm last night in the bike shed in the car park at the village hall. They've got him at the mobile incident unit for us to interview. Come on, Bill, it's time to go. Thanks, doctor."

The mobile incident room was set up in front of the village hall that morning. The trailer had offices, a holding cell, and up-to-date communications equipment and was manned by two police officers.

As Detective Chief Inspector Kaeley and Sergeant Evans walked towards the trailer, Francis Reagan rode up on his bike. "Hello, chief inspector, how is the investigation going?"

"We're just beginning, Vicar. We have started the house-to-house inquiries, and we've followed up on a number of leads. Has anybody been to see you yet?"

"Yes, one of your lads was around this morning. I couldn't be of much help though. I was at home all evening, working on an article for the *Heritage News*. I was in London last month at a conference, and I have been asked to do a report on it. The first thing I knew of any problem were the ambulance lights.

"By the way, do you know when they will release the bodies of Martha Torren and Roxanne Stevens? Only Martha's husband, George, has asked me to officiate at her funeral. I have been trying to get in touch with Roxanne's relatives with no luck so far."

"I have no idea right now. It's probably too early. It's best to get in touch with the medical examiner's office in Plymouth. They might be able to give you some idea," Kaeley said.

"Thanks, I'll do that. Good luck with your inquiries." With that, he rode off on his bike.

"Now perhaps we can go and interview our possible witness. Bill, take the lead on the questioning, and I'll just observe."

When they entered the office, they found Ned Russet lying back in his chair, drinking tea with a uniformed constable standing by the door. When they entered, the constable left, and Ned straightened up, alert. He was a man in his late fifties, as far as the experienced police officers could tell, very dirty and with months of stubble on his chin, and with an odour that would knock you off your feet. Detective Chief Inspector Kaeley quickly opened the window.

Ned was wearing a three-piece suit, a handmade shirt, a club or school tie, shoes that had been expensive, a raincoat, and a trilby hat. All these were filthy, and it was evident that he had not changed them for months. His red eyes were sunken into his head, and his nose was purplish. He was a drunk who smelled of gin and had a past he wanted to forget. He was wrapped in his own misery. All in all, he was a sorry mess of a human being.

"Mr. Russet, we'd like your help in solving a puzzle," began Sergeant Evans politely. "You see, we don't understand why you spent the night in a bicycle shed when your warm caravan was only a mile up Drovers Lane?"

"That's easy. I was on my way back from The Feathers, and I got lost! It was tumbling down, and I must have missed my turning. Then I saw this shack, and I thought to myself why not crash there for the night, out of the wind and the rain. I had no appointments today, so that's what I did," he said with a grin.

"At what time was this, sir?"

"I really can't say. Frankly, the night was a bit of a blur. I remember sitting by the fire in the pub, and then the landlord kicked me out. He said I smelled and that I kept on trying to sing. He said a number of customers had complained about me. Wretched man! I'll have to report him to the authorities. He had the nerve to tell me not to come back. But I will. I know too much about his hanky-panky with the barmaids who help out there. I am sure his wife doesn't know!" he said with a cheeky wink and grin.

"So you settled down in the bike shed. What woke you up?"

"I heard the noise of a car in the car park. I thought it might be your lot coming to throw me out. When I looked out, I saw a woman get out of the car and run towards the building."

"Then what?"

"I went back to my temporary bed. I was there for a few seconds when I heard footsteps approaching up the path. When looked out, I just saw the back of Faunus. And then he was gone. I couldn't believe it. I must have had one gin too many. So I went back to my bed to get my head down."

"Who is Faunus?"

"Faunus was a horned Roman god of the forest, half man and goat with cloven feet."

"How do you know it was this Faunus?"

"Well, the creature was tall, well over six feet, and he had hooves for feet. And he was in a hurry. That's all. Remember, it was pissing down with rain and the trees swaying in the wind. Oh, what a night!"

"You didn't see his face at all?"

"No, I was too frightened. I didn't want anyone to see me. Anyway, I was much more interested in sleeping than trying to look at him!"

"Thank you, sir," said a sceptical sergeant. "I'll just get your statement written up, and you can be on your way. We know where to find you."

"Your name is not Ned Russet, is it?" Detective Chief Inspector Kaeley said suddenly. "It's Raymond James, if I remember. You did time for fraud in Exeter prison, right? Five years, wasn't it? You were an accountant at a firm in Plymouth and walked off with half-a-million pounds. Am I right?"

A silence followed this question, and then Ned said reluctantly with a sigh, "You're right. I was released about a year ago. I came here then and wanted to forget my past. That's why I changed my name. I've been doing odd jobs for people, like gardening. Just leave me alone. I am not hurting anyone. Can I go now?"

"First, we have to take a statement from you, and then you can go. Here's a pencil and paper for you to put down what you've just told us."

Detective Chief Inspector Kaeley and Sergeant Evans left the room. "How did you know his past? It really caught him by surprise," said Sergeant Evans.

"Some years back, Plymouth police were investigating his company. They had called in the Fraud Squad at Scotland Yard, and it turned out that the chief accountant had embezzled the company over some ten years. We had a briefing later on from the team that prosecuted the fraud. It was quite an interesting case history," answered Kaeley.

"He's one crazy fellow now!" Evans remarked.

"No, I think he's clever. Remember, he was convicted of fraud and is used to building a number of scenarios to hide behind. He's frightened about something though. He knows more than what he is telling us. This business of seeing Faunus is a red herring to make us think he's mad. We'll have to keep an eye on him to make sure he doesn't do a bunk.

"Also, Bill, get someone over to The Feathers to check out his alibi," Kaeley said.

Just then, a constable came in and said that Mark Bennett was ready to be interviewed, so they left for Plymouth.

When they got to Mark Bennett's room at the hospital, he was lying in bed connected to a drip and all sorts of monitoring equipment. In a croaky voice, he recognized how lucky he had been.

"To be honest, I had no time for Roxanne, who I believe was a mischievous troublemaker, but what happened to her and Martha was an absolute tragedy. Do you have any leads at all?"

"It really is too early yet, but we have a possible witness. How reliable he is is a big question mark. Tell me, sir, I understand you asked the other members of the parish council to come early. What was the subject matter you wanted to talk to them about?" Kaeley asked.

"It was about the planning permission for that retirement home. I had found out some information in London while I was there in December. Because of my work with military intelligence, I still had contacts at Scotland Yard. I was curious about the opposition group from London called Protect the Countryside Now! which I knew had been active in other parts of country. We all had been receiving calls, often in the middle of the night, warning us about approving the plans for the home. I wanted to know whether they were a real threat or just a group of do-gooders out to cause trouble," he said between deep breaths.

"Who should we talk to in London, sir?" Kaeley asked.

Although Mark Bennett was getting tired, he pressed on. "I suggest you talk to Deputy Commissioner Bill Thomson at Scotland Yard's serious crimes division. He has information he could give if it's of help. Now I must sleep."

"Thank you, sir, we will follow this up." And with that, they left Mark Bennett to sleep and recover from the poisoning.

Their next appointment was with the Scientific and Technical Services Unit of the Devon and Cornwall Constabulary and Dr. Grainger. He was waiting for them when they arrived.

"Roxanne Stevens didn't die from poisoning but from a heart attack brought on by the poison. This was caused by the ingestion of small amount of the poison that set up an arrhythmia. The poison was Aconite, which is found in a deadly plant called Wolfsbane. There is a lot of it about. It grows in gardens and along hedgerows all over the place. We found powdered Wolfsbane root in the decaffeinated tea."

"How much of this is enough to kill anybody?" Sergeant Evans asked.

"About seven to eight milligrams. Victims would probably feel chest pains, nausea, and a tingling sensation in their fingers, which would then spread over their whole body. This would be followed by vomiting, and death would occur between one to five hours, depending on how much was ingested and the size of the individual," Dr. Grainger continued.

"Tell us about Martha Torren," Kaeley said.

"She was killed by blunt force trauma to her head caused by the rock we found near her body. It was quite heavy and brought down on her head from a height. The murderer must have been tall and strong to accomplish this. I am afraid we found very little else. The heavy rain washed away pretty much everything, including any footprints. As far as the drinks and biscuits are concerned, I'll let you have a report on them as soon as we have analysed the samples."

"Thanks, Doctor," Kaeley said as they left his office.

*　　*　　*

Linda Wilson and Jeremy Trotter were finishing their drinks at The Feathers and planning to spend some cosy time together on their way home to Okehampton. The wood where they usually went was not very inviting at this time of year, and they would have to stay in the car. Still, they reckoned this was the best they could do under the circumstances. They couldn't go back to her home because she lived with her parents, and Jeremy was married.

They were both in their thirties and had been seeing each other for about a year, but they could only get together when his wife was visiting her sick mother in London. Then it was safe. Their relationship had grown strong in the last few months, and they had to make a real effort to hide their affection for each other from the other people at the company they both worked for.

Linda thought the evening had been great. The meal was wonderful, and the after-dinner drinks were perfect. The expectation for the rest of the evening was exciting. She got wet thinking about it. Linda had gone to the ladies and taken off her panties and tights to make things easier for them in the car.

They waved good night to the landlord, who guessed at their secret, and got into the car. They drove through the village, up the hill on Drovers Lane, and into a small turning in the wood. When the car stopped, they climbed into the back and started to make love. Jeremy was a considerate and patient lover, and he slowly brought her to a peak of ecstasy. She had little trouble reaching an orgasm as he penetrated her, and they came together in unison. This was the most wonderful moment.

After a long time, she opened her eyes, and when they focused, she saw a glow through the wood.

"Jeremy, what do you think that is?"

Jeremy, sensing her concern, turned over to see. "It looks like a fire. We'd better go and see if we can help."

They rearranged their clothes, got out of the car, and walked up a path towards the glow. When they reached the fire, it had engulfed a small caravan, and there was nobody around.

"We need to go back into the village and call the fire brigade. Come on," said Jeremy.

They never saw a dark figure watching them through the trees.

* * *

That couple cannot see me, so I'll wait until they go. No point having to deal with them as well. That was a good night's work. I put pay to that drunken slob. Try to help him and he rats on me to the police! It was easy to finish him. He came waddling back from the pub bloated with gin. When I hit him with the rock, there was a look of surprise on his face. A bit of petrol thrown around the eyesore of a home and it went up quickly. I'll just carry on as normal as no one would guess. But I have to finish what I started with Mark Bennett. It's a pity he survived. He is still a threat! When he is dead, I will be free!

* * *

By the time the fire brigade arrived, there was nothing left of the caravan, except its metal frame and some pots and pans. The firemen sifted through the debris and found some skeletal remains. "Stop right there, don't touch anything else," the crew commander ordered. "We have to call in the police as well as our arson investigators."

Early the next morning, Detective Chief Inspector Kaeley and Sergeant Evans viewed the wreckage. "I don't believe for a moment that this was an accident. I bet, when the forensics come back, they'll say some sort of accelerant was used, like petrol."

"That would be my bet," said Dr. Grainger as he approach the two policemen. "Also, it looks like his head was beaten in, probably before the fire started. I'd have to get the remains to the lab and do some tests, but that's my guess."

"Thanks, Doctor, as soon as you can," Kaeley responded. "Bill, what did the couple say when they were interviewed?"

"Not much. They had other things on their mind. They saw the glow and went to investigate. They didn't see it when they turned into the wood at about eleven, and they didn't see anyone."

"We are getting nowhere!" a frustrated Kaeley cried angrily. "I know the murderer is local because he wanted our only witness out of the way. A lot of evidence points to London."

His thoughts were disturbed by one of Dr. Grainger's crime scene technicians. "Sir, I thought you might be interest in this," she said, showing him a large silver coin which was two inches in diameter. It was decorated with a Celtic knot on one side and an inscription on the other side that read "As a man is, so he sees. As the eye is formed, such are its powers.—William Blake."

"I think this was dropped recently because it looks shiny, as if new, and hasn't had time to become discoloured," she said as she put it into a plastic bag.

"Finally, I think we have something to work on," said Kaeley.

CHAPTER 34

Francis was now in a panic. His plan to dispose of Mark Bennett was a failure. Instead, he had had to kill two people to cover his tracks and a third had taken the same poison by mistake that he had meant for Mark Bennett. What a mess!

The grim irony of the situation was that he had conducted funeral services for all three of his victims in the last two days.

Sitting at his desk in the vicarage that evening, he felt suddenly very tired and lethargic. His ill health weighed heavily upon him as the stress of the past few days was beginning to tell. He was wondering whether it was worth carrying on living.

I have an urge to end things. I think it's time. I'm just too tired to go on anymore. I'm too old now to keep running, and I feel physically sick. If they come after me, I will leave this world on my own terms, not in some dark prison cell as a curiosity for the medical profession. I will go at a time and place of my own choosing. I'll wait for some sign that my time is up before I make a move.

Suddenly, he was shaken from these morbid thoughts by the sound of the front door bell ringing. He hoped there wasn't some urgent parish need that he would have to deal with.

He opened the door, and standing on the doorstep, sheltering from the rain, was Sergeant Evans.

"I'm sorry to bother you, sir, but I wanted to check with you about something. It won't take long."

"Come on in, Sergeant."

Francis ushered him into his study, and they sat down in lounge chairs opposite each other. The sergeant pulled out of his pocket a small evidence bag in which was a large silver coin.

"We were wondering if you had ever seen this before, sir. We found it near Ned Russet's caravan."

Much to Francis's consternation, he saw the coin which belonged to him. He didn't know that it was missing. He took it from Sergeant Evans and pretended to examine it.

"I haven't seen this before, sergeant. Perhaps the owner uses it as a talisman. There is a Celtic knot on one side and a very prophetic inscription on the other. Why are you questioning me about it?" he asked suspiciously.

"We're asking everyone, sir. This might have been dropped by the person who set fire to Mr. Russet's caravan. Well, thank you for your time," he said, getting up to go.

"How is the investigation going, sergeant?" Francis asked as they walked to the door.

"We have a few leads. The Chief Iinspector is going to London tomorrow to follow up on something from that end."

When Sergeant Evans had left, Francis poured himself a whiskey and contemplated his options.

They've found my lucky coin. Shit! I hope nobody recognises it. What's that inspector going to London for? I know he interviewed Mark Bennett. Maybe he told him something about Belfast. I wish I knew! I've got to get ready to go!

The next morning, Francis drove to a garden centre in Tavistock and purchased several packages of Hemlock seeds. At the vicarage, he crushed the seeds into a fine powder with the pestle and mortar. He poured the powder into a small bottle and added water to it. He shook the bottle vigorously until the powder was thoroughly dissolved in the water.

He went upstairs to his bedroom, packed a bag, and put it into the boot of his car.

Now he was ready.

*   *   *

Inspector Kinder sat in his office in New Scotland Yard in London, reviewing with Sergeant Lockhart the outstanding cases they were responsible for. Their time since their return from the Lake District had been taken up with a gangland killing in Bermondsey in South London. This had taken priority over their other cases, but they had soon wrapped it up.

"Let's take a look at the Nigel Ellis case. Brenda, what success has Detective Constable Owens had in our absence in tracing our missing man?"

"He has called all twenty-five Church of England theological colleges and the four Roman Catholic seminaries. It's taken him all this time to get the information he needed. The colleges weren't very cooperative. In the end, he found out that there were three vicars called Nigel Ellis who were all ordained at about the same time in the 1950s. One of them is dead, one is retired, and the last has a parish in Devon. The dead man was a missionary in the Far East and, according to his daughter, was an RAF intelligence officer at Biggin Hill during the war. He interviewed the retiree who had been a chaplain in the Royal Navy after serving as a seaman during the war. That also ruled him out as a suspect. He has yet to interview the vicar in Devon."

"Lean on Owens, Brenda. I want to wrap this up as soon as possible."

* * *

The vicarage telephone rang. Francis walked to the receiver in the hall to answer it. It was Dean Richardson from the Exeter diocese.

"Nigel, I just had a strange phone call from the police. They wanted to know whether you still worked in Devon. I gave them your number. They weren't very communicative about what they wanted. They must be looking into something that happened in Notting Dale. Anyway, they will be calling you. You haven't been a naughty, boy, have you?" he said, laughing.

You don't know the half of it, thought Francis. "Thanks for the heads up, Dean. I expect you're right. I've been on my best behaviour since I left London," Nigel joked back.

Time to go.

* * *

Detective Chief Inspector Kaeley walked into the reception area at Protect Our Countryside Now! in Southampton Row, Holborn, London, and showed his warrant card to the receptionist.

"I need to see Randal McGuire," he demanded.

"I'll see if he's in," she responded pertly after looking him up and down.

Fifteen long minutes later, a tall skinny woman with a cropped grey hair, who Kaeley surmised was in her mid-fifties, came into the reception.

"Mr. Kaeley, Mr. McGuire will see you now. Follow me," she said in an irritated tone without looking at him. *She doesn't like policemen*, he thought.

She walked ahead of him, past a maze offices and a row of occupied but empty cubicles. At the end of hall was a corner office. She knocked on the door and entered right away without waiting for any response. Sitting behind a big desk was a heavy-set balding man with large horn-rimmed glasses. He was in his shirt sleeves that showed off his wide red braces, and his tie was loosened. His desk was covered with scattered papers, and he was busy working on a large calculator.

When Kaeley walked in, he glanced up from his work, and a surprised look came over his face.

"My word, Sergeant Kaeley, what a nice surprise!" he said in a broad Cockney accent. "I thought you left the Met."

Recognising him, Kaeley said, "Hello, Randal. I am now a chief inspector in Devon. What are you up to these days?"

"I'm running a clean business now, Mr. Kaeley, especially after you nicked me the last time and I did time. I learned my lesson. I'm purely legit now."

"Do you call harassing people legit?"

"It's not against the law now, is it? It's within our rights to put our point of view forward," he said with an ingratiating smile.

"Who funds you, Randal?"

"Now you know I can't tell you that, Mr. Kaeley. I can't breach client confidentiality."

"Oh no. I'll tell you what, I'll talk to someone I know at the Inland Revenue about your organisation and your record. I'm sure they'd be very interested in your books."

"OK, OK. We've got a lot of individual donors, but the three main ones are environmental groups. I can give you their names and information."

"That's very good of you, Randal."

"I'm always happy to oblige," he said obsequiously.

Ignoring him, Kaeley continued, "I'm investigating a triple murder in Branton, and the information I have has led me to you."

"Murder? Murder? Now you know it's not my style, Mr. Kaeley."

"I hear your organisation is behind a protest about a convalescence home development in the area. Two of the parish councillors you've been harassing are dead, and another is in hospital, very ill."

"We pulled out of the protest at the parish level weeks ago and are concentrating on the county council. I'll tell you what, though, I'll talk to our operatives there and see whether they know anything that might help you."

"We've already talked to the Burgesses, and they know nothing."

"Well, that's all I can help you with."

"OK, Randal. Give me those names, and I will be out of your hair for now. If you think of anything, call me," Kaeley said, handing him his business card.

Chief Inspector Kaeley walked out of the PCN office and flagged down a taxi and asked the driver to take him to New Scotland Yard. Sitting in the back of the cab, he mulled over his conversation with Randal McGuire. He had to agree with the little weasel that murder was not his style, but he had to check on these environmental groups with Deputy Commissioner Thompson as Mark Bennett had suggested. These groups often had very radical people belonging to them that might take things into their own hands.

His appointment with the deputy commissioner was at two that afternoon, so he decided to eat lunch in the cafeteria in the basement. When he had selected the sandwich he wanted and poured himself some tea, he took his tray into the large dining hall and looked around for anyone he knew. He spotted Ray Kinder sitting with an attractive woman. Kaeley had been a detective sergeant at West Ham police station when Ray had been promoted to the criminal investigation department there.

"Do you mind if I joined you, Ray?"

"Good lord, George Kaeley, of course not, sit down! What are you doing here? Sorry, let me introduce you to Sergeant Brenda Lockhart."

Kaeley shook hands with Brenda and sat down.

"I thought you were in Devon," Kidner continued.

"That's right. I'm in Okehampton. I've got a triple murder on my hands. A lead we had led us to London, but looks like it's a dead end."

"Where were the murders?" Brenda asked.

"In a village called Branton." Kaeley then briefly outlined the case.

Both Ray and Brenda looked at each other.

"That's curious because we are investigating a 1940s murder in the Lake District that has led us to Branton," said Ray.

"Hasn't the Yard got better things to do than look into a case that old?" Kaeley said, laughing. "The suspects will be dead and buried by now, Ray."

"Not quite. One of them lives in Branton, a Reverend Ellis," said Ray, smiling.

"Tell me more," Kaeley said, looking serious. His demeanour had changed suddenly at the mention of a connection.

Brenda outlined their case, and Kaeley sat quietly listening. When she had finished, he let out a low whistle.

"If Nigel Ellis is your murderer, it could be that he was involved in those in Branton as well. It seems very unlikely that there are two murderers in this one small village. I'm at a loss about the motive though. Maybe that's wrapped up in the past as well. Thinking about it, Mark Bennett could have been the target all along, and the others happened to get in the way. An attempt on his life wouldn't have been made just for the development of a nursing home. That doesn't make sense. It's more personal than that. I know that Mr. Bennett was in military intelligence during the Second World War. I wonder if the connection is there.

"Ray, could you hold off doing anything until I look into a couple of ideas I have?"

"Sure. The case has waited forty years. Another couple of days won't make any difference."

Kaeley was shown into Deputy Commissioner Bill Thomson's office at precisely two o'clock.

"George, how nice to see you again! Please sit down. How can I be of help?"

Kaeley briefly outlined the case he was working on and gave the deputy commissioner the three names of the environmental groups he had got from Randal McGuire.

"I'll have these checked out and get back to you."

"There's one other thing, sir, I've got a feeling that the target for the murderer was really Mark Bennett and that the motive was something in his past when he was in military intelligence."

"Hmm. I have a contact over at MI5 that might shed some light on the matter. Have you read Mark's book?"

"No, sir."

"I would get a copy if I were you. It might give you some ideas or at least background."

Kaeley telephoned Sergeant Evans.

"Any developments, Bill?"

"Nothing this end. How about you, sir?"

"There may be a connection between our case and one the Yard is working on."

He then briefed the sergeant on what he had found out.

"There are two things, Bill. First, put an around-the-clock guard on Mark Bennett's hospital room. And second, keep an eye on Reverend Ellis. Be careful, we don't want to spook him. I'm catching the first train back in the morning."

Kaeley went to Foyle's in Charing Cross Road and bought a copy of Mark Bennett's book. That night, he sat in his hotel room and began to read it. By the time he had stepped off the train in Plymouth the next morning, he had finished it. Now he knew he was on to something.

Sergeant Evans was there to meet him with a worried look on his face.

"We have a problem, sir. No one has seen Nigel Ellis. Someone said he had seen him driving through the village a day ago, but that's the last time he was seen. I've put out an alert for him with a description of the car he was driving."

"Great, Bill! Now we've lost our main suspect. Let's go and see Mark Bennett."

They drove to the hospital and went to his third floor room. A young police constable stood at the door to the room and asked to see their identities. When they entered, Mark Bennett was sitting in a chair, reading.

"It looks like I'll be released from here tomorrow," he said. "Frankly, I'll be glad to leave."

"It's good to see you are feeling so much better, sir," said Kaeley.

"What's that constable doing outside my room?"

"There have been developments, sir. It seems that Nigel Ellis is really Patrick Duggan. Duggan's ID was found, and from what we could see, it gave some address in Belfast. This was confirmed by army records."

"What?"

"The real Nigel Ellis was murdered in the 1940s, and what remained of his body was discovered in a disused mine near Keswick. Patrick Duggan took his name and went to theological college in his place."

"So that's where he was hiding. He was in plain sight all the time, don't you see?" said an animated Mark Bennett. "When we got the information out of that Trevelyan traitor, we were able to trace him in Belfast as Tom McClure, which was the alias he used. His real name is Francis Reagan. When he ran from Belfast, he must have stolen Patrick Duggan's credentials. As an air-raid warden, he would have seen many dead people, so it was easy to take somebody's ID. We had a tip that maybe he was in the Lake District, but when we started looking for Irishmen in the area, he got wind of this and disappeared again."

"He's done a bunk again," said Kaeley. "We have no idea where he's headed or what name he has taken. We've issued an alert for him, but it sounds like he is an expert in disappearing. Have you got any ideas, sir?"

"Tell me more about what you have found out about his alias Nigel Ellis."

"Well, we know that he went to theological college in Durham. He was a curate in Hammersmith, and then he was a parish priest in Notting Dale in the late 1950s. It was a racially divided area, and there was trouble brewing. He married a nurse whom he had met at the convalescent home in Keswick during the war. According to her family, they had lost touch but met up again by accident. They were married and spent their honeymoon in Keswick, the place where they first met.

"A year later, tragedy struck when she fell down some stairs after visiting a patient in a rundown tenement. The local police said she was seen arguing with two men moments before she fell. She and the baby she was expecting died. Ellis blamed the slum landlords for the catastrophe and was very passionate about his fight with them for better conditions for his poor mainly black parishioners. He was then transferred to Branton, and from what we know, he has been an excellent and well-respected vicar," Kaeley concluded.

"I enjoyed his company," Mark Bennett said, "although I got the feeling that he was suspicious of me when I first came to Branton. In all the years I have known him, he never really gave anything away about his family or upbringing. When we searched what was left of Tom McClure's home in Belfast, we did find some magazines that had stories in them about the Lake

District, and his fascination for this part of the country was confirmed by a friend of his. That's why, in 1942, we started our search for him there and came up with Patrick Duggan.

"If I were you, chief Inspector, I would focus on that area. When you catch him, I would like to be in on the interrogation. Catching him was one of my few failures during the war, and I would be fascinated to know how he got the better of us."

When Kaeley got back to his office in Okehampton, he called Inspector Kidner at Scotland Yard.

"Our bird has flown, Ray. He may be headed north to the Lake District. The Cumbria police should check out a hotel there. It was the convalescence home at which he worked. He may be using one of his aliases or even a new one when he checked into the hotel, so they should check each single male guest."

"Thanks, George, I'll call Superintendent Davis."

* * *

Lakeside Hotel, Keswick

The previous afternoon, Francis had driven his MGB-GT up the familiar driveway to the large house which had been his home in happier times. As he entered the building, he half expected Jane to greet him dressed in her nurse's uniform and to see the matron supervising the intake of patients.

"Can I help you, sir?" a pretty receptionist asked.

"I'm sorry, my mind was miles away. I haven't been in this building since I was based here during the Second World War. I would like a room for two nights, if that is possible."

"Yes, sir. We have one overlooking the lake. We haven't got many guests at this time of year."

When he had put his bags in his room, he walked around the hotel. A great deal had changed, but he did recognise some of the rooms, especially the large ballroom which was now the dining room. He saw the large drawing room which had been the dormitory where he had rescued Jane from the grips of a demented patient.

Despite the cold weather, he walked down to the lake after dinner. The bench he used to sit on with Jane during those warm summer nights was still there. He sat down and looked out across the lake. The landscape was the same, of course, but perhaps there were more boats moored at the dock than when he was here before. There was a mist that lay over the lake caused by the relatively warm water and the cold January temperature.

He started to cry softly, thinking about Jane and his friends that were no longer alive. Because of his actions, many of them had died. These were young people who had their whole lives in front of them. They were happy-go-lucky friends who, despite the rigours of the war and the depravations of their city, enjoyed life to the full. They could no longer take part in simple joys, like dancing at the Plaza Ballroom or fishing on the Larne. All this had been cut short by him.

I must make amends to these lost friends. They took me into their hearts and homes, and I betrayed them. Now that I am dying, I will write down all that has occurred in my life as my confession so people will understand what happened to me. Then I have to end it all. I hope when I see them again in heaven, they will forgive me.

Francis was up all night, writing a report on his tarnished life, and he finished it as dawn was breaking. He then drew up a will, leaving his meagre savings to the Church of Ireland Children's Fund.

He walked down to the lake and sat on his bench. He looked out across the lake one more time. He took the small bottle of Hemlock from his overcoat pocket and swigged its contents down. Then he took the bottle of whiskey from another pocket inside his coat and drained its contents.

He sat there looking out across the lake. After a while, his feet began to feel cold. Then he couldn't move his feet, and his groin began to ache as the poison made its way up his body.

* * *

At eleven that morning, Sergeant Bader and Constable Monroe entered the reception area at the Lakeside Hotel. They asked the receptionist about the guests and whether there had been any recent arrivals.

"I checked in an old gentleman yesterday afternoon. He told me he had been here in World War II."

"What name did he use?"

She looked at her computer screen. "Francis Reagan."

"Where is he now?"

"When I came to work this morning, I saw him sitting on a bench by the lake. I haven't seen him come in yet."

The police officers walked across the lawn towards the lake. They saw a figure sitting on a bench. As they approached, they called out his name and got no answer or acknowledgement. When they finally reached him, they realised that he was dead and saw that rigor mortis had begun to set in.

Francis Reagan had finally escaped his pursuers for good.

CPSIA information can be obtained at www.ICGtesting.com
Printed in the USA
LVOW13s1529120514

385433LV00001BA/98/P